DATE DUE			OCT 0 2
4.5.'19			
GAYLORD			PRINTED IN U.S.A.

STAR TREK VOYAGER®

PATHWAYS

STAR TREK VOYAGER®

PATHWAYS

A Novel

Jeri Taylor

POCKET BOOKS

New York   London   Toronto   Sydney   Tokyo   Singapore

POCKET BOOKS, a division of Simon & Schuster Inc.
1230 Avenue of the Americas, New York, NY 10020

Copyright © 1998 by Paramount Pictures. All Rights Reserved.

STAR TREK is a Registered Trademark of
Paramount Pictures.

A VIACOM COMPANY

This book is published by Pocket Books, a division of
Simon & Schuster Inc., under exclusive license from
Paramount Pictures.

All rights reserved, including the right to reproduce
this book or portions thereof in any form whatsoever.
For information address Pocket Books, 1230 Avenue
of the Americas, New York, NY 10020

ISBN: 0-671-00346-1

First Pocket Books hardcover printing August 1998

10 9 8 7 6 5 4 3 2 1

POCKET and colophon are registered trademarks of
Simon & Schuster Inc.

Printed in the U.S.A.

For Andrew and Gina

Acknowledgments

The Usual Suspects:

John Ordover is the editor *extraordinaire,* combining patience, compassion, intellect, and insight. I thank him for the opportunity to spread my literary wings.

Rick Berman, handed the Star Trek mantle by Gene Roddenberry, has worn it with vision and integrity. I thank him for being mentor, colleague, and friend.

Brannon Braga and Joe Menoksy are fonts of creative passion. I thank them for the inspiration and the fierce loyalty they have given me over the years.

Andre Bormanis is a wealth of knowledge in all fields, and a gracious, generous human being. I thank him for sharing his intelligence and for keeping me (mostly) on the scientific straight-and-narrow.

David Moessinger, my husband, is my anchor, my rock, my heart. I thank him for being.

CHAPTER

1

TOM PARIS WAS WELL AWARE THAT BRINGING A SHUTTLE INTO A PLANET'S atmosphere was easy if you followed procedure; it only became challenging—and interesting—if you deviated from Starfleet's carefully regulated system.

He had developed a number of ways to cheat the routine, but the only one that consistently provided what Tom wanted—the ineffable thrill that accompanied danger—was what he had termed the Yeager maneuver, after an ancient but renowned pilot of the twentieth century. Now he had the chance to try it again.

Captain Janeway had deposited an away team, including the ship's senior officers, on an unoccupied M-class planet that promised abundant foodstuffs as well as time off their starship, *Voyager*. She then took the ship on a diplomatic mission to a nearby system where she hoped to secure safe passage through a part of space rumored to be rife with danger.

Tom had requested shuttle time during the away mission, not an unusual request. Logging shuttle time was required duty for every pilot, a necessary means of keeping one's skills honed. First Officer Chakotay hadn't hesitated when Tom suggested he use this downtime to log a few hours on his file.

The request was legitimate, of course, and Tom had no pangs about making it, even if he did have an agenda that had gone unspoken. The two functions weren't mutually exclusive, and he saw nothing wrong with combining them.

Now, at the controls of the *Starship Voyager*'s shuttle *Harris,* he saw the planet looming before him. It was a watery sphere, much like Earth, and the marbled blue-and-white orb gave him a few pangs of nostalgia—a fact which surprised him, for he usually found himself far happier in the Delta Quadrant than he had been at home. He shoved the feelings aside and made the necessary preparations for entering the atmosphere, which, his instruments told him, would first be encountered some thirty thousand meters above the surface.

First would come the mesosphere, where molecular structure was thin and porous, bleeding into the stratosphere, where atmospheric pressure heightened and friction became a genuine concern; finally, the descent into the full oxygen-nitrogen atmosphere and the landing. The Yeager maneuver was accomplished just at the transition from mesosphere to stratosphere.

Atmospheric flight was always done under thruster power, and as such was accomplished much as it had been with pre-warp vehicles. There were safety mechanisms in place now, of course, that hadn't been available to earlier craft, but safety systems could always be taken off line. That was the first thing Tom did as the image of the planet filled the window of his ship, growing larger by the minute.

At the point where gravity began to exert a substantial pull on the shuttle, Tom tilted up the nose of the vessel and cut the thrusters, so that the ship began sinking toward the surface tail first, without power.

And that's when his body went into an autonomic response: pulse rate increased, blood pressure heightened, and adrenaline was released. These systemic reactions were biochemical and as old as man's earliest ancestors, but to Tom Paris they provided a state of crystalline awareness that was almost hallowed. All his senses sharpened as endorphins flowed into the brain, creating a mix of fear and pleasure that were mysteriously and inextricably linked.

He stared only briefly into the black sky, which, he knew, would soon begin to change color, becoming more blue as the atmosphere thickened. From now on he had to keep his eyes down, locked on the control panel. Because very soon the shuttle would be pulled into a violent spin, and a glimpse out the window would produce instant and disabling vertigo. Then he'd be doomed.

The only way to restart the thrusters now was to get the ship into a dive, nose-down, so that air was forced through the intake manifolds, which would start the magnaturbines spinning and build up the RPMs. Atmospheric oxygen would then combine with fuel from the shuttle's tanks in a supersonic combustion chamber, providing power for the thrusters.

The ship snapped into a flat spin, whirling right over its center of gravity, like an ancient pinwheel. The force of the spin drove Tom back against the seat, his head on the outer edge of the circle.

This was the moment he'd waited for.

He could pull out of this if he functioned perfectly. He needed every sense, every instinct keen and chiseled, responding with diamondlike clarity. And that's what the fear gave him—intensified awareness that would allow him to make the moves to save himself.

The trick now was timing. He had to gauge—through a combination of skill, experience, and luck—just the right time to maneuver the nose of the ship down. Too soon and it would throw him into an end-over-end tumble from which it was almost impossible to escape. Too late and the atmosphere would be dense enough to keep the shuttle nose-up and he would continue to spin out of control, screaming into the atmosphere at a speed that would incinerate him.

His body was being slammed against the seat with increasing pressure, his head filling with blood from the centrifugal force of the spin. He forced his eyes to bore into the control panel, watching as the altitude was displayed. He was falling about fifty meters a second, three thousand meters a minute. He estimated he'd have to engage his emergency drogue field at an altitude of about thirty thousand meters, and that was coming up fast.

At thirty-one thousand meters, he realized he was in trouble. His vision was darkening and his head throbbed as blood sloshed through it. He'd better engage the field now . . . but he knew it was too soon. He'd go tumbling into an endless somersault until he and the craft became a hellish fireball.

He had to wait . . . until it felt right. But how would he know when it felt right? Maybe his judgment was becoming impaired by the unnatural rearrangement of his bodily fluids. *Go ahead,* something told him, *the altitude's close enough . . . engage the drogue field.* His fingers slid with practiced ease to the controls.

But *no!* screamed through his mind, and his fingers responded, poised over the panel, refusing to enter the command. The ship was now under thirty thousand meters. Was he heading for dangerously turbulent atmospheric levels?

Wait . . . wait . . . wait . . .

Darkness was overtaking him, and the panel was nothing more than a dim arrangement of lights that swam in his field of vision. Much longer and he wouldn't be conscious to enter the field engagement command. *Hang on, Tom . . . hang on . . .*

Suddenly, the startling image of the incident from long ago—another time when he had told himself to wait . . . wait . . . wait—ripped through his mind like a phaser, and he cried out involuntarily. He thought he was over that, had long ago purged himself of those awful sights, but there they were in his mind's eye, brilliant and indelible, shot through with colors . . . colors of fire, colors of death . . .

The shock of the memory cleared his vision briefly and he saw that he was under twenty-nine thousand meters above the surface.

Now.

His fingers danced on the controls and the drogue field engaged . . . within seconds he would feel the tug as the ship nosed down and fell out of its spin. He drew great gasps of air because now he felt light-headed and dizzy—had his eyes flicked for a half second to the window? He was sure they hadn't, and yet he was unaccountably queasy . . . why wasn't the nose pitching down? Had he entered the wrong command? The beginnings of panic crackled in his mind like arcing plasma.

That wouldn't do. Can't panic. Think. Nose down . . . why not happening . . . think . . .

He had just promised himself that if he got out of this, he'd never flirt with danger again—when the long-awaited tug pulled at him and he felt the shuttle pitch downward. In a flash, he realized that nothing had been wrong, after all, except his perception of time, distorted by his biological responses. Everything was going as it should.

Air flooded the intake ducts and the thrusters began to respond. Tom regained control and drew the shuttle into a vectored descent, then looked out to see the ripe blue sky of the alien planet, familiar and welcoming. Soon he was dropping to the surface, searching for a landing spot, telling himself that his promise not to try things like this anymore should be nullified because nothing had really been wrong, after all.

Beneath him, he saw the figures of the *Voyager* crew, tiny as dust motes at first, then gradually increasing in size as he descended.

He wasn't sure when he realized that something was wrong—maybe when he saw that several people seemed to be running in unnatural patterns, as though they were driven by some urgent need but couldn't quite figure out what they were supposed to be doing. Then he saw that a great number of them were lying on the ground, motionless.

"Paris to away team. What's happening down there?"

There was no answer. For the first time since he began his descent, Tom checked his sensors and realized the *Voyager* crew wasn't alone on the planet. There were alien life signs, dozens of them. Where had they come from?

He quickly put down the shuttle and opened the hatch, hurrying to reach his friends and find out what was happening and where those aliens were. But as soon as he stepped outside he became dizzy, and found himself lurching, staggering as though drunk. Vaguely he noted a certain sick sweetness in the air and knew it was responsible for his rubbery legs. Ahead of him, most of the away team was now slumped on the ground, though whether dead or just unconscious he couldn't tell. He saw Chakotay, the last person standing, sink to his knees, and then Tom, too, succumbed, wondering for an instant if he had survived the dangerous descent through the atmosphere only to die in this cloying poison.

When Chakotay regained consciousness, he didn't know exactly where he was. Inside a structure of some kind, for he could see walls and a low ceiling by virtue of a few lights spotted on the walls of the room; they emitted a dim yellowish light that cast small pools of illumination before being absorbed by a foreboding darkness. He raised up to a sitting position and realized the rest of the away team was in the room as well, some still lying unconscious, others sitting in a kind of groggy stupor.

His head throbbed and his mouth was parched. He couldn't seem to produce saliva. Where were they? What had happened to them?

He spotted B'Elanna Torres nearby, sitting perfectly still and staring at nothing, dark hair a matted mass and dirt smudging the Klingon ridges on her forehead. Chakotay struggled toward her on hands and knees.

"B'Elanna?"

She turned to him and stared dully. She seemed remote and uncomprehending. "Do you know where we are?" he asked.

Several seconds passed before her eyes flickered in understanding.

"Chakotay . . ." she whispered hoarsely, her throat as dry as his. "What happened to us?"

Only when she'd asked the question did he realize he didn't know. The last memory he possessed was of being on the bridge of *Voyager*—and then he woke up in this strange, dark room. "I don't know," he answered.

"I was on *Voyager* . . . and then suddenly I was here."

Around them, others were beginning to stir, moving out of their curious sleep like drowsy bears emerging from hibernation, ponderous and heavy. It occurred to Chakotay that he should get up and search the room, but his legs felt unequal to the task. He turned back to B'Elanna and saw that the Vulcan tactical officer, Lieutenant Commander Tuvok, had crawled to join them, looking as stuporous as everyone else.

"Where are we?" rasped Tuvok, and Chakotay had a moment's amusement at the thought of the disciplined, controlled Vulcan reduced to the same confused state as everyone else.

"We're trying to figure that out. What's the last thing you remember?"

Tuvok's upswept eyebrows rose and his dark forehead knotted in concentration. "Being on *Voyager*. At my station on the bridge. But I have no idea how we got here."

Chakotay felt as though his head were beginning to clear slightly, though it still ached. There were things they had to do. "We have to count heads—see who's here. Ask them if they remember anything about what happened to us."

The three struggled to their feet and moved off through the languorous bodies, each in a separate direction, exhorting their crewmates to wake, to sit up, to try to remember anything they could about their strange predicament.

A few minutes later a head count had been taken, revealing that fourteen members of the crew were present. Presumably the others were still on *Voyager*, wherever the ship might be now.

Suddenly Neelix spoke up. The orange-tufted Talaxian was wearing one of his typically garish outfits, but it looked unusually subdued in the darkened room. "A picnic," he said tentatively.

Everyone turned to him. "Picnic?" echoed Chakotay. He sensed this was important. "Are you saying we were on a picnic?"

Neelix looked momentarily confused. "I think so . . . I can almost remember the captain telling me I should pack food for . . ." He trailed off vaguely, unable to come up with anything more.

But it had triggered others' thinking. "On a planet," called out Harry Kim, the black-haired operations officer. "We all went to the surface of a planet."

"He's right," chimed in Seven, the beautiful blond human woman who had lived most of her life as a member of a Borg collective, and who had been on *Voyager* for less than a year. "The captain said we all needed to get out and stretch our legs. I remember thinking that was an odd thing to do."

Several people smiled at that. Seven had made remarkable strides in her return to humanity, but some of the nuances still escaped her. Her memory, however, fueled that of several more people, and as they all began tossing out the bits and pieces they recalled, the story began to emerge.

It was Tom Paris who remembered the sickly-sweet smell in the air, as soon as he'd opened the hatch of the shuttle, and when he mentioned it, many of the group added their similar recollections.

"It started suddenly," said B'Elanna pensively. "One second it wasn't there, and then it was overpowering."

"It must've been a gas of some kind," speculated Chakotay, "but did it occur naturally? Or were we purposely attacked?"

"The fact that we're here—wherever here is—tells me someone did it to us," offered Tom. "We were gassed and then dumped into this room."

They had found no evidence of any entrance or exit to the room— no doors, no windows, no control pad. Nothing but the bare walls and the few weak lights, nothing to give them any clue as to their location. They could be anywhere.

It was Tom, through his pilot's feel for such things, who correctly surmised where they were, although his guess wouldn't be verified for many hours, when they were finally released. "We're on a spaceship," he announced, "I'd bet anything on it. It just *feels* like a ship flying at warp speed."

This was disheartening. If they were being taken away from the planet where they had succumbed, then they were probably being taken away from *Voyager*. They had no ship and no captain, and didn't know the fate of the crew who had remained with the ship. They were boxed into a cramped, dark room with no apparent way in or out, and at the mercy of whoever had attacked them.

And they were all wildly thirsty. The gas had left them with aching heads and parched mouths, and every one of them craved a cooling drink of water, but they all sensed that was unlikely.

What none of them knew was that this was the most comfortable they were to be for a long time.

Chakotay was having a vivid and frightening dream involving a forest fire from which he was trying to escape, when a sudden lurch jolted him awake. He sat up and saw that Tom had felt it, too. "We've entered an atmosphere," said Tom. They both felt the sensation of a descending ship.

At almost the same moment, a disembodied voice filled the room, rasping and harsh. "Prepare to disembark," it announced, and then was silent.

They weren't sure how long they had been on this mysterious ship. The effect of the gas they had inhaled was enervating, and soon after the head count, most of them had fallen asleep, though for how long they couldn't be sure. Chakotay hoped that some of the mysteries were soon to be solved.

The vessel seemed to slow, and soon after there was a heavy impact which they could feel in their bones. Then nothing.

They waited, disciplined and alert, for whatever was to come next. Most felt anxiety to one degree or another, but were experienced enough not to manifest it. They stood poised, wary, ready to do whatever was expected of them when that time came.

Chakotay heard a grating noise, soft at first, but rising in volume and intensity; then one wall of their enclosure separated at the ceiling and began to lower. Intense sunlight immediately flooded in, assaulting their dilated pupils, and they all squinted or threw up a shielding hand.

Finally the top of the wall lay on the ground, providing a ramp into the hot glare of that ferocious light, so bright they couldn't yet make out what awaited them.

"Exit slowly," said the same voice as before.

Chakotay led the way, followed in an orderly fashion by the others. Gradually his pupils were contracting in the light, and he lowered his hand to see what environment, what terrain, they were walking into.

What he saw astonished him.

A vast meadow stretched before them, filled with what looked like thousands of the most miserable beings he had ever seen. Many alien species were represented, all of them emaciated and filthy, most wearing nothing but rags. Small fires burned here and there, creating an acrid, smoky haze that didn't quite serve to mask the unbelievable stench of the place.

Chakotay noted that the meadow was surrounded by a high wall of what looked to be a dark, burnished metal. At various points along the wall there were openings, each of which was manned by a humanoid figure whom he couldn't see closely enough to distinguish any features.

Beyond the wall, on three sides, rose a glowering forest of huge trees, dense and foreboding; on the fourth side a steep cliff of rocky shale loomed beyond the wall, bearing the unmistakable striations of a mining operation. And beyond the forest, which stretched nearly as far as one could see, lay a distant mountain range. This walled meadow was isolated by hundreds of kilometers of wilderness.

Stockade was the first word that came to Chakotay's mind. He turned and saw that the crew had all left the spaceship, which loomed behind them like a huge and vengeful monster, a ship that wasn't familiar to Chakotay and that bristled with armament. A ship of war. The ramp was now rising, emitting the same shrill whine of metal on metal that had accompanied its path downward.

It snapped into place, and immediately the ship trembled, then rose swiftly and almost silently into the air, where it quickly became too small to see.

Chakotay and his group watched it go, somewhat stunned that they had been dumped so quickly and unceremonious'y in the middle of this stockade without so much as a word of explanation.

"What do you make of it, Commander?" asked Tom.

"It looks like a prison of some kind. From the look of the people here, not a very benevolent one."

Chakotay looked around at the mass of wretched individuals who were watching them, some with curiosity, others with dull eyes that evinced no interest in these newest arrivals. He saw one humanoid with greenish, scummy scales and pale yellow eyes. The eyes seemed alert, and he looked to be in slightly better condition than some of the others. Chakotay walked over to him, hoping to get some answers. The scaly man watched him warily as he approached.

"What is this place?" Chakotay asked in as friendly a tone as he could summon. The man's lemon eyes darted around as though looking to see whether it were safe to answer. Finally he looked back at Chakotay and said in a guttural voice, "You don't know? It's the war camp of the Subu. We're all prisoners here."

"We don't know anything about the Subu, or their war. We were abducted and brought here while we were on a peaceful mission."

"That's true of many. You must have strayed into Subu territory. They'll take anyone who does."

"Who's in charge here?"

The yellow eyes flitted here and there again. "You'll see soon enough," said the man, who turned and scuttled away. Chakotay looked around for someone else to question, but no one else would make eye contact with him.

He was moving back toward his group, which was milling about uncertainly, when he noted a perceptible shift in the mood of the prisoners, as though an electromagnetic current had suddenly run through them. They turned away from the *Voyager* crew, seeming to busy themselves with various occupations, but Chakotay got the definite impression that they were simply trying to look busy.

Then he saw what had caused this mood swing: a door had opened in the smooth, metallic wall of the stockade and several figures had emerged from it, moving toward the *Voyager* crew. Along their path, the prisoners averted their eyes, seemingly too preoccupied to look up, but Chakotay sensed a palpable terror.

He watched the approach of the figures. There were three of them, one in front and two slightly behind, the latter two holding what looked to be weapons of some kind. They were larger than Starfleet's phaser rifles, with huge muzzles. He couldn't be sure whether they were projectile or energy weapons, but whatever delivery system they used, they were intimidating.

The three beings were equally so. He would have to characterize them as humanoid, in that they walked on legs, albeit three of them, and had heads, although they were gray, swollen, and gelatinous, with no ears, no discernible nose, and tiny faceted eyes. They reminded Chakotay of whales' heads. The beings had two appendages, like humanoids, but those were long and tentacle-like.

The trio came to a stop in front of Chakotay, who could see now that they constantly oozed a sticky slime, which coagulated quickly, coating their bodies—a function Chakotay surmised had to do with regulating body temperature. They were probably much more comfortable in the baking heat of this place than any of *Voyager*'s crew except for the Vulcans, who were accustomed to a desert climate.

An orifice opened on the head of the lead figure, and a voice spoke with the same harsh raspiness they had heard in the spaceship. "You will receive rations once a day. Water from the stream. Do not cause problems or punishment will be severe." And with that he turned to move away.

"Wait," Chakotay called out. "We don't belong here. We're travelers trying to get home, tens of thousands of light-years away, and we aren't involved in any dispute with you or your people."

The creature didn't respond, just kept moving away on its three legs, which gave it a rolling gait, a kind of trot. "Who can I talk to about this?" yelled Chakotay.

The creature stopped and turned around, and suddenly one of its tentacled arms snaked out and struck Chakotay on the neck. An instant, agonizing pain erupted on his face and he fell to the ground, pawing at his neck.

Tuvok and Tom Paris were immediately at his side, Tuvok using the cloth of his uniform to wipe away the coat of slime the tentacle had left on Chakotay's neck. As he did so, the pain began to subside, and Chakotay sat up again. "I guess I asked too many questions," he said dryly. They watched the retreating figures making their way back to the formidable metal wall, watched the studied indifference of the other prisoners, still furiously occupied with make-work activities.

The trio paused at one of the lean-to shanties, where four pitifully scrawny humanoids were busily cleaning the area, a process that seemed to involve picking up something and putting it down somewhere else, over and over. As the three Subu watched, none of the humanoids looked at them or acknowledged them in any way.

Suddenly the leader's tentacle snaked out once more, wrapping itself around the torso of one of the prisoners, who immediately began to scream and beg for mercy. "I didn't do anything! Don't take me!" But the leader plucked him off his feet and trotted off once more, with the man writhing and pleading, the two armed guards close behind.

It was a chilling event, and the *Voyager* crew was sobered, witnessing it. Chakotay turned back to the crew and set about doing what he had to do: seeing to their survival in these harsh conditions and making plans for escape.

"The first thing we need is water," he announced. Chakotay was dangerously dehydrated and he knew the same was true of the others. "Whalehead said there's a stream—everyone fan out and see if you can find it. Once we've done that, we'll start laying plans."

The others nodded and spread out. Chakotay noted that there seemed to be a vague organization to the place: it was crisscrossed with several broad paths, upon which no lean-tos rested, creating roadways of sorts. He set off down one of them, looking for anyone who might be willing to answer a few questions, and spotted a young man, barely more than a boy, cruelly thin, yellow skin shrunken around his bones, sitting on the ground. The boy looked at him with huge, sad eyes. Chakotay squatted in front of him. "Can you tell me where the stream is?" he asked quietly.

The boy stared at him, eyes reflecting a misery so profound it could not be uttered. He didn't speak, but turned his head slightly to his right, down the path Chakotay was on. "Thanks," said the commander, but the boy didn't reply.

Chakotay stood and turned to proceed down the path, but saw that his way was barred by four humanoids. These were huge men, better fed than anyone else he'd seen, but equally filthy. They had a distinctly human look except for the size of their heads, which was about twice as big as his own, giving them a fierce, ogre-like appearance.

"Shoes. Give," said one of them tersely, gesturing toward Chakotay's boots. "Clothing."

"Good morning," said Chakotay jovially. "Wonder if you could tell me where the stream is?"

The four exchanged glances and then the speaker moved forward, confrontational. Chakotay smiled at him and then quickly, coming off his back foot with a thrust up the legs, whipped his head forward and head-butted the man right in his nose. The man's legs crumpled under him and he sank heavily to the ground, nose and cheekbones crushed.

The three others started forward but suddenly Tuvok, Harry, Tom, and several of Tuvok's security guards were there with him. The three paused, uncertain. "Take him with you," said Chakotay, nodding toward the fallen man. Two of the men grabbed the fallen man's legs, and they dragged him unceremoniously off, casting dark looks at Chakotay and his friends as they went.

"I think you sent them a pretty good message," said Harry. "They'll think twice about bothering us." Chakotay wasn't sure they'd seen the last of them, but agreed that in a place like this, it was important to establish one's pecking order. A strong show against bullies would make things somewhat easier for the *Voyager* crew. At least for a while.

"The stream is supposed to be this way," said Chakotay, and saw Tom nod agreement.

"That's what I was told, too," Tom said. The group proceeded down the path, taking in the foul sights of the prison camp. Chakotay estimated that the enclosure encircled a total of about forty hectares, laid out in a roughly rectangular pattern. The camp was a long strip between the huge trees, inhabited by some ten to twelve thousand prisoners. All were undernourished, and many were ill, as well. He saw one person lying on a scrap of cloth, hawklike features shriveled and burned from the sun, skin dotted with open sores upon which insects buzzed and fed. Another lay in a soup of his own vomitus, too weak to lift his head.

Everywhere he looked, there were further examples of misery and suffering, more appalling than anything Chakotay had ever seen. Even the treatment of his ancestors on government reservations was more humane. The sun was relentless, baking them from a cloudless sky. The overwhelming stench of the place was nauseating, and he could hear a chorus of moans from the sick and wounded. It was a vision of hell.

Some eighty meters down the path the ground dipped, taking them down a slope which led to a lower level of the prison yard. There they found the stream.

It was a foul, muddy affair which stretched from one side of the stockade to the other, flowing from their left to their right, where it disappeared under the imposing metal wall. An iron grating at either end prevented anyone from getting under the barrier. The stream was surrounded on both sides by a swampy morass through which anyone wanting water would have to wade.

The real problem was that the prisoners had used the downstream portion of the stream as a latrine. A foul mass of excrement assaulted their noses, and insects buzzed heavily over it. Each member of the group felt his stomach churn at the sight.

"At least they had enough sense to use the downstream side," said Tom.

"It can still contaminate the upstream water," replied Chakotay. "That stream isn't flowing swiftly enough to prevent a backflow."

Still, they had no choice. Not to drink the putrid water was to invite sure death. They moved to their left, toward the upstream side of the creek, aware that their every step was watched curiously by nearby prisoners.

As they approached the stream, Chakotay noticed what appeared to be a blanket stretched on the swampy bank of the creek, and for a moment he thought someone had spread it there to make the crossing to the water somewhat easier.

When they got closer, however, they made a chilling discovery. "Commander," said Harry uncertainly, "I think that's a person."

13

It was. A scrawny body lay on the swampy surface, head completely submerged in the turgidly flowing waters of the stream. Tuvok waded toward it and, with one strong arm, lifted it from the watery grave.

It was an old woman, face lined with her years, hair a dirty gray, caked now with mud. Her eyes were open but sightless, and her mouth hung open in the slack-jawed grimace of death. Beneath that was another mouth, or so it seemed, until Tuvok said, "Her throat has been cut," and they saw that was true, her neck yawning with a gaping wound, out of which her life had bled.

They pulled the body to dry ground, and no sooner had they done so than it was set upon by several people who quickly stripped it of clothing and shoes, even though she wore little more than threadbare rags and the shoes were worn through at the soles. After that she lay naked, shriveled and bony, dead eyes staring up at the sun. Insects soon found her.

Chakotay noted that Harry was looking a little pale. "We have to drink," he reminded them all, and led the way to the stream from which they had just removed a dead body. He knelt down on the muddy bank and scooped water into his mouth. It was brackish and sour, but it would hydrate him, and that was the important thing.

The others did the same, reacting to the unpleasant taste but drinking nonetheless. But one of the security guards, Brad Harrison, hung back. "I don't think I'm that thirsty, sir," he said to Chakotay.

"Drink it anyway, Ensign. That's an order. We can't afford to let ourselves get weak. We have to drink what we have available, eat anything we have to in order to keep up our strength. The energy you lose from one missed meal can take you weeks to recover."

Harry smiled wanly. "You sound like Commander Nimembeh," he said. "He was my survival instructor at the Academy."

"Mine, too," said Chakotay. "Except he was Lieutenant Nimembeh when I was there. All right, go get the others and tell them to come and drink. Then we'll think about where we're going to camp."

Harry trotted off with Tom, and Chakotay tried not to look at the body of the old woman, now almost completely covered with insects.

Three hours later, spirits somewhat restored by the slaking of their thirst, the group had found a reasonably bare patch of ground, which they chose as a campsite. Soon after that an alarm sounded, numerous doors in the walls opened, and hover vehicles emerged from them. The prisoners all rose and stood alongside the paths that crisscrossed the meadow, and the vehicles moved among them, dispensing rations.

Taking their cue from the others, *Voyager*'s crew did the same, and were each handed a crumbling cake of something resembling baked grains, shot through with dirt and small bits of rock. They stared at it, dismayed. Chakotay once again led the way, breaking off a small portion, putting it in his mouth and chewing carefully to locate the stones.

"Eat up," he said as cheerfully as he could, and the group sat down and had their first meal as Subu prisoners. The torturous sun finally went down, and as night came on, the temperature cooled, bringing blessed relief. Tomorrow they would see about shelter, which might require bartering for materials, and about fuel for a fire. And they would reconnoiter the camp even more carefully, assessing the possible escape routes and methods, in preparation for what they now believed was a perfectly plausible effort. Food and water, no matter how unappetizing, had restored their optimism, and made them think that all things were possible.

"Commander," said Harry after they'd eaten and stretched out on the ground, weary after the events of the last two days. "How'd you get along with Commander Nimembeh?"

"Get along with him? Fine, I guess. I only had him during prep squad, before my freshman year started. He was tough, but everyone respected him."

Harry looked a little sheepish. "I had quite an experience with him," he said. "It wasn't a lot of fun."

"No one would ever call Nimembeh fun," agreed Chakotay. A silence fell on them, but Harry seemed to be pondering something. After a few moments, he turned again to Chakotay.

"Sir . . . if I'm prying or anything, you don't have to answer. But how was it . . . that you quit Starfleet, and joined the Maquis? I mean, to go through the Academy, and be a Starfleet officer . . . and then to give it all up—well, I just wondered how that happened."

Chakotay drew a breath. It was something he had spent a great deal of time contemplating, and he wasn't entirely sure he had an easy answer. "To tell you that, I'd practically have to tell you the story of my life."

"If you're willing to tell it, I'd sure like to hear it."

Chakotay looked around at his group. Several people were listening to the conversation, and seemed intrigued by the prospect of learning more about their first officer. It occurred to him that this might be as good a way as any to pass some time. "All right. If anybody gets bored you can go to sleep. I won't be offended."

He paused a moment to think how to start, and looked up at the night sky, dotted with stars. Suddenly an image shot into his mind, one he hadn't thought about for some twenty years, and he knew that was the beginning of his tale. "When I was fifteen, my father and I took a trip together, and it was a turning point in my life."

CHAPTER 2

"THERE WASN'T YET ONE PERSON, ANIMAL, BIRD, FISH, TREE, ROCK, canyon, forest. Only the sky was there, only the sea alone was lying under all the sky. Nothing stirs.

"Whatever might be is simply not there. But in the Otherworld, the Hero Twins are preparing to destroy the power of Seven-Macaw, so that their father, the Maize God, can be reborn."

Chakotay's mind drifted as he listened to the sonorous tones of his father's voice. They were lying on their backs atop a grassy hill in Central America, on the planet Earth, where his ancestors had evolved. The sky was an ebony blanket salted with stars that shone so brilliantly they seemed able to burn holes in his eyes. But the sight held no majesty for Chakotay. He would rather have been anywhere else.

"The Hero Twins knocked Seven-Macaw from the crocodile tree where he was perched, and then they put their father's head back upon his dead body so that he was reborn. Three gods, the paddlers, bore him in a sky canoe, concealed beneath the carapace of a turtle, to the place where the dawn of life was conceived.

"And then the First Father emerged through the cracked turtle shell, resurrected. All this happened at a place called lying-down-sky,

17

before the First Father lifted the crocodile tree on high, pushing the sky upward and centering it."

Chakotay shifted restlessly. He'd heard this tale many times before, from the time he was a small boy. He remembered being intrigued by it at first, but now, at fifteen, he was beyond such nonsense. He failed to understand his father's excitement at this strange ritual, looking up at the sky and retelling the story of creation.

But his father's exhilaration was palpable. It had begun to build as soon as he had decided on this quest, this return with his son to the planet of their ancestors, and had mounted steadily in the ensuing months. Now, as Kolopak recounted the ancient myth of the beginnings of the world, his voice was husky with emotion.

Vaguely, Chakotay tuned back in to the familiar story. "First Father had carried with him from the Otherworld a packet of maize seeds, which he scattered on the earth, and those became man. And thus was the earth created, and centered, and ordered."

There was a moment's silence, which Chakotay didn't hurry to fill. He could feel his father's awe and reverence rising like a mist, and he wished again that he had been allowed to stay behind and avoid this wearisome experience.

"Just think, Chakotay. We're here, on the night of August thirteenth, the date of creation, watching the stars our ancestors watched, seeing the hours of the beginning play out once more." Kolopak's voice broke slightly, and Chakotay felt a twinge of embarrassment for him. "The crocodile tree and the sky canoe are nothing less than our galaxy, the Milky Way. First Father is represented by the constellation Orion, which our ancestors called the turtle. Its three belt stars—Alnitak, Mintaka, and Alnilam—are the three creation stones. And Seven-Macaw, who had to be knocked from the crocodile tree in order for the maize god to be reborn, is represented by the seven stars in the Big Dipper."

Kolopak pointed up, gripped with passion. "Look, Chakotay—the Milky Way is turning from its north-south position, and the Big Dipper is falling, falling toward the horizon. In another hour Seven-Macaw will disappear, vanquished, readying the sky for creation."

Chakotay stirred restlessly. They'd already been out here for two hours, and his muscles felt stiff, needing the relief of movement. He was also hungry, and pushed himself to his feet to search his knapsack for something to eat. He knew he wouldn't find anything particularly tempting there; Kolopak had decreed that they would eat only the foods of their ancestors during this trek, so corn cakes, dried deer meat, and tubers were all he could look forward to. He rummaged in his pack and withdrew one of the corn cakes and a bottle of water. Yum.

"Would you like anything?" he asked his father politely. Maybe if he were the model child he could get out of this ordeal as quickly as possible.

"No, thank you," replied Kolopak, still gazing upward in wonder. "I don't have an appetite. I'm just overwhelmed by this."

Chakotay sat and munched his corn cake and sipped cold water. The night was warm and humid, and the cool liquid was soothing. The buzz of a mosquito seeking its own dinner hummed around his ear, and he flailed at it in irritation.

Overhead, the skies continued their inexorable display, the Milky Way "canoe" appearing to tip toward the horizon, sinking to carry the maize god to the place of creation. By dawn, Chakotay knew, the turtle constellation, or Orion, would be at the zenith, signifying the rebirth of the First Father. He knew all this, having been shown the star maps since he was a child. There was no particular amazement to seeing it in person.

"How long are we going to stay?" he ventured mildly, expecting his father to say, "Just a little while longer."

But Kolopak looked at him in astonishment. "We'll stay the night, of course, until First Father is at the zenith, at dawn."

Chakotay's heart sank. Back at their lodgings were padds with books and games that would hold his interest. Out here, on this lonely, humid hilltop, there was nothing. He flopped back onto the ground and closed his eyes, disturbed by the annoying buzz of the mosquito, still hunting for blood.

He awoke at the gentle shaking of his father's hand. Kolopak was looking down at him, face transfixed with joy. "Look, Chakotay— First Father is born again."

Chakotay struggled to a sitting position, eyes gummy with sleep, limbs aching, mouth fetid. The first faint paling of the eastern sky had begun, and Kolopak was pointing upward. Chakotay followed the gesture. There, above them, Orion's belt—the turtle constellation to the ancient people—was at the zenith, signifying the resurrection of the maize god, First Father.

Kolopak's face was shining. "It was incredible. To see this pageant replayed, just as our ancestors did—I can't tell you how deeply it's touched me. We have to come back on February fifth, the reciprocal date, and see the raising of the sky."

Chakotay stretched his stiff limbs and ran his fingers through his hair. He felt awful, cold and sticky, his stomach empty and his bladder full. The thought of going through this ordeal yet again made him shudder. He had to find some way to get out of it.

His father, relentlessly cheerful, extended his hand to help Chakotay to his feet, chattering about the power of the nightlong experience, his soul's response to participating in such an ancient and important ritual. If he sensed Chakotay's diffidence, he didn't show it. He spoke as though they had shared the night and the spiritual adventure, when in fact Kolopak had been alone.

"Let's go," his father said, with as much energy as though he had slept like a baby all night long. "We're meeting our guides soon. They'll take us into the wilderness."

Chakotay's hand went to his neck, which he realized was itching uncomfortably. His fingers discovered a thick welt there, and he dug at it until it hurt. The mosquito, at least, had had a successful night.

If the night had been long and uncomfortable, it was a time of luxury compared with the trek into the rain forest. Chakotay couldn't believe his father was determined to plunge into this malodorous jungle, replete with vicious insects and poisonous reptiles, simply to find the village of their ancestors. Who could even be sure the village still existed? There had been an exodus from this part of Earth over two hundred years ago; who knew what might have happened to those who stayed behind? They had probably become blended into contemporary human society, losing the ancient ways. At least, that was the fear that had driven his father's tribe to leave Earth and settle on a remote planet several thousand light-years away, hoping to find a place where they could preserve their customs and rituals.

This was, in Chakotay's mind, a way to insure that his tribe remained rooted in the past, clinging desperately to centuries-old traditions, instead of welcoming the new and exciting future. He, for one, was determined to embrace the twenty-fourth century, but he had yet to inform his father of that.

Now, they were slashing their way through a jungle that was oppressively hot and almost unbelievably humid. Chakotay swore he could see moisture suspended in the air, shimmering in the shafts of sunlight like a filmy curtain of water. Grotesquely huge insects hung in swarms under the canopy of trees, buzzing violently as though infuriated by the intrusion of humans. There were fifteen of them: Chakotay, Kolopak, and thirteen native guides and porters. What would have been so wrong, the boy wondered, with simply transporting all of them into the designated area? Why behave as though this were some kind of ancient safari?

Chakotay occupied his mind by trying to determine the best way to inform his father of his plans. This wouldn't be easy—he anticipated every reaction imaginable: anger, frustration, sorrow, adamancy—but he was determined to confront the issue sooner rather than later.

But how? With a prelude explaining his dissatisfaction with his father's ways, his insistence on making his own choices? Or by asking for understanding and requesting permission? He ran down several versions of the conversation in his mind, but no matter what approach he took, he could envision only a disappointing outcome.

A bright flash of movement at the periphery of his vision made him turn and then follow it. It was a lizard, orange and green, scurrying over a tree stump. Something was marked on the tree stump, and Chakotay moved toward it. He vaguely heard his father's voice admonishing him: "I don't want you wandering off . . ."

"I wasn't," the boy replied. "I was just looking at something." He heard Kolopak move behind him to look at the symbol that had been etched on the face of the tree trunk.

"Antonio," his father called. "Come here and see what my son found."

Antonio, a cheerful man in his thirties, with dark hair and a brilliant smile, joined them, inspecting the marking. "We're getting close, Kolopak. Your son is quite a scout."

Kolopak beamed with pride, making Chakotay uncomfortable. "I was just looking at a lizard and I saw it," he muttered self-deprecatingly, but Kolopak wasn't dissuaded.

"Well, your eyes saw it, no one else's did—that's the important thing."

Chakotay sighed inwardly, barely listening as his father launched into a dissertation about the symbol, an ancient blessing to the land, a kind of apologia for cutting down the tree. Why did he have to be told all this, over and over again? He had absolutely no interest in these old customs. He wandered back onto the trail, wondering how long it was until lunch, and hence didn't see the disappointed look on his father's face.

The discovery of the huge snake came shortly after they had eaten a midday meal. It was a decidedly unnerving event to Chakotay, and left him with a cold knot in his stomach.

It was Antonio who found it, a boa constrictor over three meters long, grotesquely swollen from a recent meal. The snake was torporous from its ingestion, which Antonio surmised was a small boar, or peccary. Chakotay stared in disgust, envisioning the slow devouring. The constrictor would have crushed the boar first, wrapping its coils around the pig's rib cage and then tightening slowly, inexorably squeezing air from its lungs and making it impossible for the pig to breathe. As its ribs snapped, it would pass into blessed unconsciousness.

At that point, the snake's jaws would spread wide, allowing it to envelop the boar's head, and gradually, using its powerful muscles, it would gulp the creature into its stomach. Then, worn from the effort, sated as it began to digest its meal, it would sink into languor, able only to lie on the floor of the forest until the boar was completely digested, some weeks hence. Then it would begin its relentless search for the next repast, sliding silently and surprisingly swiftly through the undergrowth until some other animal was caught within its powerful coils.

Chakotay hated snakes. As a child his nightmares were those of being pursued by giant reptiles, or of being shut inside a dwelling where somewhere, he knew not where, there was a snake that would spring at him when he least expected it. He would wake crying aloud, damp with sweat, and creep into bed with his mother and father, a place where snake dreams wouldn't dare to pursue him.

Of all the creatures Earth had spawned, these were the ones Chakotay had difficulty countenancing. They seemed to strike at some primal fear that couldn't be rationally understood; his people, after all, had been at one with all animals, and some had even worshipped the serpent, or at least put it in a position of special reverence. Their creation myth certainly spoke with awe about ancient and mysterious reptiles.

But to Chakotay they were discomfiting for reasons he couldn't articulate. The sight of one produced a slight chilling in him, a faint but pervasive sense of unease. He disliked their colorations, their scaliness, the undulating way they moved.

Now, as Chakotay was confronted with the gruesome sight of the bloated constrictor, his stomach contorted and he turned away in revulsion. He felt his father's gaze on him, but didn't care. This was just one more example of the horrors and indignities that were being thrust on him in this foolish quest for their forebears.

"Serpents have been devouring their prey here for thousands of years," offered Kolopak. "Our ancestors worshipped these majestic reptiles because of their powerful ability to shed their skins and be reborn." Chakotay could tell that his father viewed this discovery as another sign of the symbolic significance of their journey.

"Tell that to the boar," he said churlishly.

"Animals have killed each other for food since the dawn of time," Kolopak began, but Chakotay waved him off.

"Please, not another lecture about the natural order of things," he said. "I know all that. Can't we get going? The bugs don't bother you as much if you keep moving."

His father's eyes seemed sorrowful as he gazed at Chakotay, and the boy felt faintly guilty. He broke the look by slapping at the insects that buzzed about his head. After a moment, Antonio took the lead and they proceeded deeper into the rain forest.

As the afternoon wore on, Chakotay became more and more irritable. He was suffocatingly hot, damp with perspiration, covered with welts from insect bites, and tired of this endless trek through a snake-infested jungle. The cacophony of animal and bird calls that swirled around them had given him a headache, and he wanted nothing more than to be back at home, swimming with his friends in the cool green lake that was fed by mountain streams.

Gradually, he became aware that his father was saying something, something that had blended into the clamor of parrot and monkey sounds. He turned to see his father looking up, pointing toward the sky. His gaze followed. "Listen to him, Chakotay. Do you hear what he says to you?"

Chakotay located the hawk circling above them, its screech indistinguishable from that of other wild birds. He looked at his father, whose face was shining once more with joy. Kolopak looked back at Chakotay, beaming. "Do you hear it?"

Chakotay shrugged and shook his head. "He says, 'You are home,'" said Kolopak with heavy significance.

Something unloosed itself in Chakotay's mind, even as the sudden slippage of wet earth on a sodden hillside will precipitate a mudslide. He hadn't planned to say the words, but they came unbidden, and he could no more stop them than he could hold back tons of sediment single-handed.

"I'm leaving the tribe, Father," he announced, and waited heavily for Kolopak's response.

There was none. A leaden silence hung between them, punctuated by insect hum and bird call. Chakotay continued, energized by finally getting this out in the open. "I got to know a lot of the Starfleet officers patrolling the Cardassian border . . . I asked Captain Sulu if he would sponsor me at Starfleet Academy."

He was prepared for his father's distress at this revelation. Hiromi Sulu, grandson of the legendary Hikaru Sulu of the *U.S.S. Enterprise* 1701, had become a familiar figure on their homeworld, Trebus, which was near Cardassian space. Captain Sulu had warned the colonists that Starfleet was concerned about Cardassian military buildup, and had even suggested that the Indians relocate to a safer position, but of course the elders weren't about to abandon the land they had found spiritually compatible.

Chakotay was fascinated by the Starfleet officers, with their impressive uniforms and their array of technology—tricorders, phasers, replicators, transporters. They were symbols to him of life as it should be, lived in the present and anticipating the future, not linked in some unholy embrace with the past.

Hiromi Sulu was in his mid-thirties, a lithe, handsome officer who seemed to move comfortably among his crew and the inhabitants of this unusual world. He had dined at Chakotay's home on a number of occasions, and had struck up a friendship with the adolescent son of his host. Captain Sulu had three daughters, and seemed drawn to Chakotay as a kind of surrogate son.

He had befriended Kolopak as well, and Chakotay knew his father would consider it a betrayal that Captain Sulu had sponsored him without discussing it with Kolopak. And indeed, that was his father's first response: "He would do such a thing without discussing it with me?"

"I told him I had your approval. I kept him as far away from you as I could." This was true, and had caused Chakotay no end of trouble, disseminating misinformation to his father and to Captain Sulu alike. He felt faintly guilty at this manipulation, but wasn't going to back down now.

"I take it you have reason to believe you'll be accepted at the Academy," offered Kolopak, and Chakotay nodded tersely. He had to pass the entrance exams, of course, but he wasn't worried about them. Another long silence ensued.

"You've never fully embraced the traditions of our tribe, I know that. You've always been curious about other societies. And I allowed you to read about them because I believe ignorance is our greatest enemy. But to leave the tribe . . ."

"Our tribe lives in the past . . . a past of fantasy and myth."

"That past is a part of you, no matter how hard you try to reject it."

"Other tribes have learned to accept the twenty-fourth century. Why can't ours?"

Kolopak's voice was taking on a decided edge. "It is not the place of a fifteen-year-old boy to question the choices of his tribe."

"I know," replied Chakotay solemnly. "That's why I have to leave."

Kolopak scrutinized him with those burning, sorrowful eyes. "You will never belong to that other life. And if you leave, you will never belong to this one. You will be caught between worlds."

The truth of this caught Chakotay with a sudden chill, as though an icy breeze had knifed through the stifling forest. "I ask for your blessing, Father," he said humbly, but there was no answer. Kolopak stared stonily ahead, and Chakotay knew no blessing would be forthcoming.

A year and a half later he stood on a grassy plain on his homeworld, a satchel with his belongings at his side, his mother and father before him. He was minutes from transporting to Captain Sulu's ship, which would carry him to San Francisco, on the planet Earth, the home of Starfleet Academy.

The morning was cold, as though reminding the inhabitants that, although summer was just over, winter was coming quickly. Growing up, he had always eagerly anticipated that bracing nip in the air, as it seemed to energize him—probably some genetic throwback to an era when provisions must be laid in for the fallow months of winter.

"Send us messages, please," implored his mother, whose eyes, he noticed, were swollen from crying the night before. He felt both embarrassed and regretful.

"If you'd put in a modern comm system we could have instant contact," he suggested, only to be greeted by a dismissive grunt from his father. He might have known—there would be no place for sophisticated technology on this world.

He put his arms around his mother, who gulped back her tears, knowing the effect they would have on him. "I'll send lots of messages," he promised her. "I'll tell you about everything." She patted his back ineffectually.

He turned to his father, hating this moment and yet strangely empowered by it as well. He had made his choice and he was following through. He would chart the course of his own life, unbound by the past, free to explore any of the options that might lie before him.

In his father's eyes he saw only pain.

Kolopak embraced him, but it was a gesture without warmth. Chakotay tried to speak, but the words caught in his throat, and he silently cursed the revelation of emotion. He had wanted to appear manly before his father, and now his throat had clutched, betraying him. He stepped back and touched the comm device Captain Sulu had given him. "Chakotay to Captain Sulu. I'm ready, sir."

And in the disembodying moment before transport, he saw both love and anguish on his parents' faces.

"Way too slow, Cadet. Ten times around the track."

Chakotay's head whipped toward Lieutenant Nimembeh, his prep squad officer. He was sure he'd shaved several seconds off his time—his phaser had been disassembled, reconfigured, and reassembled in just under seventeen seconds. How fast did he have to be? He started to ask just that when Nimembeh spoke again. "When I give an order, you follow it *immediately*. That's fifteen times around the track."

"In my uniform and boots?" queried Chakotay, incredulous and inexperienced enough with Starfleet discipline to realize what he was buying himself.

"Make that twenty."

Chakotay moved off before Nimembeh added more, but he was indignant and furious. Run the track *twenty times* in his uniform and boots? It would be easy enough in running shoes, but the black leather boots weren't at all conducive to jogging. He'd be in blisters by the end of it. This was all so arbitrary. What were they trying to prove?

Fortunately the day wasn't a warm one—rarely was it too warm in San Francisco—and a cool breeze braced him as he trotted from the parade ground, over the immaculately groomed grounds of Starfleet Academy, and onto the track. If he were properly outfitted, it might be energizing to take this run. Just under five kilometers was a warm-up for him under ordinary circumstances.

But halfway around the first turn, he knew it would be different this time. His cadet's uniform chafed at his skin and the boots were heavy, clumsy on his feet. Eventually, they would feel like iron weights.

He set about clearing his mind, focusing on the rhythm of running, rather than on his body. He could do this, was determined to do it without complaint, because to do otherwise would give Nimembeh a satisfaction Chakotay didn't want him to have. He placed himself, in his mind, on his homeworld of Trebus, on the plains where, growing up, he had run for hours on end, seduced by the independence he felt when he was alone and the wind embraced him. He was utterly at liberty in those times, impeded by no one, obstructed by nothing. They were golden moments of his childhood, and he focused to relive them now.

For a while it worked. He discovered a pace that the boots could tolerate without punishing him, and found the stride that minimized the abrading of his uniform against his inner thighs. He recaptured the sounds, the smells of his childhood revels in the meadows and the woods. He had not realized until now how precious those memories were to him.

For ten laps it was bearable, and he couldn't avoid the rueful acknowledgment that if he had responded to Nimembeh's order immediately, he would be done now. But he was only halfway through, and there were indications that it was going to get worse quickly.

His feet had begun to protest the pounding in the leather boots. His legs had started to weary of lifting their heavy weight. But most important, his skin was beginning to feel raw in places where friction was wearing through his socks and rubbing at a toe joint, at a heel, at a metatarsal bone.

That's what would be the hardest part of this to endure. Strange that a tiny lesion in the uppermost layers of the skin could produce such pain—a testimony to the complex network of nerves that lay there. But pain could be dealt with.

Twelve laps. There were three distinct places in his feet that he could identify as blistered: left big toe, left heel, and right instep. The pain had increased geometrically in the last two laps, which didn't bode well for the next eight.

Thirteen laps. The track seemed to have lengthened horrifically, far beyond its quarter-kilometer starting point. Now it felt like a kilometer each time around. His gait had slowed appreciably, though the lessened pace didn't alleviate the pain. He clenched his jaw, determined to get through this.

Fourteen. He forced his mind to think of summers on his homeworld, when he and his friends would spend all day in the woods, playing, laughing, engaging in mock combat. In many ways they were like a pride of lion cubs, tumbling and roughhousing, but all the while honing skills for survival.

But what had driven that instinct? Members of the Federation didn't have to fight to survive anymore, didn't have to struggle or make war. What genetic predisposition compelled him and his friends to take on the role of warriors, battling for defense of home and family? Apparently something not easily lost in a few hundred years of relative peace.

Fifteen laps. His feet were now identified by three points of fire, three hot coals that were burning into the bone. He stumbled briefly but forced himself to keep going. He'd made it around that last lap by summoning visions of home. Maybe those would sustain him until the end.

His people, in the past, had been subjected to hideous tortures, many involving hot coals. The European conquerors had intimidating ways of meting out punishment, of demonstrating their authority over the "savages" they had found occupying the land they intended to claim. Chakotay had heard these stories from the time he was a small boy.

On the other hand, his people were equally well versed in such techniques, and used them with impunity against each other. Cruelty wasn't the exclusive province of the Europeans. It wasn't uncommon among his ancestors for captured prisoners to be tortured for months, even years. Sometimes the enemy was tied into a makeshift "ball," and kicked around the ball court until he died. Inventive.

Sixteen. Keep the pain at bay. If you give in to it it will be unbearable. Focus elsewhere.

His people had any number of customs involving self-sacrifice. The noble women, for instance, performed a ritual in which they pierced their tongue with a barb and pulled a length of rope through it. And just to make it an equal-opportunity culture, the noble men often pierced their foreskin, dripped blood on paper, and then burned it as a blessing to the gods.

And of course there were the ritual executions, the heart extrusions, the stonings, the disembowelments. His ancestors had little reason to accuse the Europeans of excess cruelty.

Seventeen. Pain was beginning to interfere with his ability to project his mind elsewhere. Cruelty. Was this what Starfleet was all about? What was being accomplished by this brutal exercise? Did

Nimembeh derive some sick pleasure from exercising his power over his cadets? It had struck Chakotay that way ever since he reported to the Academy and had been assigned to Nimembeh. There were twenty of them in each prep squad; for two weeks they would belong to their instructor, who was responsible for molding them into a disciplined, finely tuned unit before they actually started academic course work.

From the beginning, he had felt singled out by Nimembeh, who seemed to mete out particularly rigorous tasks to Chakotay, and to inflict especially strict penalties if the young man didn't perform up to expectations—which, he had learned, was just about always. This grueling five-kilometer run was just another in a series of disciplines to which he, and he alone of his group, had been subjected.

So Nimembeh didn't like him. But there were only three laps to go, and he would show the drill instructor he couldn't be broken quite so easily. Chakotay could endure whatever this sadist might concoct for him.

Eighteen laps. Each step sent lances of pain from his feet to his brain, and he struggled feverishly with some way to deal with it. He began to sing, summoning up remembered chants from his childhood, lamentations and invocations to the spirits which were supposed to augur well for the future. It was foolishness, of course, but he remembered being soothed by hearing the voices of his people joined together, conjurations lifted to the skies in ancient harmonies. Now, as the barely remembered chants came panting out of him, he was soothed once more.

Ahead of him, standing at one end of the track, silhouetted by the low afternoon sun, was a figure. It was Nimembeh, whose whippet-thin body and dark, bald head Chakotay would recognize anywhere. He'd come to see his charge fail, but he would not be given that satisfaction. Chakotay rounded the track in front of him, not making eye contact, seeing the familiar ebony face and chiseled features only in his periphery.

Nineteen. One more to go. He could run one more lap, one slight quarter-kilometer, even if his feet were bleeding and he felt as though he were running on knife points. He summoned in his mind's eye that dark figure standing against the sun and flung against it all his fury and indignation. Every pounding step radiated pain, and that pain fueled rage. He envisioned Nimembeh erupting into flame, consumed by the sheer intensity of Chakotay's wrath.

That vision got him halfway around. He was on the last half lap, heading into the sun once more, heading toward that dark figure . . .

Except the figure had changed. He didn't see Nimembeh's dark presence, his erect form, his studied stillness. Someone stood against the sun but whoever it was emitted a paleness, a glowing white, as though a snow-figure had descended from above. A sky spirit? One of those to whom he had been chanting? A quiver of awe moved through him.

Closer he drew, and the glow began to take form: it was a woman, dressed in white, with hair so light it looked like a cloud of milk. She was standing where Nimembeh had, looking directly at him. Was she the drill instructor's simulacrum? His gaze blurred and he shook his head to clear it; perspiration ran into his eyes, stinging them with salt. At that moment he completed his twentieth lap.

The impact on his feet changed suddenly as he ran off the track and onto the grass that surrounded it and felt, rather than saw, the difference in the surfaces. His knees buckled under him and he sprawled headfirst onto the grass, which was cool and yielding. His fingers clutched at the earth in a spasm as his feet howled with fire.

He breathed in the damp aroma of dirt and cut grass, a comforting balm that gradually appeased him. He rolled over on his back and saw the cloud-woman standing over him.

She was probably his age, with skin that was impossibly white. Her eyes were almost colorless, and he realized that she must be from another planet.

"Here," she was saying, with just the hint of an accent he couldn't identify. "I thought you might like this." She was tipping a cup of cool water into his lips, and he slurped at it hungrily, like a baby at its mother's breast.

"Thanks," he said, but his voice emerged as a kind of hoarse growl. He realized he hadn't hydrated before making that run, and might be suffering from electrolyte depletion. He struggled to a sitting position, wincing as the blisters on his feet protested any motion.

"You should get those shoes off," the woman said. "Better to go barefoot." She let him take the cup and drain the water from it, then sat back and gazed at him implacably with those impossibly pale gray eyes.

"Who are you?" he asked, as he began the uncomfortable process of removing his boots.

"Svetlana Korepanova," she replied. "Sveta for short. I'm a first-year cadet, too. From Ekaterinburg, Russia."

So she was human. He was surprised, and tried to reconcile that fact with her unique features and the almost mystical nature of her appearance on the edge of the track in the place where Nimembeh had been.

"Was my prep squad officer here before?" Chakotay asked, drawing off a sock and seeing two bloody smudges on his toe and heel.

"Yes. He stood there for almost the entire time you were running. Then he left just before you finished."

"Couldn't stand it that I lasted the twenty laps," said Chakotay with a hint of sullenness that Sveta immediately noticed.

"You think he was disappointed to see you persevere?" she asked. "What a curious attitude. He has no reason to want you to fail."

Chakotay had removed his second boot and sock, and he studied the blister on that foot before he replied. "That's not the feeling I get. I think he'd enjoy it thoroughly."

"Would you like to walk in the arboretum tonight?"

Her words took Chakotay completely by surprise. The arboretum was traditionally the location of romantic trysts of various levels of intensity, and as such the source of much titillation and curiosity by the entering cadets. It would never have occurred to Chakotay that a female might invite him on such a dalliance after having exchanged no more than a few dozen words.

"Well?" she asked quietly but with determination. "Yes or no?"

"Yes."

"I'll meet you at the entrance at nineteen hundred hours."

Chakotay had forgotten the pain in his feet, and the walk back to his quarters was euphoric.

If Chakotay had thought that there was nothing more in store for him than a romantic interlude, he had miscalculated. Not that Sveta wasn't passionate, for she was, in a straightforward, unabashed way that left him breathless and awed. But she turned out to be a complicated young woman, possessed of many aspects, some of them seemingly contradictory. Affectionate and compassionate, she exuded a concern for others that Chakotay found extraordinary. On the other hand, she held strong opinions about many things, and had a stubborn streak that wouldn't be dislodged with a photon torpedo and a tart tongue that could sting like a scorpion.

He frequently found himself on the receiving end of that sting.

"Let me see if I understand you," she said musingly. "You kept making your bed the way you wanted to, rather than the way Starfleet says you should, but it's your dorm officer's fault for putting you on report."

"You don't understand at all. The bed looked perfectly fine, just as neat as regulations called for. Most people couldn't tell the difference. And my room was spotless."

"I should hope so. You don't even have a roommate to contribute to the mess." It was true. One of the few fortunate things that had happened at the Academy was that he had not been assigned a roommate, and occupied two-person quarters in solitary splendor. Chakotay, who valued his privacy, couldn't have been happier.

Today, he and Sveta were sprawled in a window seat of one of the Academy's study rooms, overlooking the San Francisco Bay. Just a day before, sunlight had danced on the water and aficionados of the old and pervasive sport of sailing had taken advantage of the inviting weather, careening around the bay in small craft with brightly colored sails. They had looked to Chakotay like dozens of vivid birds, skimming and dipping among the waves.

Today, the weather that he would learn was far more characteristic of the area had arrived: the skies sagged darkly, and a cocoon of fog obscured the vast Golden Gate Bridge, which still spanned the bay. The day looked as bleak as he felt. Being put on report was not a good way to begin his Starfleet education, and could damage his prospects for a command track, all because of arbitrary and overly exacting rules.

Sveta didn't seem to understand this, and frankly he was getting frustrated trying to explain it to her. She just kept staring at him with those gray-white eyes, implacable, refusing even to try to comprehend his side of it.

Like right now, over the matter of making beds. Chakotay frankly thought it was a waste of time to do it at all—why make a bed when one is going to get right back in it a few hours later? He'd never made a bed as he was growing up, and his parents had never suggested he should. They understood which things were important and which weren't.

It wasn't as though he were refusing to do this pointless task. He understood that Starfleet had rules and he was willing to abide by them.

But weren't there reasonable rules—and those that were completely ludicrous? Starfleet seemed a slave to the latter, and surely there was a point at which one just didn't let oneself be manipulated by slavish adherence to ridiculous policies.

"What's so important about a mitered corner, anyway?" he continued, still irked by the dorm officer's insistence on conformity.

"A mitered corner," Sveta replied, "is a technique that's hundreds of years old—"

"And I suppose that makes it instantly superior," interrupted Chakotay, but she ignored him.

"It's what Starfleet has chosen as the way we're to make beds. That's the only thing that matters."

"Why is it the only thing? Doesn't common sense enter into it? If my bed looks just as neat as the next one, why isn't my method as good as Starfleet's?"

For a brief instant, he thought he saw her lips tug in amusement, but it might have been a trick of the light. He hoped so: he disliked the thought of being an object of scorn by this perverse woman.

"Were you indulged a great deal as a child?" she asked now, changing the subject, a tactic he'd observed in her before. He wasn't about to play into it.

"What does that have to do with what we're discussing?" he queried.

"You behave very much like someone used to getting his own way."

Irritation bubbled into aggravation. Sveta had a way of picking at a point, like someone worrying a scab until it began to bleed. "I had a very disciplined upbringing," he stated, and recognized the hint of defensiveness in his voice. "I had to do all kinds of things I didn't want to. My father insisted on steeping me in all the history and tradition of our tribe, and taking me on pilgrimages and teaching me all kinds of old myths. I wouldn't have done any of that if I'd had a choice."

She regarded him evenly. "Then why are you so contrary?"

He blinked. "Did you use that word on purpose?"

"What word?"

"Contrary."

"It's just how you strike me."

"That's a term in our tribe. I've always been called a 'contrary.'"

"Because you always swim against the current?"

"Something like that. My father says it started when I was born feet-first."

She smiled, but there was no condescension in it. It was tender, and its sweetness melted him. "Starfleet will be very good for you, Chakotay," she said softly. "But you have to allow it to reach you."

She leaned over and kissed him lightly on the mouth, then gathered

33

her padds and was gone. He stared after her, tasting her lips on his, wondering when he'd see her again and what she'd meant by her last statement.

When Chakotay was given his class assignments, he was relieved to see that Nimembeh had given him high marks for his prep squad experience, but distressed that several bad reports from his dorm officer had resulted in his being denied entry to the pre-command class. He appealed to his faculty advisor, but was told he'd have to clear the bad reports from his record before being allowed to take pre-command. The only way to do that was to avoid being put on report for the rest of the semester. Chakotay seethed inwardly, knowing there would be no recourse.

Negative thoughts and disagreeable feelings enveloped him, and he decided to go back to his room, where at least he could be alone and possibly shed this annoying mood. The dormitory was deserted, as he'd hoped it would be, with most students going through the process of getting their class assignments. The halls were blessedly quiet and Chakotay looked forward to the haven of his quarters. He entered the security code into the panel beside his door and entered as it slid open.

A blue-skinned creature was standing in his room.

They stood facing each other in a moment of mutual surprise. Chakotay noted that the young man was hairless, his skull covered in the same blue skin as the rest of him. A line of demarcation ran down the middle of his face from the top of the skull to his neck. He was rounded, if not plump, and he stared at Chakotay with eyes that were small and bright.

"You must be my roommate," the blue person said with what Chakotay thought was excessive enthusiasm. "I'm Chert. Are you human? I'm Bolian."

Chakotay felt his spirits sink. His good fortune was over; they'd assigned him a roommate. He took a breath and tried to appear more welcoming than he really felt. "Yes, I'm human. My name is Chakotay."

"Chert and Chakotay—alliterative names, I like that." Chert burst into a shrill giggle, which sounded like a horse neighing in pain. Chakotay's nerve endings felt as though they'd been rasped. "I was transferred from Fillmore Quad because some upperclassmen were assigned single rooms. Oh, well, I was getting lonely by myself. It'll be much nicer having a roommate. What are your interests? I hope you're a chess player, I think I could tolerate anything in a roommate except one who doesn't play chess. And what about music? Do you know Bolian music? It's an acquired taste, I'm told, but once your ear accustoms itself to the dissonances, you'll be bored with anything else. You wouldn't happen to have any snacks, would you? Moving over here has famished me."

Chakotay groaned inwardly. How could he bear this prattling fool? He wouldn't have an instant of peace, not a moment's quiet with this garrulous blue man. He would have to draw the lines from the beginning. "I don't have any snacks and I don't play chess and I'm not fond of music at all. So it appears we have nothing in common. If you'd like to petition for another roommate, I won't protest. We'd both be better off."

It was a harsh statement, and Chakotay felt somewhat guilty, but reminded himself that every word he'd spoken was true. He prepared for wounded feelings.

But Chert was unfazed. "No need, no need. I can teach you chess. And I'll introduce the music gradually and softly, you won't even know it's happening. Before long if I don't play it you'll be asking me to. And from now on I'll make sure to keep us supplied with snacks. I like sweet things, do you?"

"What courses did you draw?" asked Chakotay, hoping at least he wouldn't have to encounter this bombastic fellow in class.

"Thermodynamics, Engineering Analysis, Duonetic Systems Design, and Warp Field Theory," replied Chert ebulliently. "I'm heading for the engineering track." This was good news to Chakotay, because it meant their lives wouldn't intersect in the classroom. And if he used his room only for sleeping, maybe he could get through the year without killing this gibbering oaf.

At the end of that year, Chakotay had decided to leave Starfleet Academy. He had served a full school term laboring under Starfleet's rules, and he didn't intend to spend the next three in the same fashion. He had worked harder and trained longer than anyone he knew, but he kept getting put on report for not adhering strictly to some regulation or another. Even his roommate, Chert, clucked with concern over his improprieties. "You've got to be more careful or you'll never graduate. Why is it so hard for you to pay attention to details? I'll be happy to make your bed for you, but I can't follow you around to make sure you follow all the rules. Want a doughnut?"

Chakotay vowed that his first year would be his last. Once he returned to Trebus in June, he would announce his refusal to return to San Francisco. He wasn't entirely certain what he would do with his life, but he'd figure something out.

And, in fact, he told his parents just that when he went home. There was a joyous celebration the night he returned, with tables set up in the meadow, laden with food. His parents were, of course, completely supportive of what he wanted to do. "We never wanted you to go there, Chakotay," his mother assured him. "Your place is here, with your people, helping to preserve the traditions we've kept alive. It's time you began to think of taking a wife. I noticed tonight that Philicia was watching you carefully. She's a lovely girl, very intelligent. You should get to know her."

Chakotay sighed. He'd known Philicia since he was a baby. She was sweet, but he had absolutely no interest in her other than as a childhood acquaintance. She was insular and predictable, her world-view extending only as far as her place in this tribe on this planet. He didn't see how he could spend a lifetime with someone like that.

For that matter, what would he do if he didn't return to the Academy? The thought of staying here and working to preserve his people's traditions was stultifying. He'd entered the Academy in order to escape just such a fate. How could he return to his parents' world so submissively?

He spent the summer wrestling with the decision, enjoying the rough and tumble of games with his friends. He and the young men he'd grown up with would lie under the summer stars, looking up at their twin moons, reminiscing about childhood and laying plans for the future.

It was the latter that left Chakotay feeling uneasy. It seemed all his friends, like his parents, like Philicia, envisioned a destiny no broader than staying on this planet, mating, procreating, and starting the cycle all over again. To Chakotay, it was a disturbing thought.

But what alternative did he prefer? He found it difficult to envision any except staying put or returning to the Academy. He'd heard of itinerant traders, vagabonds who roamed the stars, a footloose existence that took them where the solar winds blew them. And there were freight haulers, who carried goods between the star systems, minerals here, medical supplies there, a constant crisscrossing of space to insure the survival of people who lived on planets that didn't have the natural resources necessary to sustain life.

Would that be satisfying? A nomadic life in space, a peripatetic existence, rootless and ungrounded? He thought not. But *what,* then?

Would he ever find anything satisfying? He wished longingly that he had come out of his mother headfirst, like everyone else, rather than beginning life, and continuing it, in such a contrary fashion.

In the end, he asked his father to help him choose. In truth, he wanted someone to make this choice for him; he was too young, too inexperienced to make it for himself. He needed a helping hand.

"I'll do whatever you say," he said to Kolopak one day in late summer, when the heat rose in shimmering planes from the ground, and all the animals were still, taking refuge from the searing sun. Chakotay was confident his father would make his decision. Hadn't he spent his life trying to tell his son how he should live?

But Kolopak squinted into the sun for several moments as Chakotay felt a drop of perspiration trickle down the left side of his neck to his shoulder blade, then down his back. Finally, his father turned to look at him, his eyes, as always, shining with love when he regarded his son.

"The time is past when I can make your choices for you," he said. "You must choose your own path now, for only you can walk it."

Chakotay deflated. Now, when he *needed* guidance, his father wouldn't provide it! There must be some cruel irony at work here. All his life he had chafed under his father's control, and now when he was ready to accept it, it was withheld.

"But I don't know what path I want to take. That's the problem."

"You must look within yourself. The answers will be there." And Kolopak walked away.

Chakotay knew what he meant. He was suggesting Chakotay embark on a vision quest, abetted by the Akoonah, technology that had been developed to help one explore one's own unconscious. What his ancestors had achieved through fasting and smoking potent hallucinogens, his people today could accomplish safely, through a neuroelectric stimulator.

Chakotay had always resisted the vision quest, for it was part of a tradition that he eschewed. But today, in the throes of his ambivalence, it sounded almost tempting. In a moment's decision, he went to the small chamber of the house, the habak, which was dedicated to inner exploration.

His father had brought him into that room many times, pointing out artifacts, explaining rituals. Chakotay, of course, had turned a deaf ear to all of it. Would he even remember, now, what to do?

His eye traveled the walls of the room, adorned with ancient writings. He knew that some of them described the creation myth, the story of the First Father and his raising of the sky. For the first time, he actually looked at the symbols, to see if he could decipher what he knew of the story.

It was all gibberish to him.

Ancient artifacts were everywhere—carvings and figurines, fetishes and amulets. And, in the center of the room, a small bundle that held his father's most precious spiritual talismans. Chakotay sat and unwrapped the leather hide, revealing several decorated stones, an oddly shaped bone, a disk of feathers.

And the Akoonah.

The Akoonah was a flat piece of technology upon which Chakotay must lay his palm. He knew he was supposed to chant a ritual prayer, but from what he understood, that was just for ritual's sake. The journey inward was actually induced by the Akoonah, which stimulated the neurons of the hypothalamus, producing a lucid REM state.

Ignoring the artifacts in the bundle as well as the ritual prayer, Chakotay placed one hand on the Akoonah and focused his eyes on the row of fetishes in front of him. At first he felt nothing, but then a faint tingling sensation drifted through his hand, and then through his whole body. He began to feel a contentedness, a sense of well-being that was unfamiliar. He liked this blissful sensation, and hoped it would continue. His mind relaxed, and he felt himself entering willingly into a euphoria.

Gradually, he became aware that his surroundings were changing. The row of fetishes were becoming formless, vague. Their colors melted somehow and rearranged themselves, even as the very quality of the air began to change. It was cool and sweet, assuaging his cares, pacifying his anxieties. If only he could feel like this forever, without having to make uncomfortable choices . . .

Colors melted still further and swam in constantly shifting patterns until they settled once more into recognizable form.

He was in a secret spot within the forest. He knew this place well; he had found it as a child, a small clearing where the stream pooled and leafy fronds obscured it from prying eyes. It was a place he came to when he wanted to be absolutely alone, a place where he felt safe.

Chakotay smiled. It felt good to be there. Even though there was a rather large green-and-yellow snake coiled right in the middle of the clearing. He felt no apprehension, none of his usual trepidation. He simply stared at the reptile, amused at this strange irony. Did his unconscious have a sense of humor?

"Are *you* my spirit guide?" he asked of the snake.

"Am I?" the serpent replied to his mind, in a voice soft as a breeze through the trees.

"I thought that was how this worked. I'd take this journey and find a spirit guide."

"I wasn't aware there were rules and regulations. This is your journey. It will be what you want it to be."

"That can't be true. I don't like snakes. I wouldn't have chosen you."

The reptile's forked tongue darted out, testing the air, his lidless eyes glittering. "Then don't. What would be more to your liking?"

Chakotay pondered. "Something—more powerful. A bear, perhaps."

The snake's voice in his mind was amused. "If that's what you wanted, where is it?"

"How should I know?" Chakotay was beginning to feel annoyed. "I don't know how this works."

"You came here easily enough," the snake's voice said lightly. "You must be at least somewhat receptive to what you find."

"I came here to get answers about my future."

"Oh, your future. That's very important."

Chakotay felt foolish speaking like this to a snake. But he made no move to leave the clearing, and he still felt no anxiety about being in some proximity to the creature which had caused him uneasiness all his life. "If you're my spirit guide, then guide me. What do I do? Go back to Starfleet Academy or stay on my home planet?"

The snake uncoiled beautifully, and flowed around the edges of the clearing. Chakotay turned to watch it, fascinated by its easy muscularity. "That's a hard one," it said as it glided along the ground. "Go or stay home? Go or stay home?"

Chakotay felt a stronger sense of annoyance. It sounded very much to him as though this lowly snake was making fun of him. He doubted *that* was how spirit guides behaved. "Well?" he asked at last, when it seemed that nothing further would be forthcoming from the serpent, which continued its relentless progress around the clearing, circling and circling and circling.

"Well what?" it responded.

"What answer do you have for me?"

"I don't have any answer for you."

"Then what's the point of my being here?"

"I don't know. Why don't you ask the bear?"

And with that, the brightly colored coils disappeared into the leafy ferns, leaving Chakotay alone in the clearing with only the sound of the trickling stream for company.

Frustrated, he turned in a circle. "Is there a bear?" he called out, but there was only silence. "A wolf? An eagle?" He'd heard of those noble animals serving as spirit guides. But there was no response.

"A parrot, perhaps," he called out, determined to conjure up a guide he could accept. "Or a macaw. I know the creation myth."

The clearing was still except for the sound of trickling water. Even the usual forest noises were silenced. He stood for a few moments trying to think of another animal.

"All right," he said finally, "it doesn't have to be a powerful animal, or a noble one. What about a raccoon, or a beaver? A woodchuck. A prairie dog."

He imagined he heard laughter in his mind, but of course that wasn't possible. He waited.

"All right, have it your way. How about a snake?"

The green-and-yellow serpent erupted suddenly from the water, something trapped within its coils. It was a fish, which the snake was methodically suffocating. The fish struggled only briefly against its fate, then went limp. Chakotay watched, fascinated, as the snake opened its mouth and began to ingest the fish. The fish seemed to be larger than the reptile's mouth, but the snake widened its jaw in order to accommodate its meal. Gradually, with successive gulps, the fish disappeared down the snake's craw, leaving a huge lump directly behind its head. Then it turned to Chakotay.

"Were you indulged a great deal as a child? You behave very much like someone used to getting his own way."

Chakotay felt a chill as he heard Sveta's words repeated to him. It was hard to remember that everything that was happening was in his own mind, that all the memory and experience of his life was available to anyone or anything that might inhabit this strange landscape.

"Is that a clue?" he asked sincerely. "Are you saying I should go back to the Academy, where Sveta is?"

"I'm not saying anything. All of this is coming from you."

"But I don't know what to do. I need an answer."

"It's an answer you have to provide yourself."

"Then what's the point of coming here?"

"Good question. Maybe it's to confront something you can't confront in the external world. Out there you can point the finger at others, blame them for not making things easy for you. In here it's a little harder. There's only you."

Chakotay contemplated this. This annoying snake was certainly frustrating, but he would feel awfully foolish suggesting to anyone—including himself—that an imaginary snake had let him down by refusing to make his decision for him.

"I've always been a contrary," he said. "If I'm here, I want to be there. If I'm there, I want to be here. I don't know what to do about that."

"Then I guess you'll stay that way." The snake's muscles gulped once more, and the lump of fish moved slightly farther along its body.

"I'd like to change that. I just don't know how."

"Then I guess you won't be able to." Another gulp.

"I'm trying to work this out," said Chakotay irritably, "and I thought you were supposed to give me some help. 'Spirit guide' does imply guidance, after all."

"I'm hurt. You're accusing me of not doing my job."

"Exactly. You're not guiding me."

The snake lifted its head slightly and extended its forked tongue once more. "People used to think my tongue was the poisonous part," it said. "It's actually my sensing organ. I sense a big hulking presence in front of me, and I sense that it's a hopeless mass of confusion. I sense it would do anything other than make a decision, including indulging in a perfectly pointless argument with a figment of its own imagination. I see little hope for this presence. Now, if you'll excuse me, I have to digest my meal."

And the snake coiled itself again, lowering its head to rest, preparing to spend the next several days in a torpor, consuming its recent meal.

Chakotay sat down on the ground and stared at it. Somewhere in what it had said there must be an answer, but he couldn't figure out what it was. If this was all the help one got from a vision quest, he failed to see why it was so important to his people. Did they all go through these exercises in frustration and then report to the world that it had been a satisfying, productive experience? Was it all a sham, a ritual perpetuated for its own sake—as he suspected most of their rituals were—and lacking any intrinsic value?

He stood up in the still silent clearing. "All right, I'm ready to go now," he announced.

Nothing happened. He remained in the clearing, the water pool trickling softly, the snake coiled and still. This was bothersome, but not really an impediment. This was his clearing; he'd discovered it and he knew the way out. He turned to follow the path he'd worn between the ferns over the years.

There was no path and there were no ferns. The shape of the clearing had changed subtly, and seemed more thickly thronged with underbrush. He tried to force his way through, but the brambles were thick and impassable.

He wasn't going to be able to get out of there. This was something he hadn't counted on—how did one leave a vision quest? He knew his body was actually sitting in the habak of his house, palm lying on the Akoonah. But here, in his mind, there was no Akoonah, no way that he could think of to break the hold of his vision.

He sat down again and contemplated the snake. It was completely at rest, all its bodily functions slowed in order to channel its energy into digesting the fish. It was in its own version of a trance. Chakotay was on his own.

That, he realized, seemed to be the message everyone was giving him. No one was going to help with this difficult choice; no one would even suggest which path might be more desirable. He and he alone must choose.

With that realization, a great weight seemed to be lifted from him, and he felt himself return to the euphoria that had preceded his arrival at this place. The green of the forest began to run, smearing into kaleidoscopic patterns once more, and again he felt buoyant and weightless. Was that all it took? Understanding, on some gut level, that only he was master of his destiny? It seemed too easy . . . until he remembered that just moments ago, it was an impossibly difficult idea to embrace.

The forest glade had swirled out of existence and its colors were shifting into cohesive forms once more. A pleasant humming in his ears grew louder and louder until—

—he opened his eyes. He was in the habak, surrounded by artifacts that had been a part of his people for thousands of years. His hand was on the Akoonah, and now he withdrew it, slowly. The sensation of euphoria was still with him, and he was loath to lose it. The stillness of the clearing pervaded his senses, and he remembered the coiled body of the snake with fondness, feeling somehow empty to be apart from it.

Curious.

He rose and sought out his father, who was tending his garden, lush now in late summer with fruits and vegetables, the seeds of which had been brought from Earth two hundred years ago when several native tribes emigrated to Trebus. Kolopak looked up, holding a bright golden tomato in his hand, smiling with satisfaction.

"I'm harvesting lunch, Chakotay. This will be delicious in a salad."

Chakotay wasn't much interested in a tomato. He regarded his father with a serious mien and said, "I've made a decision. I'm going back to Starfleet Academy. I intend to graduate."

Kolopak nodded once, then studied the yellow tomato. "Is this enough, do you think? Or should we have squash as well?"

"Squash," answered Chakotay without hesitation. It really wasn't terribly hard to make decisions, once you put your mind to it.

Three years later, Chakotay graduated from Starfleet Academy with honors. He had eventually excelled in his studies and his extracurricular activities.

But there was little joy in the process. All around him, he saw his friends and classmates responding with enthusiasm to their regimens, finding wonder in knowledge and pleasure in activity. They laughed, they fought, they played jokes on each other, they fell in and out of love, they alternately despised and worshipped certain instructors, and in general entered into Academy life with vitality and ardor.

Chakotay was on the periphery of those experiences. He had friends, but none was intimate. He participated in wrestling events and had a rackful of medals to show for it, but he found no satisfaction in those victories. He was always asked to participate in group outings, and occasionally did, but frequently demurred. He was popular even though he didn't seek out friends.

Only one person held a particular fascination for him, and that was Sveta, whose cool and knowing manner intrigued him. She seemed to see into him in a way no one else did. She challenged him, confronted him, debated with him—and then would smile that enigmatic smile and slip away, not to be seen for days. She began to assume the aspect of a mythological being in his mind: the Ice Maiden, alluring and mysterious.

His closest friend was probably Chert, who was undaunted by Chakotay's darker moods and who deflected any rebuff with a cheerfulness that was irresistible. Chert might have been the only person with whom Chakotay felt genuinely comfortable, for he was the one person to accept him unconditionally, edges and all.

On many occasions Chakotay came close to leaving. Often he felt he wanted nothing more than to escape this burdensome life and go home again.

But he never did. Every time he contemplated that move, sense memory of the quiet clearing in the woods overwhelmed him, and the liberation he had felt then—when he realized he was alone, and alone could decide his life's course—returned to him. He had made a choice; he would not unmake it. And so, almost by default, he finished school and entered into the life that Starfleet provided.

The first skirmish was hardly deserving of the title—an encounter, actually, almost not worth noting and certainly not a harbinger of everything that was to come. There was little to suggest that Cardassia would become the major influence in Chakotay's life.

He was a lieutenant aboard the *U.S.S. Vico,* an aide to Captain Roger Hackney, a dour, wiry man with a leathered face and intense dark eyes that reflected both astuteness and cunning. Hackney was what in an earlier era might have been called a "man's man," preferring the company and comradeship of other males. He was married, had two sons, and from all indications adored his wife; however, with most females he was quaintly gallant, a behavior which covered the fact that he was uncomfortable with them. He had taken an instant liking to Chakotay, and the younger man had risen swiftly in the chain of command.

Chakotay was on the bridge of the *Vico* when they first detected the alien ship. "Sensors show an unidentified vessel approaching on an intercept course, one-point-six light-years away," he warned Hackney.

"Anything like it in the Federation database?" queried Hackney with interest. They had been charting a far-flung sector of the Alpha Quadrant for a month, and anything that broke the tedium was welcome.

"It might be Cardassian, but if it is it's a class of vessel we haven't encountered before." Chakotay noted his sensors and then added, "They're scanning us as well."

"Put the ship on screen as soon as we're in visual range." Both of them realized that the same kind of dialogue was probably occurring on the alien ship as well, each scanning the other, wanting clues, hoping to absorb as much information as possible before actually making contact. Chakotay felt his senses go alert and wary at the prospect; Cardassians were known to be dangerous and unpredictable.

"Here it is, Captain," said Chakotay, and a faint image appeared on the viewscreen, barely discernible among the stars.

"Magnify," said Hackney, but Chakotay had already entered the command, and now the image took shape: a massive, tripartite warship with extensive—and powerful—weapons systems.

At that moment they were hailed, and the image of the ship was replaced by that of a Cardassian: tall and rangy, the man had thick cords outlining his broad neck and temples, and black eyes that glittered like obsidian.

"State your purpose, Federation vessel," the man said without preamble.

"I'm Captain Roger Hackney of the Federation starship *Vico,*" said Hackney in the standard introduction. "We're charting this sector for our astrographic database."

"You are perilously near Cardassian territory," replied the man, who had not given them the benefit of a name by which to address him. "I am transmitting the coordinates of our borders to you and I urge you to respect them."

Chakotay and Hackney both looked down at their consoles and studied the incoming data transmission. Hackney frowned and looked back at the screen.

"We're aware of your stated territory, sir. There have been a number of encounters between our ships and yours. But I must say there's an astonishing amount of flexibility to your borders. This transmission seems to indicate that Cardassia has swollen considerably in the last month."

"Are you disputing our claims?"

"Just trying to understand them. The last reported border we have in our charts was two light-years from here."

"The current coordinates are correct."

"Is the Federation Council aware of this?"

"It is not our duty to report to the Federation Council. We are autonomous and will not be bound by the constraints of foreign cultures."

"I'm only suggesting a spirit of cooperation," replied Hackney easily. "Staying in communication could lessen the chances of unpleasant misunderstandings."

The reptilian eyes narrowed. "Are you threatening me, Federation Captain?" Chakotay noted that the Cardassian ship had suddenly powered its weapons systems. He looked to Hackney, who had seen the move but didn't order him to follow suit.

"Not at all. As I said, just trying to communicate."

"Let me communicate this: It would be best if you left Cardassian territory now."

Hackney and Chakotay exchanged a quick glance. The Cardassian borders had magically shifted yet again.

"Are you suggesting we're now *inside* Cardassian territory?"

"Of course. See for yourself." Instantly, a new flood of data was transmitted to indicate that the coordinates the *Vico* now occupied were well within Cardassian space. Chakotay felt anger begin to rise in him; this was a blatant bullying technique, purposely transparent. Did the Cardassian think they would stand for this, that they would skulk away like chastened dogs? He brought the ship's weapons on line, sure that Hackney would give that order.

"Belay that," said Hackney quickly, with a dark look. Reluctantly, Chakotay powered down the weapons.

"A wise move, Captain," purred the Cardassian, whom Chakotay was beginning to dislike intensely. "Far better to power your propulsion system and back off."

"I hope your government will consider establishing diplomatic relations with the Federation at some point," said Hackney. "Unfortunate incidents like this could be prevented."

"The only unfortunate thing about this incident is your insistence on talking instead of acceding to my demands."

"We have no intention of causing an incident, and we will withdraw. But my government will be notified about this encounter."

The Cardassian smiled, a mirthless expression that conveyed menace more than anything else. "A prospect that causes me to quake with terror," he droned, and then his image blinked off the viewscreen and was replaced with the sight of his ship, weapons still powered.

"We shouldn't let him push us around like that," Chakotay said instantly. "Our ship is as powerful as his—we could have made things difficult for him."

Captain Hackney cast an understanding look at his young officer. "Of course we could have. But to what end? Our orders are to map space, not cause incidents that could escalate into something worse."

"We didn't cause anything—that Cardassian was the one juggling his borders."

"That's a nicety that would go largely unnoticed if we started trading phaser shots with him." Hackney gave Chakotay a friendly clap on the shoulder. "When I was your age, I would've felt the same way. What you'll learn as you get older is that it's almost always smarter to avoid violence than to provoke it."

Chakotay sank into a moody silence, his mind combing history for examples of times when violence had been the only solution to a problem, and when appeasement had only prolonged the inevitable and allowed the enemy to gain ground early on. They were abundant. And yet he knew his captain was correct in his assessment of this situation. One Starfleet survey ship and one Cardassian cruiser weren't going to affect their governments' policies one way or the other, and the only thing that could come from a skirmish between them would be a further deterioration of relations between the two entities. Better to back off.

But something in him still burned, an ember of resentment that he couldn't quell, no matter how hard he tried.

In the long run, of course, Starfleet's enlightened policies couldn't endure. Cardassian ships kept nibbling away at the outer edges of Federation space in an intentional and well-orchestrated effort to provoke retaliation and, since they were frequently dealing with civilian colonists rather than well-disciplined Starfleet personnel, began achieving their goals. Disagreements became altercations became skirmishes became battles. The Cardassian border territory disintegrated into a series of hot spots, growing in intensity until the Federation had no recourse but to respond militarily.

It was at this time that Chakotay was transferred to the *Gage,* and posted to defend Federation space in Sector 21749. It was at this time that he learned everything he needed to know about warfare.

He fought Cardassians in space; he fought them on land; he fought them, on more than one occasion, hand-to-hand. He knew moments of terror and of triumph, of bitter cruelty and noble sacrifice. He saw friends die and he saw friends kill. He learned that one can take a life as dispassionately as one can blow one's nose, even if one is, on some more fundamental level, forever changed because of it. He had become inextricably linked to his ancient past: he had become a warrior.

That realization brought him neither joy nor sorrow. Somewhere in the course of the nearly four years he spent in warfare, he lost the capacity to feel much of anything at all. He was unaware of this at first, as it was a gradual process of self-protection, an incremental slide into indifference. When at last he realized he had lost the ability to experience any strong emotion, he was relieved, and didn't miss the days of intense feeling. In this way, he could survive.

When, at last, there was a cessation of hostilities—not an end to war, in that war had never been declared—he was given an extended leave and he returned, for the first time in years, to his homeworld. He found it remarkably changed. Everything was smaller than he remembered—was that postage-stamp meadow really the vast playing field of his youth?—and the people astonishingly unsophisticated. His childhood friends were stolid adults with children of their own, and he found himself barely able to find a common ground for conversation. The boys he had romped with in the forests had become stodgy and colorless, younger versions of his father and every other member of the tribe he had ever known. He wondered how any of them would fare against the Cardassians.

There were any number of celebrations to mark his return, but Chakotay felt disengaged from the festivities. Music did not cheer him, food and drink were tasteless, and the companionship of his friends and family seemed shallow and unimportant. He found them all naive, oblivious of the situation in the worlds around them, caught up in their own concerns, their own lives, their own minuscule problems.

One night he wandered away from a party in his honor and went to sit alone in the fields, looking up at the two crescent moons hanging low in the sky. He was thinking of nothing in particular, but simply had to remove himself from the endless, banal conversations that punctuated the celebration. A footfall behind him made him flinch and he leapt to his feet.

It was his father. "Sorry. Didn't mean to startle you."

"I'm fine."

Kolopak gazed up at their twin moons reflectively. "The sisters are dancing tonight," he intoned. This was the phrase used when the two moons were in proximity, the smaller one seeming to dance in conjunction with the larger. "Good things happen when they prance together."

It was an innocent statement, a variation of which Chakotay had heard a thousand times as he grew up, but tonight, for whatever reason, it struck him as intolerably ignorant. The position of the two moons was entirely predictable, charted by astronomers, their orbits entirely a matter of gravitational dynamics. He felt a peculiar fury rise in him.

"Why do you say things like that?" he challenged, and heard his voice, harsh and dark, slice through the night. His father stared at him, stunned at the intensity of the question. But Kolopak, as always, tried to respond harmoniously.

"It's just part of the lore of our people," he began, but Chakotay didn't let him get any further.

"It's foolishness. Ancient myth. Those aren't two sisters in the sky any more than the Milky Way was a canoe. But at least our ancestors didn't know any better—they didn't have telescopes and astronomers and space travel to show them the difference between reality and fantasy."

Kolopak's black eyes burned into him through the darkness. "Chakotay, you've been wounded by your recent experiences. Your soul is troubled—"

Everything his father said was enraging Chakotay. He erupted once more. "My soul is fine because I don't have a soul. I have a mind, and a body. That's it. I won't be endowed with some vague attribute that's an outgrowth of ancient ignorance."

"Whatever part of you you care to acknowledge has been wounded. You're full of rage, and it's crippling you."

"If you'd seen what I've seen you'd be full of rage, too."

"I know that. But I would take steps to heal myself."

"Just how would you propose to do that?"

"I would go on a vision quest."

Chakotay threw up his hands in a gesture of exasperation. "A vision quest. Wonderful—that would solve everything." He whirled back to face his father, anger still boiling in him. "Don't you see that I'm not like you? That I can't be, I'll never be? Why do you keep trying to push me into this world that isn't mine?"

"It is yours. You just don't realize it yet."

How could Chakotay respond rationally to a statement like that? How could he carry on a dialogue with someone who could see only one point of view? He shook his head, bitter and weary. "Fine. I'll be sure to let you know when I get around to realizing it."

"I know you will." His father's voice was as calm as a moonlit night after snow has fallen and everything is stilled. It gave no evidence of ire, or hurt, or condemnation. And that made Chakotay all the more frustrated, because it gave him nothing to feed his wrath.

"Good night, Father. I'll be leaving tomorrow. It's time I returned to the real world."

His father nodded, and Chakotay strode off into the night, continuing the argument in his head with a father who was much more belligerent, and much more satisfying, in that he let Chakotay argue him into chastened defeat.

The next morning, when he was ready to leave, his father was nowhere to be seen. His mother stood with him, her eyes grave and solemn. "Your father is in the forest," she told him. "He thought it best if he didn't try to say good-bye to you."

A ripple of guilt shimmered over Chakotay, but he forced it away. "Please tell him I asked about him," he said, and she nodded. Then she took his face in her hands and held it tightly for a moment.

"No one can find your way for you, Chakotay, or clear it of stones before you set off. You must find your way. But we will be here, to help, if you need us."

His eyes stung briefly and he blinked away the sensation. "I don't mean to hurt you," he began, but she covered his mouth with her fingers. "You owe us no explanation," she said gently. "Love requires none."

He nodded and then touched his commbadge. "Energize," he said to the starship waiting in orbit, and his homeworld shimmered out of his vision. It was not the last time he was to see it, but it was the last time he cared to remember.

It was years before Cardassia and the Federation were able to finalize a treaty that officially dealt with the disputed area between their territories. It was controversial, creating a demilitarized buffer zone which belonged to neither power, and which ideally would have been unpopulated. But a number of worlds in that zone had already been occupied, generally by hardy pioneering people who were self-reliant and stubborn, and who had no intention of abandoning the homes they'd created. Among these were Chakotay's people, who had searched for years to find the planet that was most suited to their needs, and with which they were spiritually at one.

And so these people decided to stay where they were, despite the urging of the Federation, and the insistence by Starfleet that they would not be able to protect them from attack. The inhabitants of colonies and outposts throughout the demilitarized zone responded with one unified voice that they didn't care, they were staying put.

Chakotay, by now a lieutenant commander aboard the *Gettysburg,* found himself in an unaccustomed position: defending his people's actions. He was serving under Captain Madolyn Gordon, an energetic, cheerful woman whose good nature belied her toughness, her tenacity, and her intimidating intelligence. She had curly brown hair that bobbed up and down in response to her habit of punctuating her arguments with short, sharp jerks of her head. She and Chakotay spent long hours engaged in debate on a wide-ranging number of subjects, the latest of which was the Cardassian treaty.

"It's concessionism," insisted Chakotay, as they drank coffee in her ready room. "The Federation shouldn't be required to abandon its own colonists."

"Those colonists were given every opportunity to resettle. They would have been moved by Starfleet to any of a number of planets that were virtually identical to the ones they left."

"That's easy to say when it's not *your* homeworld. These settlers have made an investment in their colonies, with their labor and their energy. My people went through an exhaustive process of determining their spiritual affinity for the planet they finally decided to settle. It may sound easy to the bureaucrats to relocate everyone to 'identical' planets, but in fact it's incredibly disruptive."

"Your people have absolutely no protection against any Cardassian attacks. Doesn't that concern you?"

"Of course it does. That's why I think the idea of a demilitarized zone was fallacious in the first place. Cardassians won't respect it— they'll be in there in a minute, trying to force our settlers out. It would've been far better to draw a definitive border and then protect everyone within the confines of our territory."

"Maybe you're being unfair to the Cardassians. So far they've lived up to their word. The planet we're headed for, Bajor, was occupied by them for over fifty years." Gordon's curls bounced heavily as she nodded her head heatedly. "They've withdrawn and given the Bajorans their autonomy once more."

"After destroying their culture and their infrastructure, and decimating the population."

"But they're gone now, and Bajor is rebuilding."

"Captain, mark my words. We'll all come to regret this demilitarized zone. It's bad politics and bad military tactics. Remember, you heard it here." He smiled at her and she smiled back, gray eyes twinkling. They had a genuine affection for each other and enjoyed these jousting matches mostly as an intellectual diversion, and often switched sides just for fun.

But once he'd seen Bajor, Chakotay found his feelings calcifying.

He had experienced brutal savagery during the war, and though that ordeal had certainly damaged him, he believed he had, over the years since, managed to recuperate. Visiting Bajor was like ripping open old scar tissue only to find that, underneath, the wound has never properly healed.

The Cardassians had followed a scorched-earth policy before they left. Cities that were once graceful and inviting had become vast ruins. Dwellings were ravaged, public buildings razed, temples burned. Nothing in this behavior had benefited the Cardassians; they could just as well have packed up and left the cities intact. Instead, in pointless savagery, they laid waste.

One thing that seemed to have proliferated and thrived on Bajor was the saloons. Built by the Cardassians, they found increasing popularity among the Bajorans who sought respite from the horrors of their existence. Depressed after his tour of the once-beautiful planet, Chakotay sought the same palliative. A dark, quaintly ornate room, festooned with garlands and banners that bore an air of faded elegance, was probably more depressing than uplifting, but the darkness obscured the desperate decorations. Chakotay went to the bar and ordered ale.

The bartender set a glass before him and then a frosty dark bottle that was beaded with condensation. It looked wonderfully cool, and Chakotay rubbed the bottle over his face before he poured it. When he quaffed the first mouthful, he felt the first bolstering moment of that grim day. The ale was delicious, strong and faintly sweet, but with a tart aftertaste that lingered pleasantly in the mouth. He was never much of a drinker, and his people eschewed the use of alcohol entirely, but he was glad he hadn't adopted that particular prohibition. He would have hated to have missed the experience of a drink of ale as good as this at the end of a day as bad as this.

He was halfway through the bottle when he felt movement and a presence at his side. Before he could look up, he heard a silky voice in his ear, cool as a mountain rivulet. "Hello, Chakotay. It's been a long time."

Recognizing the voice instantly, he whirled to find Sveta, the Ice Maiden of Russia, sitting next to him. She was as otherworldly as ever, remote, poised, confident. And incredibly beautiful. He felt his pulse quicken and heard his voice stammer as he spoke.

"Sveta! What—why are you—I can't believe you're here!"

She smiled in that serene way and laid a dainty hand on his arm.

"I'm here because you're here," she said, waving off the bartender, who had approached with a questioning look. "I heard you were touring Bajor and I set about finding you."

He eyed her clothing, which was civilian. "Aren't you in Starfleet anymore?" he queried.

"No. I served eight years and then I got married. We settled in a colony on Riva Prime."

Chakotay felt himself grow immediately somber. Riva was one of the planets most devastated during the war, subject to repeated attacks by the Cardassians. He was silent, waiting for Sveta to tell him more.

"My husband was a farmer. He loved the process of planting, growing, reaping. It was an almost holy occupation to him." Her voice had taken on a faraway quality as she seemed to move back in memory. "We had two children, twins—a boy and a girl. We thought we had everything . . . we used to wonder how it was we were so fortunate. We loved each other, we had a perfect family, we had an occupation that gave us pleasure."

She looked into a mid-distance for a moment, and Chakotay had the feeling he didn't want to hear what was next.

"You know that Riva was a prime target during the war. Starfleet did its best to protect us, but the Cardassians were determined to occupy our planet and mine the valuable pergium ore there. Eventually, there was no letup." Another silence ensued, and Chakotay could sense her trying to find a way to continue. She looked up at him with sad eyes.

"You know what's coming. There's no point in embellishing anything. The Cardassians attacked our settlement while I was away trying to procure medical supplies. My husband and my children were killed when our settlement was wiped out by an orbiting battle cruiser."

Chakotay didn't know what to say. "I'm sorry" was inadequate. He'd heard countless stories like this over the past years, and he never knew how to respond, so usually he simply kept quiet. Sveta turned her gaze directly to him, and stared at him with those unsettling pale eyes.

"That tragedy ignited something in me, Chakotay. I swore to avenge them, and that cause has given me a reason to live."

"But it's over now."

Something hard and flinty happened on her face. "Don't be naive.

It's just beginning. Do you think Cardassia has given up just because there's a treaty?"

"Of course not. But Starfleet's out of it."

"Good riddance, as far as we're concerned. We'll make more progress without them."

"Who's 'we'?"

She glanced around carefully, then leaned in toward him. "A group of freedom fighters is beginning to band together. We've even taken a name—the Maquis."

"Maquis?"

"The name of ancient French resistance forces during a conflict on Earth known as World War Two."

Chakotay had studied ancient Earth warfare, but was unfamiliar with the French name. The whole thing had a faintly adolescent sound to him. But Sveta was leaning even closer, her voice clear and intense.

"We intend to defend our homes. It's obvious to us that Cardassia intends to harass us mercilessly and try to force us out. We aren't going to let that happen."

"Good for you. I wish you well."

"Your homeworld is in the demilitarized zone. Surely you have feelings about this."

He felt himself take a deep breath. It was impossible to explain to her, in one sitting, the complexities of his relationship with his people. "My people will do what they do. They don't pay a lot of attention to me."

"Join us, Chakotay. We need trained, disciplined people like you. Many of us are former Starfleet personnel. You could be in a leadership position—we need you."

"Sveta, I wish you the best. But I'm part of Starfleet. I have no intention of leaving—even if I don't agree with them about the treaty."

"What is that supposed to mean? You disagree with them but you'll continue to follow them, like a sheep?" Her voice had taken on an uncharacteristic passion. "I don't remember you as that hypocritical."

"This isn't my fight, Sveta. I won't take it on."

She eyed him briefly, then nodded. "If you change your mind, you can reach me this way." She slipped a padd into his hand and stood up. "It really is your fight, you know," she offered, and then she walked out, her tall, slim body proud and straight.

Chakotay finished his ale, but it had turned sour somehow, and the aftertaste was bitter.

Captain Gordon's face was pale but she was composed. "We have incomplete reports because the situation is chaotic. And of course, we have no official presence in the zone."

He nodded, trying to turn himself to stone. He didn't want to hear what he knew he was going to hear.

"But the attack on Trebus was sudden and devastating. Apparently there's widespread destruction. The Federation will send in a humanitarian ship with food and medicine, but Starfleet can't go near the place."

"Can I join the supply ship?"

She looked directly at him. "Officially, no. You're part of Starfleet and your presence would be illegal. Unofficially . . ." Her voice trailed off and he understood what she was saying.

"Captain, I request a leave of absence. I haven't taken vacation for quite a while and I need a few weeks off. Do I have your permission?"

"Granted. How soon do you want to leave?"

"Immediately."

"Good luck, Chakotay. I'll hold good thoughts for you."

He nodded, unable to get a word past the lump that had formed in his throat. He headed for his quarters and began to pack.

Four days later he was on his homeworld.

Of the village in which he had grown up, nothing was left. Only piles of rubble, some still smoking, gave any indication that once it had been a place where gentle people lived in close harmony with the land.

There had been nothing gentle in their destruction. Thermalite weapons had incinerated the village, creating a firestorm that had raged at sixteen hundred degrees centigrade, a temperature at which iron melted. The stone of their dwellings had been transformed into glass, fused into desperate shapes, gnarled and twisted as though the stone itself were convulsing in agony.

The people were essentially cremated, turned in moments of searing agony from happy, peaceful villagers tending their crops and playing with their children into puddles of ash that scattered in the winds of the firestorm. There would be no good-byes, no burials, no mementos of loved ones. They had simply vanished.

Chakotay stood in the devastation of his home village, absorbing every image that assaulted his senses. A vile odor permeated the air from a smoky film that hung over the site, the residue of the thermalite weapons. He would remember that smell forever.

The grotesque, twisted shapes of fused stone stretched before him, a vast detritus field of contorted forms, an ugliness that stained the earth. He would remember that sight forever.

But what was most painful of all was the stillness. Once, this village had hummed with the sounds of daily activity, of people working, talking, singing. The laughter of children at raucous play was always present, in the meadow and the woods, the shrill, exuberant sounds of young people rollicking with eagerness and headlong daring, witless of the cruel future that awaited them.

He would hear that silence forever.

Though it was a hot day, and the moist film of smoke that hung in the air exacerbated the warmth, Chakotay was strangely chilled. An iciness had penetrated him, had consumed his heart and his mind, a cold steel of determination: *I will avenge them.*

It had been easy to find Sveta. In fact, she was waiting for his transmission. She had heard of the Cardassian attack on Trebus, and knew Chakotay well enough to surmise that he would be contacting her. The rest was easy. She procured a ship for him, not the most splendid or the most up-to-date, but packed with weaponry and defensive features. It was a guerrilla ship, meant for fast, daring raids, quick battles, and swift escape. He named it the *Liberty.* The first time Chakotay sat at the controls, he felt at home.

And then Sveta put him in touch with Seska.

He heard her before he ever saw her. He had been sent by Sveta to Bajor, where there were an ample supply of willing recruits for the Maquis, Bajorans whose long subjugation by Cardassia had ignited in them a murderous desire for vengeance. Sveta had learned that a woman named Seska was one of those, and Chakotay was to bring her into the fold.

At the periphery of one of the towns on Bajor had once been a magnificent outdoor arena, a graceful oval built into the side of a mountain that was studded with huge trees, spreading a lacy canopy over the terraced seating area. The Bajorans had used it for celebrations of the arts, and for various rituals of their Prophets. Cardassians, during their occupation, had made it the scene of punishment and execution of dissidents. Now it was in ruins.

Chakotay had been told he would find Seska among those ruins at the moment sunset becomes twilight, and when that time arrived, he approached the now-crumbling arena, which had been all but destroyed by receding Cardassian troops. A ring of columns still stood at the top of the auditorium, proud sentinels of survival on a planet that needed every symbol of courage and resilience it could muster.

From somewhere behind those columns came the sound of a woman's voice, singing. It was haunting in the sunset haze, a strong, husky voice that had the ability to convey powerful emotions: longing, valor, despair, determination. He didn't recognize the melody, but he stood for some minutes, rapt, listening as this muscular voice captivated his senses.

When it stopped, he approached, feeling somehow abject, humbled by the intensity of her song. He saw her at last, standing, facing the sunset, which was exploding in a profusion of orange and pink, her body straight and proud, gazing up at the violent sky with a concentration that was almost palpable. It was a moment of potent communion, and he was silent, respecting its sacredness.

Finally, she turned. Her face was as strong as her voice, beautiful in the way a powerful animal is beautiful. Her dark hair was swept back but loose, like a mane, and her black eyes glistened with some inner fire, opalescent.

"You're Chakotay," she said simply, and he nodded. "Seska," she informed him.

And then she walked straight to him, put strong arms around his neck, and kissed him full on the mouth.

It was the most electrifying event of his life. Everything coalesced into that one moment: the brilliantly turbulent sunset, darkening now into slashes of purple, the proud clear voice raised in defiant song, and the anguish Cardassia had inflicted on each of them. Lightning flashed between them, igniting some deeply smoldering eroticism into a raging, heedless lust.

An hour later, they were engaged in a pitched battle about whether or not to venture into Cardassian territory on their first sortie.

And thus was their relationship born, of hunger and need and conflict, and so did it continue, until the time Chakotay realized he could not captain a ship and carry on an affair with one of his crew, but that time was surprisingly long in coming.

The first time he killed as a Maquis, it was with his bare hands.

He and his crew, which had grown now to a small but fierce band of some fifteen hardened, well-trained members, had heard that a rogue

Cardassian ship had put down on one of the uninhabited planets in the demilitarized zone. It seemed clear that they were going to establish a settlement there, in clear defiance of the Federation treaty. Chakotay had determined that they would make that decision a regrettable one.

Surveillance had told them that the Cardassian band was small, not more than twenty, and was clustered together in a tropical forest in the southern hemisphere. As usual, Chakotay and Seska were in conflict about just what to do.

"They don't realize we know they're on the surface," she said spiritedly. "They don't have a ship in orbit and they won't expect us. We could annihilate them all with one photon torpedo."

"In the first place, we only have three torpedoes. I'd rather save them for the times we really need them. In the second place, I have no intention of slaughtering them—just letting them know we won't let them put down roots here."

She looked at him with unconcealed contempt, an expression she had perfected. "I didn't realize you were so gutless, Chakotay. Are you willing to be so chivalrous to the people who massacred your family?"

"I won't sink to their level."

The argument raged for some time, as their arguments usually did, but in the end Chakotay prevailed. They would quietly encircle the Cardassian camp, spike the perimeter with their own isotane gas, and ignite it. The Cardassians would be forced to transport well away from the area or be asphyxiated. They would not be injured, but would get the unmistakable message that their presence wouldn't be tolerated. Seska had acquired enough of the deadly gas on the black market to allow them to repeat this maneuver several times, until the Cardassians abandoned the planet.

Chakotay and five others—not including Seska, whom he left in charge on the ship—transported to the surface under cover of darkness. Their sensors had indicated that the Cardassians were all within the camp, probably eating and getting ready for bed. They had been safely ensconced for several weeks and had become relaxed, assuming that since no one had bothered them so far, no one would.

The group spread in a ring around the small settlement, each armed with canisters of isotane gas. When they were set, the others would transport back to the ship and Chakotay would stay behind a moment longer, in order to ignite them.

The jungle was a fetid place, devoid of animal life, rank with the odor of rotting plants. Why the Cardassians had chosen this location was something of a mystery, but Chakotay assumed it was precisely because it was so unlikely. It took him nearly half an hour to set his canisters, because making his way through the slimy undergrowth was time-consuming. Although the planet had a sizable moon, a cloud cover partially obscured it, and there was little ambient light, making his progress even more difficult.

Finally he had placed the final canister, and received the brief signal from each of the others that they had done the same. He returned the signal that would transport them to the *Liberty,* and then prepared to ignite the isotane.

It would require activating the first canister simultaneously with the second, after which a chain reaction would set off the others in the huge circle. He had synchronized the transponder on the second unit, and was on his way back to the first, one part of his mind wondering what kind of decaying plant could produce such a malodorous smell.

Suddenly the ground opened beneath him and he plunged straight down.

He crumpled to the floor of a pit that he estimated to be about twice his height. Mercifully, it had contained no spikes, no acid bath, none of the surprises Cardassians had been known to put at the bottom of their traps. He looked up toward the opening, where the faint light afforded by the moon created a small rectangle of gray. It didn't look so far; he might be able to climb out, which he preferred to contacting the *Liberty* and having to transport back to the ship. He wanted to ignite the isotane canisters as quickly as possible.

Then he heard something moving in the pit.

Not wanting to guess what it might be, he risked turning on his wrist beacon, and shined it right into the just uplifting head of a large serpent. From his Starfleet training, he identified it as a Cardassian nephrus snake, which had obviously been brought here by the illegal settlers. It was a mottled brown color with an abnormally thick, muscular body and an elongated, wedge-shaped head and one un-blinking eye, which now fixed him in its flat gaze. Unlike the reptiles of Earth, it depended on its eye to detect its prey, and it bore some resemblance to alligators and crocodiles in that it had teeth and a powerful jaw. It was known to be a fierce predator, more than capable of crushing a man to death, and had probably been kept hungry by the Cardassians. At the moment, it was about three meters away, at the opposite side of the pit. He wondered briefly if he had developed any special rapport with reptiles now that he had a snake as a spirit guide, but then decided he'd better not put that thought to a test.

"Chakotay to *Liberty*. Beam me up right away."

He waited, still eyeing the snake, which was, unfortunately, attracted to the light and was beginning to rouse out of its torpid slumber. But Chakotay had no intention of shutting the light off and staying in the darkness with the serpent, even for the few seconds it took to transport.

Then he realized those seconds had already passed. He touched his commbadge again. "Chakotay to Seska. Do you read?"

No answer. It occurred to him that the Cardassians must have done something to mask communications from the pit, but he quickly realized he didn't have time to try to figure that out because the snake was on the move. Although he had always been taught to value the life of any living being, he drew his phaser. The snake, he was sure, didn't value his life.

But whatever damping field prevented communications also prevented weapons fire.

He disliked turning his back on the thing, but he had to try to climb. He shone the beacon up one wall of the pit and saw a smooth, graded surface that offered no handhold. He looked back and saw that the snake was uncoiling, wedge head lowering to the ground. He looked back to the next wall, quickly ran the light over it, and found it as smooth as the last one. The third wall, the only other one he could reach without running into the snake, was just the same.

In mounting desperation, he played the light on the pit wall behind the snake and saw his only opportunity embedded there: a stubble of tree root that protruded from the dirt wall.

But that meant he had to get past the snake.

It was moving toward him, now, slowly, its one eye fastened on the beacon strapped to Chakotay's wrist. He quickly unsnapped it and set it on the ground in the farthest corner from the serpent, light pointed directly at it. Then he moved slowly away from the light.

The serpent kept its eye on the beacon. It seemed mesmerized, confused, heavy body undulating sluggishly along the floor of the pit, as though wary of this bright intruder. Chakotay kept moving away from the light and the snake, inching his way along the wall, ready to make his leap for freedom. When the serpent's head was less than a meter away from the light, he bolted for the far wall.

From the corner of his eye, he saw the snake's head turn at the sudden movement, but it was apparently baffled enough to hesitate. Chakotay charged for the wall, but tripped over the coiled tail of the serpent and went sprawling. Heart pounding, he scrambled to his feet and flung himself at the far wall, grabbing for the tree root.

It pulled out in his hands.

He glanced back and saw that the snake's head was now pointed in his direction, and its long ropy body was in the process of reversing course. He began scrabbling at the wall of the pit, digging into it, looking for something that might hold his weight, but he kept pulling out only handfuls of dirt.

The reptile was beginning to move more quickly now, having refocused on its proper prey. Over his shoulder, as he clawed at the wall, Chakotay called out, "You're supposed to be my spirit guide!" But the snake seemed unmoved. Chakotay grabbed a clump of damp dirt and flung it at the snake's head. It landed solidly, right on the eye, and the serpent twisted slightly, momentarily blinded.

Chakotay's scrabbling fingers suddenly found something solid— another section of tree root, just over his head. He dug furiously at it until it was exposed, and then clutched at it, pulling. It held. Without checking again to see if the snake was heading toward him, he hauled himself off the floor of the pit and drew his legs under him.

He looked down to see that the snake was just beneath him, grotesque head lifted off the ground, peering up at him. Fortunately for Chakotay, its heaviness prevented it from lifting any more of its body; it couldn't reach him so long as he clung like this to the side of the pit. But how long could he do that?

Light from the beacon still illuminated the trap, and he looked upward, willing another handhold to be present. He saw it in the shape of a rock that jutted sharply from the dirt wall. He was able to get a firm grip with one hand, then another, and to use the tree root as a step for his feet. Now he was well off the floor of the pit and almost within reach of the top.

Beneath him, the snake had begun to emit a strange squeal, unlike the sound of any animal he'd ever heard, something between an owl and a pig. The sound made his stomach clench in a sudden, violent spasm, and he became even more desperate to get out of the pit.

The faint light from the moon silhouetted something on the lip of the pit above, a shadow-shape that formed a loop of sorts. He hoped it was the curling root of a tree, and he hoped it was sturdy. If it weren't, there would be no second chances.

The only way to reach it was to jump. He found the sturdiest grip he could with his feet, then bent his legs slightly. With the squeal of the snake growing louder, he sprang upward with as much strength as he could muster, grabbing for the dark circle above.

His hands found it, grabbed, slipped slightly, then held. His entire weight was now supported by the loop, which felt that it must be part of the root of a tree. He hoped it was an old, well-established tree whose root would hold him, or he would plunge back into that dreaded pit and into the coils of the now-angry snake.

It held. He began walking his feet up the wall, and finally was able to fling one hand onto the surface, grabbing for purchase, finding the extension of the tree root and using it to pull himself farther out.

Suddenly a dark shape loomed above him and a searing pain erupted on the back of his hand. A heavy-booted Cardassian soldier had driven his heel into Chakotay's hand as it clutched the root of the tree. If he let go of it, he would slide back into the pit.

That thought gave him an instant surge of strength. As the Cardassian lifted his leg to deliver a vicious kick at Chakotay's head, he swept out with his other hand, grabbing at the leg and deflecting the blow, toppling the Cardassian off balance. As the soldier unwound himself and got to his feet, Chakotay pulled himself the rest of the way from the pit, and then rolled quickly as the Cardassian dived for him.

They collided, pounding at each other in a silent, deadly contest, punctuated only by the eerie wailing of the snake's cry, still emanating from the pit. The Cardassian was going for Chakotay's eyes, Chakotay for the other's throat. They kicked and clawed and rolled on the ground, grunting and huffing like water buffalo, each knowing he was fighting for his life.

Chakotay was a big man, but the Cardassian was bigger, and hadn't just used all his strength trying to climb out of a pit. His blows took their toll on Chakotay, who felt bones shatter in his jaw as the soldier landed a solid punch. Chakotay summoned every reserve of strength he had and shoved the Cardassian off him onto an outcropping of rock, then dived on top, fingers finding the corded neck.

He quickly realized that wasn't the way to dispatch a Cardassian. He couldn't get his hands around the wide bands of cartilage. He gave one quick chop to the throat and heard a heartening grunt of pain, and then, using his grip on the man's neck cords, let out a huge yell and began hammering his adversary's head against the rock.

The Cardassian kicked at him, raked his face with his hands, thumbs probing his eyes, but Chakotay kept screaming and pounding, smashing the man's skull against stone, all the rage of his pain driving him, ignoring the sudden pressure he felt on his eyeball, twisting his head to elude it, pounding, pounding, remembering his violated home, his parents, the friends of his childhood.

He wasn't sure how long the man was still before he realized it. He dropped the neck cords and shoved himself off the Cardassian, whose head lolled awkwardly to one side, the back of his head a matted sponge of blood and bone.

Exhausted, dizzy, perspiring, gasping for breath, Chakotay put his hands on his knees and bent over, needing blood to his brain. Things stopped spinning and he slowly stood upright, hearing once more the strange plaintive cry of the trapped snake. It was hungry, and had been denied a potential meal. How long would the Cardassians keep it down there, starving?

He knew others might have been alerted, but he wasn't going to resist the sudden compulsion. He stripped the Cardassian of clothing, and then dragged his body to the pit and rolled it in. There was a sudden cessation of the serpentine squealing, and Chakotay peered over the edge.

The wrist beacon was still illuminating the pit, in which the massive reptile was slowly entwining the Cardassian's body in its coils, not realizing that its work had already been done. No matter. In time, it would feed.

He moved to the first isotane canister and activated it, used his tricorder to insure that the chain reaction had begun, and then touched his commbadge. "Chakotay to *Liberty*. One to beam up."

In the seconds before dematerialization, it struck him that in Starfleet's mind, he was now not only an outlaw, but a murderer.

Afterward, there was no particular remorse for the act, which, though passionate, was in self-defense. But what enveloped him instead was far more profound, and far worse.

He had somewhat expected that taking a Cardassian life would expiate the rage and grief that he felt after the destruction of his home village. He had promised vengeance, and had taken it. A debt had been paid.

But there was no satisfaction in it. Instead, the leaden weight of an awful realization had lodged in his heart, crowding out everything else, spreading, eating like a cancer through his mind, consuming everything.

His last words to his father had been spoken in anger.

Kolopak had died with the memory of his son's furious rejection of everything he stood for. His soul had been burdened by the venom of Chakotay's anger, his death tainted by that estrangement. His father believed in an afterlife—was he now doomed to carry that last awful moment with his son throughout eternity?

It was unbearable. Chakotay moved in a daze, thinking of nothing else, feeling nothing else, stunned and distraught. He announced that they would take a brief respite from their guerrilla actions, and they put down at one of the secret strongholds the Maquis had established on friendly planets. Chakotay shut himself in his quarters under the pretense of scrutinizing future plans, but in fact he was in the grip of a paralyzing apathy, unable to wrench his mind from the overwhelming guilt that had enveloped him.

Seska, of course, tried desperately to draw him out, preparing food for him herself and bringing it to his quarters, where it usually went uneaten. She'd even scoured the planet for edible mushrooms to make him a soup which he favored, certain he would show some enthusiasm for her efforts.

She entered the spartan quarters of the stronghold and put the tureen down in front of him, lifted the lid, and stood waiting for his gratitude.

He tried to offer a smile, but it was wooden and off-center. "Thanks" was the best he could offer. She regarded him for a moment and he hoped his silence would induce her to leave, but she stayed put. She placed her hands on his shoulders, kneading the muscles with strong fingers.

"You're so tense . . . you need to relax," she said suggestively. Her hands went to his face and she leaned to kiss him. He turned his head.

Stung, she backed off and he rose, facing her. "I've been thinking this for a long time," he said, "so it's not a sudden decision. It's not right for us to have an affair."

Her eyes widened in shock and surprise. "Why not?" she queried, and he heard in her tone the willingness to fight. He held up his hand as though to block any further statement.

"Not while we're working together like this. It interferes with the work we're doing."

"No, it—" She was prepared to debate, but he wasn't going to get drawn in.

"Don't. Please." There was an edge to his voice that she heard, and she subsided. There was a long moment between them, and then she took a breath.

"You've been under a lot of stress. I understand. If you need some time off, that's fine. I just want you to know I'll be here when you're ready."

It seemed easier to accept this than to assure her that wouldn't happen, so he gave her a curt nod, and thereby kept her hopes alive— a mistake, as he was to learn years later.

As his malaise continued, he desperately wished he could ask his father for advice. What could he do to shake the terrible languor that had beshrouded him?

When he realized the answer, he chided himself for not having realized it immediately. He procured an Akoonah from the people of his planet and prepared to go inward, where his father had told him all answers would lie.

"Akoochimoyah . . . Akoochimoyah . . ." This time he used the ritual chant of his people, and slipped easily into the vision, finding himself almost instantly in the woods of his homeworld once more. He looked around for the snake, eager to tell it of his adventure with its more malignant relative, but the brightly colored serpent wasn't in evidence. He began walking, searching for the clearing, but the landscape had changed somehow, and he no longer felt he knew just where he was.

Further, the sky had darkened, and a wind began to swirl the leaves and kick up dust. The temperature dropped noticeably, and Chakotay was no longer comfortable. Something was amiss.

He heard footfalls behind him, and turned to peer into the dark woods, but he could see nothing. Then the sounds of steps came from another direction entirely, and he whirled, trying to locate the unseen presence.

Footsteps began sounding from all directions, all around him, getting louder and louder, like rumbling thunder. He turned in circles, fearful, awaiting the appearance of a dread apparition, realizing now that this inner journey was to be his punishment for his anger and disrespect toward his father.

He would accept whatever happened. He deserved whatever the quest might bestow on him.

He closed his eyes, listening to the deafening sounds, feeling the forest floor vibrate with the intensity of the steps of thousands of beings, marching inexorably toward him.

Then there was silence.

He opened his eyes and saw his father standing before him.

Chakotay's knees suddenly buckled and he staggered, sinking onto the damp floor of the forest.

"Hello, Chakotay." It was indeed his father's voice, his father's wise eyes and gentle countenance, his voice which rang with love. Chakotay felt his eyes sting with gratitude for this chance to see him once more.

"Father," he said in a choked voice, and saw Kolopak smile and put a warm hand on his shoulder.

"You're surprised, I know. You didn't expect to see me."

"I had a spirit guide. I thought . . . I don't know what I thought."

"Apparently you need me, as well."

"How can that be?"

"It could only be if that's what you want."

The rush of joy Chakotay felt was so intense he almost lost consciousness. Never had he been so elated, so exuberant. He hadn't lost his father, after all—he was there, inside him, accessible, for the rest of his life. He felt a laugh begin in his throat and he opened his mouth to shout it out, but instead he burst into tears.

He sat on the forest floor, sobbing, as his father knelt by him and held him. He cried out his pain, and his loss, and his confusion, and when he was done he looked up at Kolopak with swollen eyes, and saw his father smiling at him.

"Things will be better now," he promised, and Chakotay knew that, as usual, his father was absolutely right.

The arrival of several new people to the *Liberty* was the beginning of a series of problems. Each of them had their strengths, to be sure, but their presence caused other difficulties which, although subtle, were to have a far-reaching impact on the crew.

The first was B'Elanna Torres, the half-Klingon engineer they rescued from Cardassians. She brought a wealth of technical expertise to the group, but her arrival seemed to send Seska into a paroxysm of jealousy. Seska tried to disguise it, and insisted she had nothing but the highest regard for B'Elanna, but it was clear she was deeply threatened by this new female presence.

The recruiting of Tom Paris to the *Liberty* was a move Chakotay at first approved, then gradually came to regret. He was a first-rate pilot, but he had an arrogance that was annoying, and Chakotay also began to wonder if he could be trusted. He'd lied about the deaths of three of his friends in order to save himself from censure; he lacked strong character. And it was clear he was attracted to B'Elanna, which only served to complicate the tangled emotional relationships he had to deal with.

When Chakotay had heard there was a disenchanted Starfleet Vulcan who might be interested in becoming a freedom fighter, he responded with alacrity. He'd had a Vulcan on board earlier, a pilot named Setonak who had returned to his home planet to recover from wounds, and Chakotay had always appreciated the calm and steadying presence on his bridge. Tuvok was much the same, a seasoned and unflappable veteran whose cold logic Chakotay found valuable, especially among this group of hotheaded rebels.

Things had come to a head with Tom Paris fairly early on. Chakotay had ordered the ship for its first foray into Cardassian territory, a short reconnaissance run to test the perimeter for defensive measures. Things had gone well and they had actually gathered some data on a weapons depot that was secreted on a small moon, and were heading back to the demilitarized zone when they stumbled on a surveillance probe.

"It's scanning us," said B'Elanna from her post on the bridge.

"Send out a polaron beam, see if you can block the scan—" Chakotay had begun, when suddenly the probe exploded before their eyes.

"What was that?" B'Elanna asked.

"That was me," replied Tom Paris, with the cocky edge to his voice that Chakotay had come to dislike.

"What's that supposed to mean?"

"I fired on it. Took it out."

Chakotay's wrath began to well up, though he tried to keep his voice calm. "I don't remember ordering you to do that."

"I took it on myself—"

"On my bridge I give the orders. You don't take it on yourself to do anything. Is that clear?"

A flush emerged on Tom's cheeks, and Chakotay knew he was angry as well. "I didn't realize this was a mini-Starfleet. I thought we were expected to think on our feet."

The fact that Paris was challenging him in front of the others added to Chakotay's ire. "Thinking is one thing. Acting without an order is another. All you've managed to do is alert the Cardassians that we're here. Stop arguing with me and start getting us the hell out of here."

The two men held a bitter look for a long moment, then Tom finally turned away and began working his controls. From that point on, things were tense between them, until the point that Tom abandoned them. It was good riddance as far as Chakotay was concerned.

Of course, that was all before the great adventure that had changed their lives, before the flight into the Badlands that ended with their strange experience at the hands of an entity known as the Caretaker, before he met and joined forces with the captain of the ship *Voyager,* before his Maquis group and her Starfleet crew combined and then became stranded in the Delta Quadrant, before he learned that Tuvok was in fact an agent working for Starfleet who had infiltrated his ship—and before fate ironically threw Tom Paris right back in his lap, probably for the rest of his life.

But it was all made worthwhile by one thing: having met and worked beside the remarkable woman named Kathryn Janeway.

CHAPTER 3

W<small>HEN</small> C<small>HAKOTAY</small> <small>FINISHED TALKING,</small> <small>HE REALIZED THAT EVERY ONE OF HIS</small> group had been listening, rapt. "I didn't mean to go on and on," he apologized, realizing he had revealed more about himself than he had ever expected to.

"That was interesting, sir," said Harry sincerely. "Commander Nimembeh did the same thing to me at the Academy—ordered me to take laps in my boots. But the outcome was a little different."

"Tell you what, Ensign," replied Chakotay, "tomorrow night you can tell us all about it. Maybe by then we'll even have a campfire to tell our stories around."

"I didn't have nearly as interesting a life as you. Everyone will be bored."

Chakotay clapped him on the shoulder. "I doubt that. I'd especially like to hear your experiences with Nimembeh."

Harry finally agreed, and they all went to sleep, feeling closer, more bonded, at the end of this day than they had at the beginning.

Harry's sleep was fitful, because the night life of the camp was not a tranquil one. There was a chorus of cries and groans that was even more disturbing in the dark than it was during the day. In the distance he heard the shouts of conflict, and then a horrible shriek. He glanced up at the wall to see if this behavior provoked any response from the guards, but there was none. Apparently they were content to let the roiling mass of prisoners see to itself, dispensing rough prisoner justice.

Harry tried not to let himself think of home, of the quiet gardens his parents cultivated, of the soft music his mother played on an ancient instrument, of the utter harmony and serenity of that life. It was far away now, and he'd been through one severe test after another since he'd joined *Voyager*. He was harder, tougher, more capable than ever. He could survive this latest challenge, *would* survive it. Fleeting memories of Nimembeh flickered in his mind and he felt a moment's nostalgia for the man who had once been his tormentor.

He turned over on the ground, looking for a comfortable position. The ground didn't seem to have retained the heat of the day, and felt damp. The night air was as chilly as the daylight had been scorching. The elements weren't kind on this planet.

He wasn't sure when he realized someone was crawling toward him. A dark shape about fifteen meters from him, silhouetted by the flickering light of someone's fire, moved with agonizing slowness toward the outer periphery of the *Voyager* group, where Harry lay. Once he spotted the prowling form, Harry's senses were alert. He saw the huddled shape, on all fours, picking its way through a scattering of other sleeping forms, stopping occasionally as though to gauge its progress and assess whether its stealthy approach had been detected.

Harry watched intently, breathing deeply as though he were sound asleep. The creeping form was now only about three meters away, still stopping every few seconds and looking around, testing the air like an animal. Harry couldn't see any of its features, only a black shape that moved against the background of the distant campfires.

When the dark form reached his feet, it stopped, and was still for a long moment. Harry waited, tensed, ready for the being to make its move.

When it came, it was anything but what he expected. A hand reached out and gripped his leg gently, the soft touch of a cat's paw, while the other tugged smoothly at his boots. Swiftly, he sat up and lunged forward, grabbing for the hand holding his leg.

He heard a surprised gasp, and then he flung the person on his back, quickly straddling him and shoving both arms over his head into the ground. "Nice try," he began.

And then he realized he was looking at a young woman, barely more than a girl, who was staring up at him with terrified eyes. "Don't hurt me," she breathed.

Harry instantly leapt off her, and had time only to notice that she had hair as black as his own, a heart-shaped face, and unusual eyes that flashed with a strange color which he couldn't clearly make out in the darkness. And then she was gone, springing up and scrambling off like a wild animal suddenly set free.

That brief glimpse of her face haunted him for the rest of the wakeful night.

"Let's go. Everybody up." Chakotay's voice knifed through Harry's sleep like a cleaver. Harry realized he had finally fallen asleep, and deeply, only now to be roused by his commander. He opened scratchy eyes to the bright glare of the sun and realized the air was already baking hotly. His mouth was cottony.

"There are things we need," continued Chakotay when everyone had shaken off sleep and was sitting or standing. "Containers for storing water. Materials to build shelter. Fuel for fires. It's usually possible to barter in a place like this. I'd suggest you offer your jacket or your undershirt. If you give away your shoes you might be in trouble."

"What about our commbadges?" asked B'Elanna.

"Some of us can offer commbadges, but I don't want to lose more than two or three. I'm not sure they'd be as desirable as good clothing, anyway."

Tuvok joined in. "No one should venture off alone. No fewer than two people in a group, preferably three or four."

And so they set out for their first full day in the place their captors called Area 347, but which the *Voyager* crew quickly dubbed Hellhole. Harry moved out in a group that included B'Elanna and her young Vulcan engineer, Vorik. Harry didn't tell anyone, but he had a double agenda on this day: bartering for the items they needed—and finding the young woman who had crept up to him last night.

It was Vorik who first succeeded in trading with other prisoners. He approached a seedy gathering of small, gnomelike creatures who had built a rather sizable lean-to and seemed to have any number of pots and pans and other artifacts strewn around their area.

"My jacket is made of synthetic polyfibers which provide insulation against both heat and cold. It is of superior construction and can be expected to hold up against the harshest elements, as well as resisting wear and tear for some time to come. It is stain-resistant and can be rolled up to become quite a comfortable pillow, as I can attest after last night."

The wizened little beings stared at him, openmouthed. Vorik's unflappable Vulcan presence seemed to mesmerize them. He stripped off the jacket and held it out in front of him. "I will accept fuel, containers for liquid, or any building materials you might possess."

Ten minutes later they walked off with an armful of jars and pitchers, a large tarpaulin, and four squares of dried dung to use as fuel. It was a good beginning. But even after each of them had managed to trade, and they carried their booty back to camp, Harry had yet to spot the young woman from the night before. The likelihood of finding, among these thousands, one person he'd only glimpsed in the light of a flickering fire was, he admitted, remote. But he suspected that she must not have been far from the place they made camp, and if he kept looking, he might find her.

The away team's morning was a successful one, and the afternoon was spent constructing two shelters which, while not luxurious, were large enough to accommodate them all and offer protection from the elements. When Chakotay asked for volunteers to fill the water containers, Harry was first in line. Something inside him said he would find her during this foray.

He almost missed her. She was huddled on the ground, back against a tree stump some ten meters in front of the muddy marsh, knees drawn up to her face, head bowed. She was dressed in a kind of caftan, a dark robe that enveloped her small body. It was the black hair that made him slow down, then he saw a corner of her cheek, and he squatted down next to her.

"Hello," he said, and was sorrowed to see that she started and drew back at the sound. Her eyes, in the daylight, were glittering, prismatic disks of orange and yellow, but even in their strangeness he could see fear.

"I won't hurt you," Harry assured her, and was gratified to see that she seemed to relax slightly. "I'm the one whose boots you tried to steal last night. No hard feelings."

She turned away, chewing on a lip that was cracked and sore. Her face was grimy, her hair a matted mess, but to Harry she possessed an unearthly beauty. "Do you have a name?" he asked. "I'm Harry."

The response was so soft he could barely hear her. "Coris," she said.

"Are you part of a group? Do you have friends here?" She shook her head, and Harry saw a moistness gather in her unusual eyes.

Harry held his hand toward her. "Come with me," he offered. "You'll be safer with us."

There was a long silence, and then she reached out a hand and took his. It was tiny, again reminding him of a cat's paw. He pulled her to her feet, which were bare and swollen. She reminded him of a fragile bird, all bone and feather, heart beating wildly, ready to fly at a hint of danger. She stood patiently by the marsh as he and the others filled their containers with the murky water and then headed back down the road they called Broadway, toward their camp.

Coris said nothing during the entire walk, but kept her eyes fastened on the ground in front of her. When they reached their camp, Chakotay spotted her and raised an inquisitive brow, at which Harry shrugged sheepishly and said, "She followed me home, sir."

Chakotay smiled and said nothing else, and so young Coris the Saccul became part of their group.

Rations that evening consisted of a handful of wet mush that smelled foul and tasted worse. It was full of bulbous sacs which, when punctured, ran a thin green juice that was bilious. Yet the crew from *Voyager,* and their new guest, ate it as though it were rice pudding. They were realizing that the grain cake from the night before wasn't adequate nourishment for twenty-four hours, and they were famished.

They had lit small fires against the chill, and their temporarily filled stomachs had once again given them a sense of well-being. They were alive, uninjured, and had shelter; tomorrow they would begin investigating the possibilities of escape.

Chakotay turned to Harry. "It's your turn to be storyteller, Harry," he said. "Let's hear about your trials with Nimembeh."

"Like you said last night, Commander, it goes a little deeper than that. It's kind of—about my whole life."

"I told you mine—we'd love to hear yours."

Harry glanced quickly at Coris. Something made him uncomfortable launching into his life's story in front of her. She was stretched out on the ground, head cradled in her arms, looking more contented than she had this afternoon, eyelids flickering shut against the welcoming heat of the fire. She was going to sleep.

Relieved, Harry turned to the others, and saw they were waiting eagerly. He guessed that here, in this hostile place, even the unremarkable story of Harry Kim's life was a welcome distraction. He determined to try to make it sound as interesting as possible.

CHAPTER

4

THE FIRST MEMORIES WERE OF MUSIC. THE STRUMMING OF THE P'I P'A AND his mother's delicate voice, wafting through shafts of sunlight that dissected the room with gentle planes of gold.

He stood in his crib, pudgy arm extended, fingers straining to reach the motes that swam in the sunlight, hearing the tranquil sounds of his mother's voice as she sang.

The enticing motes danced just out of his reach. It was a problem that required a solution, even if fifteen-month-old Harry Kim couldn't yet think of it in those terms. He wanted the tantalizing little specks in the same way he wanted nourishment: it was an unnamed need and it drove him powerfully. His hands clasped the rail of the crib and he tensed his arms, squeezing tightly, as though testing his own strength.

Out. He wanted out. These bars were keeping him from what he wanted. His small body, rather than his mind, suggested the answer, as his toes found friction on the slats of the crib and he felt himself crawling higher, higher . . .

Instinct told him he was about to fall, to pitch headfirst onto the floor below. Clutching the top rail tightly, he stretched his body along it and then shifted his grip so that his fingers now curled toward the crib, rather than toward the room.

The rest was easy. His toes climbed down the slats on the outside of the crib and, when he could go no farther, he released the top rail one hand at a time, clasping the slats hand over hand, and in this way lowered himself until he could drop easily to the floor.

He crowed with delight. That was fun! He stared up at the crib, wondering how to get back in so he could re-create the climb to freedom, but quickly realized reversing his course would be considerably more difficult. The urge instantly left his mind, and he turned to the first object of his desire, the fluttering motes that rode the sunlight. All the while, his mother's singing, and the beguiling sound of the ancient instrument, flooded the room.

He toddled somewhat awkwardly across the floor—this new upright mobility had been achieved only a short time ago—and reached toward the first pool of light he encountered. His fist closed around the specks and he drew his hand close. But when he opened it, nothing was there.

This was a puzzle. But he knew from experience that many new tasks required attempting them over and over. That had been true of his first locomotion, on hands and knees, and certainly was the case when he learned one could put one foot in front of the other and travel much more quickly (this method also freed the hands for grabbing things, another plus).

But grabbing the motes was proving a difficult task. No matter how many times his fingers closed around the flickering specks, they disappeared by the time he opened his fist. This caused him no anguish—Harry would not suffer a moment's anguish throughout his charmed childhood—but simply redoubled his determination to succeed.

So focused was he on his task that he didn't notice that the music had stopped. It was such a constant in his life that its presence or absence didn't call attention to itself. And so it was that his mother opened the door and found him standing in the middle of the room, clutching and unclenching his fist, trying to capture the sparkling bits of dust that were illuminated by the streaming afternoon sun.

She laughed, a sound not unlike the delicate tones of her singing. Harry looked up at her and he laughed, too. "How did you get down there?" his mother asked merrily, but Harry couldn't understand her.

He understood only the joy and love that glowed from her like the streams of lemon sunlight that illuminated his room.

Every birthday was a vast celebration. Grandparents, aunts and uncles, cousins, in-laws, and friends jammed the beautifully appointed Kim home in Monterey. He remembered his first birthday, the first awareness of a cake topped with candles, the first gooey mouthful of frosting. Faces crowded round him, laughing eyes peering, murmured sounds of laughter, soft voices urging him to blow candles, to eat the cake, to tear paper from a massive pile of presents. It was then that one of his relatives presented him with a small bundle of fur that meowed comically, at which Harry pointed and said, "Mousie," a word he had just learned from hearing his mother read to him, and Mousie was the cat's name from that point on.

On each birthday, the adults would drink a joyous toast, acknowledging the specialness of this princely child. On his fifth birthday, Harry asked his mother why they did that.

Her soft hand reached out and caressed his cheek, brushed his dark hair away from his forehead. "We waited such a long time for you," she said, gazing at him with shining eyes. "We'd given up any hope that you might come. So when you did, it was a miracle."

"Where did I come from?" Harry asked, and was curious about the small ripple of laughter that trickled around the room.

"From here," his mother said without embarrassment, patting her stomach. "I carried you inside me, safe and protected for nine months."

"I remember that," the boy said, and was surprised by an even greater swell of laughter.

But his mother seemed to take him seriously. "What do you remember?" she asked evenly.

"Warm . . . and dark . . . floating . . . it felt good. But coming out was hard."

His mother and father exchanged a bemused glance, but made no utterance of contradiction. If Harry said he remembered being in the womb, they accepted it.

They accepted everything about him, always. Harry, who could remember all of his childhood as clearly as he remembered the last hour, had no recollection of ever being censured, admonished, or denied. His childhood was a womb of another kind, sheltering him from sorrow and affliction, from obstacles and misfortunes. He was loved, cosseted, rewarded, supported, and approved, and though some under such tolerant handling might have become self-indulgent monsters, he grew instead into a child known for his sweetness and patience.

He would sit for hours with his father, watching as John Kim painted elaborate, delicate designs on porcelain with a tiny brush, colorful flowers with trailing vines that wound around and around until the plate or vase was completely filled with color. It was one of several ancient arts that John practiced, and their home was filled with beautiful artifacts—intricate carvings in jade, lustrous sculptures in bronze, exquisite painted porcelain. Each piece was produced slowly, with infinite patience, with thorough appreciation of the process involved in creating a work of art. It was work not to be rushed, and Harry, sitting quietly hour after hour, watching, seemed to have inherited his father's quiet forbearance.

His mother started to teach him the fingerings of the P'i P'a when he was three and was amazed that he already knew them. He had watched her play, studying her fingers as she moved them over the strings and learning the correct positions without even realizing it. He played it as easily as he breathed. His mother, astonished, immediately envisioned him as a concert artist on the ancient instrument, which had enjoyed a resurgence in popularity during the twenty-fourth century.

As it turned out, it would not be a stringed instrument that captured Harry's imagination, but a reed, which he had first encountered in the form of a clarinet when he was seven. He had eyed the slender tubelike apparatus in the music school to which his mother took him and, with his teacher's permission, had picked it up and attempted to produce a sound.

Nothing came out. Surprised, for he had never picked up a musical instrument he couldn't play almost immediately, he tried again. This time there was a rush of air and an ungainly squeak that didn't sound musical at all, but more like the squeal Mousie had made once when he had inadvertently stepped on her tail.

Harry was intrigued. This simple-looking device was a challenge, something he didn't often encounter, and he determined to master it. He announced this to his mother in a firm voice, and though she was disappointed in his choice, she didn't question him. If Harry wanted to play the clarinet, he had her support.

And so his parents endured months of squawking, squeaking efforts to produce a mellifluous sound. Mousie had no tolerance for the learning period; whenever Harry withdrew his clarinet and began to puff into it, Mousie would scurry to the opposite end of the house and hide, all but clamping her paws over her ears to keep out the strident sound.

But gradually, the persistence paid off, and within a year Harry was playing a repertory that included Mozart and Weber. By the time he was ten, he was transporting regularly to New York, where he played in the Juilliard youth symphony, while studying music theory, composition, and orchestration. He was considered a prodigy, and the instructors saw a limitless future for him in music.

When he was fourteen, his life took an unpredictable turn that changed it forever.

"How much farther is it?" asked Harry, breathing heavily and perspiring in the hot August sun. The cloth he had knotted around his head was already damp.

"Not too far now," replied his father, marching ahead of him on the foot trail, with pencils, charcoals, and sketch pad carried in a pack on his back. They had been hiking for almost two hours in the Sierra Nevada mountains, and Harry was secretly wishing he hadn't agreed to accompany his father on this expedition, though he would never have said so because such a statement might hurt John Kim's feelings. Harry's feelings had always been treated with delicacy and caring, and he tended to respond in kind.

"It's a long hike, I know," John was saying, "but you'll agree it's worth it when you see this little lake. I don't think most people even know it's there. It's off the hiking trail and so small it's not on most maps. But it's the prettiest spot I've seen on this earth."

Harry's father had traveled extensively, and so this statement carried weight. Besides, Harry enjoyed his father's company, and liked to see him sketch, even if the price was a long climb on a hot day. He carried his clarinet in his day pack, and looked forward to practicing on the shores of a jewel-like lake in the pine forests of the Sierra Nevadas.

Fifteen minutes later, they reached a ridgeline and John pointed downward. Below them nestled a pool of blue, completely surrounded by tall conifers. It seemed both magical and inviting, and Harry was glad he'd come along.

"That's it, Harry," said his father. "It's only about a ten-minute walk down to the lake. We can have lunch on the shore."

He took one step and then disappeared from view as the trail collapsed beneath him.

It happened so quickly that it took a moment for Harry to absorb the event. He peered over the ridgeline and saw his father, far below him, tumbling downward, out of control, and finally slamming into a huge boulder and coming to a stop.

Then he didn't move.

Harry's throat constricted with fear and he looked around as though someone might have magically appeared to help. But he realized with awful clarity that he and his father were alone in this wilderness, and now his father was unconscious—or worse—at the bottom of a steep incline. Harry had to act.

He scrambled onto the trail past the point where it had collapsed and began hurrying down a long, snaking series of switchbacks, checking occasionally to see if his father had perhaps regained consciousness and was walking around, unharmed after all. But each time he peered downward, he saw the still form lying exactly as it had been since it had cracked against the boulder.

It seemed to take forever to reach him, and Harry could hear his heart pounding in his ears as he maneuvered his way toward his still-prone father. Again, he looked around through the trees, wishing someone would suddenly appear in the woods, someone older, who would know what to do about an emergency like this. But the woods were empty.

Fearful, he hurried toward his father, mind scrambling to remember some of the emergency medical procedures he'd learned in school. Don't move him, that was foremost. You could exacerbate a spinal injury by moving someone.

What else? First see if he's breathing, if he has a pulse. Harry could see his father's chest rising and falling, but he extended his fingers to check for a neck pulse, anyway, just to follow the procedure he'd been taught.

Okay, he was breathing. That was good. But his eyes were closed and he wasn't moving. He must have hit his head on the boulder against which he now lay. Maybe he had a concussion.

Now what? Harry felt panic rising in him as he mulled over his options. He could start running, back along the trail they had taken this morning, and summon help. But that would take hours, even if he could run the whole distance, which he doubted. And it would mean leaving his father alone out here, which he was afraid to do. There might be animals, bears, mountain lions. He couldn't leave John Kim unprotected.

Briefly the thought occurred to him that he might not be much protection against a bear or a mountain lion, but he willed the notion away.

Nearby, the water of the small lake lapped gently at the shore. Water, that was something. He pulled off the cloth that was knotted around his head and ran to the lake, dipping the scarf into the cold water, soaking it through. Then he ran back to his father and applied the cold cloth to his forehead. Surely that would accomplish something.

But his father did not respond. He lay with terrible stillness, eyes closed, mouth parted slightly, a dribble of saliva trickling down one cheek.

Harry sat heavily on the ground, fighting anxiety, trying to remain calm. He'd have to go get help, there was no other choice. He remembered his father's drawing materials and found them scattered on the ground from the tumble down the ravine. He used a charcoal to write a message on the sketch pad, telling John that he'd gone for help, and not to move from this spot.

He put the sketch pad where it would easily be seen and then put his hand on his father's forehead again. It felt clammy, and an icy squeeze of fear clutched at him. He turned and looked once more into the woods, for the magic rescuers that would come to his aid and handle this terrifying situation.

And there they were.

There were four of them, young men and women several years older than he, dressed alike, in drab jumpsuits that had the feel of a uniform. Metal badges were worn over their hearts.

They caught Harry by surprise, but he had no feelings of alarm. They seemed benign and purposeful, and were in fact hurrying toward him as though sensing his situation.

"What happened?" asked one of the young men as he moved quickly toward John Kim's unconscious form.

"He fell," replied Harry, pointing upward. He was experiencing a vast feeling of relief now that these samaritans had appeared. They were older than he, more knowledgeable. They moved with purpose and dispatch. They would know what to do.

One of the young women was passing a device over his father's body. "It's a concussion," she said calmly. "We have to get medical attention."

The first young man briefly touched the badge on his chest. "Noftsger to base camp. We have an emergency situation."

A voice replied: "Go ahead, Cadet."

"We've encountered civilians who've had an accident. A man, forties, has sustained a concussion. He needs medical attention."

"Stand by to transport, Noftsger. We'll be taking your whole team."

"Aye, sir." The young man knelt to Harry's father and put his hand on the man's shoulder. One of the females put her hand on Harry's, and within seconds they had dematerialized and were transported to a building that seemed still to be in the mountains, but was sleekly styled and teeming with people: more of the young people in jumpsuits, and older men and women wearing uniforms of black and red. One of these moved immediately toward Harry and his father, passing a device over John just as the young woman had done.

"Get him to the infirmary," said the older man, and the boy known as Noftsger said, "Aye, sir," and knelt once more, touching John's shoulder. "Energize," he said, and the two dematerialized.

"How did he get hurt, son?" asked the man.

It had all happened so fast Harry hadn't been able to assess who these people were, where he had been taken, or what he should do now. "He fell," he stammered, and then blurted out, "Who are you? Where is this place?"

The man smiled and put a hand on Harry's shoulder. "Sorry. I thought you knew. Cadet Shanak, take our young friend to the mess hall and get him some lunch, and fill him in on Starfleet's survival program."

"Aye, sir," said the woman known as Shanak. She was Vulcan, dark-haired and dark-eyed, with brows that swept upward at the outer corners. She regarded Harry coolly and gestured down a hallway.

"Starfleet?" said Harry in surprise. "I thought all that was in San Francisco."

"Headquarters is there," she replied, "and the Academy. But there are facilities all over Earth. We do survival training in the Sierra Nevadas, and there are two base camps like this one to coordinate all the teams."

"You go to Starfleet Academy?" asked Harry curiously. He'd heard of Starfleet, of course—who hadn't?—but only as a distant and not entirely well-understood entity. Harry's life had been proscribed and insular, defined by family, by art and music, and his awareness of this legendary organization was unformed.

Shanak gave him an imperious glance, but it didn't carry any sense of ill will. It was just who she was. "Yes," she replied simply. "I have just begun my second year."

A thousand questions flooded Harry's mind. "How did you decide to go to the Academy?" he began. "What do you have to do to get accepted? How long does it take? Is it hard to get in?"

Shanak looked at him imperturbably. "I made my choice when I was a small girl, and I began working toward the goal then. It is extremely difficult to be accepted. There are thousands and thousands of applicants from all over the Federation, so the competition is great."

"So . . . how did you do it? What do you have to do?"

"As I said, I began as a small child. I reviewed the curriculum of the Academy and I structured my schoolwork to focus on that curriculum. I devoted myself to studies and the activities I knew would serve me well in the event of my acceptance. I allowed nothing to interfere with my chosen course."

Harry took this in with a heavy heart. That morning, he was barely aware of Starfleet. Now, all he wanted in life was to become part of it, to be accepted at the Academy and become one of these proud, capable, supremely proficient cadets. But if it required the kind of lifelong devotion Shanak had given it, he was much too late in making this decision.

All through lunch, he peppered her with questions, which she answered in her cool, composed way. And when she received a communication to take him to the infirmary, he questioned her all the way on their walk there.

John Kim was sitting on a cotlike bed, and smiled as Harry and Shanak entered. To Harry's relief, his father looked perfectly healthy, and his smile was as warm and ready as ever. "These good people have me good as new, Harry," he said. "We owe them a debt of thanks." He opened his arms, and Harry ran into them, so glad to see his father well that he didn't even feel embarrassed by the display of affection.

From that day on, Harry had but one goal: to be accepted at Starfleet Academy.

His parents were admittedly puzzled by his strange epiphany, and not a little concerned by the prospect of his becoming a space adventurer. Having been blessed with his birth after having given up on the possibility of ever having a child, they had fantasized a future in which he would remain a constant part of their lives. He would marry, of course, and have his own children, but that would be done within the geographical confines of their family community. The Kims had many relatives, and they all lived within a hundred kilometers of each other. It had never occurred to Harry's parents that he would stray farther than that.

Starfleet personnel, they knew, were often in deep space for years at a time. In some instances, their spouses and children were able to accompany them, but such provisions were not made for grandparents, or aunts and uncles and cousins. The prospect of a Harry Kim in Starfleet was that of an absentee son.

But when Harry began talking about nothing but Starfleet Academy, they concealed their fears and threw themselves into offering whatever support they could. They urged him to speak with his school counselor about his new goal, and to determine what he would need to do to achieve it. They arranged for tutors in those subjects which Harry had heretofore taken lightly. They did their own reading about Starfleet's history, so they would be able to discuss it intelligently with their son.

Harry, for most of his life, had put his energies into music, and was woefully lacking in science and mathematics. He had studied only what was required, and that in a desultory fashion. He much preferred art, and literature, and history.

But to stand even a chance of entering the Academy, he would have to shore up those other disciplines: biology, chemistry, physics, astronomy, and anthropology just for starters, as well as mathematics. He'd been exposed to algebra and geometry, but the vast array of mathematical studies that loomed before him was like a dark, impenetrable forest, terra incognita.

He gave up every other aspect of his life in order to study. His clarinet stood unplayed on its stand; the P'i P'a rested in its case. He allowed himself one social outing a week, usually the Parrises Squares game at his school. He did not date. He kept his place on the volleyball team because he knew athletic participation was a requirement at the Academy. He had one burning, single-minded purpose: to become a part of Starfleet.

He was vaguely aware that his parents were worried, and whenever he allowed himself to see the situation from their vantage point, he understood their concern. He had become a recluse. He didn't go out with friends, he didn't attend concerts anymore, he didn't dance or ride hovercycles or do any of the things the other young people his age were wont to do. He was trading part of his adolescence in order to pursue his dream.

And yet not once in the four years of his arduous preparation did he regret his choice. Nothing about it felt as though he were being denied; rather, he had a greater sense of purpose than he had ever imagined possible. Everything had always come so easily to him—love, approval, musical prowess—that he enjoyed taking on this overwhelming challenge. He used parts of himself that he'd never tapped before, muscles of the mind that had lain fallow for too many years. He felt an edge, a sharpness, in his thinking that hadn't been there before.

And, to his great surprise, he found that once he tackled their labyrinthine depths, science and mathematics were utterly fascinating. There was a purity, an exactness, to both disciplines that was as refreshing to him as a plunge into a cold pool on a hot day. He loved literature, especially poetry, but realized now that while poems were good at posing questions, they rarely provided answers. Good literature made you wonder, set your mind to bubbling with the possibilities of this or that, led you to ponder ideas heretofore imponderable.

But it provided no absolutes. In physics, force equals mass times acceleration. In chemistry, a compound contains two or more elements combined in a definite proportion by weight. In calculus, the derivative of x squared is two x. Once you solved a problem, it was solved. The square root of forty-nine wasn't somewhere between six and eight, it was seven. Period.

Harry found this incontrovertibility comforting. It was firm ground rather than shifting sands, and that kind of stability was pleasurable to him. He redoubled his efforts, learning to get by on less and less sleep each night in order to have more time for study. He could feel his mind growing, expanding, stretching to touch truths he had never dreamed of. It was an experience far more appealing than sleep.

And so it was, three weeks after his seventeenth birthday, that Harry Kim transported to San Francisco to take the entrance examination for Starfleet Academy.

He sat in a vast room lined with long tables, at which sat four hundred people just like himself: seventeen- and eighteen-year-olds with the blistering desire to enter Starfleet Academy. This test session was just one of many that would be held in San Francisco, and there were similar tests held in locations all over the Federation, for the thousands and thousands of young people of many different species who wanted one of the coveted places in next year's freshman class.

The test lasted eight hours, with one ten-minute break in the morning, another in the afternoon, and an hour for a lunch that none of the test subjects really tasted. It covered a vast array of subjects: Federation history, astrophysics, interstellar treaties. It was the most grueling day Harry had ever spent in his life.

But when it was all done, he felt good. Nothing had seemed beyond his capacity, nothing had come as a surprise. His years of arduous study had stood him in good stead. He transported home that evening, exhausted but elated, and told his anxious parents that he'd done as well as he possibly could have. They erupted in smiles of relief, and his father made them tea while he told them about the rigors of the exam.

Then the waiting began. No one would be notified of the test results until everyone who had applied had had the opportunity to take the examination. It might be weeks before that information came from some of the far-flung outposts of the Federation. Then, after the results were in, the second phase of selection would begin: those who had made it past the written test would be given an oral examination. This was actually the more difficult aspect of the process, and the thought of it made Harry's stomach lurch. It was one thing to write answers in a padd, and quite another to sit in a room with three Starfleet officers and respond verbally to a barrage of questions. He knew they would be judging not just on the answers he gave, but on his personality, his composure, his articulateness—all of them important factors to consider when grooming Starfleet personnel.

His tutors had been giving him verbal exams for three years in order to prepare him for the process, and he determined to use the weeks of waiting to hone his abilities. He wanted to be as impressive as possible when he appeared before the examining committee. The more he practiced, the better he would be. So he devoted every waking moment to answering test questions orally, focusing on presenting himself in the best possible light. He recorded himself on his console and reviewed his performance, critiquing himself severely. He studied a dictionary and thesaurus, increasing his vocabulary substantially.

In January, he received a communiqué from Starfleet Academy. It came as a transmission on his personal console, and when he saw the notification of the message, his throat constricted and his fingers tingled unpleasantly. Four times he started to key the control that would open the message, but at the last minute withdrew his hand.

Finally, he went to his mother, who was singing as she prepared dinner.

"I have a message from the Academy," he told her, and heard his voice catch inexplicably.

She whirled, excited. "What did it say?"

Harry hesitated. He felt suddenly foolish, unaccountably childish. This wasn't how a prospective Starfleet officer should behave; he should have boldly opened the message and shouldered the responsibility of whatever it said.

But his mother knew him too well. She brushed his hair from his eyes, and said, "Why don't I come with you while you open it?" Relief flooded him and he nodded.

But even with his mother, his pillar of strength, at his side, it was hard to force his fingers to open the message. They were shaking as he keyed the controls, and when the message flashed on screen, he wanted to close his eyes and squint them open gradually. But he made himself look at it.

The first word was "Congratulations." At that, Harry let out a whoop and his mother gasped. He pulled her to her feet and twirled her around the room, laughing with a manic intensity. Nothing else mattered; he had made the first cut.

Finally he sat down again and they read the entire communiqué, which announced that he had passed the written examination in the highest percentile and should report to Starfleet Academy for the oral exam in February. In under three weeks, he would face the second battery of tests.

But Harry felt strangely relaxed about the oral. The written exam was the difficult one, the one that weeded out most of the applicants. Far fewer failed to make it past the verbal interview, and Harry had been practicing assiduously. This obstacle held no fears for him.

In February he transported from his school to Starfleet Academy, wearing a suit his mother had just replicated for him and feeling quietly confident. He arrived early and strolled the manicured grounds of the Academy, imagining himself next fall as one of the uniformed cadets; it was an easy picture to conjure. He felt immediately at home here, as though he belonged. This oral examination was the last hurdle before he achieved the goal he had worked so hard for.

He reported for his interview at thirteen hundred hours, and took his place across a table from Admirals Brand, Strickler, and Kel-Nah. They were friendly, with easy smiles, and Harry quickly relaxed. They began to pepper him with questions about astrophysics, which he answered with rapid-fire accuracy. They moved through the sciences, then into history, literature, government. He felt strong and articulate, never at a loss for words.

Finally, the question every applicant got, the one Harry had been waiting for. "Why do you want to attend Starfleet Academy?"

Harry was ready for this. He launched into his carefully prepared answer, one which spoke of Starfleet's hallowed history, its legendary heroes and heroines, its explorations and discoveries. He cited specific instances of achievement and lauded the Starfleet people involved. He closed by saying he wanted nothing more than to be a part of this proud history.

The trio of admirals nodded and smiled. They rose and shook hands with Harry and said he would be notified after all the examinations had been conducted. He left ebullient, and wandered the grounds for a while longer, feeling a sense of belonging that was palpable. Cadet Harry Kim. It had a good ring to it.

"Get out of my azaleas!" The voice was ratchety and cross. Harry turned toward it to see a thin, wizened man with some kind of gardening implement in his hand. He was staring at Harry in pique, pointing toward the ground.

Harry looked down to see that he had wandered off the path and was in fact standing among a bed of flowering plants. He moved back onto the path. "Sorry," he offered. "My mind was someplace else."

"Oh? Where might that have been?"

"I was thinking about next year."

"What about it?"

"I'm going to be a cadet next fall."

"Really. Don't ever remember those announcements coming out until April."

"Well, I don't mean I've been told. I'm just . . . pretty sure it will happen."

"How's that?"

"I just had my oral exam. It went very well, if I do say so."

The man grunted and moved to the place where Harry had stood in the azalea bed, and began turning the soil slightly as though to erase his footprints. "I have my doubts," the man growled, and then walked away without another word.

The encounter left Harry strangely uneasy, though he couldn't put his finger on just why. The man was just a gardener, a laborer, but something in his attitude, his brusqueness, had destroyed Harry's euphoric mood. He reported to the transporter room with deflated spirits and when he got home he was exhausted. He fell into bed and took a three-hour nap, but when he woke up he was as tired as before.

The news came on a Saturday in mid-April. Harry, along with the thousands of other applicants, knew the day the freshman class would be announced, and surprisingly he slept well the night before. The transmission came in in the late morning, and he almost opened it immediately, but then thought about his mother. She had been at his side when he expected bad news; it was only fair that she share in this moment of fruition. His father was out of the country on one of his many travels, but had made them promise to contact him as soon as they got the word.

He found his mother in the garden, pretending to be busy dead-heading flowers, but knowing she was as aware as he of what this day meant. "It's here," he said simply, and she rose from the flowers, a muscle twitching in her cheek. "It'll be okay," he promised her, and they walked into his room.

"Dear Mr. Kim," the transmission began, "there are many ways in which we evaluate applicants for Starfleet Academy. One factor is test scores, and yours were excellent. Nonetheless, we regret to inform you that you have not been accepted for admittance in September. We feel you will not fit comfortably with this year's cadets. You are free to apply again next year."

Harry stared at the screen, reading the message over and over, as though it might change on the fourth or fifth reading. Beside him, his mother was silent, and he realized he would have to give some response to this devastating news.

"I guess . . . I guess that's it," he said, trying to keep his voice from cracking. He felt his eyes begin to sting and he willed the moisture away, refusing to compound this awful moment by crying in front of his mother.

He felt her hand on his arm, and he covered it with his own. She had been his friend, his confidante, his strongest advocate since he was a baby. He derived strength from her, and he needed that strength now. He clutched at her hand, trying to feel the succor that flowed from her.

"I've been accepted at a couple of other schools. It's not like I have no place to go."

"Will you reapply next year?"

"I don't think so. If I couldn't make it with all the effort I put into it, there's not much point in trying again."

To his surprise, his mother stood up suddenly, her eyes flashing. "You will not quit," she said with greater firmness than he'd ever heard. "I won't allow that. You've worked too hard, put too much into this. You will apply next year."

Harry was speechless. His mother had never insisted on anything. She had never imposed on him, never demanded anything of him. But there was no mistaking the steel in her voice.

"I don't even know why they turned me down."

"Then you have to find out."

"How do I do that?"

"However you can."

And with that she left the room, leaving Harry absolutely dumbfounded.

It was perhaps not the most orthodox way to investigate, and Harry wasn't entirely certain why he was doing it. But a week later he was on the grounds of Starfleet Academy once more, looking for the gardener. He wandered for several hours, but the grizzled old man wasn't to be seen. For a few moments he had an eerie feeling that the man didn't really exist, but was some kind of supernatural phenomenon that had appeared only as a dark omen foretelling Harry's doom.

If he perpetrated the same crime as before, maybe the wraith would appear. So Harry finally walked into the azalea beds and began plucking at the fading blooms. He had been doing that for only about four minutes when he heard the grumpy voice.

"Hey! What do you think you're doing?"

"Deadheading," replied Harry instantly. "Can't let the plant go to seed—it'll think its work is done and stop blooming." This was a process Harry was intimate with, a litany he had heard from his mother since he was a toddler.

The old man cocked his head sideways and regarded Harry with faint curiosity. "You're the one who was here a few weeks ago. Took your oral."

"That's right. And failed. Just like you thought."

The man snorted, but made no further comment. Harry walked closer to him. "What's your name?"

"Boothby. What's yours?"

"Harry Kim."

"Not many young folks know diddly about flowers. Much less deadheading."

"I know a lot of things. But that didn't get me into the Academy." Harry felt foolish now that he was here. Was he really concerned with this gardener's opinion? On the other hand, it couldn't hurt to ask.

"Mr. Boothby, you seemed to know I wasn't going to get in. Why was that? What was it about me that told you I wasn't going to make it?"

Boothby squinted at him, gnarled face screwing up like a wrinkled prune. "Cocky," he spat. "Arrogant. Too sure of yourself."

"Me?" This description was so at odds with Harry's view of himself that he found it hard to accommodate.

"They always ask why you want to be in Starfleet. What'd you answer to that?" asked Boothby.

Harry launched into his carefully prepared answer, but he was barely into it when Boothby waved a hand, stopping him. "You think that's what they want to hear?" he asked contemptuously. "A lot of empty flattery about how great Starfleet is?"

"I wanted them to know I value the organization. Respect it."

"How would that make you different from anyone else?"

"I—I—"

"They're not interested in hearing you praise Starfleet. They're interested in knowing who you are. In finding the man you'll become."

"I told them I wanted to be part of that proud tradition—"

"That's what I'm talking about. 'That proud tradition.' Nobody talks like that. It sounds rehearsed."

"Well, I worked on my answer. I wanted it to be smooth."

"Better if it was real."

Harry had absolutely no answer for that. He felt crushed, defeated. All the work he'd put in hadn't helped him, it had hindered him. He thought he'd sounded so polished, so articulate, and instead he'd come off as a phony. He knew in his heart Boothby was right. The old man had spotted it right away, recognized his carefully cultivated image for what it was: a façade.

He was staring at an azalea plant as though it were the most absorbing thing he'd ever laid eyes on. He didn't want to think about anything else, didn't want to contemplate coming back to the Academy. His humiliation was too profound.

"Johnny Picard went through the same thing," offered Boothby casually. "They turned him down the first time. Always thought he was better off for it."

Harry turned and stared at him. "Jean-Luc Picard? Of the *Enterprise?*"

Boothby snorted. "He was Johnny when I knew him. And once he got in he got in more trouble than any seven cadets I ever knew. But he turned out all right."

Harry was amazed. Jean-Luc Picard, the legendary captain of the flagship, had been denied entrance when he first applied? And wasn't a model student? It was hard to believe, and yet Boothby's words had the dry ring of truth.

Boothby's bright eyes were on him, focused like a phaser beam. "Most folks don't come into the Academy perfect," he intoned. "This place is about coming out in better shape than you went in."

Harry stared at the old man, heard the rightness in his words, and felt as though an enormous burden had just been lifted from him.

"Way too slow, Cadet. Ten times around the track."

Harry stared at Commander Nimembeh, his prep squad officer, then down at the phaser in his hands. He'd disassembled, reconfigured, and reassembled it in under twenty seconds. Wasn't that fast enough? He looked back up at Nimembeh and tried to figure out what to say, but Nimembeh spoke again. "When I give an order, you follow it *immediately.* That's fifteen times around the track."

"Like this?" queried Harry, perplexed. He was in his cadet's uniform and boots, not in running gear.

"Make that twenty."

Harry started moving. He was still carrying the phaser, but he was afraid to put it down or ask what he should do with it for fear the officer would keep adding to his laps. Twenty was bad enough.

Harry began a slow trot. He was in good shape, having played volleyball since he was twelve, but running had never been his long suit, and he knew twenty laps around the track in his uniform and boots would be a killer. What's more, it was a rare hot day in San Francisco, the late-August sun steaming the city through moisture-laden air.

As he rounded the track for the third time, he was already in trouble. At the far end, he saw Nimembeh standing, watching him, trim body erect, sun glinting from his smooth black head. Harry already disliked him intensely, and from what he could tell, the feeling was mutual. Nimembeh picked on him, required more from him than from the others in the prep squad. And this running in boots was ridiculous!

Harry made it eleven laps before he couldn't go any farther. He collapsed on the grass at Nimembeh's feet, feet burning, lungs on fire, consumed with thirst. "I can't, sir," he gasped. "Do whatever you have to, but I can't go another lap."

"Report to sickbay, Cadet" was Nimembeh's response. "Make sure there's no danger of heat exhaustion."

"Aye, sir," said Harry gratefully. Maybe the commander wasn't a heartless monster after all. Harry went to sickbay and was examined by a Starfleet doctor who passed a tricorder in front of Harry and inquired casually as to how Harry had become so dehydrated.

Harry told him briefly, and when he mentioned Nimembeh's name, he thought he saw the corner of the doctor's mouth turn up slightly, but probably he just imagined it.

Harry had hoped for a roommate from a species other than his; it seemed to him that was part of the point of Starfleet. But he had been paired with a tall young man from Kentucky, George Mathers, with close-cropped light brown hair and eyes almost the same color. His mother had warned Harry that after being an only child, and having his own room for all his life, he might have trouble tolerating a roommate. Harry was apprehensive about it, too, and was determined not to be difficult, but was relieved that George was unfailingly pleasant and even-tempered. From the beginning, they got along well and never argued about anything.

So far, his Academy experience was everything he'd hoped. He had spent the last year catching up on some of his adolescence, doing the things he had refused to do in high school when he was so obsessed with gaining admittance to the Academy. Having been refused served to free him from that obsession, and he set about to become a more well-rounded person. He became more social, dated several young women, and fell in and out of love with at least two of them over the period of several months.

Once when he attended a Ktarian music festival he sat in the wrong seat by mistake, and when the correct occupant came along, he fell in love with her in a nanosecond. She was voluptuous and tall, almost as tall as he, with raven black hair that was long and thickly curled, and a face that was so perfect, so symmetrical, that he caught his breath.

In another nanosecond he decided she would never go out with him and he put her out of his mind. It was a year of such mercurial romances.

He read for pleasure, not for test scores. He returned to the clarinet and began playing improvisational jazz, something he'd always avoided, preferring to stick strictly to music that was written out, note for note. He found that he enjoyed the freedom of improvisation, and now played the clarinet for pleasure, with no particular goal in mind.

And the following spring he had retaken both the written and the oral examinations for Starfleet Academy and passed them with, in Admiral Strickler's words, "great distinction."

The first hint of trouble came after their two-week prep squad period, as he and George reported to the sports stadium with the rest of the freshman cadets to pick up their class assignments. There was a palpable sense of eagerness in the air as the young people anticipated their placements. They knew they had been carefully scrutinized during their prep period, and were being classified on the basis of those evaluations. There were occasional yelps of delight from a cadet pleased with the results, and the rarer shake of the head by one who wasn't. But all accepted the judgments as being in their best interests, and vowed to work within the system.

But Harry was stunned by what he read on the padd that was handed to him.

He had been put on probation for his first semester because of a report from his prep squad instructor. Nimembeh! The steely-eyed commander had given him an "unsatisfactory" rating for the prep period, and now he couldn't choose a career track until he'd eliminated his probationary status. He turned to George, adrenaline flaring.

"Do you see what Nimembeh did to me? I'm on probation!"

George's eyes registered surprise and sympathy, which fed Harry's feeling that he had been unjustly treated. But George, as usual, was upbeat. "You'll get that wiped off in no time, Harry. You're smart, and organized, and you'll do well in your classes. What did you draw?"

Harry glanced back down at the padd. "Integrated Systems Management, Nonlinear Control Theory, Subspace Communication Analysis, and Environmental Regulation," he replied, and began to feel better. He'd been given classes in the Operations track, which

93

was what he would have chosen had he had the opportunity. Maybe this wouldn't be so bad. He'd already chosen volleyball as his extracurricular athletic activity, and he'd always done well in that sport. The only other requirement was Basic Wilderness Survival, which every cadet had to take each year.

"I've got Systems Management and Control Theory, too," said George, scrolling his padd. "And Statistical Analysis, tennis . . . and . . ."

His voice trailed off and he looked at Harry with a curious expression. "Get this. I drew Nimembeh for Wilderness Survival."

Harry glanced down at his own padd and his worst misgivings were fulfilled. So had he. The man who had put him on probation would be his instructor in a course that everyone said could be either an exhilarating adventure or a nightmare experience. Harry had no doubt as to which it would be for him. But at least George would be there to share the pain.

The group of six materialized somewhere in the Sierra Nevada mountains. In addition to Harry and George, there were two Vulcan females, Slisik and T'Passa, a human male, Kevin O'Connell, and one male Klingon, Tagar. They had spent four weeks under Commander Nimembeh's tutelage, studying survival techniques and continuing their physical training. Harry had thrown himself into the course, determined to reverse Nimembeh's adverse opinion of him. Now, on this survival mission, he was sure he could finally win his way back into the commander's good graces.

"Well, we know what to do," Harry said, having decided to take charge from the beginning. "I'll offer to be group leader unless anyone has a problem with that."

The Vulcan women's eyebrows lifted simultaneously. "Are you the logical choice?" asked T'Passa quietly. There was no threat in her voice.

"It's as logical as any other. But as I say, if anyone else wants to volunteer, I'm open to that."

George chimed in with support. "I probably know Harry better than anyone else does, and I think he's absolutely the right choice. You can count on him to keep his head no matter how tough things may get. He's patient, and fair, but still decisive. He gets my vote."

That seemed to be enough for everyone else, and Harry began giving orders immediately. "First we should try to determine our position as accurately as possible, then figure out the best route out of here. Kevin, you'll be the navigator. Give me an estimate based on the sun, then again after the stars come out."

Kevin O'Connell was bookish and cheerful, the perfect person to grapple with the problems of navigation. His apple cheeks broadened in response to the assignment, and he set about gathering materials to determine their position. Harry turned next to the Vulcans.

"You'll be responsible for finding us shelter for tonight. With any luck we'll be starting out by tomorrow, but it'll be cold in these mountains at night and we'll need to sleep warmly if we're to maintain our energy."

The Vulcans nodded briskly and moved off to reconnoiter the area. Harry turned to George. "Do a preliminary scout and find out if we're up against any unexpected kinds of hazards." George nodded and moved off through the woods.

That left Tagar, who was standing at a remove from the rest of the group. His gaze was fierce and penetrating, as though to show everyone what a formidable warrior he was. Harry moved toward him, wondering why it was so important to the Klingon to assert himself in this way. But he realized that defensiveness might be a natural response to what was still an unusual situation. There hadn't been more than a handful of Klingons at the Academy in the last ten years, even though relations between the Empire and the Federation had thawed. Tagar probably felt very much alone, and Harry decided to treat him in as welcoming a way as he could.

"All right, Tagar, you've got the most important job of all. Finding us food and water."

"That will not be a problem."

"Glad to hear it."

"Unless anyone here has qualms about what they eat."

"I don't think we can afford to have any."

"Very well." Tagar moved off and Harry mentally reviewed their situation and planned his next moves. He had only one goal: to get this group out of the wilderness and back to the staging ground in record time. He intended to prove to Nimembeh that he was not just a good cadet, but one of the best ever to attend the Academy. That would take some doing, because Nimembeh had continued to hold Harry in some kind of disdain, demanding more of him than of others and disciplining him more severely when he failed to meet expectations.

And so this survival test was supremely important to Harry, his opportunity to make Nimembeh look at him in a new light. So far he'd done everything by the book, and he intended to keep doing just that. Nimembeh wasn't going to be able to fault him on anything.

Each cadet had been given one item of gear: together they had a cord saw, a knife, a small bucket, a flint and steel, a small shovel, and a sheet of plastic. Nimembeh had remarked that frankly, he thought these items gave them too much luxury. If ever they were in a true survival situation, who was to say they'd have any of those things? But most of the cadets, he informed them, had been raised taking twenty-fourth-century technology for granted, and without some implements, no matter how rudimentary, they probably wouldn't make it out of the wilderness. It was the kind of challenging remark that intensified Harry's desire to show the commander that he wasn't just another soft cadet, but a tough and disciplined leader.

He saw O'Connell eyeing a piece of wood he'd driven into the ground, and walked over to him. The young man's Irish eyes shone with pleasure as he reported to Harry. "I've established an east-west line using shadows," he said, indicating a mark on the ground which designated the tip of the first shadow he'd charted.

A second tip was now marked as well, and O'Connell had drawn a line between the two to indicate the east-west trajectory. "I'll have the north-south orientation in about half an hour," he added. "I need a sighting after noon before I can determine it."

Harry nodded. This was rudimentary navigation; anyone could have made these calculations. But O'Connell was fascinated by problem-solving, and Harry knew he would apply himself to this process with such diligence that they could probably map the area once they were done.

He heard sounds of activity within a stand of conifers, and found the Vulcan women hard at work fashioning a shelter. They had discovered a rocky outcropping that provided a natural roof, and were busy adding sides to it by laying long slender branches and thatching them with leafy boughs. They would no doubt add a heat reflector and perhaps even a floor of pine needles.

A glint of sunlight on something bright caught his eye and he followed it into a clearing. There Tagar had already constructed a solar still by digging a pit approximately three feet deep, placing the bucket in the bottom, stretching the plastic sheeting over the opening, and then weighting it with a rock so that the plastic formed a cove with the apex directly over the bucket. The sun's heat would raise the temperature of the air and soil under the plastic, hastening vaporization of the water in the soil. When the air under the plastic became saturated, the vapor would condense in tiny drops on the undersurface of the plastic. The drops would run slowly down the sloping underside of the plastic and drip off into the bucket.

Harry was reasonably sure they would soon find a stream—streams were prevalent in these mountains—but admired Tagar's thoroughness in insuring that they would have a water supply until a stream was located.

"I have already located several varieties of fungus," the Klingon said without looking at him. "They should provide adequately for our nutritional needs. However, I plan to hunt and trap small game as well."

Tagar was following survival training to the letter. Wild fungi, or mushrooms, were the first food one was taught to seek in the wilderness. They occupied a place in the food chain somewhere between meat and vegetables, providing protein, fat, and carbohydrates, all of which were necessary to sustain life. And they could be eaten raw, eliminating the need for a fire. It was important, of course, to avoid the poisonous varieties, but they'd all been drilled repeatedly in recognizing the deadly Amanita family, responsible for most of the recorded fatalities from eating mushrooms, and taught to recognize the abundant harmless fungi.

Tagar continued to fine-tune the still, all the while avoiding Harry's eyes. It was as though he wrapped himself in a protective cocoon of indifference, letting little of himself out and none of the outside world in. It wasn't an attitude Harry thought appropriate in a team situation like the one they were experiencing, and he decided he'd have to find a way to break through Tagar's defenses. He intended to do more than simply bring this group back intact; he wanted them to bond, to be cohesive in the way groups can become when they share difficult circumstances. A good leader would find ways to make that happen.

A small yelp of surprise caused him to turn and dash toward the shelter that Slisik and T'Passa were constructing. But when he emerged from the conifer grove, he saw only T'Passa. His heart sank, for he knew what had happened.

One of his group had been "killed."

They were being monitored, of course, by Academy personnel, to make sure no one got into serious danger, but also so their comportment in the wilderness could be evaluated. If the group made a

97

serious mistake—one that might prove fatal in an actual situation—a member was dematerialized and transported back to the camp at the staging area. The group was graded on the number of cadets that made it "alive" to the camp, and now he'd already lost one.

T'Passa was, of course, singularly unruffled by the event. "I assume she was transported to the staging area," she announced coolly. "One minute she was right here beside me, and then she was gone."

Her demeanor exasperated Harry. "I know she's been taken back. That's obvious. But why? We're following procedure exactly."

T'Passa began inspecting the shelter she and her recently departed comrade had been constructing, looking for errors. Harry began pondering every step of their operation, trying to figure out where he'd gone wrong.

"I find no mistakes in the construction of this shelter," the Vulcan announced confidently. "The error must have come in another phase of the operation."

Harry found himself getting irritated. This icy Vulcan wasn't the group leader, he was. He'd be the one to take the blame for any failures, he'd be the one Nimembeh would lambaste. It was easy for T'Passa to shrug off responsibility, because in the long run, she wasn't accountable. He was. And now, only an hour into the expedition, he'd already lost a member.

Why? He moved quickly to O'Connell, who was drawing in the dirt with a stick. "We've lost Slisik," said Harry tersely, and was comforted at the distress that flashed on the cadet's face.

"What did we do wrong?"

"I can't figure it out. We're doing everything we should—determining our route out of here, finding shelter, food, water . . . it's all been right by Starfleet protocols."

O'Connell inspected the markings he'd made on the ground. "I'm sure I've done this properly," he said worriedly. "I estimate we're almost due east of the staging area. I'll get a more accurate measurement tonight, with the stars, but we should proceed west until I can triangulate our position more closely."

Harry squatted on his haunches, mind working furiously. Could it be George? Had his roommate done something that violated protocol, and for which he was now being punished? He stood up and marched in the direction George had taken for his reconnaissance.

Five minutes later he heard something crashing through the brush. He stood behind a tree in case the noisemaker was a bear, but in seconds he spotted George, face flushed from exertion, just meters from him. Harry stepped from behind his tree right into his room-mate's path. George stopped abruptly, startled.

"Harry—you could give a person a heart attack," he gasped.

"And you could raise the dead with all the noise you're making," shot back Harry. George's eyes widened slightly at the ire in his friend's voice, and Harry had a moment's remorse. "Sorry," he muttered. "We've lost Slisik. We've made a mistake and I can't figure out what it is. What have you been doing?"

"Reconnoitering. I haven't found any indication of people, but there are droppings and tracks that indicate wildlife in the area, including bears and coyotes. And there's a deep ravine directly east of us that would be difficult to cross."

Harry stared at him. There was nothing unusual in what he was reporting, nothing to indicate he'd made a mistake that would warrant the removal of one of their band. *What were they doing wrong?*

He waved at George to follow him and they made their way back to the others. Harry gathered them all around. "From now on, no one goes off by themselves. If you have to leave the camp, take someone with you. We can't risk someone going off and making an error. If we use the buddy system, we'll have checks and balances."

He was aware of T'Passa's dark eyes fastened on his with what looked like disdain. Suddenly he realized that she was the only remaining female—did she think that she had to perform the necessary bodily functions in the presence of one of the males? He felt himself flush with embarrassment.

"Not, of course, that anyone's privacy will be violated. That is, privacy in certain . . . uh . . . in those instances where . . . ." He felt himself stammering and hated his inability to handle this matter with the proper aplomb. He turned to T'Passa, trying to regain his composure and appear authoritative once more.

"You need have no fears," he announced solemnly, hoping that would clear the matter up. He was rewarded with an icy stare.

"What could you possibly be talking about?" she asked with that Vulcan aloofness that always made Harry feel about six years old.

"Never mind," he said ineffectually. "If you're happy, I'm happy."

"I do not experience happiness," she stated, "any more than I experience fear. I confess to being baffled by your statements." Several of the others, Harry realized, had been stifling laughter, and now couldn't contain it any longer. Muffled giggles erupted.

Warmth burned on his cheeks as embarrassment flooded over him, and he felt for a moment like a small child who's made a social gaffe and drawn the bemused attention of all the adults. He forced himself to sound as composed as possible.

"I think we all have the same goal here—to get all of us back to the staging area without anyone else being removed. Let's pull together on this, all right?"

Four pairs of eyes fixed on him, four young faces nodded solemnly. Harry took a breath, satisfied. He was back in control.

Five days later, only he and Tagar were left. George had been the next to go, followed by T'Passa a day after that. O'Connell had dematerialized in front of them only minutes before, as they were striking their shelter after a meager breakfast of berries and water. Harry had been hungry for days, his stomach mumbling in protest and finally lurching unpleasantly whenever he did put food into it. He knew he had become noticeably weaker, and his mood was irritable.

When O'Connell disappeared, Harry couldn't contain a furious howl of protest, and he drove one fist into a palm, needing to physicalize his frustration. Tagar regarded him impassively, then continued to sweep the area with a leafy branch, in order to erase any evidence that they had been there.

"What is it?" snapped Harry, pacing the ground in irritation. "What are we doing that's so wrong? How could we lose this many people?"

"I don't know," said Tagar. "But I think in one more day we can reach the staging area. We must keep going."

"Of course we keep going. Did I say anything to suggest we wouldn't?" The words came out more harshly than Harry meant, but he didn't care. He wanted nothing more than to solve this mystery before they reached the staging area and Nimembeh's formidable presence. He noted that Tagar drew up slightly at the tone in his voice, and for a moment he thought the Klingon might protest, but he locked eyes with his last remaining team member, glaring, and eventually Tagar muttered something guttural under his breath and turned away. "Let's go," Harry muttered, and they proceeded down the brushy, ragged slope, the sun at the back of their left shoulders, heading west.

The march, when O'Connell had been with them, was at least full of a certain energized spirit. He was voluble and witty, and kept them all amused with stories of his ancient ancestors, of their poetry and passion, of the "terrible beauty" that was Ireland. O'Connell was a natural storyteller, and the hours seemed to pass quickly as he chattered on.

Now, a tense silence bound Tagar and Harry. Only the sound of their footsteps through the chaparral and manzanita of the western Sierras competed with the occasional bird call. The tall conifers were well behind them now, as were the mountain streams. Here, in the foothills, on the final descending slope toward the staging area, there was only scrubby vegetation, which ripped at them, scratching exposed skin and leaving it susceptible to insects and infection.

They walked for over four hours without exchanging a word. Then Harry signaled that they would stop for a midday meal—if you could designate more berries and water as a meal. He had kept his eyes roaming for other edible plants all morning, but had seen nothing in this sere vegetation that would provide nourishment.

He sat and opened his pack, pulling out the few berries that remained from his collecting efforts of several days ago. He lifted his hand, offering some to Tagar, but the Klingon was standing above him, looking at the meager offerings with disdain. He shook his head brusquely and marched off, presumably to find something else. Harry nibbled at the berries, trying to savor each one, but felt his stomach recoil as the bits of dry fruit reached it. He drank a tiny swallow of water; Tagar's solar still hadn't produced much the previous day, and they were strictly rationed.

He heard Tagar pushing toward him through the underbrush, and looked up to see what he'd found. Tagar's hands held a squirming mass of what looked like white maggots, and Harry's stomach soured. Tagar held out the writhing mound to him, and Harry saw they were grubs, beetle larvae. He knew they could be a good source of protein, but he couldn't imagine at this point putting any of that pale, gelatinous, undulating cluster into his already queasy stomach. The driest of berries would be preferable.

"This will feed both of us for several meals," pronounced Tagar.

Harry shook his head. "I'll pass," he replied.

"That is not an attitude conducive to survival."

"I'm doing fine, thank you."

Tagar grunted and began shoveling the grubs, still squirming, into his mouth. Harry felt gorge rising in his throat and he turned away.

"Are all your people this squeamish?" Tagar challenged, the words somewhat obscured because of the mass of larvae in his mouth.

Harry whirled on him, a retort on his tongue, but suddenly Tagar shimmered and dematerialized.

101

Harry was alone, having lost every member of his squad, every cadet who had agreed he would be their leader, and who looked to him to get them out of the wilderness. Every one of them had been "killed."

He was in despair. He sat on a stone and held his head in his hands, trying once more to determine what he was doing wrong. On the ground, a few grubs that had dropped from Tagar's hands still twitched, until, with a heavy buzz, flies began to swarm around them.

Harry stood and stalwartly moved off, determined to continue his trek and complete the assignment. Better to walk into the staging area alone than to wait for his own humiliating dematerialization. If he could keep a steady pace, he estimated he would arrive at the base camp no later than midmorning tomorrow.

By late afternoon he was weak and stumbling. The berries had provided little in the way of nourishment, and he'd had only tiny sips of water. The October sun was uncomfortably warm now that he'd left the sheltering bowers of the tall pines, and he knew he was becoming dehydrated. His mind was fuzzy, unfocused, and he couldn't seem to get a fix on just what he should be doing. So he kept going, one foot in front of the other, marching steadily forward, down toward the staging area.

When sunset came and light began to fade, he realized too late that he'd failed to scout for more food. It would be doubly difficult at night. And what about water? How could he have forgotten these essentials? Panic began to stir in him, and he consciously quelled it. He had to stay calm, to think clearly.

The next thing he knew he was waking up, limbs cramped from cold. When had he fallen asleep? He was sprawled on the ground without shelter or cover, and his hunger was palpable. He heard rustling noises in the brush, and stood quickly, suddenly fearful of what might be coming to attack him.

The moon was at third quarter, and cast enough illumination that he could see somewhat. He decided to keep walking. He could sleep when he got to the base camp. He told himself to forget hunger and thirst, and to pretend he'd just had a massive feast. Only slightly buoyed by that image, he continued his faltering march toward Nimembeh.

But after an hour, he couldn't go on. He sank to his knees, head swimming, mouth parched, nauseated. He stared at the vegetation around him, trying desperately to remember if any of it was edible. But his mind wouldn't concentrate properly, and kept drifting off to other settings, other times. He remembered a wonderful celebration his family had held when he was about six. He remembered long tables laden with food, stews and breads and soups and fruit and the most succulent baked goods. There was something with apples, warm and running with juices. Had it been one of his birthdays? No, there would have been a huge cake, and candles for him to blow out . . .

He didn't know how long he'd sat there, fantasizing about food. But he couldn't allow it to continue. He had to keep going. With effort, he shoved himself upright and took one step, then another. The ground felt spongy, and his footing was uncertain. He tottered slightly in the chaparral—

—and then tumbled to the ground at Nimembeh's feet, having been transported from the foothills.

He was in one of the permanent structures at the staging area. Briefly he wondered if it was the same one he and his father had been taken to, only five years ago, when his desperate desire to be part of Starfleet was born.

Nimembeh stood above him, legs planted firmly, hands on his hips. Harry's eyes traveled up and saw the dark, smooth-domed officer looking down at him with no discernible expression.

"There's this to be said for you, Cadet," intoned Nimembeh. "You didn't manage to kill yourself."

Harry struggled to his feet and was handed a flask of water. He drank greedily, knowing that drops were running down his chin but not caring. The water was cool, silver in his throat. He had never tasted anything so delicious. He was vaguely aware that a hypospray had been planted against his arm and an injection transferred.

"A nutritional supplement," explained Nimembeh stonily. "You were suffering from lack of adequate nutrition."

Harry sagged. He had failed in every way. His entire team had been "lost," and he himself was rescued because if he'd been allowed to stay in the wilderness, he would have perished. How had it come to that?

"What did I do wrong?" he asked Nimembeh sincerely. "I lost my first cadet within minutes after we arrived, and averaged one a day after that. But we all thought we were going by the book."

"Had you been moving through enemy territory, I doubt you would have lasted that long. I might as well have landed a troupe of acrobats, wearing bright costumes, who proceeded to thrash through the woods calling every possible attention to themselves."

Harry recoiled. He realized what Nimembeh was saying, but the injustice of it galvanized him. He drew himself to his full height. "With all due respect, sir, when we were sent on this excursion, there was no mention made of its being an evasive situation. We all assumed it was merely a test of our ability to survive."

"An assumption shared by most of your peers," observed Nimembeh dryly. Harry looked around and saw a room full of dispirited cadets—the other team leaders, he presumed. Only one group, off in a corner, seemed to be somewhat animated.

"You mean . . . everyone else lost their team, too?" asked Harry, somewhat mollified to know that this humiliation was not his alone.

"One team took the appropriate evasive tactics and survived intact."

Rancor rose in Harry. He faced Nimembeh, cheeks flushed, all the desperateness and frustration of the past five days making him uncharacteristically confrontational. "Sir, the parameters of the situation should have been made clear. We couldn't be expected to operate properly if we didn't know exactly what was going on. This simply wasn't a fair test."

Before Harry had gotten the last word out, Nimembeh's hand had struck, clasping Harry's arm around the wrist, holding it firmly. The commander was a small, lean man with not a millimeter of excess fat on him, but he was surprisingly powerful, a tensile strength that came from within; his grip felt more solid than titanium. Startled, Harry stared at him. Nimembeh's dark eyes burned through him, and his voice was like a phaser beam in its intensity.

"Not a fair test? I'm sorry you were put at a disadvantage, Cadet. But consider this: If ever you find yourself in enemy territory, I won't be there to make it clear to you what you should and shouldn't do. You're going to have to learn to think for yourself, to anticipate the situation, to expect the worst and prepare for it. There won't be any convenient transports back to base camp, no hyposprays to protect you from malnutrition. You may find yourself completely on your own, in hostile territory, and there won't be any room for excuses in a situation like that. You won't be able to say to the person who has phasered you to death that the situation just wasn't fair. Do I make myself clear?"

Harry could only nod, chastened under the withering harangue. But Nimembeh wasn't done. "I am responsible for turning out cadets that know how to survive in any situation. Any time any one of my people dies in the field, a part of me dies with them. I won't have my people making mistakes that can be fatal. My people will have all the training, all the mental focus, all the tenacity to help them make it out of the worst of situations."

Again, Harry nodded. "Yes, sir," he said humbly, but Nimembeh didn't release him from his brutal grip. "Now, Cadet, tell me what you did wrong."

"Sir, we should have taken cover immediately and assessed the situation. We should have traveled mainly at night, and not lit fires. We should have avoided the ridges of hills where we could be silhouetted and spotted. We failed to employ a leading scout. We followed none of the procedures for evasive maneuvers." Harry eyed Nimembeh with as much dignity as he could summon, hoping this recitation would satisfy the commander and make him release his crushing grip. But Nimembeh held on as firmly as ever, and Harry began to feel tingling in his fingers from lack of circulation.

"What else?"

What else? There was more? Fatigue and bewilderment combined to tongue-tie him. He tried to make his mind grasp what other infraction he might have committed, but he couldn't find it. He stared at Nimembeh helplessly. "I . . . I . . ."

"Do you know what else you did wrong or not, Cadet?"

"I don't, sir."

"You foolishly refused to eat food that was available to you. You let your personal aversions dictate what you would ingest. Because of that, you became weak and disoriented from malnutrition. You must eat everything, no matter how repulsive it may seem to you, because even one lost meal can cost you weeks of lost strength. If you are going to survive, you must eat—no matter what it is."

Harry could only nod and stammer, "Yes, sir." Even though he was taller than Nimembeh, he felt like a small boy, looking up into his father's eyes. Except that his father had never castigated him like this, had never reprimanded him, had never made him feel demeaned and humiliated. He had always been treated with dignity and acceptance, from the time he was a toddler. For a moment the unfairness of it all made his eyes burn, but the further humiliation of Nimembeh's seeing him with tears chased the moisture away. He realized that his fingers were now numb from the manacle-grip around his wrist.

"Sir, I've lost sensation in my fingers," he said with what he hoped was proper deference.

"Cadet, your fingers are mine. All of you is mine. And I want you to know you've become a special project for me. From now on, if you turn around, I'll be there. If you turn on your desk monitor, there'll be a transmission from me. If you want to take a leave, or change your room, or wipe your nose, you'll have to go through me to do it."

"Can . . . can you do that?"

"I can and I will."

Harry was weak from exhaustion and pain. The prospect that loomed before him was so frightening that the only consolation he could find was in the knowledge that he could simply leave the Academy. But, as though reading his mind, Nimembeh removed that option as well.

"If you're thinking that you'd rather leave the Academy, you're right. You can turn yourself into a victim and a quitter. And no one would even notice that you were gone."

Harry looked down at his fingers, which were visibly swollen now. They seemed like the appendages of some entirely different entity, an alien being that had somehow begun to occupy the end of his arm. He thought of his mother, suddenly, and her response if he dropped out of the Academy at this point. He looked up at Nimembeh.

"Yes, sir. I'm yours. Will you let go now?"

A charged moment passed, and then Nimembeh dropped his wrist, which fell heavily to Harry's side as he did so. The young cadet resisted the impulse to rub his fingers with his opposite hand, as though that would somehow denote weakness and cause Nimembeh to revile him even further. He gently stretched them, wincing as blood rushed to the tips once more.

"Report to me at oh-six-hundred Monday morning. We'll set up your training regimen."

Nimembeh turned on his heel and walked away, erect and proud. Harry stared after him, now finally kneading his painfully throbbing fingers, wondering if there were any appeal to this program Nimembeh was levying. Could he talk to his group leader? His academic advisor? There had to be a way out of this.

Harry quickly discovered that all avenues to an appeal from Nimembeh's regime were closed. This "special project" was not unprecedented at the Academy; in fact, there were usually several cadets a year singled out in this fashion. The only recourse was to leave the Academy, and Harry knew he'd rather face Nimembeh than his mother.

He discussed the whole thing with George, who was unfailingly sympathetic and comforting. "I can't believe this is happening," moaned Harry. "He has approval over my academic schedule, my sports program, my extracurricular activities, my leave time—he was right: I can't blow my nose without going through him."

"I don't understand it. Why would he single you out? I could fathom it if you were some discipline problem, or disruptive, or a problem in some way. But you're about the most perfect cadet I know."

Harry smiled. This kind of statement, he'd learned, was typical of George. Frankly, his ego needed that kind of rebuilding after Nimembeh had gotten through hammering at him. George's attitude toward him was more like what he was used to from his family—approving and supportive.

"I've asked around, but no two people have the same answer. Nimembeh takes on a 'special project' cadet now and then, but there doesn't seem to be any common thread as to the kind of student he chooses."

"You're just lucky, I guess."

Harry smiled. He knew he was lucky to have drawn George as a roommate. Some of the cadets he'd met would've driven him crazy, but George and he got along amazingly well. In fact, without George, he wasn't sure he could have survived Nimembeh's harsh regime.

It quickly became clear what the commander expected of him: more than his all, on every occasion, in every aspect of his student life. He set goals that were rigorous and demanded that Harry meet them; failure to do so met with harsh disciplines. He drove Harry physically, academically, and emotionally. Without George's calm, stolid presence, his unending reservoir of succor, Harry thought many times he might have quit.

Nimembeh's schedule for Harry was so grueling that it left little time for socialization, so Harry did his best to keep his mind off the female cadets. This wasn't easy, as there were hundreds of bright, eager, talented and quite beautiful young women at the Academy; but Harry had learned strong self-discipline during his adolescence, when he had devoted himself to his studies in order to be admitted.

"Who needs women," he laughed ruefully to George, "as long as we have each other?"

It was simply easier, and far more comfortable, to take a night off with George than to go to the effort of inviting a young woman he barely knew, make an evening of strained small talk, and then face the prospect of deciding whether or not he wanted to repeat the process. With George there was no awkwardness, no struggle to make conversation, no effort at all. When he had time on a weekend to transport home—a rarity—George often came with him, and his family had all but adopted his roommate as one of their own.

And so Harry was unprepared for what happened to him on a windy spring day in April, when San Francisco sparkled like crown jewels after a series of thunderstorms had blown through, leaving the air sweet and brisk, the streets and building glowing with dampness.

On this beautiful day, Harry was in a dark, cavelike building on an impossible quest. Nimembeh had ordered him to procure a book that wasn't available in any form except the ancient one of printed, bound pages. Harry frankly thought that anything worth reading should be available on padds, but Nimembeh had insisted he find the centuries-old tale of a British sea captain who had piloted his men to safety after having been put overboard after a mutiny.

Old books were rare commodities on Earth. A few serious biblio-philes had collections, but these were privately held and carefully guarded. Only one possible source existed in San Francisco, a huge, multistoried building in the Embarcadero, lined with rows of old bookshelves, and onto which were jammed a chaotic, disorganized array of books—of all kinds, on all subjects, fiction, history, art, cooking, everything one could think of.

But there was virtually no way to locate a specific book. The building was manned by cheerful volunteers who claimed a love of old tomes, and who in fact read them almost constantly, but who had no idea just what books were in their keeping, nor how to find one that might be there. "It's a browsing place," said one robust, ample woman with neatly cut white hair and kindly gray eyes, and a rectangular tag on her bosom which read HARRIET. "There's nothing more soothing than wandering around the stacks, just picking up a book that catches your eye and poring over it."

"Yes, ma'am," said Harry, a bit desperately, "I'm sure that's true. But I have to find one specific book. Isn't there any way to do that?"

Puzzlement registered in the woman's eyes. "Charlotte," she called to another volunteer, "this young man wants to find a particular book. Do we have any way to do that?"

Charlotte, who was a vision in neutrality—beige hair, beige eyes, beige sweater and skirt—seemed equally bewildered. "I don't know of any," she said vaguely.

"You mean the books aren't catalogued?" asked Harry incredulously, which produced gentle laughter from both women. "Oh, no, of course not," said Charlotte. "There are millions of books here. How could we ever catalogue them?"

Perspiration began to collect on Harry's forehead. He wasn't going to go back to Nimembeh and say he'd failed. "Maybe you've noticed the book I want," he offered politely. "In your browsing, I mean."

"What is it, dear?" asked the older woman sweetly. "I've rummaged through these books for years."

"It's called *Men Against the Sea*. It's the story of a Captain Bligh—"

"After the mutiny," the woman chimed in eagerly. "It's part of the *Bounty* trilogy. A thrilling story."

Harry's heart quickened. "Then you have it here?"

"I have no idea. I read it when I was a child, in Ohio. I wonder whatever happened to that book?"

Harry's spirits plummeted again. This was maddening—how could he convince Nimembeh he'd done everything he possibly could, and had come up short? But Charlotte had held up a finger, as though thinking of something, her pale beige forehead wrinkled in concentration. *"Bounty . . . Bounty . . ."* she was muttering. "I think I've seen it . . ."

"Where?" asked Harry quickly. He stared at Charlotte, willing her to remember.

"Was it on four? Or six? I think it was on an even-numbered floor. And it was near a window, because I remember looking up and seeing one of Starfleet's hovercraft passing by." She smiled at Harry, pleased with herself. He waited politely for her to add to her recall, but nothing more was forthcoming. He drew a breath.

"So it's probably on floor two, or four, or six—"

"Or eight. That's if I'm right about it's being even-numbered."

"And somewhere near a window."

"I'm fairly certain. That is, if it was the book I was looking at when the Starfleet vessel went by. It could have been another one."

Harry stared at her, wordless. Then he nodded and thanked them, mentally calculating the time it would take to search for the book with that vague description of its possible location. As he climbed the old and worn stairs to the second floor, he realized he could spend all day and night in this place without success.

Two hours later he'd given up on the second floor and climbed to the fourth, where he began sneezing. Dust had collected on the vast array of books—didn't their air-filtration system reach to the fourth floor?—and was irritating his nose. Great. Trapped in a fruitless quest for a book that might not even be there, and invaded by allergens as well.

He had headed for the window wall and begun his systematic search when, in the third aisle, he saw her, standing against a bookshelf, an open volume in her hands, reading.

It was the woman in whose seat he had mistakenly sat when he went to the Ktarian music festival.

Her fierce concentration on the book seemed to endow her with a quality of mystery, and he found himself stopped in his tracks, staring at her, as intimidated now as he'd been when he first saw her weeks ago.

Her eyes lifted and briefly caught his, then flickered back to her book without showing even a passing interest in him. But to Harry the look was electrifying, and he could feel the effect in the marrow of his bones.

He forced himself to resume his search, carefully poring over the rows of books, checking the angle to make sure he could still see a window from where he stood.

Then he went back to the third aisle and glanced down it. The woman was gone.

He felt a momentary regret, then shrugged his shoulders. He was there on a quest, and didn't need distractions. It was just as well this beautiful young woman had slipped out of his life once more. He headed for the as-yet-unsearched fifth aisle and began again. Then soft footsteps caught his attention and the black-haired woman rounded the corner of the aisle and began browsing just opposite him.

Harry felt the air around him become suddenly close, and it was difficult to breathe. He glanced over his shoulder as the woman moved slowly in his direction, eyes scanning the books. He tried to concentrate on his own task, but was overwhelmingly aware of her presence as she inched, inexorably, closer and closer.

From the corner of his eye, he saw her arm extend and her hand remove a book from the shelf. His mind worked desperately to think of some clever way to start up a conversation, but everything he thought of sounded trite and forced. He didn't even want to mention the music festival because he was certain she wouldn't remember him.

Finally he decided on just saying hello and asking if she were looking for a specific book, too. He turned, smiling, and saw that she was now reading the book she'd removed from the shelf.

It was titled *The Bounty Trilogy.*

A small, undignified squeak emitted from Harry's mouth and the woman looked up curiously. "That's the book I need!" he all but shouted. "I've been looking for two hours."

She eyed him dispassionately. "I've been looking for this book for *years,"* she retorted, closing it and starting to move away.

"Wait, wait, please, you don't understand. I *need* that book. My instructor ordered me to find it, and I can't tell him I failed."

She gave him a cold look. "You Starfleet people are so arrogant," she said with spirit. "You think you're superior to everyone else, that you deserve to be treated like royalty." She turned away again.

"No, don't go, please. Please." She stopped and turned slowly back to him, as though something in his voice had reached her. Harry felt like a babbling, inarticulate child. "It's not that way at all. I've got this commander, Nimembeh, and he makes my life miserable but I've got to do what he says or leave the Academy. And he said to get that book. I didn't think I'd ever find it—what are the odds you'd want it, too?—and I'm begging you to let me have it."

His sincerity and his desperateness had caught her attention. Her dark eyes dropped to the book and then lifted again to Harry. "My father had this book," she said softly. "He read it to me before I could read for myself. He said there were lessons in it that would stay with me forever. I didn't know what he meant at the time. Then he died, and all his books were given to a museum. As I got older, I remembered what he'd said, and I started looking for it."

Harry stared at her. What she had said moved him tremendously, and suddenly her need to have the book eclipsed his own. He'd just have to deal with Nimembeh. He gave her a wan smile. "Then you should have it." Then he could think of absolutely nothing else to say, and so he turned away from her and started down the aisle.

"Wait," she said. He turned back, and was startled once more by her ethereal beauty. "Maybe we could compromise," she said, her voice velvet in the dusty room. "You could take it so your instructor would be satisfied. And when you're done with it, you can return it to me."

Harry's gratitude was immense. This beautiful creature was also generous! He looked at her, falling in love in that instant, and took a breath to thank her.

And began sneezing.

She had laughed, and they'd left the bookstore together, walking for hours in the fresh spring day, talking and talking, exploring each other with all the eagerness and energy of young love. He learned that her name was Libby Lattimore, that she studied art, that she loved cats, that she ate an orange every day, that her mother was a noted author who lived in England and that they talked frequently, and that she'd dated some Starfleet cadets and found them arrogant and full of themselves and had promised to avoid them in the future.

And she did remember him from the music festival.

Harry found her fascinating. He loved the sound of her laughter, which was rich and throaty. He loved the way her nose turned slightly sideways at the tip, the way her dark hair bounced as she walked. He loved her sensitivity, her caring, her sweet nature.

He loved everything about her.

But when he returned to his room that night, holding the ancient copy of *The Bounty Trilogy* in his hands, he found he didn't want to tell George about her. How could he do justice to this wonderfully unique person? He was afraid he'd sound foolish, puppy-like, the victim of an adolescent infatuation. He wanted George, his best friend, to meet Libby and to see for himself how special she was.

"Want to visit an art gallery with me?" he inquired casually of George, who had been studying calculus, a subject with which he struggled.

"Sure," replied George, agreeable as ever. "What's the show?"

"Paintings," said Harry.

"Paintings? As in two-dimensional canvases coated with oil-based pigments?"

"That's right."

George looked at him with a dubious expression. "Are they old?"

"No, they're done by a young artist. Very promising."

"I'd have thought just about everything that could be explored on a canvas has been. Many times over."

Harry shrugged. "Can't hurt to check it out. The opening is tomorrow night."

"You mean Nimembeh will give you the night off?"

Harry held up the book. "I pulled off the impossible. I think he'll be sufficiently impressed."

And so he was. Nimembeh was so impressed, in fact, that he gave Harry a week's respite from his scrutiny, the first time that had happened all year. Harry was free to go to Libby's opening with George.

The art gallery was a spacious building on Market Street, and by the time the young cadets got there it was already teeming with people. Harry and George worked their way through the crowd, Harry looking everywhere for Libby, but finding no sign of her.

Her artwork, however, was extraordinary. Harry was frankly unprepared for the effect it had on him. The showing was a study in contrasts: huge canvases, covering entire walls, with images of dark, preternatural creatures, powerful and mysterious, engaged in strange rituals that seemed to have sprung from genetic memory. But other walls contained tiny miniature paintings done in such delicate realistic detail that it was hard to believe both had been done by the same artist.

Even George was impressed. "I was wrong," he stated firmly. "These are outstanding. Who's the artist?"

"Her name is Libby Lattimore," said Harry, hoping the pride in his voice wasn't too evident. "She should be here somewhere." Harry looked around the room again and finally saw her, talking with a group of middle-aged people who seemed to hang on her every word. She was wearing a white jumpsuit that accentuated the blackness of her hair and the red of her lips. She was stunning.

"That's her," he said eagerly, and noticed that George was staring at him somewhat curiously. "Come on, I want you to meet her." He started making his way through the crowd, assuming George was right behind him. As he neared the group, Libby spotted him, and he saw her wrap up her conversation with the others and head toward him, clearly as glad to see him as he was to see her. She reached out her hands and took both of his in them, and gave him a quick kiss on the cheek.

"I'm so glad you're here," she breathed. "It's a madhouse, but people seem to like my work."

"It's incredible. I mean that—I had no idea."

She beamed at him in response, and he turned around to introduce George, only to find that his roommate wasn't right behind him. Harry looked back and saw him standing in the same spot, watching them, a strange expression on his face. Harry waved at him impatiently, and finally George moved toward them.

"This is Libby Lattimore, the artist," said Harry proudly. "My roommate, George Mathers. He said your work is outstanding."

Libby extended her hand. "Thanks so much for coming, George. Harry's talked on and on about you."

George made what looked like an attempt to smile, but to Harry it seemed forced. What was wrong? "You're very talented, Miss Lattimore," said George formally. "Thank you for the opportunity to see your work."

George didn't talk this way, thought Harry. Why was he so stiff and formal? Harry was baffled, but also disappointed. He wanted these two people, the two he most cared about, to like each other and to get along. But George was almost icy.

Now he turned to Harry with a façade of good cheer. "Well, I better get back to calculus. I have an exam day after tomorrow and I need every minute I can get. Nice to meet you," he added to Libby, and then he hurried off through the crowded room.

"Did I say something wrong?" asked Libby, obviously having noticed his strange demeanor.

"Of course not. Maybe he wasn't feeling well." Harry looked into Libby's black eyes and immediately forgot about George. They spent the evening together, Harry feeling unaccountably proud as he heard the accolades heaped on Libby from all who saw her work, and he didn't think about George and his unusual behavior until late that night, when he returned to his room at the Academy, aglow with thoughts of Libby and the sweet memory of their first kiss.

He entered quietly, in case George was asleep, and indeed the room was darkened. But he spotted his roommate sitting in the window seat, staring out at the trees in the quadrangle of which their dormitory was a part. George was silhouetted against a sky that was illuminated by a half-moon.

"George? You all right?"

George didn't turn his head to answer. "Fine," he said unconvincingly. Harry looked at him, reminded of his earlier behavior at the gallery.

"I thought you might not be feeling well," Harry said. "You left so abruptly."

George finally turned toward him, and in the moonlight Harry could see naked anguish in his eyes. "I've been a fool, Harry, and it's a little tough to admit that to myself."

"What are you talking about?" Harry was genuinely puzzled. There was a long silence in which Harry could hear George breathing, as though he weren't quite getting enough oxygen.

"When I saw you with that woman tonight, it was clear how you feel about her. And—I just didn't realize."

"Realize what?"

A sound of exasperation emitted from George, half a laugh, half an ironic expletive. "Are you so dense, Harry? Do I have to spell it out?"

Harry felt trapped and confused. He couldn't imagine what was making his friend act like this, couldn't wrap his mind around whatever it was George was trying to say. "George, please, I honestly don't understand."

George stood up, the moon catching one side of his face while the other remained in darkness. His one visible eye looked immeasurably sad. "I love you, Harry. I'm *in love* with you. And I thought you felt the same way."

Harry stared at him, suddenly understanding everything, realizing that he was the one who'd been a fool. It had never occurred to him that George had made this assumption about their relationship. And he blamed himself for not seeing the obvious.

"George, I'm sorry. I've been pretty stupid."

But George was shaking his head. "I made assumptions because I wanted to make them," he admitted. "You didn't date women, you seemed to enjoy my company, we did everything together . . . I interpreted those things in the way that made me happy."

"But there was never anything romantic between us . . ."

"I wanted there to be. But I told myself it would come with time. And I liked being with you so much that I didn't want to take the risk of pushing it." He shook his head ruefully. "If I'd been honest with myself, I'd have known I was fantasizing. But I didn't want to admit it. I loved you too much."

An immense wave of friendship, of caring and concern and, yes, of love, swept over Harry. He went to his friend and put his arms around George, who responded in kind, and they stood like that for a long time, locked in a healing embrace. Then George pulled away. "I have to request a change of rooms," he said quietly. "It'd be too difficult to live with you now. I hope you understand."

"Of course I do." Ineffable sadness enveloped Harry, and he felt a palpable sense of loss, the only such pain he'd experienced in his life since Mousie had died years earlier. "I want to be your friend, George. Can we still have that?"

George took a breath, looked away from him. "I hope so. In time. But not right away. I have to . . . to get over you."

Harry would have done anything at that point to take George's pain from him, to suffer himself rather than see his friend anguish. But he knew George must walk that path by himself, and could only hope that when he was done, they could be friends again.

Three years later Harry stood with his classmates in the stadium of the Academy, listening to Admiral Brand inform them that they had now graduated and were setting forth to represent Starfleet throughout known and unknown space. It wasn't a particularly inspiring speech, at least not to Harry, who was simply glad to be finally out from under Nimembeh's tutelage. In the four years of his college experience, Nimembeh had been unchanging: flinty, impervious, exacting. Not once had he offered an encouraging word, a compliment, a sympathetic utterance. Now, at last, Harry could look forward to getting away from him.

But where he would be going was another question. Harry was caught in a dilemma and didn't know how to resolve it. He'd even sought the counsel of Boothby, the groundskeeper, as he had on numerous occasions over the years. Boothby's practical, down-to-earth common sense always seemed to clear away doubts and confusion.

But even Boothby hadn't been able to help him with his current situation.

"I've got two ways to go after graduation," he said to Boothby one overcast day as the old man planted a flat of impatiens. "I can stay here in San Francisco, with Starfleet Command, as a design specialist in the Engineering Corps. Or I could become the operations officer on a small starship."

"Which do you want to do?"

"That's the problem—I can't decide. I've always wanted to explore space, and it's a terrific opportunity to become an ops officer right away."

"But?"

"But that would take me away from Earth. Away from San Francisco."

"From the tone of your voice I'd imagine it's the young woman you're thinking of."

"Yes. We've gotten . . . very serious. And it's not going to help our relationship for me to be gone for months at a time."

"That's a problem."

"I know it's a problem. That's why I'm talking to you."

Boothby looked up at him, grizzled face squinting, bright eyes searching his face. "Think I've got the answer, do you?"

"You always seem to."

Boothby cackled briefly, then continued to insert plugs of small, multicolored flowers into damp soil. "Well, sorry to disappoint you, but seems to me this is the kind of decision only you can make. You have to decide what's really important to you and decide accordingly. No one else can see inside your heart."

And that was it from Boothby. He also talked it over with George, whose friendship he had cherished over the four years, and who always seemed wise beyond his age. George was adamant in his opinion. "Stay in San Francisco. Marry Libby and have a family. You two have something special between you, and you don't walk away from something like that."

But Libby had yet another opinion. "I won't be the cause of your giving up something you've worked so hard for. If what we have together is going to last, it has to be strong enough to endure some minor separations. There are a lot of married people in Starfleet, and they seem to make it work. I don't see that we should be any different."

His mother and father refused to commit themselves, although Harry knew that they wanted him to stay nearby. His faculty advisor, Commander Moffat, helped him to see the advantages of either choice professionally, but carefully avoided recommending either one.

And so Harry was alone with his problem. And as he listened to Admiral Brand drone on and on during the graduation ceremony, in his mind he was no closer to a decision than he had been a month ago. But he'd run out of time: the choice had to be made today. He'd heard of the ancient custom of tossing a coin, which was common when there was still currency, and considered some equally random way of resolving this dilemma.

Admiral Brand finally finished talking, the ceremony concluded with loud cheers, and Harry stood waiting for Libby and his parents to make their way through the crowd that was streaming from the stands. As his eyes searched the teeming masses of people, they fell on Commander Nimembeh, who was standing to one side, alone, his presence as formidable as ever. He was looking right at Harry.

Harry walked over to him, impelled to have a final statement, to bring to some kind of satisfying closure the travail of the last four years. "I made it, sir," he said to Nimembeh, his tormentor. "You did everything you could to make me quit, but I held out. What I'd really like to know is whether that makes you happy or if you're disappointed."

An expression Harry had never seen before flickered over Nimembeh's face. What was it? There was a slight tug at his lips—a smile? Was the man mocking him?

"You've made me proud, Ensign," the older man said flatly. "I expect you to continue to do just that."

A sudden and unexpected emotion flooded over Harry, the realization of the gift Nimembeh had given him. He had arrived at the Academy a pampered and spoiled child. Nimembeh had seen that and spent four years toughening him up, turning him into a man—a man of whom he could be proud. Harry was moved, so much so that he could hardly speak.

"Sir," he began shakily, "what do you think I should do? Stay in San Francisco or take the posting aboard *Voyager?*"

Nimembeh's coal-like eyes glinted at him. "I didn't spend four years on you so you could sit at a desk, Ensign," he said, and then turned and walked away, erect as ever.

And thus was Harry's decision made. A week later he had joined *Voyager* at *Deep Space Nine,* and walked into Captain Kathryn Janeway's ready room. "At ease, Ensign, before you sprain something," she said wryly, and so their adventure began. Harry had endured many losses during their long odyssey through the Delta Quadrant, for he missed Libby, and his parents, and George, and all the people who had been a part of his life. But one of the regrets that he lamented the most was that Nimembeh would never know how well Harry had learned his painful lessons.

CHAPTER

5

HARRY LOOKED UP TO SEE EVERY EYE ON HIM—INCLUDING THOSE OF Coris, whose orangy disks caught the light of the fire like mirrors. Everyone was utterly silent, rapt. Harry had a moment's discomfort, thinking briefly that they were embarrassed by his tale of youthful inadequacy, but soon Chakotay moved to him and put a hand on his shoulder. "I wish he could see you now, Harry," and in his voice the young ensign heard warmth and approval.

They moved into the shelters after that, stretching out on the ground, young animals strangely at peace after Harry's tale of innocence and initiation. Coris followed Harry without a word, and curled up next to him, back to back. Within minutes, he was asleep.

Coris lay awake for a long time, listening to the steady, sonorous sound of Harry's breathing. Her mind was awash with thoughts and sensations, swirling from the stimuli of this remarkable day.

She had fully expected the man in the gold and black uniform to beat her for having tried to steal his boots. When instead he had brought her to his shelter, she assumed she would be raped first.

When she was treated with decency and courtesy, she hardly knew how to respond, and was suspicious of the motives of these people, these Voyagers. She didn't speak for fear of setting them off, sure they were simply trying to catch her unawares. In this part of space, no one befriended a powerless girl unless they expected something in return.

It was only after listening to Harry's story, which was so suffused with love and compassion, that she began, somewhat tentatively, to believe that these people were different, that they were as good and decent as they seemed. It was a concept that her mind all but refused to accept, but it was so provocative, so enticing, that she couldn't resist it.

Of course, it could still turn out that they wanted to use her in some fashion, and that would be no surprise and no disappointment. It was what she expected. If if turned out otherwise, that would be the shock. She would simply bide her time and see which it was to be.

Finally, after some hours, she fell into a fitful sleep, and dreamed of her grandmother, the only person who had ever shown her love.

"We must create a reasonably accurate map of the entire stockade," said Tuvok to the group that assembled within one of the shelters the next morning. The day had dawned overcast and raw, with a chill breeze that held the hint of rain. B'Elanna felt the cold in her bones, and focused on what Tuvok was saying in order to take her mind off the nippy weather. The group had gathered to discuss the next step in their survival: escape.

It was a daunting task. The wall surrounding the camp looked unassailable. The guards possessed sophisticated and lethal weapons. They were surrounded on all sides by thick forest and had no idea how far they were from civilization, if any—the prisoner-of-war camp might be the only habitation on the planet. And they still had no clue as to the whereabouts of Captain Janeway or *Voyager* and the rest of the crew.

But one step at a time. They would map the stockade, looking at details of terrain, geological elements, location of guard posts, and anything else that might be useful as they made their plans.

B'Elanna found herself with Chakotay and Brad Harrison, heading for the corner of the stockade they had designated the southwest. This was territory no one had ventured into yet, a rolling, undulating part of the meadow, teeming with ragged prisoners. B'Elanna felt many curious eyes on them as they made their way along the rough road they had dubbed Main Street, which ran the length of the stockade, perpendicular to Broadway. She was aware that her group was better dressed and better fed than anyone in the prison camp, and that they would be objects of both envy and resentment.

"How about it, B'Elanna?" queried Chakotay. "Are you going to tell us your story tonight?"

B'Elanna felt her cheeks flush. "I'm not much of a talker. Better pick someone else."

"I've never known you to be at a loss for words," retorted Chakotay, and she shot him a quick glance, seeing that his lips were turned up in a characteristic grin. "We've heard the tale of two men—time for a woman's story."

"You might hear some things that would shock you," she said wryly, and his grin became wider. "I'd be interested in hearing just what those might be," he shot back. "I bared my soul pretty completely, and Harry was painfully honest. It wouldn't do for you to be anything less than forthcoming."

B'Elanna declined to respond. If she didn't commit, maybe he'd choose someone else tonight. But she didn't have time to think beyond that, because they became aware of a shouted tumult ahead of them. A cluster of prisoners off the road to their right was gathered around something, or someone, they couldn't see. B'Elanna thought this was in their favor; if the crowd was distracted, they could go about their business more easily.

A tide of prisoners was now streaming toward the knotted mass, and the shouting became more intense, a cacophony that rose into the dank morning air like water vapor from a forest floor. What was happening? B'Elanna had to sidestep to avoid being run down by a trio of pale, scrawny humanoids who were covered with sores, but who were apparently desperate to get to the scene of whatever was happening.

Ahead of them, a filthy, hunched old man was waving at the approaching crowds, beckoning them toward the growing cluster of observers. As B'Elanna and the two men neared him, he scrutinized them, puzzled. His nose was huge, and hooked, like that of a predatory bird. Long, stringy hanks of dirty gray hair hung from his head, and he twisted one nervously as he talked.

"Are not you wishing to see the fracas?" he asked, in a voice that sounded like a death rattle. "Myself will I hold the wagers, for you be not wanting to trust any others."

"What's happening?" asked Chakotay, and the man seemed even more surprised.

"Do not you know that this is the sometime waited-for challenge by Loord the Noarkan against the brute Troykis? Many suns in the waiting, with ill attitudes climbing ever so high. Will not you wager? And if may I offer, Loord is much determined to depose Troykis. Assume his victory and reward will be reaped."

"No, thanks," B'Elanna said. This was the perfect time for them to do their mapping, when so much attention was going to what sounded like a grudge fight.

The old man shrugged and immediately lost interest in them, waving a bony talon toward others who were hurrying along. B'Elanna, Chakotay, and Harrison stayed on their course for the southwest corner of the stockade, feeling something like salmon swimming against the stream.

The southwest quadrant of the camp had thinned out considerably, although not everyone had gone to see the fight. Those who were too old, too infirm, or too sick remained sprawled on the ground, their suffering unrelieved by the prospect of witnessing combat. B'Elanna noted that there was a rise to the land here, giving them a better overview of the camp than they had had before. The three climbed to the highest point, a knoll topped by a clever shelter of wood and thatch, and surveyed their new surroundings.

"Quite a sight," murmured Chakotay as they took stock. From their vantage point they could see the entire camp, a vast, sprawling ribbon of squalor contained inside the foreboding walls of the dark metal stockade. Thousands of beings swarmed the meadow, sluggish fire ants, pulsing, undulating, as though the mass of prisoners composed one organism, one entity that throbbed with torpid life.

Now they could see the "arena" where the fight was taking place, a circle of hundreds of prisoners surrounding an open space some thirty meters in diameter. Within that ring hunched two beings who circled each other warily, eyes locked on one another, ready to spring at the other or dodge a blow. They were a study in contrasts, as one was dark and shaggy, covered from head to foot with a mat of hair, while the other was fair and smooth-skinned. B'Elanna wondered for a moment which was the challenger and which the champion, then dismissed the thought as irrelevant. It was a silent drama enacted a hundred meters from them; only the sound of the shouting spectators rose to the distant knoll on which they stood.

They turned their attention to their task, and were busy estimating distances and topographical features when they saw something the crowd watching the fight didn't. One of the side portals of the stockade wall had opened, and through it emerged a phalanx of four guards, loping toward the arena area on their three legs.

"Uh-oh," said Harrison, and without knowing why they did it, they aped the behavior of the prisoners the day they'd arrived, pretending to busy themselves, collecting bits of rock and grass, as though this task were the most important in the world.

They kept an eye on the drama below, however, sensing that it would soon encompass more than the battle in the ring. The spectators of the fight were still oblivious of the approach of the guards, engrossed in the duel that was unfolding. The two combatants were now locked in a grip, rolling on the ground as the cries of the onlookers swelled to a wail.

What happened next was truly horrible, and would haunt B'Elanna's dreams for a long while. The three of them ceased their aimless activity and stared, appalled, at what was transpiring below them.

As the guards approached the cluster of spectators, whose backs were to them, they raised their massive weapons and opened fire. A stream of yellow energy vapor emerged and flooded the backs of the unlucky periphery. The people hit by the vapor burst into flame. The tumult that had been athletic exhortation became shrieks of agony as the guards cut a swath through the clumped mass, bodies falling aside and then writhing and rolling in fearful torment.

The guards quickly broke through to the open ring, as the spectators realized too late their fate and began to run, panicked, stumbling and tumbling over each other in their desperate efforts to escape. The combatants themselves looked up in shock, their bodies still locked in struggle, a pose they would share in death. The guards trained their awful weapons on the pair and incinerated them.

A panicked riot now ensued among the remaining spectators. Those at the rear of the circle opposite the guards had some chance of escape; among them B'Elanna saw the ragged gray locks of the wager-maker, who scuttled into a shelter and disappeared.

But few others were as fortunate. The guards spread out, putting their weapons on continuous fire and swinging them in widening arcs, cremating anyone in range. Burning bodies fell to the ground, twisting, tormented, trying in vain to extinguish the cruel flames that were consuming them. Hideous cries resounded from the burning mass of bodies, and the stench of burnt flesh rose like a miasma.

B'Elanna's eyes lifted to the rest of the camp, and was astonished by what she saw. Everyone not directly involved in the slaughter was working feverishly but doing nothing, taking absolutely no notice of the carnage that was occurring. Heads did not lift, eyes did not seek out the events that played out around the awful arena. There was a kind of mass denial, a refusal to acknowledge the hideousness of what was being done. B'Elanna guessed that experience had taught them that the safest behavior in such circumstances was to feign indifference.

She was unable to do so. She stared, unmoving, horrified, sick, her mind struggling to encompass the horror to which she was witness. The bodies were continuing to burn, even after they had stopped their agonal writhings, burn hotly, until nothing was left but a skeleton to which was affixed hunks of charred meat.

The guards finally stopped firing and simply stood, watching as their victims perished. When they were satisfied that a sufficient number had been punished, they turned back toward the portal in the wall through which they had emerged, and loped back to their posts.

It had taken minutes. Retribution for whatever offense had been committed had been swift and dreadful, but was it expected? B'Elanna wondered if the prisoners knew they were risking such awful punishment, or if the guards behaved unpredictably, changing the rules without warning, on a whim. She couldn't imagine the fight taking place so openly if they had even vaguely suspected the consequences.

The next event was even more hideous.

As soon as the guards were done, prisoners set upon the charred bodies, ripping black flesh from the bones and consuming it. B'Elanna felt her stomach contract, her vision blur. Nausea flooded her, and she put her head down, bringing blood to her brain. In a moment, she felt slightly better, and turned to her companions. They were as pale as she imagined she was. Perspiration beaded Harrison's face, and his eyes were haunted. Chakotay stared solemnly down toward the newly created crematorium, one vein in his temple throbbing.

Finally he turned to them, and said quietly, "You do what you have to to survive. Let's keep going."

B'Elanna found herself relieved. Work, purpose, activity—those time-honored elements would help to eradicate the sights and sounds they had just experienced. Do your job, fulfill your responsibility, keep going. In the end, that was always best.

* * *

That night it was a sobered group that ate the unappetizing rations—grain cake again—and huddled around the small fires. B'Elanna, Chakotay, and Harrison had told them briefly and tersely what they had witnessed; most were unaware that anything *had* happened, so complete was the denial of the other prisoners, though most had noticed the acrid stench that had permeated the already odoriferous air in the stockade.

"We could use a change of subject," said Chakotay quietly. "B'Elanna, maybe you could take our minds off this place for a while."

B'Elanna found that she wasn't reluctant to chronicle her life, and was in fact almost eager. She would do anything that would take her away from this wretched site, from the searing memories of what she had seen this morning. Even if that meant speaking of the greatest pain that had ever assailed her.

CHAPTER

6

OF HIS LEAVING, SHE REMEMBERED NOTHING.

Of the time before his leaving, she had only the most vaporous of memories: a strong, deep voice . . . arms with dark hair curling on them . . . jumping into those arms from a platform in a lake . . . the scent of the plains of Nessik after a summer rainstorm . . . her hair being tied in tight braids . . .

. . . and the voices, subdued and angry, that made her stomach twist and her hands turn strangely wet. Their arguments.

Of the time after his leaving, and of her mother, she remembered too much.

"B'Elanna, *HighoS!* Come out this minute. I won't let you hide in your room like a cowardly puff cat."

"I'm not coming." Her voice sounded anything but brave, eight-year-old B'Elanna admitted to herself, but she determined not to give in to her mother this time. This time, she would do what she wanted.

"You can't let them shame you into hiding. That's not how Klingons behave."

"I don't care! I'm not Klingon!"

There was a brief silence, and then the rattling of the door to her bedroom. "B'Elanna—open this door immediately." Her mother's voice had taken on a new and more definitive tone. It was one with which B'Elanna was familiar, and which ordinarily struck dread into her heart. Today, she steeled against it. She had activated the electronic lock on the door, and she would stay in her room until she died. How long did it take to starve to death? No matter. However long it took, she would stay right where she was, under her bed with her stuffed cat, Gato, beside her. They would lie like that forever, until her body rotted away and only the bones were left, small skeleton fingers still clutching Gato's fluffy pelt.

Moments later, she heard the door open and saw her mother's feet and legs as she entered the room. The legs moved toward her, and then her mother's face, ridged and bony, appeared in her view.

"Come out from there. I won't have you hiding."

Dismayed, B'Elanna scrunched forward and emerged from her safe place. How had her mother gotten in?

As though she'd read her mind, Prabsa Torres stared at her and said, "It doesn't do any good to activate the lock. I can disable it whenever I want. What if there were a fire and I had to get you out? Or you were sick and couldn't open the door?"

What if I wanted to starve to death? thought B'Elanna, but the thought went unspoken. She just wanted to get through this as quickly as possible.

Her mother sat at her desk and looked at her with black eyes probing. "Well? Do you want to tell me what happened? And why do you have that dirty scarf around your head?"

B'Elanna's hand went instinctively to her forehead. She tugged the scarf—a scrap she had found discarded on the street—farther down in defiance. "Nothing's going on. And I'm wearing the scarf because I like it."

Something seemed to drain from her mother, and her next statement was softer, less challenging. "You left the house to go to the park an hour ago. *Not* wearing a scarf. Then you came running home as though you were being chased by Fek'lhr himself and slammed into your room. Something happened to upset you, and I want to know what it was."

"Nothing."

"Were the other children taunting you?"

In spite of herself, a sharp breath escaped B'Elanna's lips. Taunting her? No, not at all. That would be something she could confront. But the *indifference* the others showed her—how could anyone confront that? It might as well not exist. Except that it did, as clearly as though the children of the outpost on Nessik were shouting it aloud.

"No, they weren't."

"Did you get in a fight?"

You'd be proud of me if I had, thought B'Elanna, but that idea went unspoken as well. "No. No fight."

"Did you fall? Get hurt?"

"No."

Her mother looked at her with increasing exasperation. "We could go on like this all day. Just tell me what happened."

"I already told you—nothing."

Prabsa drew a sharp breath, clearly vexed. She looked for a moment out the window as though to gain control of herself, and then she began speaking.

"Once, when Kahless had been walking in the desert for eighty days . . ."

B'Elanna rolled her eyes. Not this again. Not another Klingon story with a lesson to be learned. Why did her mother inflict these morality tales on her? What good did she think they did? They were foolish, empty stories that B'Elanna found embarrassing. She couldn't believe her mother actually thought she might learn something from them. They were all alike—long, rambling legends featuring the exploits of one Klingon hero or another, all ending with some nugget of wisdom by which, she assumed, her mother thought she should live.

As her mother droned on, her mind wandered, back to the park and the scene of her latest humiliation. A group of little girls—pretty girls, human girls—were playing there, practicing the ball-kicking techniques of Pre-Squares, the game that provided the foundation for the adult sport of Parrises Squares.

No one was better at Pre-Squares than B'Elanna. It had come naturally to her, an unlearned ability that had allowed her to conquer effortlessly the intricate patterns of ball-handling that took the others hours of practice. She would fly down the field, hair streaming behind her, Squares ball hovering low to the ground, completely under her control. A giddy feeling of freedom rushed over her every time she broke away from the pack.

Her teachers praised her.

Her classmates ignored her.

That afternoon, she had stood on the sidelines, hoping to be invited into the practice game, certain someone would want her skills on their side. But no invitation came. She stood there, by herself, gazing longingly at the group of spirited children, for almost an hour.

Finally, just about at the time she'd decided to give up and go home, the antigrav ball came skimming in her direction, out of control of either of the teams. She caught it on an ankle, then the opposite knee, and before she knew it, she was off and running, deftly maneuvering the ball, driving it with total command down the field. The familiar exhilaration consumed her and she focused on her goal, keeping the lively ball zipping from knee to elbow to ankle, using her arms to guard against defenders, for surely the others would be after her, trying to maneuver the ball away from her.

She had taken the ball the full length of the field before she realized no one was coming after her. She crossed into the Square, then turned and looked behind her.

The others were standing where they'd been when they lost the ball, forty meters away, staring after her but making no move to follow.

They were just ignoring her. She was nobody. She didn't even exist.

She felt the ridges in her forehead begin to flush—she hated that, they always looked worse when they reddened—and she dug her fingernails into her palms, trying to calm herself and alleviate her mortification. As casually as she could, she carried the ball back down the field, stretching herself erect, walking with as much dignity as she could muster.

As she approached, the girls looked at her with no visible emotion. She tossed the ball toward them. "Guess somebody lost control of it," she said flatly, and watched as one, then another, of the girls tried to rein in the errant sphere. Then she turned and walked away from them.

She was only a few meters away when she heard the whisper. "I hate those bones in her head," someone said, obviously thinking she was speaking too softly to be heard but unaware that B'Elanna, as part Klingon, had keener hearing than humans.

Now, at home, her mother's voice was still droning on, but from its rising inflections she knew the story was coming to its conclusion. "And so Kahless came out of the wilderness, and entered the world once more, choosing to live among the people he was dedicated to lead, even if it meant suffering the pain that others inevitably bestow. That was the lesson he learned from the serpent of Shrika."

She looked up to see her mother gazing down at her quizzically, apparently trying to judge the effect of this fable. Then Prabsa knelt down, and her ridged face was suddenly level with B'Elanna's, dark eyes peering at her, pointed teeth all but overflowing her mouth. B'Elanna recoiled.

"Do you understand what Kahless learned?" her mother asked. "That a Klingon can't hide from his destiny. That confronting your fears will conquer them, but flying from them gives them power. Do you understand that?"

These were all just so many words to B'Elanna, but she nodded solemnly, hoping her mother would accept this acknowledgment. Her mother's eyes probed her for a minute more, then she took hold of B'Elanna's shoulders. "I won't let you be weak, B'Elanna. All I can give you is a sense of your own strength, and I *will* do that."

Her mother didn't understand. B'Elanna didn't want to find her Klingon strength. She wanted to be consoled, and reassured. She was only a little girl, after all.

"We're going to have a party," Prabsa said. "Invite all your classmates. We'll go to the lake. You have to show them that you won't be intimidated."

A *party?* Terror rose in B'Elanna with astonishing swiftness. She couldn't imagine anything worse. Didn't her mother realize that human children wanted nothing to do with her? How could she invite them to an outing at the lake? No one would come.

Her mother stood up. "Just let me know how many to plan for. And you can choose the menu."

Prabsa reached over and gently removed the scarf from B'Elanna's head, then brushed her hair up and away from her forehead. "You're such a beautiful girl," she murmured. "You mustn't cover yourself up."

And then she was gone. B'Elanna clutched Gato tightly to her chest, ridden with despair. She wasn't going to risk further humiliation by trying to arrange this awful party. She just wouldn't do it.

But she knew it wouldn't matter. Her mother would then take over, issuing invitations through the parents, who would be too polite to refuse, and so the event would take place, an agonizing afternoon in which everyone would pretend they were having a good time, the human children desperately eager to get away from them so they could snicker and gossip about the Klingon women: the friendless, belligerent child and the overbearing mother, whom they surely found the ugliest creatures they'd ever seen.

* * *

The first thing she noticed about Qo'noS, the Klingon homeworld, was the noise, and it was the noise that continued to assault her during the entire time of their visit. From the time they arrived, she longed for the quiet of Nessik.

The Terran colony at Nessik was, for all the loneliness it imposed on her, a serene and orderly place. Houses were clustered in beautifully landscaped parks which were tended by those who enjoyed gardening, and those people seemed beset with a kind of genial competition, each trying to make his or her assigned section the most abundant, the most breathtakingly lush. Each walkway, each path, was immaculately maintained, and animal life of every kind abounded.

These idyllic surroundings lent an atmosphere of harmony and tranquillity. Walking through these parks, one could hear the call of songbirds, or the distant sound of children playing, but that was all. There was an ineffable stillness that permeated Nessik, a calming aura that quieted the mind.

This was an assessment that B'Elanna could never have made until her visit to the Klingon homeworld at the age of ten, when her mother decided that it was time she come face-to-face with her heritage, and booked transport from Runii to Minis Prime, where they were able to procure space on a freighter bound for Gostak, which was just inside the confines of the Klingon Empire, and were then able to find a shuttle that would take them to Qo'noS.

It was a long, wretched journey, and B'Elanna hated every minute of it. She had never traveled in space, and it left her faintly nauseated. Their accommodations were never more than spartan, at best, because her mother foolishly abjured her right to take Starfleet ships, and procured only civilian transportation. The food was uneven and their fellow travelers a rough lot of polyglot species.

All during the flights, Prabsa had extolled the wonders of Qo'noS, telling B'Elanna rapturous stories of the things she would see: historical battle sites, splendid cultural centers, natural wonders that defied description. She chattered on and on, B'Elanna by habit tuning her out for long stretches, about the richness, the diversity, of Klingon society. Prabsa herself hadn't been back to Qo'noS for over ten years, and she was all but giddy with anticipation, sleeping little, nibbling at her food, and babbling endlessly about home.

"We'll go to the shrine of Kahless first," Prabsa said in one of a myriad of itineraries she concocted and then threw out. "That's obligatory, and it sets the proper atmosphere for everything else. Or maybe the battlefield at Mithrak should come first, so you'll have an understanding of the context Kahless sprang from."

All of it sounded dreadful to B'Elanna. Battlefields? Shrines? She could relate to none of it. She knew her mother assumed that, after ten years of hearing the history, the myths, the legends, the stirring tales of valor, she was sufficiently inundated in the Klingon past to appreciate its present. Prabsa couldn't know how completely her daughter had shut out her ceaseless teachings.

They were disgorged from the final shuttle flight into a vast spacedock thronged with people, all of whom seemed to be talking at the top of their voices. B'Elanna clung to her mother's hand as they made their way through the crowds, her mother entering into the verbal fray right along with the rest.

"Move aside . . . we're passing through . . . watch yourself, ghargh, your smelly feet are in the way." Prabsa kept up this oral bombardment as they pushed and shoved their way across the huge floor of the docking area, hurling insults to anyone who was in their way, snarling with what B'Elanna assumed was feigned rage when people failed to move aside, and in general behaving as rudely as everyone else there.

B'Elanna was horrified. She had never seen people conduct themselves in this way, had never known these kinds of crowds, where people all shouted and reviled each other, where there were no rules of decorum, no manners. Her ears began to ring from the din, and her arm ached where her mother clutched it, dragging her through this mass of pulsing, chaotic Klingonhood.

Finally they were at the transport area, where once again her mother pulled her into a group that was ready to dematerialize, ignoring the shouted protests of the transport engineer and steadfastly planting herself and her daughter within the group. Prabsa and the engineer exchanged a volley of insults that made B'Elanna want to shrivel into herself for shame, but finally the man backed down and they were transported to the surface.

Things didn't improve there. Crowds were *everywhere* on Qo'noS, a hurly-burly mass that never seemed to move in a discernible pattern or toward a common goal. The masses were swirling eddies of movement, here, there, anywhere, as though a common madness had struck them all and impelled them to move against any tide they encountered.

And they continued to yell. Even general conversation, B'Elanna realized, was conducted at an earsplitting level, often with loud guffaws of laughter punctuating the cacophony.

The edifices of Qo'noS were certainly imposing. The buildings all loomed large, and dark, ornately constructed and richly appointed, a dazzling display of architecture as an expression of national ideology: gazing at vaulting towers and pillared courtyards, one couldn't escape the sense of haughty pride, of strident militancy, of reverence for ritual and tradition.

By the time they reached the home of B'Elanna's maternal grandparents, she had a terrible headache. She longed for the quiet of her garden on Nessik, the call of a single bird the only sound to disturb a summer night. But inside the home, she found, things were as disorderly as everywhere else.

"Look at her!" bellowed her grandfather Torg, a huge, barrel-chested man with long, unkempt hair, and a full beard and mustache that seemed full of bits and pieces that B'Elanna didn't want to identify. He leaned down and picked her up as easily as if she were a piece of cloth, lifting her high in the air above him. Her stomach quailed.

"She's a little runt of a thing, isn't she," he continued, turning so that everyone in the crowded room could get a good look.

"She's just a bit scrawny," assessed a gray-haired woman as she scrutinized the child in the air. "A month of good Klingon food and she'll fill out nicely."

Suddenly, Torg tossed B'Elanna upward and she began to fall, her stomach clenching with fear before she felt herself caught from behind by another huge Klingon man. "I'm your uncle Kor," he thundered, specks of spittle bursting from his mouth as he did. "You've got more family here than you can imagine." He plopped her down on the floor, where she reeled slightly and tried to keep her balance, and then stared up into a panorama of faces, old, young, big and small, all with their eyes locked on to her as though they were missiles and she were the target.

"Does she talk?" roared one of the younger men, producing a fierce howl of laughter from everyone—including her mother, a fact that made her feel as though an icy dagger had pierced her heart. Here, as on Nessik, she was alone and friendless, an object of scorn and ridicule, with no one to take her side. So she was surprised when the gray-haired woman spoke again.

"She's been traveling for a week, you lummoxes. She's tired and hungry. Make way while I get her some food." This, she was to learn, was her grandmother, B'Kor, who pushed her way through toward B'Elanna and grabbed her with a strong hand and led her through the group—which did have the good grace to part and not make her fight her way through—to a room where a huge table stood, laden with more food than B'Elanna had ever seen in her life.

"Here, little *be'Hom,* I'll make you a plate. We'll get you fattened up in no time." B'Kor was pulling morsels of food from the vast array, most of which was unfamiliar to B'Elanna. A few dishes she recognized as those her mother had made, but most were an exotic array of roasted meats, strange vegetables, runny cheeses, and—to her dismay—dishes of creatures who seemed still to be moving.

B'Kor had piled her plate until food was dropping off the edges, and she put it in B'Elanna's hands with a huge smile that showed her twisted Klingon teeth to full advantage. "When you're done with that I'll cut a big slab of blood pie. You've never tasted better."

When I'm done with that I'll be dead, thought B'Elanna as she eyed the huge platter with some apprehension. She'd never seen that much food on a plate before. She couldn't possibly get it all in her stomach. She felt arms on her shoulders propelling her into yet another room, this one full of trestle tables and benches, and she realized she was to take a seat and begin gorging on this massive plate of food.

She sat and tried to distinguish the various edibles before her. She was disconcerted that one pile of yellow mealy things seemed to be squirming, and tried to cover them with a piece of dark bread. Other young people then began to join her in the room, which she soon realized was designated for the children. There were boys and girls of all ages, from toddlers to adolescents, all with unfettered energy and high spirits. And loud voices.

A boy that she judged to be about five years older than she sat opposite her, his plate piled even higher than hers. He had dark, flashing eyes and a smile that would have been attractive if it hadn't been for his teeth. "Be sure you try the blood pie. Aunt B'Kor makes it better than anyone in the family."

"Not so, you *QIp.* My mother Toksa's is far better." This was from a girl just about B'Elanna's age who sat down next to her. The benches were filling fast with noisy young people, and B'Elanna strained to tune in to the two near her.

"I'm K'Karn, your second cousin," said the boy. "This deluded child is my first cousin, Lanna. When she's a few years older she'll have more experience by which to judge blood pie. She's just a stripling now."

B'Elanna saw Lanna's ridges flush and realized she wanted to be liked by this dashing young boy, was infatuated with him. And she could understand why; K'Karn had an air of genial confidence that was infectious. Even B'Elanna was drawn to him, but she couldn't for the life of her think of anything to say to him. She began to pick at her food, realizing for the first time that there were no utensils. This didn't deter the others, who were plunging into the meal with both hands, tearing meat from bones and licking greasy fingers with gusto.

She chewed a few pieces of bread as she listened to K'Karn and Lanna banter back and forth. K'Karn was describing his latest exploits in mock battle, his preparations for the Ascension rites. Lanna seemed enthralled, asking him questions, urging him on. But finally he turned again to B'Elanna.

"Tell us about you, cousin." He smiled. "What is life like for a Klingon on Nessik?"

The question caught B'Elanna like a blow to the belly. Never in her life had anyone made such an inquiry, never sought her opinion, her feelings, her reaction to her own life. Her father had disappeared and her mother proceeded to tell her how she *ought* to live her life, her teachers were not unkind and treated her as they did the other children, and the children of course ignored her. But no one had ever asked that most simple of questions: What is it like for you?

Her eyes stung and she blinked fiercely in order to keep any moisture from escaping, but K'Karn and Lanna both realized what was happening. There was a stunned silence, and B'Elanna knew in the next moment they would move off, embarrassed by this weak cousin, and leave her alone once more. That she could endure; that was familiar.

But to her surprise K'Karn rose and crossed round the table to her, taking her arm and pulling her upward. "Come on, cousin, this isn't a night for tears. Lanna, let's show her the caverns."

And they escorted her outside, one on either side, chattering as though nothing were amiss even though tears were spilling over B'Elanna's cheeks.

An hour later, they sat in an amazing, glowing cavern, whose walls were studded with tiny mothlike insects that were iridescent and beautiful, casting a light from within. B'Elanna had told them both of her life on Nessik, of her nonexistence, her isolation, her utter and complete rejection.

When she was done, K'Karn's face had hardened, and he rose to his feet, seething with energy, pacing the floor of the cavern, low growls occasionally punctuating his diatribe. *"VeQ ngIm,"* he snarled. "Humans don't have the courage to settle things in an honorable fashion. You should challenge them, B'Elanna, and then they'd know immediately who was superior."

This was startling advice. Challenge them? To what? B'Elanna felt confusion invade her mind, but K'Karn didn't seem to notice.

"How is your warrior training coming? What level of fighting skills have you achieved?"

"Warrior . . . training?" B'Elanna had no idea what he was talking about.

"Surely you've begun by now, at least the martial skills," said K'Karn, as though it were the most natural thing in the world.

"No, I . . ." B'Elanna felt herself stammering. She was suddenly embarrassed to admit to him that she had no desire to train as a Klingon warrior, no *intention* of doing so. "There isn't any place to train," she said quickly. "We're the only Klingons, after all."

"Then you must stay here and enter the training program at Ogat as soon as possible. You can live with Aunt B'Kor—she'd love to have a young person in the house again."

B'Elanna had no idea how to respond to this outlandish suggestion. Live here, on this crowded, noisy, chaotic world with inedible food and rude people who pushed and shoved and yelled their way through life? It was an unbearable thought, and she panicked at the thought that others, the grownups, might get wind of it and think it a wonderful idea.

"I can't do that—I couldn't leave my mother."

"Maybe she'll move back here. No one ever understood why she left in the first place. Her roots are here, B'Elanna, and so are yours. This is your true home."

A panic so complete it overwhelmed everything else took firm hold of B'Elanna Torres. She lost sight of the fact that this relative was offering her what she had never had—acceptance, kinship, support—and could only imagine the terrors that awaited her on this planet of wild people. She stood up, pulse racing, mouth dry.

"I'll talk to my mother about it. Thank you."

K'Karn and Lanna rose to join her, and the two of them babbled endlessly on the walk back home about the fun they'd have together when B'Elanna moved here, hunting, fighting, and preparing for their warrior rituals. By the time they reached the home of B'Kor and Torg, B'Elanna was sick to her stomach.

The scene in the house didn't help any. The adults, it seemed, had been drinking ale, and had become even more raucous. Two men were amusing themselves by running at each other from opposite sides of the room, heads down, and ramming each other as hard as they could. These blows left them reeling, but seemed to afford great sport to the others, who let out rousing cheers each time they butted heads. The noise level was higher than ever, with loud music of some dreadful cacophony permeating everything, and the scent of greasy meats and strange, pungent spices seemed to clog her nose, and then everything began to revolve, slowly at first, then faster and faster, and she struggled to stay upright but then a blessed darkness overtook her.

She awoke in a huge bed, her mother sitting by her side pressing a cool damp cloth to her forehead. B'Elanna's head throbbed and her throat ached strangely. In her mouth, she tasted the acid aftertaste of vomitus—she had thrown up. Had she done that in front of everyone? It was too embarrassing to contemplate.

"Feeling better?" her mother asked gently. "I should have realized your stomach might not adapt so quickly to Klingon food. Something didn't sit right with you."

B'Elanna knew it was more than food that didn't sit right with her, and she couldn't hold it back—she had to know if living here was even a remote possibility.

"Is this our true home?" she blurted out. "Are we going to stay here? Have we left Nessik forever?"

Prabsa looked at her curiously. "Why ever would you ask such questions?"

"K'Karn said we should live here. That I should begin my training as a warrior. Is that going to happen?"

An unusual expression came over her mother's face, both amused and serious at the same time. B'Elanna had no idea what it meant. "No, it isn't," Prabsa said, and B'Elanna's relief was so overwhelming she had trouble concentrating on anything that followed.

"Nessik is our home. I have my laboratory there, and it's important to me. I love my family, but I decided long ago that my place wasn't here, on the homeworld. And I still feel that way." There was a small pause, and then she continued. "If you'd like to consider living here, I'd understand. You might be happier among family."

"No, I don't want to stay here. I want to go back."

Prabsa studied her daughter for a long moment, then simply nodded and dipped the cloth into cool water once more, wringing it out and placing it on B'Elanna's forehead. *"Puq Doy',"* she murmured, "such a tired little girl." It was a moment of uncommon closeness between them, and B'Elanna felt the dark question unfold in her mind like a black flower. Now was the time to ask it, now, when her mother seemed forthcoming, yielding: *Why did my father go away?*

She trembled on the edge of that shadowy abyss, wanting to ask but afraid of the answer, and so remained silent, listening as her mother hummed a plaintive tune, cooling her face with the pleasantly damp cloth, and finally she fell asleep for a long dark time during which she did not dream, or if she did she retained no memory of it.

Acceptance by the young people of Nessik, when it came, arrived in a manner wholly unexpected, in the summer she turned fourteen. She had become aware that adolescence hadn't been kind to some of her human peers, many of whom became ungainly and silly. Some put on weight and others were reed-thin; a few had erupted with dreadful pustules on their faces until a series of medical treatments could return the clarity of their complexions. Behavior changed, too, in strange, unpredictable ways that seemed to leave the air around them charged with an untapped energy.

B'Elanna was unafflicted by these changes. She did not develop pimples, though she developed breasts, and her body was lithe and supple as a result of the swimming she did every day in the huge lake near their colony. It was in, or on, the water that she was happiest. She was a strong swimmer and her redundant lungs gave her the capacity to stay under water for incredibly (to humans) long periods of time, and she enjoyed the wonder it produced in the other children. She also loved to sail, and had a small racing sloop that she had learned to maneuver with great skill. This predilection also set her apart: most of the young people preferred hovercraft, which were faster and easier to handle. But B'Elanna enjoyed the challenge of mastering the difficult waves, of conquering the elements, which, if one wasn't up to it, could prove not only dangerous but fatal. Each time she set forth, she told herself it could be her last, and that to survive she would have to sail with consummate skill. These thoughts were strangely titillating to her.

While she still had no true friends, the young people her age no longer shunned her, and had become (perhaps at their parents' insistence) at least civil. She made no effort to move beyond that cordiality, and was content to keep largely to herself, studying hard and excelling in her grades. While adolescence seemed a time of turmoil for her classmates, it was for her a time of relative equanimity.

At least for a while.

As a child she had developed a protective barrier that allowed her to block out whispered remarks and unkind comments, and so she remained largely oblivious of any notice paid to her. This remained true as the young men of her school had begun to stare at her in unaccustomed ways, whispering among themselves when she walked by. She had no way of knowing that this serene aloofness made her all the more desirable to them.

Late one afternoon in that summer she walked to the lake and set out in her sloop for a small island some five kilometers away. It was a favorite place, full of brooks and glens and shady nooks which she had discovered as a child and where she played out fantasy games in which she was, variously, a princess, a famed explorer, or a poet, each of whom was adored by millions, and whose company was always sought. Now that she was older, the island still had the power to bestow those magical feelings on her. If she no longer dreamed of being a princess, another dream had been forming in her mind, one that was just as unlikely: she thought of attending Starfleet Academy as her father had.

This might have been so remote a possibility that it would never have occurred to her had she not been told by her mother that a Klingon actually had been accepted at the Academy, a boy whose parents had died at Khitomer and who had been raised by humans. This knowledge began to burn in her, a tiny flame at first, but gradually gathering heat and intensity.

She would go to the island and imagine herself at the Academy. She had a book, left behind by her father, with pictures of the fabled school, and she had pored over them for hours, trying to familiarize herself with the environs, imagining herself walking along those manicured walkways, attending classes in those imposing buildings, even sailing in San Francisco Bay, which the book assured her was a favorite pastime of residents there.

It was no more than a ten-minute sail to the island, as the wind on the lake was gusting powerfully. She was drenched in spray by the time she beached the craft, but she felt invigorated.

She made her way to a beautiful little clearing near a stream which ran over smooth stones, and sat in her favorite spot, leaning her back against a smooth-barked tree. She closed her eyes and tried to decide what classes she would take. She didn't really dream of a career in

Starfleet, a likelihood that somehow seemed out of reach, but convinced herself that she could attend the Academy and simply study what she enjoyed. Art, for example, and literature. What heaven to be able to read and read and receive college credit for it!

She also wanted to study the history of Earth. She had been drowned in Klingon history by her mother's endless stories, and she longed to know more about her other heritage, the one that seemed nobler. Of ancient kings and queens, of the millennia-long struggle for human rights, for democracy, for peace—of the long road toward the paradise, the jewel of the Federation, that Earth was now.

She had never visited Earth, but felt that she knew it, somehow, had walked its farmlands and climbed its mountains. It was an Eden that she longed for, and Starfleet Academy was the route to that Eden.

The snap of a twig on the ground interrupted her reverie and she stood quickly, alert. Sometimes others brought hovercraft to the island, but they usually stayed on the beaches, never venturing so far inland. Who would be disturbing her special place now?

She heard the rustling in the brush of what seemed like several people, and heard murmuring voices. She waited, senses heightened but unafraid, until they moved into the clearing.

Two boys from her class, James Chesney and Robin Beckett, stood before her. When they were much younger, the two had teased her unmercifully, but no more so than any of the others. It was just something young boys did. As they had grown older, the two had at least treated her neutrally, which was fine with B'Elanna. James had even once helped her work out a difficult physics problem, for which she had always been grateful.

Now, they seemed unaccountably nervous. James had short blond hair and a smattering of freckles; they seemed etched on a face which was strangely pale. Robin was a redhead, cheerful and sturdy, but today he hung back, clenching and unclenching his hands.

"Hello, B'Elanna," said James, and his voice sounded faltering, almost cracking. She stared at him in bewilderment.

"Hello," she answered casually. "What brings you two here?"

"We were out on the hovercraft and saw you beach your boat. Just thought we'd say hello."

"Well, you've done that," she said, curious as to where this conversation was going.

There was an uneasy silence. Robin contented himself with gazing around the clearing, as though it were an object of fascination. James shrugged and smiled. "I have some orange juice in my pack. Are you thirsty?"

"Thanks."

James extracted three containers of juice from his pack and handed one to B'Elanna. It was cold, and sweet, and she was grateful for his thoughtfulness. "Want to sit down?"

"Sure," he replied, and Robin hurried to join them. "How did you do on that term paper Wheezer assigned us?" James queried. Wheezer was a teacher in their school, a man who had the habit of breathing through his mouth, thereby emitting a hoarse, wheezing sound. He had been referred to as Wheezer during his entire three-decade tenure at the Nessik school.

"I'm working on it. I'm just not very interested in Bolian literature. Too frivolous."

"I kind of enjoy it. It's funny."

"Some of the writers try to be funny, but it's like they're working too hard at it." She was beginning to realize there was probably no purpose to this visit, just a happenstance encounter among school-mates.

"Did you read the story about the farmer's wife who kept sneaking out in the middle of the night?"

"I thought it was stupid." The story had been a trivial accounting, a fairy tale actually, about an amorous wife who was dissatisfied with her husband and who sought the friendship of a supernatural being, a woodsprite. It was fanciful but silly, with a heavy-handed moral about faithless wives. B'Elanna had found it nothing short of moronic.

"Really?" said James, as though this topic were of intense impor-tance. "Didn't you identify with the wife?"

"What?" B'Elanna retorted in disbelief. James looked vaguely confused at this response, and ran his tongue over dry lips.

"Well, I mean . . . she was so passionate. And frustrated. Her husband just wasn't satisfying her."

She stared at him, not sure who was more confused now. "James," she asked pointedly, "what are you saying?"

He flushed, and his freckles temporarily seemed to disappear. He wet his lips again but his eyes danced off her, avoiding her. When he spoke, his voice was cracking again, uncertain. "Aren't Klingons . . . I mean, we heard . . . well, they're very passionate."

Robin suddenly stood, embarrassment apparent in his expression and his posture. "I'm going back to the hovercraft," he said over his shoulder as he barreled out of the clearing. B'Elanna resisted the temptation to giggle. It was so obvious now what was going on, and she felt an infusion of power, knowing she was in control of the situation. She put her fist under her chin, contemplatively, and leaned toward James.

"What about human girls?" she asked silkily. "Are you saying they're not—passionate?"

His face had seemingly acquired a permanent blush. "I . . . wouldn't know," he croaked, rubbing his hands on the sides of his pants. "Listen, I better go now. Robin's waiting."

She put out a hand and touched his thigh to stop him. It had an electrifying effect. He sat rigidly still, as though afraid to twitch even a muscle. "Don't go yet," she purred. "I'm interested in what you're saying."

"You are?"

"Yes. It's fascinating. Tell me what you know about Klingons." Her voice had become low and throaty, inviting.

"Well . . . I guess . . . they're supposed to have very strong urges. Almost uncontrollable."

"Really? Where did you hear this?"

"You know . . ."

"No, I don't."

"Just . . . around."

"That's so interesting. Uncontrollable urges . . . sounds pretty powerful. How do they satisfy these urges?"

"Well, I'm not sure, exactly. They have to find someone who can take it. I mean, it's supposed to get violent."

"Mmmmm." She looked at him for a moment, dark eyes peering through her thick lashes. "Are you saying you might be someone who's up to it?"

James tried to control what seemed a paroxysm of anxiety. He rubbed his hands on his pants legs again, and wet his lips. "Maybe," he said, but his voice cracked dreadfully as he said it.

"I'll bet you are," she whispered, as she drew closer to him. She put her hands on his arms and drew him upward, standing, mouth very close to his. James was all but hyperventilating.

Then, in a movement so swift it seemed instantaneous, she had flipped him onto his stomach, put a knee on his back, and held his arms extended from his body. "B'Elanna!" he huffed. "What'd you do that for?"

"Shame on you, James Chesney," she said purposefully. "Shame on you for thinking so little of me. Did you think I'd be taken in by that crude approach? Didn't you realize how *obvious* you were? Did you really think I have such uncontrollable urges that I wouldn't see through you?"

"I . . . I . . . didn't mean any harm . . ."

"Then you don't think it causes harm to insult someone like this?"

"B'Elanna, I'm sorry—"

"Listen to me. If you want to spend time with me, I'll consider it. But you'll have to treat me with respect. You'll have to ask me on dates, and take me to dances, and all the things you'd do with human girls. I am not some Klingon slut you can corner in the woods and have your way with. Do you understand me?" Where these words came from, B'Elanna didn't know. They just poured out of her, a stream of pent-up indignation that had been years in the accumulating.

"Yes."

"If you want my company, you're going to have to treat me very, very well, with more dignity and appreciation than you've ever treated anyone. Do you understand that?"

"Yes, I do."

She released him, then, and stepped back, watching as he got to his knees and then rose, looking at her with a clear expression of awe.

"Go home and think about it. Decide whether or not you want to get to know me."

Without replying, James dashed out of the clearing, and B'Elanna was sure that would be the last conversation they would ever have.

But when she got home, there was a message from him on her comm console. He very politely invited her to a concert that would be held in the park three nights hence. He promised her she could trust that he would treat her in the manner she deserved.

And he did. James became her friend, her confidant, her defender. He wouldn't allow an ill word to be spoken about her, and he extolled her virtues and abilities to everyone. He gave her a validation that she had never had before, and so her last years on Nessik were the most stable and fulfilling she had ever known.

With James's enthusiastic support, she applied for admission to Starfleet Academy, and set about fulfilling the rigorous requirements. James also wanted to be schooled on Earth, but had made his primary application to a small and ancient school in Indiana, DePauw University, a highly respected liberal-arts school.

James's friendship nurtured B'Elanna at a pivotal point in her life, and she valued it immensely. But she was never unaware of the fact that she was, from those first fateful moments, completely in control of the situation. It was an empowering feeling, but the message it had given B'Elanna was of the potency of sex. She was convinced that had James Chesney not lusted for her, he would have ignored her. But what she could do with this knowledge, this power, she had no idea.

Her first stroll through San Francisco was emotionally overwhelming. It seemed at once sweetly familiar and wildly alien, for while many of the sights she had pored over in books and pictures were just as she had expected, nothing had prepared her for the reality of the jewel-like city by the bay. It was more beautiful, more energetic, more charged with activity and determination than she could have realized. Everyone she encountered seemed imbued with a sense of purpose, of mission, that she found exhilarating. She wanted to steep herself in those same energies, to take on some noble challenge, to accomplish grand and unimaginable goals. As she walked the hilly streets of San Francisco, she felt capable of anything.

Two months later, she wondered why she'd ever come to Earth.

She had been completely unprepared for the rigid disciplines in place at Starfleet Academy. Her fantasies of taking only the courses she enjoyed, of reading simply for pleasure, evaporated. Every minute of a cadet's day was programmed, planned, and charted, and any off hours were consumed with studying. Every teacher seemed to think his or her course was the only one the cadet was taking, and piled on so much work it was impossible to stay abreast of it. She got by on no more than three or four hours of sleep a night, a feat that was easier for her than for many species, but that ultimately became debilitating.

And she missed James. She realized she had taken his friendship for granted, hadn't appreciated how it buoyed and sustained her. Now, in its absence, she was unbearably lonely. But she had never developed socializing skills, and didn't really know how to go about making new friends. Flipping them to the ground and lecturing them didn't seem to be reasonable options at the Academy.

She and James spoke together frequently at first, and then, as happens, less and less as time went by. He was clearly absorbed in his studies, and his new friends, and eventually they had little in common to talk about. With sadness, she acknowledged that they had moved far apart.

She began to challenge her teachers, questioning regulations, confronting precepts. Her temper grew more intense and less controlled, and with each outburst she felt herself becoming more isolated. She had no one with whom to share these feelings; her mother had opposed her coming to the Academy in the first place, and she had made no real friends here. And so she did what she had done for most of her life: relied on herself, and tried to figure out what she was going to do with her life.

The night was cool, as she had been taught would be the case on Tresorin III. She had also been taught that she would be lucky to get off the planet alive. To come there alone was probably foolish, but she needed to test herself.

The first assailant burst out of the woods, which were shrouded in heavy fog. He was so large his armored body brushed the tree branches as he plowed through the forest, giving B'Elanna time to react and prepare for his attack. Without that slight warning, she knew, he would probably have overpowered her before she could turn to face him.

The moves that would save her took shape, not as conscious thoughts, but as instinctual reactions: crouch low, ready to spring . . . anticipate his first blow . . . use his bulk against him . . .

His head was huge and grotesque, plated like his body but misshapen and distorted so that it lacked any symmetry. Tufts of a furlike substance erupted in patches among the plates, and his eyes gleamed like laser points. He was emitting an earsplitting bellow from an orifice that was dripping a foul-smelling gelatinous substance.

Just the type to take home to meet Mother, B'Elanna thought as he lunged, and before she could wonder where *that* thought had come from, he was on her.

His first blow was predictable, a slashing-downward chop from his right arm. B'Elanna grabbed it as it descended toward her head and used his own momentum to take him down, flipping him onto his back and then kicking him solidly in the throat. He clutched at it, gasping for air through the crushed windpipe. He would fight no more.

This time, there was no telltale sound to warn her of the attack. The second assailant was behind her before she could register his approach, and she took a staggering blow to her left shoulder. Pain rippled down through her arm and hand, little shock waves of anguish that made it all but impossible for her to focus on what she had to do.

The blow had driven her to her knees, and she continued the motion, rolling in a tight ball away from the armored attacker, trying to collect her wits. She tried to push upright with her left arm, but found it was, for all intents, useless; it was nothing more than a thousand tiny fire points, and failed to respond to any command she gave it.

She saw the sweeping kick coming at her head and barely threw up her right arm in time, intercepting the kick and finding purchase with her hand on one of the armored plates. It was surprisingly spongy in texture. Using her legs to drive upward, she toppled the monstrous assailant, who fell to the ground like a giant tree, smashing his face against rocky shale.

B'Elanna massaged her left arm, hoping they were done with her, but doubting it could be that easy, and was proven right when two of the aliens—even larger than the first two—crashed from the woods at opposite ends, galloping toward her, bellowing like Tovian bulls.

She made a quick decision and turned toward one of them, running directly at him, head down. Her small size was actually an advantage with a creature so tall, as he had to bend down to get at her, throwing himself slightly off balance.

He was also somewhat perplexed that she was coming at him, and hesitated slightly as she neared. Then he roared again, and bent down to strike at her small, compact form, just as she dived at his knees. He went sailing over her head and landed directly in the path of the other, who stumbled over the crashing form.

These guys are big, she thought, but not too bright, as she rotated into a flying kick.

And felt her leg almost torn from its socket.

She screamed involuntarily and fell heavily to the floor, muscles and ligaments straining against the force being applied to them by yet another assailant. Without even knowing what she was doing, she rotated with the force, turning her body in the same direction in order to take the pressure off her hip socket. Then she was free of his grip and the pain in her leg triggered an overwhelming response: rage. Fury pulsed through her like a wildfire, igniting everything in its path, turning her into a woman possessed, ferocious and inexorable.

Her hand clutched at the ground beneath her, grabbing for the shale, breaking off a shard of it and then swinging it upward, right at the distended head of the creature, right toward the orb that seemed to be its eye, driving the rocky stake deep into the mass of pulp, plunging it the full length of the shale until her fingers touched the eye.

Then she pulled it out and whirled toward the others, who lay in a tangled heap on the ground, and drove the spike into the eye of the first one she reached, listening with satisfaction at the bellows of pain she was causing. Something feral was loose in her now, a heat to the blood that burned away restraint and urged her to slake her blood-thirst.

"Computer, delete program," said the disembodied voice behind her, and everything disappeared—the woods, the rocky ground, the assailants, and the shale spike that had become her weapon.

Gasping for breath, she whirled, crouched, ready to take on this new presence, to destroy it as thoroughly as she had destroyed the marauding aliens.

Standing in the empty holodeck was a Starfleet officer, Commander Stern. He wore the red uniform of command, which did not become his florid complexion. He was balding, with only a fringe of brown-gray hair around the sides and back. He spoke quietly, but his voice was steel. "That's enough, Cadet."

B'Elanna stared at him, trying to reconcile the officer's presence there, swimming up from a consuming fire, forcing her mind to reintegrate what felt like disparate elements: This is a holodeck, that is an officer, I am Cadet B'Elanna Torres.

I'm in trouble.

"This is an unauthorized use of the holodeck, Cadet," said Stern. "What's going on?"

B'Elanna took a deep breath, tried to get her racing heart and her breathing under control. But her voice came out ragged and gasping. "Sir, I'm just putting in my self-defense exercise time. Five hours a week, required."

Stern's gaze, from pale blue eyes, was cool. "Sensors indicated a holodeck program being run without the safeties in place. That's strictly forbidden."

She started to feign innocence, but hated the thought of lying to this fussy little bureaucrat, and instead lifted her head, looking him directly in the eye. "I know that, sir. But sometimes I like to push myself just that extra bit harder. After all, there won't be any safeties when we're on actual missions."

"The Academy has rules for a reason, Cadet. It's not your place to decide whether or not they work for you."

B'Elanna felt anger simmering in her again. Authority for authority's sake. Everything in her rebelled against these gratuitous expressions of control. Who did this icy-eyed autocrat think he was? Rules, rules, rules. That's about all she'd heard since she arrived at the Academy a year and a half ago. She took another deep breath and tried to quell these rebellious feelings. "Sorry, sir. It won't happen again."

He was still staring at her, pale eyes squinting. "You're Torres, aren't you?"

"Yes, sir."

"If I remember correctly, you're already on report for causing a melee on the hoverball court. I'll check the logs, but if I'm right, this means a four-day suspension."

"Don't bother checking. It was me." Her voice was surly, even to her ears. Stern's eyes snapped to hers.

"And that'll be another day for insubordination."

Every pore of her body cried out for her to leap on him, fingers raking his face, thumbs plunging into the sockets of his eyes until he was left writhing and sightless on the floor. But with supreme effort, she managed to hold herself still and return his gaze. "I understand, sir."

"Report to your quarters."

"Yes, sir." She exited the holodeck without looking at him again, imagining the satisfaction of squeezing his eyeballs in her fists until they ran like jelly.

When she entered her room, she felt the dark gaze of her roommate, a compact young woman named Mary Ellen Regan, known as Mellie. She was, in B'Elanna's mind, the most perfect person she'd ever met. Strikingly lovely, she was also intimidatingly intelligent and talented in any number of fields: she sang, she played the flute, she was a graceful gymnast. She made B'Elanna feel unworthy and even unclean.

"You've gotten another transmission from Mexico," said Mellie. "It's logged on to your console. I thought you'd want to know."

"Thank you." B'Elanna, still smarting from what she considered Commander Stern's unprovoked punishment, marched to her bed and flopped down on it, arms under her head, gazing up at the ceiling. Mellie regarded her carefully.

"A bunch of us are going to take a picnic dinner to the park. Would you like to come?"

"I'm on suspension. Confined to quarters."

"B'Elanna, I'm sorry. What happened?" Mellie's concern was genuine, but B'Elanna didn't feel like recapping the incident in the holodeck.

"Let's just say I messed up again."

"Is there anything I can do to help?"

"I really just want to be alone. Don't worry about me—I'll be fine."

Five minutes later, Mellie had departed, and B'Elanna heard the laughing calls of a group of her peers as they left the quad and moved off into a balmy evening, enjoying the camaraderie and ebullience of youth. B'Elanna felt as though she were a hundred years old, trapped in her room, isolated and bereft.

Her eyes flickered toward her console. She knew very well who was transmitting from Mexico, and the knowledge hung over her like a pall. She stared at the darkened monitor, knowing all she had to do was press a few controls and she could access the series of messages.

She lay like that for almost forty minutes, then rolled off the bed and moved toward the console and, with studied casualness—though for whom she was feigning indifference she wasn't sure—she activated her comm system to play the messages she had been saving.

The man whose image appeared on the screen was in his late forties, hair dark and wavy, flashing eyes almost black, smile broad and warm. He was, in B'Elanna's eyes, almost unbearably handsome, and she felt a wave of something foreign and ineffable rise in her. It wasn't pleasant, turning her hands clammy and her stomach queasy. She drew several deep gulps of air.

"B'Elanna," the man said, "I've been in deep space for over a year and I just learned you were at Starfleet Academy. I'm so proud of you . . . I'd love to visit you. Please let me know if that's all right."

That was message number one, which had come in months before. Each succeeding transmission—and there were seven in all—was increasingly urgent. She had replayed each one over and over, night after night, without responding. Tentatively, she tapped the control that would play the latest one.

"B'Elanna, it's possible you're out in the field, or sick, or on leave. But I'm reasonably sure those things aren't true and that you've chosen not to answer me. I'm sorry for that . . . it hurts me . . . but I can understand it. I wish we could talk, so I could explain some things to you. I didn't leave you and your mother because I didn't care about you, I swear to you. Now that you're grown, maybe I could put things in a context that would make what I did understandable. Maybe even forgivable."

There was a pause as the intense black eyes stared at her. "I love you, B'Elanna. I've missed you every day of my life. I'd do anything if we could find each other again. Please—don't shut me out."

The screen went dark and B'Elanna deactivated the console. Her chest felt constricted, as though pressed by stones. Her stomach twisted like a loose eel, forcing gorge into her throat. Her fingers hovered over the controls that would allow her to reply to these messages, and she told herself that when she'd counted to ten, she would do it. She counted to ten seven times before she admitted she wasn't going to be able to summon the courage.

She made her way on trembling legs to her bed, and fell on it in a dead weight. The room began to spin dizzyingly, and she closed her eyes, trying to draw air into her lungs. She felt fevered, ill. She turned on her stomach and pulled the pillow over her head, trying to insulate herself from this onslaught of feelings, and presently she fell into an unquiet sleep.

She waked a few hours later. A cool breeze was pouring through the window as the ubiquitous San Francisco fog gathered for the night. She felt calm once more, her head clear and focused. She realized she had made a decision in her sleep, and it had cleansed her of the anguish she was experiencing.

She was leaving the Academy. She was going somewhere far away, many sectors from here, maybe into another quadrant. Any place where she could be sure her father couldn't find her.

"More power! More power! What are you doing down there? I need more power!"

B'Elanna sighed and brushed her hair out of her eyes, leaving a dark smudge on the ridges of her forehead. It was impossibly hot in the engine room, and sweat stung her eyes and dampened her shirt. "I'm doing the best I can, Mesler. It won't help to yell at me."

The Bolian's voice on the comm was shrill and tinny. "I'm on a strict deadline! This cargo has to be at its destination by seventeen hundred hours! We'll never make it!"

He was giving her a headache. "If you'd maintained these engines the way you should've, we wouldn't be in this mess. I can't work miracles."

"Klingon fool! You claimed you were an engineer! I've been duped!"

Irritation gave way to anger. B'Elanna swung out of the engine room of the Bolian freighter and climbed four ladders to the cramped, utilitarian bridge. That's about all the ship consisted of: bridge, engine room, and four decks of cargo space. She and Mesler, the pilot, were the only crew, which suited B'Elanna just fine. It was all she could do to deal with Mesler; if she could've found a situation where she was the only crew member and could devote herself solely to the ship's systems, it would've been even better.

Now, she burst into the bridge and was gratified to see the rotund, blue-faced Bolian jump in alarm at her unexpected entrance. His eyes widened with apprehension as she stood before him, fist raised.

"If you ever . . . and I mean *ever* . . . call me a Klingon fool again, do you know what I'm going to do to you?"

Mesler's face took on a green tinge as he stared up at her. "Don't get yourself upset, Torres . . ." he began, but she barreled on.

"Feel this?" she asked as she put one hand around the back of his neck and applied pressure to the sides of his neck with her fingers. "It's a pressure point—see how it makes your mouth pop open? I could reach in right now, twist your fat tongue out of your throat, and eat it. And that's just what I'll do if you ever denigrate my heritage again."

"All right, all right," he croaked, squirming under her grip. "Just do whatever you have to to get those warp engines at peak efficiency. We can't afford to lose any more time."

B'Elanna dropped her grip and turned on her heel. "You'll get them when you get them," she growled, and made her descent once more to the engine room. The problem was in the freighter's aging warp propulsion system, and she'd had to be endlessly creative in order to keep the ship running. Now she wasn't sure how she was going to remodulate the plasma injectors in order to restore warp speed, but a little bubble of an idea was forming in her brain. She stared at the injectors as the bubble swelled, and then it was full enough for her to grasp and roll around her mind, testing it for weaknesses.

The injector open-close cycle was variable, from twenty-five ns to fifty ns. Each firing of an injector exposed its corresponding warp coil to a burst of energy to be converted into the warp field. At warp factors one through four, the injectors fired at low frequencies, between thirty Hz and forty Hz, and remained open for only short periods. If she didn't try to restore the full range of their cycle, and required only low firing frequencies, the ship could achieve warp speed if Mesler didn't try to push it faster than warp four. It would have to do.

She was ready to make the final modulation on the injectors when a muffled shriek over the comm system made her snap her head up, and then suddenly a rush of air disturbed the warm closeness of the engine room and a man materialized in front of her.

A Cardassian, to be specific, weapon drawn and pointed right at her. The cords of his elongated neck stood out, rough and fibrous. The bony cartilage that gave his face the appearance of a topographical map was distended and shiny—a sign, she knew, of aggressive posture.

She backed away from him slightly, arms in front of her, showing no hostility. She was about to ask him what he was doing there, but he spoke first.

"Your cargo, Klingon. Where is it?"

B'Elanna bit her tongue. She hated it when people addressed her simply as "Klingon," and hadn't tolerated the appellation from the pudgy Bolian pilot. But this Cardassian warrior was another matter. He was dangerous.

"We have four decks of cargo. It isn't that difficult to find."

His dark eyes flashed slightly at her impudent tone, and she felt him assessing her with barely disguised disdain. "Be careful, Klingon. Your people may be brave warriors, but you are a lone woman and unarmed. It would be more sensible to cooperate than to antagonize."

B'Elanna tossed her hair out of her eyes and glared at him. "What gives you the right to demand cooperation? You've boarded our ship illegally. We're in Federation space and you have no authority here. I'm going to register a complaint with the Federation Council."

His eyes narrowed and the start of a patronizing smile curled at his lips. "You're a plucky one," he murmured. "I've always enjoyed strong-minded women. But you are no navigator. This ship is in the demilitarized zone which buffers Federation and Cardassian space."

Torres stared at him. She was sure he was wrong, but unless that could be proven, they were in trouble. Starfleet offered no protection to the denizens of the demilitarized zone. Cardassians, knowing that, routinely took advantage of the situation to harass the tenacious colonists who had refused to leave their homes. She and Mesler could hope for no reinforcements from Starfleet, and were essentially at the mercy of this pompous Cardassian soldier.

Nonetheless, it seemed wrong to show weakness. She kept her eyes locked on his and lifted her chin. "I'm afraid you're wrong. I can prove to you that we're still in Federation space and that you are the trespasser." She took one step toward her console and felt a hand clasp her arm firmly and swing her back around. Suddenly she was drawn closely to the Cardassian and could smell a musky odor coming from him.

"You don't move unless I tell you to move," he said, extremely softly, and that quiet tone was somehow more menacing than a snarl. She stiffened, forcing herself to look at him once more.

"Let go of me," she said, just as softly, but hoping the timbre of her voice was as threatening as his. But he didn't move, keeping his tight grip on her upper arm.

"I don't think so," he said, and in his tone she heard complete authority and confidence. The voice of a man who was used to getting what he wanted. "I enjoy the feel of you. You're wonderfully . . . firm."

In spite of the heat of the engine room, B'Elanna felt a chill. What did this man want? Were there others? What was going to happen to her?

She endured the touch of his hand as he squeezed her arm lazily, staring at her with the proud look of possession. She felt herself become faintly nauseated; she wanted to shrink from him and curl up into a ball, shutting him out. But she willed herself to stand proudly, unyielding.

He smiled indolently, continuing to rub her arm, never relaxing his firm hold on it. "First I want to see your cargo. You may lead the way." And he released her. He had become languid, fluid. Clearly he had more on his mind than cargo. Her mind began to race, trying to plan a strategy.

"The cargo decks are this way. Should I lead you?"

"Please." He still had the weapon, and raised it slightly to remind her of his dominance. She turned her back on him and moved toward the ladders. She climbed upward, uneasily aware that he was right behind her, and she imagined his gaze on her.

As soon as she could, she swung from the ladder and onto the lowest cargo deck. Crates were stacked in neat rows—credit the Bolians with tidiness, anyway—which filled the shadowy confines of the space. One solitary light source in the rear of the room provided the only illumination. They could have had ten times the light for the same energy output, but Mesler for some reason claimed that one light was enough and that frugality was a virtue to be championed.

"Open one of the crates," ordered the Cardassian as soon as he had joined her on the deck.

"You'll have to speak to the pilot," she retorted. "This is his ship, his cargo. You'll need his permission before you touch anything."

The Cardassian's easygoing smile played again on his mouth. "Your pilot lies in a pool of his own blood," he informed her quietly. "I suspect he's being skinned. Bolian skin is considered a rare treasure on our homeworld. Our women particularly enjoy its suppleness."

B'Elanna's stomach turned to ice. She tried not to register the shock she was feeling, but knew she couldn't fully hide it. She drew several full gulps of air, trying to counteract the light-headedness that had overtaken her. She looked back at her captor and saw that he was smiling easily, assessing her.

"Shocked? Disgusted? I thought Klingons were made of hardier stock."

"I am only half Klingon. I am also human. And, yes, I am reviled at what you're saying. It's barbaric. Savage."

"It was my understanding the people of the Federation are too open-minded to make judgments on the cultural predilections of other species. It would seem that you are a poor representative of both your genetic strains."

Nausea was threatening to overcome B'Elanna, and she drew in more ragged gasps of air. It was as close and warm on the cargo deck as it had been in the engine room, and she felt the room begin to spin. "Sick . . ." she gasped, and sank to her knees, lowering her head to bring blood to it. She felt the Cardassian kneel beside her, felt the caress of his hand on her back. She looked up at him.

"Thank you," she murmured. "If I could just sit here a minute . . ."

"It's quite all right, my dear," he said softly. "Gather your senses. In the meantime, I'll inspect your cargo." She nodded, still not looking up, trying not to think of poor Mesler, who was an annoying little man but essentially a decent one, and who did not deserve to die violently on the bridge of his hard-won vessel. Gradually, her head began to stop swimming and her stomach stopped roiling. She looked up.

The Cardassian stood over her, Starfleet weapons in his hands. It was such an unexpected sight that for a moment she didn't realize the implications. Then, she gasped.

"I suppose you're going to say you didn't know this ship carried weapons," he intoned.

"Of course I didn't. Mesler said we were taking humanitarian supplies to the colonists in the demilitarized zone."

"I suppose one might classify phaser rifles and photon torpedoes as 'humanitarian,'" he said. "Depending on one's political stance."

"I have no political stance. And I didn't know anything about those weapons."

To her dismay, he approached her, knelt down beside her, and stroked her cheek with his corded hand. "Proud little Klingon," he breathed. "Don't be afraid . . . I am Gul Tancret, and I will put you under my protection."

B'Elanna lifted her eyes to his. She felt clearheaded now, focused. She knew exactly what she had to do. "My name is B'Elanna," she breathed. "You're very gracious, Gul Tancret, and I appreciate your kindness. I'm alone now . . ."

His hand dropped to her neck, her shoulder, her back, stroking and caressing. She was aware that his breathing was deepening. She picked up his other hand in hers and began sniffing it, the instinctual Klingon prelude to mating. The gesture seemed to arouse him, and she heard a low moan escape his lips. She nipped gently at his hand with her small white teeth—thank goodness she hadn't inherited her mother's Klingon teeth—and heard him moan again.

Her legs tensed under her as she readied herself. She drew one long breath of air (knowing it would be interpreted as passion), and then suddenly drove upward like a shuttle being launched. Gul Tancret's head snapped back and he tumbled off balance, sprawling in an ungainly heap on the deck. Caught completely off guard, he struggled to regain himself, but by then B'Elanna was on her feet and swinging a flying kick at his temple.

She felt her boot make contact, felt the bone in his forehead collapse, saw Tancret crumple. Then saw him shake himself, swing his head toward her, and focus on her with black eyes flaring. He erupted toward her, arm cracking her calf with such impact that she cried out. Her leg went numb and she stumbled backward, trying to regain her footing and ready herself for his next attack. But she had no purchase on the decking; his second blow caught her on the jaw, and she went reeling, pain streaking along the whole left side of her face.

She scrambled on the floor, seeking refuge behind the weapons crates. She looked desperately for the open one, on the chance she could snatch a phaser, but she was nowhere near it, and to open another would give him time to strike again.

She shoved at a stack of crates and, to her delight, they toppled, blocking his path for a moment. She scurried through the maze of cargo, glad now for Mesler's frugality and the darkness of the room. She heard Tancret plowing through the toppled crates and worked her way farther into the gloom.

Suddenly, there was a muffled rumble, and the entire deck trembled. A sound of voices in the distance, excited calls of alarm. There was another rumble, and several stacks of the cargo crates collapsed. B'Elanna now realized she was in danger of being buried if she stayed where she was. Carefully, she began to move toward the open center of the room once more.

Then the voices were closer, shouting, tumultuous, and she heard the distinctive sound of phaser fire. Quickly she worked the closure on one of the crates and pulled out a rifle, feeling complete for the first time since she'd encountered the Cardassian.

Cautiously, she edged her way forward, listening carefully. She heard the voices of humans, crisp and urgent. Then there was another of the violent shudders, the room shook, and she felt the stack of crates just next to her begin to lose stability.

She dived into the center of the room, weapon skittering across the floor, just in time to escape being crushed by the collapsing cargo containers. She rolled to her feet, arms in front of her, ready for battle.

A human male stood in front of her, a look of astonishment on his face. He was darkly handsome, and wore a strange marking on his temple. Gul Tancret and two other Cardassians were sprawled on the deck, unconscious or dead. "Who are you?" the human barked.

"Engineer . . ." B'Elanna began, but winced with the effort to speak. She realized her jaw had been broken, and her hand involuntarily moved to it, pressing gingerly.

"Is the propulsion system on line?" She nodded. "Come with me," he ordered, and began to descend into the engine room. She followed him unquestioningly, knowing somehow he was a friend.

Two hours later, her ship was in orbit of Riva, a planet in the demilitarized zone, along with its valuable cargo, which was immediately unloaded onto the surface.

She was in a small compartment on board the Maquis ship *Liberty,* being tended by a Bajoran woman whose hands were strong and gentle, and who wielded the osteogenic stimulator with deft skill. "That was quite a blow you took," the woman observed. "It's a wonder you didn't lose consciousness." She paused briefly, then added, "Most would have."

B'Elanna started to reply, but the pain in her jaw was still too severe. "Shhh," whispered the Bajoran. "Don't try to talk yet. It'll be a little longer before the bone is regenerated."

A few moments passed, with the affable hum of the stimulator the only sound. Finally, the woman spoke again. "I'm Seska. The captain of our ship is Chakotay. He's the one who found you." Seska smiled to herself, and B'Elanna immediately sensed a change in this woman when she mentioned Chakotay. She was softer somehow, more vulnerable.

"You're lucky it was our ship that found you. It took incredible courage to engage that Cardassian ship, but Chakotay is the most fearless captain a ship could have. He didn't hesitate."

"The load of weapons we were carrying might have been an inducement," replied B'Elanna, noting that she could speak without pain now.

Seska frowned slightly. "We could've taken the cargo and left you to the Cardassians," she retorted, "but Chakotay doesn't behave like that."

"Believe me, I'm grateful," B'Elanna replied. She didn't want to antagonize these people. She was only too aware that she was alone and friendless in this part of space, and couldn't afford to alienate her rescuers.

Before Seska could reply, the door to the compartment opened and Chakotay walked in. "How's the patient?" he inquired, and B'Elanna noted the imperturbability in his voice. This man was unflappable, she realized, but at the same time she had the distinct impression he could be as stern and rigorous as necessary.

Seska smiled at him, and B'Elanna once again sensed a change in her, a responsiveness that somehow suggested intimacy. "Healing nicely," she said. "She's a strong one."

B'Elanna felt Chakotay's dark eyes inspect her. "We're grateful to you for bringing the weapons through. I'm sorry Mesler had to die. He was a good friend."

"I didn't know anything about the weapons," replied B'Elanna. "I thought it was humanitarian supplies. I was just the engineer on that ship."

Chakotay smiled slightly. "Mesler was trying to protect you," he suggested. "Though I doubt the Cardassians would've believed you."

A flashing memory of Gul Tancret lanced her mind, and she

couldn't suppress a slight shudder. "I want to thank you. For saving me. I can only imagine what would've happened to me."

He put out a gentle hand and held her shoulder. B'Elanna was vaguely aware that Seska was watching this gesture intently. "Our friends on the surface have asked us all to join them tonight. To celebrate this supply of weapons. Will you join us?"

B'Elanna nodded, not wanting to look at Seska to see what the Bajoran thought of this invitation. Chakotay's hand rested on her shoulder for only an instant more, and then he was gone, leaving the room somehow charged with the strength and power of his presence. B'Elanna glanced at Seska, and saw her looking after him, longing emanating from her like mist rising from the floor of a deserted forest.

That night they gathered in the camp of the Maquis sympathizers on the surface of Riva. It was a summer's evening in the planet's tropical hemisphere, and the breezes carried the wild fragrance of pungent blossoms. The dwellers on Riva had set up tables in a woodland clearing near a rocky stream, which cooled the air and lent a pleasant murmuring music to the evening.

There were perhaps thirty inhabitants of Riva and twenty-five crew from Chakotay's ship, who mingled easily. The tables were laden with food: a thick stew that B'Elanna was pleased to note was laced with chunks of a flavorful meat, for she often craved real meat, but could rarely find it; huge slabs of freshly baked bread; bowls of ripe fruit; and a dry, spiced ale that complemented the stew wonderfully, and brought a pleasant inner warmth that dispelled her uneasiness.

Chakotay had stayed by her side all evening, introducing her, praising her courage against the Cardassian Gul, giving her credit for bringing the much-needed supplies to their group. She felt the object of adulation, and though at first it made her uncomfortable, she gradually began to enjoy the feeling.

But she was always aware of Seska's presence, hovering near Chakotay, on the periphery but near enough that if he had sought her, she would be there.

He didn't seek her.

His attentions were focused on B'Elanna, patiently explaining the purpose and the activities of the Maquis. His passion for this cause—the protection of the rights of the abandoned colonists in the demilitarized zone—was profound. B'Elanna found herself stirred by his commitment and curious as to its origins.

"Why are you so devoted to this cause?" she asked him. "You're risking your life for these people. There must be a reason."

Chakotay looked away from her and she saw his face cloud slightly, and he seemed to wrap himself in some invisible, protective coating. She felt an almost physical barrier between them, and it was unnerving.

Finally he looked back at her. "It's a long story. I'll tell you someday."

She wasn't about to press him further. The sound of a stringed instrument began to drift on the summer breeze, and B'Elanna looked to see where it was coming from.

Seska was holding the alien instrument, a round, bowl-like apparatus with at least ten or twelve strings, strumming it with quiet skill. Then she began to sing, her proud, compelling voice ringing through the night, the song one of both strength and lamentation. B'Elanna leaned back against a tree and gave herself up to the sensations: the nurturing warmth of the summer night, the wild fragrance of alien blooms, the full stomach and the ale-induced lull, and the sound of Seska's voice, clear and transcendent, wafting on the scented breezes, singing of the loss of dead comrades and the solidarity of brotherhood.

An ineffable emotion began to suffuse B'Elanna. It was vague and unfamiliar, and she couldn't identify it, couldn't even tell if it were similar to anything she'd ever felt before. She had a sudden, vivid memory of sitting in her father's lap as a child, safe and protected, listening to her mother tell a story of a legendary Klingon hero. What was his name? She couldn't remember any longer. But in that moment, secure in her father's arms, hearing her mother's mythic tale of courage and honor, she had felt as she did at this moment.

She glanced toward Chakotay, who was listening solemnly to Seska's haunting song, his face betraying no emotion. She leaned toward him and whispered, "Chakotay, could your ship use a highly qualified engineer?"

When he turned to her and smiled, her heart hammered in her chest, and she suddenly identified the unfamiliar emotion she was experiencing.

It was happiness.

In the dreams, he came to her at night, taking her sometimes tenderly, sometimes in a feral hunger, but always because he loved her. He whispered of his passion, his adoration of her, his determination that they be together always. She would never again be lonely, or sad, or afraid, because he would be with her. He would never abandon her.

She would wake aroused and unsatisfied, but, for a few moments, enveloped in a drowsy cocoon of well-being. He loved her. He would stay with her.

And then the vaporous mists of sleep and dream would evaporate, and she remembered where she was. She lay on a hard cot in cramped crew quarters on board the *Liberty,* captained by the man of whom she dreamed. The man was a friend, who respected and trusted her, and who valued her abilities as an engineer.

But not the man who loved her.

Soon after she joined the Maquis, Seska caught her look toward Chakotay, and correctly interpreted it. She had waited until she and B'Elanna were working, alone, on a damaged shuttle they'd "salvaged" from a Federation ships' graveyard.

As they struggled to repair the vessel's driver coil assembly, Seska spoke casually. "How do you like it so far? Serving with the Maquis?"

B'Elanna was instantly wary. She didn't dislike Seska, and she respected her abilities, but there was something in her voice as she asked the question that aroused suspicion. It was too offhand, more casual than the question warranted. B'Elanna shrugged. "It'll do," she replied.

Seska seemed hurt. "We're starting to have a real impact. Cardassia has registered a formal complaint with the Federation about us. People can't ignore us any longer—we're a force in the demilitarized zone that has to be taken into account."

"Then I guess we're doing our job."

Seska looked at her with accusation in her eyes. "You don't really care, do you? To you, this is just a job, a way to pass your time. It's not a cause like it is for the rest of us."

"I've never been one for causes." She was beginning to get annoyed. What was Seska up to? Why was she challenging her like this?

"If Chakotay knew that, he might have second thoughts about your being aboard."

B'Elanna's head whipped toward her. Suddenly she understood perfectly. Time to pick up the gauntlet. She faced Seska squarely. "Are you in love with him?"

The bluntness of the question caught Seska off guard. There was a brief startled flicker of the eyes, and a glance away as she gathered herself. But she was off balance for only that second. She turned back and fixed B'Elanna with a smug gaze. "He's in love with me," she stated decisively, and waited for B'Elanna's response.

Torres eyed her with what she hoped was impassivity. "I'm surprised," she said. "I've seen the way you look at him, but I've never seen him return that look. In fact, I've never seen him treat you as anything more than a valued crew member."

"We've been having an affair for more than a year. But we know it's best to keep that a secret. It might create tension among the crew."

"He's a very good actor. Better than you."

A bright flush appeared on Seska's cheeks and her eyes glittered in a way that made B'Elanna unaccountably afraid. There's a lot going on inside this woman, she thought, and decided to stay alert in her dealings with the Bajoran.

"Chakotay's able to hide his feelings well. That's just the way he is. But . . . Bajorans are very passionate people." She paused to let that assessment sink in, then continued. "It's harder for us to hold in our emotions."

"Seska . . . why are you telling me all this?"

Seska busied herself with one of the six toroids of the driver coil assembly. "It seemed only fair to let you know the situation. In case there were any doubts."

A droplet of anger was beginning to boil in B'Elanna, but she willed herself not to reveal it. That's what Seska wanted, and to give her that satisfaction would be intolerable. She maintained a studied coolness. "Frankly, I've never thought about it one way or the other. What you and Chakotay do in your spare time isn't of any interest to me. I can't imagine that you thought it might be."

She felt Seska's eyes on her, but didn't look back. "Have you aligned the toroids?" B'Elanna asked casually. "We're never going to get this shuttle operational if we don't stop talking."

And the rest of the afternoon passed in silence.

Six months later, Chakotay returned from a hurried and secret visit to Earth with a sullen young human in tow. His sandy blond hair was wayward and his blue-gray eyes frankly assessed every woman he saw.

B'Elanna disliked him on sight.

Chakotay had recruited him to replace Setonak, their Vulcan pilot, who had been injured during a fracas with the Cardassians and who was recuperating in a medical facility on Vulcan. B'Elanna missed

Setonak, whose stoic restraint was calming to her. She wondered if she could ever learn to control her emotions in the way that Vulcans had. She'd often thought of talking to Setonak about his mental discipline, but that very discipline made him impervious to approach.

And now, in his place, was this arrogant whelp, this Tom Paris. What could Chakotay have been thinking?

They clashed right from the first. She resented his appraising look at her, as though she were an ornament whose value he was deciding. She disliked the seductive timbre of his voice, which seemed to imply that they were in a bedroom rather than an engine room. And most of all, she hated the fact that he was trying to tell her her business.

"All I'm saying," he drawled, "is that if you'd just keep the vectored exhaust director at its narrowest setting, I could probably increase my maneuverability by about thirty percent."

"And if you knew anything about venting exhaust, you'd know that would cause a buildup that would not only start producing toxic fumes in Engineering, but might overload the reaction chamber and cause a nasty little explosion. Why don't you stick to piloting, and let me handle the engines."

He grinned at her, which nettled her further. He seemed coated in some defensive shield, deflecting any comment or criticism. It was impossible ever to know what was really going on inside him, for he presented only this surface self, carefree and impervious.

"Torres, what say we call a truce? I won't try to tell you your business, you don't try to tell me mine—and maybe we can be friends. You might like me if you get to know me."

"A truce is fine. But I'll pass on the friendship part."

He shrugged and moved away. If he was disappointed, or wounded, he didn't show it. She found herself unaccountably irritated by that trait, without realizing that it was one she wished she could develop as well.

It was because of Tom's skill as a pilot that they began to explore a region of space known as the Badlands.

It was a violent, churning, dangerous region, full of plasma storms that could destroy a ship in an instant. Many of the crew disliked entering it, even though it provided protection from both Cardassian and Starfleet vessels, both of which were loath to follow.

But B'Elanna found that she derived a secret thrill from the Badlands. She loved the roiling, dramatic clouds, the tendrils of trailing plasma that threatened to destroy them. She liked to watch

Tom Paris maneuver his way through the storms, brow knit in concentration, skillfully guiding their ship away from danger. He was a good pilot, that she had to admit.

And she suspected that he enjoyed this challenge as much as she did. The whole experience triggered a rush of adrenaline in her—a condition that had always been like a narcotic for B'Elanna. Danger heightened her senses, elevated her mood, gave her a sense of excitement that had always been pleasurable. She sensed the same in Tom.

One day they were mapping the area for future use. B'Elanna, Tom, and Chakotay were on the small bridge, along with Yuri Terikof, their navigator. Yuri was a wiry, dark-ringleted man with small bright eyes and a prominent nose which combined to give him a strangely avian look. He was also completely fearless, and an inspiration to them all in situations of battle. The ship was being battered by the intense storms, and B'Elanna suspected Chakotay was on the verge of giving the order to retreat from the Badlands.

Suddenly, unexpectedly, they were sailing as smoothly as a child's boat on a tranquil pond.

She and Chakotay exchanged surprised looks. "Are you an even better pilot than I thought, or did we just leave the Badlands?" Chakotay asked Tom.

"We're still inside," replied Tom, "but we've come into an area where there aren't any storms."

"I can get clear sensor readings now," added B'Elanna. "It's an area approximately eight hundred million kilometers across— completely free of storms."

"Like the eye of a hurricane," muttered Chakotay, intently scanning his own console. But it was Yuri who spotted the most interesting aspect of their discovery. "What's this? A belt of planetoids? Captain, this isn't on any Federation map."

"Then it looks like you've made the find, Yuri." Chakotay grinned. "How does 'the Terikof Belt' sound to you?"

Yuri's bright eyes sparkled even more as he smiled with childlike pleasure. "It sounds great," he admitted. "But I don't think a Maquis discovery is ever going to be entered into Federation cartographical charts."

"You never know," B'Elanna replied. "I think you should send a subspace message and register it." She smiled to herself to think of the consternation this bold gesture might cause the stuffy Federation officials, who might balk at naming a ring of planetoids after a

Maquis renegade, but who would feel ethically obligated to acknowledge that he found it first.

"Hold that thought," interjected Chakotay, still scanning his console. "A couple of those planetoids look like they might be M-class."

This posed interesting possibilities. If they could form a base camp here, in the middle of the Badlands, it would be far more secure than anything they could ever find in Federation space.

"Shall we check it out?" asked Tom. Chakotay nodded tersely in reply. B'Elanna had noticed lately that there seemed to be tension between the captain and the pilot, though she hadn't witnessed any specific incident that might have caused it. Tom was irritating enough to cause tension with anyone, B'Elanna thought, and assumed that Chakotay had simply become frustrated with Tom's cheeky attitude.

Presently they were in orbit of one of the M-class planetoids, scanning for the salient characteristics. "Breathable oxygen-rich atmosphere," intoned Yuri, "photosynthetic flora is abundant, and sensors indicate substantial bodies of potable water. Sounds like home."

That last remark produced no response from the people on the bridge, but B'Elanna assumed they all had a similar response: these were people who had no real home, not anymore, not after they decided to thumb their noses at the Federation's peace treaty and try for a different kind of justice. So that paltry little planetoid in the Badlands would do as well as any.

Chakotay was clearly thinking the same thing. "Let's take an away team. Tom, B'Elanna, Yuri, you're all with me. And I want Seska to come, too."

And within minutes they were standing in a meadow on one of the loveliest worlds B'Elanna had ever seen. Great forests stretched for kilometers, rich and verdant, rolling into foothills and then mountains which were snow-tipped. Sweet grasses blew on the meadow, producing a heady fragrance that reminded B'Elanna of the jasmine fields on Nessik. The sky was an azure blue, startlingly deep, and an occasional pink-tinged cloud drifted by.

They were silent for a few moments after materializing, taking in the surprising beauty of the place, each indulging in private thoughts that conjured up memories of earlier times, childhood times when the world was not so complicated and the sight of a fulsomely blooming woodland was enough to gladden the heart.

Such thoughts made B'Elanna feel vulnerable, and it wasn't a pleasant feeling. She turned to the rest of the group, and her voice, when she spoke, was harsher than she'd intended. "Well, what do we think? It's pretty, but can it be of any use to us?"

The others reacted as though they'd been jolted out of a reverie. She saw Seska, in particular, flash her an irritated glance. Chakotay turned in a circle, absorbing the grandeur of the meadow and the forests. "I think it can," he breathed. "If we put up a few structures, we could have a base camp that's absolutely safe from Starfleet. We could get out of the ship from time to time . . . stretch our legs . . . breathe some fresh air."

There was a tone to his voice that B'Elanna caught, something that spoke to his appreciation for the outdoors, and she regretted her sharp words earlier. Who was she to spoil their enthusiasm for this halcyon planetoid?

"It wouldn't take long to put up a few buildings," she offered. "There's plenty of wood here, which we could mill with phasers. I'd volunteer to be part of a construction crew."

She noticed Tom Paris looking bemusedly at her, but she studiously avoided his eye. If he thought there was something quaint about her being able to build a dwelling, let him.

"I think that's a hell of an idea," said Chakotay, with noticeable enthusiasm. "You're all volunteers. You can get started right away."

"I think I'm needed on the ship," protested Seska. B'Elanna knew right away that was a mistake on her part; Chakotay wouldn't appreciate having his order challenged in front of others. And, indeed, he turned to her, tight-lipped, clearly displeased. "I'll make those decisions, if you don't mind," he said with his quiet firmness, and it was all B'Elanna could do to suppress a smile.

The morning was uncomfortably hot by eight hundred hours; two hours after that it was almost unbearable. They were all perspiring profusely and had stripped down to minimal clothing. Only the nearby stream, which cascaded from a mountain lake high above them, and into which they plunged several times an hour, made the situation tolerable.

After Chakotay refused to let her accompany the ship to Bajor, where they would resupply, Seska had retreated into a sullen pique, which was fine with B'Elanna. She was finding it increasingly difficult to make conversation with this woman, who was so clearly threatened by her presence.

Yuri, on the other hand, was as unflaggingly cheerful as always, chatting easily, making jokes about "his" belt of planetoids, and generally making the situation as pleasant as he could.

That left Tom Paris for her to cope with.

Tom disturbed her in a way she couldn't quite comprehend. He always made her feel vaguely like a piece of livestock on display, and she certainly resented his appraising looks. But she'd been looked at like that by men for much of her life. There was something else in Tom that grated on her, but she couldn't figure out just what it was.

Now they were working side by side in the insufferable heat, building one wall of the structure while Yuri and Seska were off milling logs with phasers. The wood of the trees they were using was dense, and the logs were heavy. B'Elanna's shoulders and arms were already protesting, and they had hours of this labor to go. She wiped sweat out of her eyes with a forearm and bent her legs as they struggled to lift a two-meter log into place. They'd almost succeeded when B'Elanna lost her grip and the timber went crashing to the ground.

"VeQ ngIm!" she spat, and heard Tom chuckle. She turned and glared at him. "What's so funny?" she asked sharply.

"You—sounding like a Klingon mercenary. Just seems incongruous, somehow. You're not like any Klingon I've ever known."

"I hope not."

He looked at her quizzically. "What's that supposed to mean?"

She drew a breath. She was never comfortable talking about herself, and Tom was about the last person she would want to discuss her most private feelings with. "Let's get this log up," she countered, hoping he'd get the hint. They heaved once more and the log took its place on top of the last one. The wall was steadily growing.

"Is your father Klingon? Or your mother?" He wasn't going to drop it.

"My mother."

"Is your father Starfleet?"

"If we have to talk, could we talk about something else?"

He looked at her solemnly for a moment. "How about a dip?" he suggested. "Time to cool off again."

She took a breath and then nodded. It really was too hot to work for any length of time without taking steps to cool themselves. They stripped off their gloves and headed for the stream that ran through the woods.

"You know, we were at the Academy at the same time," Tom said casually. Her head whipped toward him.

"I didn't know you."

"I wasn't that noticeable. But everyone was aware of you. There aren't that many Klingons who attend the Academy."

Irritation nibbled at her. Did it have to be like this? Was she always going to be defined by her lineage? "My father was Starfleet," she said. "I never laid eyes on him after I was five years old, but his name did get me permission to take the entrance exams."

"Why didn't you see him after you were five?"

She sighed. He was certainly in an inquisitive mood today. Maybe she could dispatch all his questions at once. "He left us."

She felt his blue eyes on her and resisted the impulse to look back at him. "Why?" he asked.

There was that funny little constriction of her heart, the one that seemed to clench her every time that particular question arose. "I don't know," she replied honestly. She could hear the stream ahead, through the trees, and was glad this conversation would soon have a natural break.

They had reached the stream, a cold, lush current nearly ten meters across which ran swiftly on its pell-mell course toward a valley below. At this point in its descent, it leveled briefly, forming a large pool which, though still flowing, was less turbulent than its extremities. B'Elanna waded right into it, gasping slightly at the shock of the icy chill on her sun-warmed body, hoping the plunge would divert Tom from this relentless pursuit of her past.

He followed her, half-diving into the cold pool, surfacing quickly and spitting water like a blowing whale. She laughed, and the tenseness of the previous moments was dissipated. He playfully shoved a spray of water toward her and, enjoying the childlike abandon, she splashed him back. They continued in that way, laughing and choking, forgetting the stifling heat of the clearing as they frolicked like bear cubs.

Then she submerged. She was a strong swimmer, and knew she could catch him unawares, circling him and coming up behind him. She reached for his legs and upended him, toppling him into the water in a heap. She surfaced to enjoy the spectacle, careful to stay out of his reach. He came sputtering to the surface and immediately looked around for her. She smiled and ducked under once more. She would lead him on a chase he couldn't win.

The water was colder beneath the surface and the currents stronger, but neither was problematic. B'Elanna knew where she was headed: a series of boulders that formed a mazelike arrangement in the center, deepest part of the stream. She pulled strongly toward them, unable to see in the rushing water, but guided by memory and instinct, and soon made contact with one of the stones. She clasped it firmly and dragged herself past it and into the field of boulders.

The water was quiet within this maze, the huge stones deflecting the current. B'Elanna felt an immediate sensation of tranquillity as she moved lazily among the forest of stones. Given her lung capacity, there was no doubt in her mind that she could outlast Tom Paris.

Fluttering like a fish among the huge boulders, she smiled to think of Tom's consternation when she failed to reappear. It was not a nice trick, certainly, but he was pushy and arrogant and deserved to be shaken up a little. He'd find out she was not someone to be taken lightly.

She found a handhold on one of the stones and was surprised that it wobbled slightly. She had thought these stones were firmly embedded in the channel. But after it shifted slightly, it settled once more into its footing. B'Elanna continued to wind her way through the rocky corridors.

The collapse of the boulders happened so gently she was almost unaware of it at first. There was a sense of motion in the water—a lazy roiling that conveyed no alarm—and then movement from above made her lift her head, even though she could see nothing.

Only vague surprise came over her as she felt the pile of stones lower gently on her, like a feather-cloud of soft blankets. She was pushed softly to the silt bed of the stream and covered by a network of smooth boulders. There was nothing violent about the act, nothing that seemed brutal or dangerous. It was like a delicate caress, casual and soothing.

Except that she couldn't move.

She didn't panic. There were minutes to go before she would need to breathe again. There would be a way out from under this stony covering and she would rise to the surface to delight in Tom's astonishment.

She maneuvered her body as best she could to find a point of leverage. The stones were cradling her so softly it seemed impossible they could resist her efforts to push them off. But try as she might, with both legs and arms, she couldn't budge them.

Still, she felt no fear. There was an unreality to the situation that kept her in a state of disbelief. She expected at any moment to feel the stones yield to her and float off, as they might in a dream.

She didn't know how much time had passed before she realized they might not. She had tried everything to shift her granite shroud, but the boulders hadn't moved so much as a millimeter. Soon, she would have to breathe. If not, she would die.

But strangely, this thought didn't energize her. In fact, her mind began to wander, and she stopped straining at her rocky tomb. Images of childhood swirled in her mind, but unlike most of her recollections of her youth, these produced no anxieties. Why had she always been so angry? It seemed so unnecessary now. Her father had gone, and she lacked friends . . . but her mother was always there. Always. Her mother had taught her to be strong . . . stronger than any of the other children . . . smarter . . . why had she allowed those human children to make her feel unworthy? Why did she drive them away?

Drive them away?

The thought flickered in her mind for a moment like the wings of a desperate insect trapped in a cobweb. She had created her own isolation. Here, in this tranquil pool, soon to be her grave, the thought had the clarity of beautiful crystal. She had yielded to her Klingon temperament, and therein lay her undoing.

She could have behaved in a more human way. Her life would have been free of anguish, she would have had friends, she would have been loved. Why did insight come too late?

Vague memories of her father drifted through her mind . . . he was on the floor on hands and knees, she sitting astride him shrieking with a toddler's delight . . . he was pulling covers over her, kissing her cheek and saying good night . . . his cheek scratchy on hers . . . he was calling to her to jump . . . jump from the dock into the lake . . . he would catch her . . . he would keep her safe . . . he would protect her and love her . . .

Why had he gone away? Why wasn't she ever told?

Then she realized: She could have known. If she had answered his messages at the Academy, she would have that knowledge. He had offered to share it, wanted to explain, wanted to see her and perhaps even love her again.

But she hadn't had the courage to contact him.

And so she would die here on this forsaken planetoid never knowing the great mystery of her life, never having the opportunity to force her Klingon fierceness into submission and to become as human as she possibly could. And it would have been so easy . . .

She felt sleepy. Was this what it was like to die? This drowsy peacefulness? Why was it so feared, then, if it was this easy? Of course her mother had always taught her that the best death, the honorable death, was in battle. And that might not be as gentle as this. She'd heard tales all her life of glorious Klingon battles, and the heroes who died in horrible, if honorable, circumstances. Better this placid death, this serene acceptance of the inevitable. She could do without honor . . .

A pressure, a weight, was lifted from her and she imagined this was the moment of death. A release of earthly bonds, a lightening, and then the journey—where? Was there a destination? Or would oblivion follow, a nothingness? That might be preferable to the unknown . . .

Then she realized that the lifting of pressure was her release from the network of boulders. A hand was pulling at her arm—it hurt!— tugging and tugging until she thought her arm would be pulled from its socket, and then suddenly she was ascending through the waters of the stream, choking, gasping, taking water into her lungs, thrashing wildly but held in an inexorable grip until she broke the surface.

Tom was pulling her toward shore. She was coughing wildly, trying to expel the water she had sucked into her lungs. And she was freezing cold. This was altogether more unpleasant than the watery tomb had been.

Tom flung her onto shore and crawled after her. She looked up at him between coughing bouts and saw that his face was pale, his sandy hair hanging in sodden tendrils over his eyes. "Okay," he was saying, "okay, you're going to be all right."

The hacking bouts diminished and she struggled to a sitting position. She felt queasy and her throat burned from coughing. She tried to speak, but the effort triggered another eruption of coughs, and the sour taste of the stream water stung her mouth. Tom rubbed her back helplessly.

Finally, she was able to talk. "Thanks," she rasped, and felt horribly guilty at the trick she had intended to play on him.

"I can't believe you're still alive," he said, and his voice reflected his concern. "You were down there forever. Until those stones fell, I didn't even know where to look."

She took several deep breaths. Gradually, her body was beginning to feel normal again. "Tom," she croaked, "can we send a subspace message from the shuttle?"

He shook his head. "Not through the plasma storms in the Badlands. We'll have to wait until we rendezvous with Chakotay."

She got to her feet. "Then let's get that cabin put up. I have to contact someone in Mexico."

He looked at her quizzically, but she had already set off through the woods. She wanted to finish their task as quickly as possible. The answers to the great questions of her life were within her grasp.

That was almost the full extent of her interaction with Tom Paris before he disappeared. A day later they were attacked by two Cardassian vessels and, while the *Liberty* managed to destroy them, it was left badly damaged. Chakotay had sent Tom in a shuttle to bring help, but Tom never returned. So much, thought Torres, for loyalty.

Chakotay had returned from Bajor with a new crew member, a dark Vulcan named Tuvok. B'Elanna welcomed the return of a Vulcan to their midst, but her mind wasn't really on Maquis activities at the moment. She told Chakotay she had to send some subspace messages and he gave his permission, warning her only to disguise the location of the transmission origin.

She spent some time working on a routing scheme that would conceal the whereabouts of the ship sending the messages, then created two separate transmissions: one to her father in Mexico and one to her mother on Nessik.

It would be several days before the messages could wend their way from relay station to relay station and reach their destinations, and several days more before a reply could be expected. But five or six days wasn't too long to wait to get the answers she sought. B'Elanna felt almost at peace. A reconciliation with her mother and a relationship with her father were tangible possibilities, well within her grasp.

She found her longing for Chakotay had abated somewhat, and she felt almost friendly toward Seska. She sensed a balance to her life that had always eluded her. She had several conversations with the Vulcan Tuvok, and found him as calming an influence as Setonak had been. She looked forward to knowing him.

Two days after she had sent her messages, the ship suddenly went to red alert and B'Elanna bolted from the crew's mess to the bridge. Tuvok was there, and Chakotay. "Cardassian ship approaching," Chakotay said, and she heard the tension in his voice. Scanning her own station, she saw that it was a Galor-class warship, the most heavily armed of all the Cardassian fleet.

They leapt to warp, but the warship was already within range. Phaser fire began pummeling them. Tuvok released a photon torpedo, which did them some damage, but they kept coming.

"We have to get back to the Badlands," Chakotay said, just as a volley of fire ruptured a coolant conduit.

But the Badlands was not to be sanctuary for them that day. Amid the plasma storms, with which they were familiar, was another lurking anomaly, their first indication of which was a brilliant flash of light.

"What was that?" queried Chakotay.

"Curious. We've just passed through some kind of coherent tetryon beam," replied Tuvok.

"Source?"

"Unknown. Now there appears to be a massive displacement wave moving toward us . . ."

They watched their monitors as a strange, foglike phenomenon swept toward them from behind. "At current speeds," announced Tuvok, "it's going to intercept us in less than thirty seconds."

They tried to outrun it, but it swept relentlessly toward them, quickly overwhelming them in a light that dazzled, then blinded them.

And so it was that the *Liberty* was plucked from the Alpha and into the Delta Quadrant, where the crew was eventually thrown together with the crew of the *Starship Voyager,* and B'Elanna, in spite of all her efforts to avoid it, was reunited with Starfleet.

Almost immediately she was reminded of all she didn't like about the institution. It manifested itself in the person of Captain Kathryn Janeway, who stood for all the lofty principles that Starfleet represented, but who made a decision that severely impacted every member of both crews: she destroyed the technology that brought them to this part of space, and which could have returned them home.

"Who is she to be making these decisions for all of us?" B'Elanna had erupted when she realized Janeway intended to destroy the Caretaker's Array.

"She's the captain," said Chakotay simply, and B'Elanna had no choice except to watch as *Voyager* fired tricobalt devices that demolished the Array and thereby prevented the warlike Kazon from being able to invade the gentle Ocampa people.

And that meant that all the myriad loose ends of her life at home would be left dangling. She'd never be able to talk to her mother and father, never have her questions answered, never reconcile the conflicted feelings that lay within her. She was on a Starfleet ship surrounded by Starfleet personnel, butting right up against all the regulations and protocols and restrictions that had driven her from the Academy in the first place.

This was going to be a long, long journey.

CHAPTER

7

B'ELANNA LOOKED AROUND AT THE FACES OF HER FRIENDS, WHO WERE staring at her intently. "I hated her at first. I was furious because she'd cheated me of the life I thought I wanted."

She was silent for a moment, staring into the flames of their small fire. Then she looked back at the others. "But eventually I realized I had no one to blame but myself. All my problems came from inside me, not from the captain. She'd done a very noble and courageous thing. I just happened to be there, like all of you."

She didn't make eye contact with Chakotay. She was a little embarrassed at having revealed her once-powerful feelings for him. And she didn't look at Tom Paris. They'd been through so much together, but she'd never told him that she'd once been infatuated with Chakotay. She hoped he'd understand.

Tuvok abruptly interjected, changing the subject entirely. "After assessing the situation, I believe the most successful option we have is to construct a tunnel."

But this brought an immediate response from Coris, who was sitting next to Harry. She'd become a fixture among their group since he'd brought her back with him from the stream, but B'Elanna hadn't heard her say much of anything, certainly not with such firm authority. All eyes swung to her.

She looked better than she did when Harry first found her. More rested, less like a frightened animal. Her startling eyes caught the light of the flames and seemed to be on fire themselves. "They have sensors which penetrate to a depth of ten kilometers, and below that is solid psilminite. If you try to dig, they'll know it immediately."

"How do you know?" asked Harry.

"I was nearby when the guards discovered a tunnel some others had constructed. The guards made a point of telling everyone within range how foolish it was to try to escape, because of all the sensors."

B'Elanna, who was more than happy to turn the discussion to subjects other than her life and its tangled emotional web, began considering other possibilities. "Too bad we don't have a transporter," she said, half joking. "We could just beam ourselves out."

Coris took her seriously. "But the sensor net is said to extend beyond the enclosure for another hundred meters. You'd still be detected."

"As long as we're wishing for transporters, let's wish for one that would take us beyond sensor range."

"What do you figure we'd need to make one, Harry?" This from B'Elanna, who was now seriously considering the idea.

"A lot more than we have, that's for sure. A matter-energy converter, some phase transition coils . . . a power supply, control circuitry . . ."

"Anybody seen anything like that around the camp?" queried Chakotay, and the question brought somber chuckles. Not likely.

"But if we took apart our commbadges, we'd have plenty of control circuitry," mused B'Elanna, intrigued now by the challenge. "And who knows what there might be in this camp? We've only been looking for certain items. Maybe there's a way to do this."

Her enthusiasm was contagious, and the mood of the group lightened. Inspired, B'Elanna considered all the ramifications of this fragile plan. "We should move our shelters," she noted. "We're right in the middle of the camp now. If we're able to build a transporter, it would be primitive. We'd have a shorter distance to beam ourselves if we were closer to one of the walls."

Chakotay had started to agree when Coris interrupted once more.

"No," she said, "they'll know what you've done. They watch for escape attempts. If you move for no reason at all they'll be suspicious. They'll inspect your shelters every day."

Her words hung heavily in the chill night air. B'Elanna didn't doubt them, and was sure no one else did, either. But Tuvok wasn't about to see this plan shattered.

"Then we must concoct a compelling reason to move," he announced calmly.

"A fight," said Tom Paris immediately, and B'Elanna shot him a smile. Leave it to Tom to come up with that solution. But even Tuvok saw its logic.

"Continue, Mr. Paris," he intoned.

"We stage an altercation. A big one, that turns into a brawl. There's anger, and hostility. When the fight is over, most of us move one of the shelters to another location. Close to the wall. It'll look like bad blood between us has caused the move."

B'Elanna could see Chakotay running that plan through his mind, testing it, then turning to Coris. "Would the guards see through a ploy like that?"

The young woman pondered the question. "Maybe not," she said slowly. "There are fights all the time here, squabbles over territory, people being displaced. It might work."

"Let's try it," said Chakotay. "First we decide who goes and who stays."

Everyone was willing to accept Chakotay's decision on that matter, although Brad Harrison and his partner, Noah Mannick, asked to stay together, a request Chakotay was happy to accommodate. They had only recently become a couple and were still in the early flush of romantic intensity.

"All right, who fights?"

"Sign me up for that part," said Tom, and B'Elanna smiled again. She understood his feelings. It felt good to be planning something, to be active, to take steps to be in control of their destiny once more. They spent over an hour planning tomorrow's altercation, going over every detail until the plan was clear in everyone's mind. That night she slept more soundly than she had for a long time.

Tom Paris, on the other hand, slept fitfully. He was eager for morning to arrive, to get this plan going. To *do* something. When gray dawn finally broke, he was up before the others, sipping on brackish—but necessary—water, nibbling some of last night's rations that he'd saved for morning. Hunger was a constant now for all of them, and he believed it was important for them to start their escape plans sooner, rather than later. With so little food, they would gradually become weaker and more susceptible to disease and injury. And in a place like this, even a minor illness could be life-threatening, the slightest abrasion become infected and lead to death. Now was the time to act.

His impatience would help kindle the role he was to play in their carefully concocted drama. He allowed it to energize him, pacing nervously, driving fist into palm, talking to himself, until he felt a tensile strength forming deep inside, a coil of pure energy ready to burst forth.

He began kicking at the ground, muttering, tapping into old angers, remembering the rages and resentments of the past. Then he spotted Chakotay, seated on the ground and breaking off a portion of a grain cake he, too, had saved from the night before.

Tom marched over to him, stood above him, challenging. "I'm hungry," he announced.

Chakotay looked up at him and shrugged. "Should've saved some for this morning," he said quietly, and stuffed the chunk of foul mush in his mouth.

Tom's arm snaked down and closed over Chakotay's wrist, twisting it backward until the remainder of the grain cake could be pried loose. Then he quickly devoured it. Chakotay leapt to his feet. "What the hell do you think you're doing?" he said bitterly, shoving at Tom's chest. Tom swiped his hands away, and then they were into it, shoving and grappling, finally falling to the ground and rolling, punching, pounding on each other like crazed enemies.

The others were soon involved. Tuvok shouted at them to desist, but was ignored. Neelix began to exhort Tom, and Harry became outraged, and soon they were fighting, too. B'Elanna and Brad yelled at each other, prompting Noah to start berating B'Elanna, and before long the whole contingent was engaged in a melee that drew considerable attention from nearby prisoners. Only Tuvok and Vorik did not participate, and stood firmly, calling on their comrades to come to their senses, finally wading in and splitting up the combatants, chastising them, trying to restore order.

Tom kept one eye on the guards within the walls. They didn't want to disrupt the camp to the point where the guards felt the need to emerge and incinerate them. Gradually, the fight abated, and as people withdrew, they did so in two distinct groups: one included Tom, B'Elanna, Neelix, and Seven; the second, facing them squarely, consisted of Chakotay, Harry, Coris, Brad, and Noah. Tuvok and Vorik, true to their Vulcan natures, were neutral.

"You try that again, you'll have to go off and fend for yourself," Chakotay began, but Tom cut him off.

"That's what I'm going to do anyway," Paris shouted. "And these people are with me." He looked around at the group behind him. "Right?"

There was an answering affirmative chorus.

"Good," said Chakotay. "Take one of the shelters and put it up as far from here as you can get. Then don't get in my way again."

Tom nodded to his group and they began dismantling one of the shelters. A curious but spare crowd had gathered around them. Tom was sure altercations like this happened frequently, but it was probably still a relief from the squalid monotony of life in the camp. Fortunately, the incident had been minor enough not to arouse the ire of the guards, though they had undoubtedly noticed it. He hoped the brawl would mask their true intent.

Within an hour they had dismantled the shelter and were ready to move. Tuvok stood and made a pronouncement to Chakotay. "Commander, I think it best that I accompany this group to insure they keep their distance. And to keep their volatile natures in check."

"Agreed," said Chakotay. "Vorik, what's your choice?"

The young Vulcan pondered, as though making a decision he had not thought about before this. Finally, he turned to Chakotay. "Sir, I will go with Commander Tuvok. It may be that the presence of two Vulcans would enhance the atmosphere of rationality. But I would like permission to return here from time to time, as well. I have taken no part in this altercation and hope I would be welcome here."

"Of course," said Chakotay. "Anytime." This was the plan they had devised to keep communication between the two groups, and Tom just hoped it wasn't transparent. "Let's get out of here," he said, and turned his back on Chakotay.

In their mapping session of yesterday, Neelix had spotted a bare section of ground at the periphery of the campground, not more than twenty-five meters from the wall, and immediately adjacent to the twenty-meter-wide "free zone," a band of ground that encircled the camp just inside the walls, and into which no prisoner was allowed to venture.

The unoccupied segment of land was flanked by a sprawling

complex of lean-tos that seemed to belong to a cohesive group. There were probably fifty of them, tall, graceful humanoids with skin so black it looked as though they'd been smeared with coal. By contrast, their hair was white, and was pulled back and secured. They had a neatness about them that denoted fierce pride, for staying groomed in a situation like this was nearly impossible. Tom rubbed his own stubbly cheeks, grizzled after several days of not shaving.

Tuvok took charge of the group, directing the setting up of the shelter. It would have to conceal their efforts in constructing a transporter, and so they were careful to make it occupy as much area as possible. A great deal had to happen under that shelter.

Tom was pounding a stake into the ground to secure one corner of a tarpaulin when he felt a presence behind him. He turned and looked up to see one of the lanky black humanoids looming over him, blocking the sun. Tom stood, hoping they weren't going to have to fight these people. Not only was the *Voyager* crew outnumbered, but the men of the white-haired species were at least a meter and a half taller, with long, powerful arms. Tom and his group wouldn't last long in combat with them.

"I am Tassot Bnay of the Rai'." His voice was impossibly deep, like the roll of distant thunder. "What is your intention in occupying this ground?"

Tom, who was tall himself, had to crane his neck up to look at the man. "We had a falling-out with the rest of our group. Thought it was better to separate than to keep fighting. We have no quarrel with you and we'll keep to ourselves. Hope that suits you."

The man nodded curtly, but made no effort to leave. "There are those who blame us for their suffering. We must be on guard against retaliation."

This intrigued Tom. "Why would anyone blame you?"

"We are the Rai'. It is our war with the Subu that has resulted in the establishment of these camps."

"Ah." This was the first Tom had heard of the other players in the battle, and he wanted to know more. "What's the conflict about?"

"War is always about power. And power derives from the acquisition of territory. The Subu have taken worlds from many species, who acquiesced rather than fight. Then they encountered us."

Tom nodded. There were usually two sides to any story, even those involving war, but he found himself respecting this tall, proud man who had seemingly come on an errand of peace as soon as the *Voyager* crew had moved in.

"We take Subu prisoners; they take us. My group will stand a chance of being set free in a prisoner exchange. But other species, such as yourselves, have no such hope. We are also resented for that fact."

"Has anyone ever escaped from here?" Tom asked casually, returning to his task of pounding the stake.

"There is nothing to escape to. A vast wilderness surrounds this place, thick and impenetrable. Beyond that—more wilderness. The planet is uncivilized."

"Hmmm." Tom tried to make his grunt as neutral as possible. But Tassot squatted down to be more nearly at his level, and fastened his dark, unblinking eyes on Tom's.

"Punishment for escape attempts is brutal. And there are ample rewards for those who turn in potential escapees. Let those facts guide your actions."

"Thanks. I'll keep that in mind." Tom looked at the stake, then back toward the huge, dark man next to him. "But it sounds like you're saying the only way out of here—is to die."

Tassot was silent for a prolonged moment. Then he said, "Because of the sensor net, there are few options for getting beyond the walls. But if someone were to escape it is unlikely the guards would pursue. They know that one would not survive for long in the wilderness." He let that sink in for a moment, and then added, "One can die quickly . . . or slowly. Remember that."

And then he was gone, rising and moving off with surprising grace given his size. Tom considered the warning ambivalent. The man had told him that punishment for the attempt was harsh—but then pointed out that if they got out, the Subu were unlikely to come chasing them. Which message was he sending? Tom thought about it for a while, but then realized they weren't going to abandon their escape attempts and sit quietly, waiting to starve to death. That was a slow death, too, but worse than that, it was passive. To Tom, that made it intolerable.

The day had been spent searching for duotronic components. By nightfall, they had found nothing except a weak and fading trans-tator. They were doled their daily rations—a damp and rotting root of some kind, which nonetheless was the best-tasting meal they'd been offered—and hoped tomorrow would be more successful. A fire was lit and they all drew round.

Tom thought Chakotay's idea of having people talk about themselves was a good one. It had distracted them all from their circumstances—and it was interesting to hear what people would reveal. He'd learned more about B'Elanna last night than he had in over three years of knowing her.

So he turned to Seven, whose life was still enigmatic to all of them. "How about you, Seven?" Tom prompted. "Want to let us in on your past?"

Seven regarded him with her cool poise. She had lost much of the disdain she had exhibited when she was a Borg, but there was still an unsettling remoteness about her. She had yet to fully reconnect to the humanity into which she had been born.

Her beautiful face, clear-skinned but still bearing two Borg implants, blue-eyed, topped with ethereal blond hair pulled smoothly back, grew pensive in the firelight. "There's little I remember," she said in her direct way. "We were on my parents' spaceship. My mother schooled me . . . I read a great deal. But that was long ago. I had my sixth birthday on board. They sang 'Happy Birthday, Annika.' And then the Borg took us."

She looked down and everyone was silent for a moment. Seven was still dealing with the trauma of her assimilation, and no one wanted to push her into recollections that were too painful. She looked up after a moment, delicate shadows from the fire playing on her face. "I don't have specific memories from my time with the Borg. It all runs together, memories, impressions, sounds . . ."

Many of those memories, everyone realized, would be of assimilating other species, and not the kind of events that would make for good listening. Tom was sorry he'd asked Seven to speak, and hoped he hadn't made her feel awkward or uncomfortable.

But the beautiful Borg was staring right at him, not at all hesitant. "I think you should speak instead," she announced in her forthright way, a statement which caught Tom somewhat off guard. But the rest of the group quickly sided with Seven.

"Good idea," said B'Elanna wryly. She had peppered Tom with questions about his life ever since their friendship had started developing, and he had managed to answer in the vaguest of terms. That would be his instinct in this instance, too, but after Chakotay, and Harry, and especially B'Elanna, had been so honest, so intimate—anything less from him would seem cowardly.

The thought of releasing some of his buried feelings was suddenly appealing. He was aware, as were they all, that this prisoner-of-war camp might be the occasion in which they weren't able to cheat death, and if that should prove the case, Tom wanted, finally, to unburden himself. For the first time in his life, he felt confessional.

"Okay," he said to the group. "I don't know how this will come out. But here goes."

CHAPTER

8

"TOM! TOM, WAIT UP!"

The voice rang through the cool morning air in Buchanan Quadrangle and Cadet Tom Paris turned to see his friend Charlie Day trotting toward him. They had grown up together in the Portola Valley, competing genially with each other all through school in both sports and academe and finally both earning coveted acceptances to Starfleet Academy. They'd been on campus for a month now, gradually adjusting to the grueling Academy routine.

Charlie jogged up to him, his round, cheerful face wreathed in a toothy smile, dusty brown hair managing as always to look shaggy and unruly in spite of the regulation haircut, big brown puppy-eyes radiating warmth. Charlie had a face that always made Tom feel good, no matter what his mood might be.

Now, Charlie's gaze made a quick sweep of the quadrangle, as though to insure their privacy from eavesdroppers. "I can't say this is for certain," he said conspiratorially, "but Bob Dehan heard it from Jim Bradley who heard it from the trainer."

Tom knew what was coming, but as he didn't know quite what he wanted to do about it, he chose to stay noncommittal. "Coach Patton made the final cut?" he said carefully.

Charlie leaned in closer to him, all but bursting with the good news. "He did—and we're both in." He clapped Tom solidly on the shoulder and Tom had to work not to wince; Charlie's face, round and doughy, was deceiving. He was a superbly conditioned athlete, body lean and muscled, quick and lithe as a Varkan jungle cat.

"I knew you'd make it—nobody can cut around left flank like you—but Dehan swears we're both on the team." He stood smiling at Tom, buoyant with anticipation. "You know what this means, don't you? It means the team has a real shot at being Parrises Squares state champions. Maybe even the nationals. But whatever you do, don't tell your father until Patton makes it official. Okay?"

It was only now, Tom realized, that Charlie began to notice his lack of enthusiastic reaction. A slight puzzled frown appeared on his brow and he stepped back slightly as though to scrutinize his friend. "Try to control your excitement," he muttered, "people might notice."

Tom drew a breath. He'd known this moment was coming and he'd chosen to ignore it until it came. Now he honestly didn't know what he was going to do. As he looked into the cherubic face of the friend he'd known since he was a baby, he felt miserable. And tried to prolong the moment of decision a bit longer.

"Of course I'm excited," he began, "but I had a late night. Big test in geomorphology this morning."

He wondered if Charlie believed him. His voice sounded hollow in his own ears and he suddenly wanted to get away from his friend, to run until he fell, exhausted.

"You aren't having second thoughts, are you?" queried Charlie. "We've been waiting for this chance ever since we started playing."

Tom was feeling worse and worse. Charlie was right—they'd trained for years to make the team at California's Academy Institute, Starfleet's preparatory school, and led it to divisional championships their last two years. How could he tell Charlie he wasn't sure he wanted to be on the team now that they were at the Academy?

"Charlie," he equivocated, "let's not start celebrating until we know for sure, okay? No point in setting ourselves up for a letdown." He smiled with what he hoped was reassurance, and kept talking before Charlie had a chance to reply. "I'll see you tonight. Got to hit the library before that exam." And he moved away quickly, leaving Charlie standing, slightly perplexed, in the center of the quadrangle.

The next day, he received a summons to his father's office.

Commander Klenman, the clipped British woman who had been his father's aide for years, smiled warmly at him when he entered.

She was a diminutive woman with iron-gray hair and a strong jaw. Her dark eyes were sparkling with some ill-kept secret, and Tom wondered briefly how, if she were ever captured by an enemy, she could fail to telegraph everything she knew.

"He's just finishing a transmission with the Vulcan ambassador," Commander Klenman said crisply. Or maybe it wasn't so much that she made the statement crisply as her aristocratic accent gave that impression. Tom had always liked Klenman, who had virtually seen him grow up, often attending school functions in his father's stead when the admiral was otherwise occupied.

Tom took a seat and the commander smiled at him. "How's the first month been?" she asked.

"A little rough. I'd be a liar if I said otherwise," Tom answered. "I'm learning to get by on less sleep than I thought was possible."

"Every first-termer says that. But things usually begin to settle down after a few months. As you get into the routine."

"Do you know what my father wants with me?" he probed. A summons from Admiral Owen Paris was something to make even seasoned veterans quail, and his son frankly felt no different.

Klenman's smile broadened. "No idea," she lied. And at that point the door to his father's office opened and Admiral Paris appeared, smiling just like his aide. "Good morning, Cadet," he intoned with false formality, "come in, please."

Tom followed him into the office, which was, as always, festooned with pictures of him and his sisters. Seeing that array always made Tom feel vaguely uncomfortable, and he wondered what others thought when they scanned the desk full of family portraits. That Owen Paris was a proud father, a devoted family man?

Now his father was shaking his hand, his eyes squinting in a smile, cheeks quivering slightly as he pumped Tom's arm. "I wanted to be the first to congratulate you," he said. "I made Patton withhold the announcement until I had a chance to talk to you."

Even Tom couldn't deny there was unabashed pride in his father's voice. He'd heard that tone all his life, as long as he could remember, and didn't doubt that his father had expressed pride in the way Tom rolled over in his crib.

"I couldn't be happier about this, Tom. You and Charlie Day are two of only six first-termers to be named to the Parrises Squares team."

Okay, thought Tom, this is it. Take it slow, no need to rush. Take a breath. Smile.

"Thank you, sir," he heard himself saying, his voice echoing in his ears as though he were listening to someone else entirely. "But . . ."

His voice caught in his throat, and he hated himself for revealing his nervousness. He coughed, hoping that might somehow explain the crack in his voice. "Actually, I'm not sure I'll be accepting a place on the team."

His father stared at him. A long moment passed, and then the admiral said, merely, "I see."

"It's a huge commitment, for one thing. Everybody knows Coach Patton makes you eat, sleep, and breathe the sport. I think I'd rather concentrate on my studies this year." There—that sounded perfectly reasonable.

Admiral Paris scrutinized his son, a gaze Tom knew well. He held his father's eye levelly, trying not to succumb to the impulse to keep talking. That's what his father did: intimidated people into giving themselves away with that unrelenting stare of his. Finally the admiral spoke, and Tom felt a small twinge of triumph that he hadn't yielded first.

"You're required to participate in a sport. If not Parrises Squares, what will it be?"

Well, his father knew how to cut to the point. Just as well, it had to come out some time. Tom inhaled.

"I'm going out for a new sport. Well, an old one, actually, but the Academy's never competed. Downhill skiing."

Tom admired his father's self-control. Not a twinge, not a blink indicated his attitude about this statement. He just kept his neutral gaze bearing down. "Skiing. Didn't realize you had any interest. Never even mentioned it."

Tom knew his father was upset. He always spoke in that terse, clipped way, dropping the subjects of sentences, when something had gotten to him.

"It's something I've been thinking about. The chance to be on the Academy's first team ever, kind of help build it from the ground up— it appeals to me."

"You've never even been on skis."

"As a matter of fact, I have. Quite a few times, when Mom took us on vacations to Lake Tahoe." A small pause, and then Tom couldn't resist adding, "You were never able to make it. Too busy."

His father's eyes took on a flat look. "I see. And you're pretty good, are you?"

Tom shrugged. "Not as good as I'll be with more practice. We're transporting to the Andes this weekend to start the regimen."

"Is there a young woman involved?"

Tom desperately wanted to smile at this—as though this insane decision could only be motivated by his attraction to a female—but he employed his own self-control and remained stoic. "No, sir. That is, there are women, as well as men, who are joining the team, but there's no one I'm especially interested in."

"I see," his father repeated.

A faint and ineffable sensation of something he couldn't identify began to glow in Tom. His father was flummoxed. He was repeating himself with nonphrases because he didn't know how to contend with this unexpected rebellion.

Admiral Paris rose and walked to the wall of pictures on his wall— the one with the lineage of Starfleet Parises, the veritable nobility of the Federation. He stared briefly at one of them, then turned to face his son. "Well, your mother will be disappointed. She was your biggest fan at the Institute, and I know she was looking forward to cheering you on at the Academy."

Liar, thought Tom. You're the one who's disappointed, and you can't even admit it. "I'll talk to Mom," he said. "She'll understand."

"Of course. She cares about your happiness. No matter what it costs her. As you mature, maybe you'll develop that kind of compassion."

"I'm sure I will, sir," said Tom. He wasn't impervious to the idea that his mother might be disappointed by his choice, but he also felt sure she would be just as proud of his downhill racing as she would be of his playing left flank. His father was just using every ploy he could come up with to affect his decision. The warm feeling, still unidentified, glowed brighter in Tom.

"I'll just ask you to think carefully before making a final decision. It's a tremendous honor to be on the P.S. team as a first-termer. You don't want to discard that offer lightly."

It would have been easy to acquiesce to this simple request. But the small flame that burned in Tom was inextinguishable. "I've thought very carefully, sir," he said with what he hoped was quiet dignity. "My decision is made."

A heavy silence for a moment, and finally Admiral Paris said, "Then I'll respect it."

The flame burst into a veritable conflagration. Tom couldn't quite understand the feeling: he had clearly disappointed his father, whose opinion of him had determined most of the course of his life, and he had fully expected to leave this meeting wretched with conflicted emotions.

Instead, he felt a palpable triumph, a sense of victory. As he exited his father's office and waved a cheerful good-bye to Commander Klenman, he suddenly identified this new and giddy feeling: it was power.

The ancient sports of downhill and slalom racing had lost popularity somewhere in the late twenty-first century, some time after traditional skis had been abandoned and bare-shoe skiing was the accepted norm. But even then, the sport had been almost entirely supplanted by snowboards and racing was losing favor to increasingly acrobatic aerial skiing. And of course, hoverboards made them all seem quaint and old-fashioned.

But a few diehards in Europe and Scandinavia kept the older ways, skating on the long slats that seemed so eccentric to many, passing down the skill to their children, who passed it down, so the sport was maintained in various pockets of the world.

Tom's mother was the one who first introduced her children to what was then considered an archaic activity, but of her two daughters and one son, only Tom showed any interest in it. He was ten when he first slid down a gentle slope at a resort near Lake Tahoe, under the guidance of Henri Islicker, a patient gentleman from Switzerland who was trying to reintroduce the sport to Americans, one child at a time. Islicker was a grandfatherly man with a great shock of white hair, a neatly trimmed white beard, and brilliant blue eyes. Tom liked him instantly, sensing a patience and lack of judgment in the old man that made him unafraid to risk embarrassment by attempting this unusual sport.

There were scant few children who cared to try this unaccustomed activity, with its awkward skis and ungainly poles. But when Tom first stepped into the boots, he felt instantly confident, sure that this was something he could do, and would enjoy.

That first run was down a slope that declined no more than five or six degrees, but to young Tom, it was thrilling. The caress of the cold breeze on his face, the white of the snow and the deep green of the pine trees etched against an unclouded winter blue sky, the scent of conifers—all these sensations combined to create a euphoric effect in the young boy.

Within a day Islicker had taken him onto the more difficult slopes and watched admiringly as Tom carved turns as though he'd been skiing for years. It was, Islicker told him, a natural talent that could never be taught, simply enhanced.

By the end of that week they were on the most advanced of the slopes, skiing powder where no one had been before them, Islicker being careful to instruct Tom about the danger of avalanches, what conditions to look out for and how to avoid them. Tom absorbed all this, and kept up with the courtly old gentleman turn for turn.

His mother brought him back seven more times over the course of the next eight years, and those few occasions were his only experience on skis. Each time they had returned to Portola Valley, he had wanted to tell his father what he'd been doing, but some instinct told him that his father wouldn't think much of this strange old sport, and so he kept quiet. He focused instead on Parrises Squares, which his father supported with passion.

Now, his clandestine experiment with skiing had provided the instrument of his first challenge to his father, though Tom didn't think of it this way in the beginning. Only later, after the incident in the Vega system, did he trace back the events and begin to understand why joining the ski team had been such a heady experience for him. He was playing out a drama as ancient as Oedipus.

The Academy ski team was a motley group at first, consisting of six men and four women, all of whom were human (off-worlders generally thought the sport truly bizarre), only one of whom was more competent than Tom. That was Odile Launay, a young woman from Beziers, in southern France, whose father had been one of those European ski enthusiasts trying to revive the sport. Odile had grown up on the slopes of the Pyrenees, and was as graceful a racer as Tom had ever seen.

She also had the most amazing green eyes, two large emeralds set in an oval face as milky white as a pearl, offset by a cloud of hair that was somewhere between blond and red, and which Odile referred to, laughing, as *"jaune commes les fraises,"* or strawberry blond.

Tom was determined to develop no feelings for her other than the camaraderie of fellow team members. He could admire her skiing, respect her determination on the slopes, and enjoy her thoughtful analysis of their practice runs.

But he would not think about those eyes, or about the full pink lips which she would bite from time to time when she was concentrating, kittenish white teeth making a dark pink indentation which sometimes stayed on her mouth for minutes.

He would not even *notice* things like that.

"You could cut tenths of a second off your time if you would only work on your prejumping," she would observe, with that delectable accent that Tom could have listened to all day. "You are so stubborn, Tommy. *Pourquoi?*"

"Maybe I need a strong woman to show me the error of my ways." He grinned, and was gratified when she didn't look away, but rather lowered her lashes slightly, so that she seemed to be peering up at him through a fringe. He felt his legs become uncertain.

"You are saying that you want me to coach you?" she inquired innocently.

He sighed. How would he last for a year keeping his distance from this delightful person? "Yes, dearest Odile, I would love for you to coach me—in skiing, in French, in life and love and all good things."

She eyed him with bemusement, her adorable nose wrinkling slightly, tender mouth pursed. "You can take nothing seriously, Tom. How will we succeed if you have no commitment to the skiing?"

"I *am* committed, I swear I am. More than you could ever imagine."

And he tried to keep his concentration on the sport, but as he followed Odile down the practice runs of Andermatt or Chamonix or Whistler or Crackenback, her lithe body in the formfitting ski suit made his pulse quicken.

I need, he thought, *les douches froides.*

The fledgling ski team didn't particularly distinguish itself that first year, but it didn't embarrass itself, either. The women fared best, placing third in four of their meets and almost taking second in one. Odile actually had the fastest time in several of her runs.

Four of the men focused on slalom, while Tom and a gentle but powerful Finn, Brunolf Katajavuori, were the downhillers. Tom and Bruno had a friendly but ardent competition, each pushing the other to the limit, topping and retopping each other with neither one gaining the clear edge.

Bruno was a tall, big-boned man with sand-colored hair, pale brown eyes, and a fair complexion with permanently ruddy cheeks. His thighs were the size of small tree trunks, giving him plenty of muscle strength to steer turns confidently at high speed.

"How'd you get legs like that, Bruno?" Tom asked enviously. "You could kick holes through titanium with those things."

"You were raised soft," joshed Bruno. "We lived in the mountains, and my parents made us ski to school every day. It wasn't so bad going, because it was downhill. But it was miserable climbing back." He whacked his hand on his massive thigh. "It did great things for the legs, though."

For the final meet of the season the team transported to Wengen, in the Jungfrau district of the Swiss Alps. It was the site of the legendary downhill course known as the Lauberhorn, which Tom and Bruno would ski in competition with seven other schools from around the world. It was just over forty-six hundred meters long, with a drop of slightly more than a thousand meters. This gave it a vertical gradient which averaged about twenty-seven percent, or fifteen degrees. However, there were sections with a gradient of almost ninety percent, or forty-two degrees. This was like skiing straight down.

The day of the competition dawned gray and raw, with an icy wind that snapped nastily at exposed skin. Tom didn't like skiing in these conditions, but he accepted the fact that if you chose a winter sport you'd better be prepared for winter weather.

Things hadn't improved by the time he and Bruno transported to the top of the run. Even in his polytherm suit, Tom felt the cold, and he knew his muscles were tightening in response. He kept flexing and stamping on the ground to keep himself as limber as possible. He glanced over at Bruno, who didn't seem affected by the weather.

"Don't you even feel the cold?" Tom inquired.

"This isn't cold," Bruno replied mildly. "When the mucus in your eyeballs freezes—that's cold."

Four racers, from Austria, Peru, Canada, and Switzerland, preceded Tom down the course, with the Austrian clocking the best time at 2:21:63. This was well short of the world record of 2:20:04, which had been set over three hundred years ago when downhill racing was still a wildly popular sport.

Tom's best time on this run was 2:22:87. He'd have to ski a personal best—by well over a second—in order to overtake the leader.

He crouched at the top of the run, within the starting hut, muscles tensed, determined to rise to this occasion. The cold faded away, as did any sense that other people occupied the space. For the seconds before the starter's chime, Tom was alone on the mountaintop.

Then he was off, springing forward, driving to accelerate right from the top, then bending into a low egg position, shoes parallel, knees and feet apart, hands tucked together in front of his body in an effort to provide as little aerodynamic resistance as possible. He felt the adrenaline surge he always got at the top of a run.

Direction flags denoted the course boundary, red on the left, green on the right. But Tom knew the course by heart. He could stay tucked for nearly five hundred meters on a plunge that averaged a sixteen-degree incline and pick up good speed before he hit the first gates. Those would commence shortly after the first steep plunge of forty-one degrees, when speed had approached maximum.

It was one of those days when he felt at one with the whole experience: he was no longer aware of the cold or the wind, he saw no distractions in his peripheral vision. Skis and poles seemed natural extensions of his own body, and were controlled effortlessly. He felt fluid, jointless.

And yet he felt powerful, too. His legs were strong, as strong as Bruno's, tireless, ready for whatever challenges lay ahead.

He approached the first of the "bumps" that would propel him airborne briefly. He wanted to spend as little time in the air as possible, as the line of travel while airborne is longer and eats up valuable tenths of seconds. He anticipated the jump carefully, knowing he had to time the prejump exactly: too soon and he might land before he had cleared the bump; too late and he would be thrown higher in the air than if he hadn't jumped.

Just before he reached the lip of the slope edge, he drew his knees up beneath his body, lifting his shoes off the snow and clearing the edge at the lowest possible height. Then immediately, he stretched out his legs to get his feet back on the snow, flexing forward and downward to absorb the shock and acceleration.

Part of his mind said a silent *"merci"* to Odile for making him work on this maneuver, for he lost almost no time in the air. Almost immediately, he saw the first of the gates.

Control gates were set to limit average speed, and were marked with orange flags. They had to be at least eight meters wide, and he had to pass through them with both feet. The gates forced a skier into a series of turns, slowing him and forcing him to come out of the egg position in order to have better balance and quicker reactions on the turns.

Initiating turns at high speeds was easier than at slow speeds, because a racer's higher kinetic energy supplied a lot of the turning force. But steering those turns was much more difficult, and that's where the legs came into play. Muscle strength was essential to counteract centrifugal force produced by the turn and hold an accurate line.

As he swung into the series of gates, Tom realized that one of the things he loved about skiing was the *effort* it required. He'd tried hoverboards, and they were fun and certainly called for an agility, a lightness of touch, that was demanding. But racing on skis was *work*. It took all his strength to knife the edge of his ski into the snow to keep himself from spinning out of control or go tumbling in a sprawl of arms, legs, and poles down the steep incline.

On this day, the turns seemed to carve like butter. His edges were strong, but not so deep as to cost him time. He felt as though he were flying. There was no sensation of wind, just the exhilaration of streaking through the air, unfettered, part of the air and the sky and the snow, a headlong flight that was so smooth, so perfect, he might have been falling through space.

He sensed—no, more than that, he *knew*—that this run was undoubtedly a personal best. He might not overtake the Austrian, but he would be able to say that on this day, he had excelled.

What happened next he couldn't explain. For no reason, no stimulus that he could identify, his eye focused for a fraction of a second on the spectators that lined the course. There weren't that many, and maybe that's why he could see whom he saw.

A figure in Starfleet winter wear, bundled against the cold, a sandy mop of hair tucked under an insulated cap, chiseled features in a stern face, a face that was looking directly at him.

His father.

His father had never come to a meet. Had he actually made the effort, taken the time to transport from San Francisco to Jungfrau in order to see his son compete?

The moment of effortless euphoria was gone. Tom was suddenly aware of everything around him, the cold wind, the shuddering bumpiness of the icy snow, the muffled sounds of people calling out to him. His mind snapped from its state of bliss into a a rude awareness of the now, and suddenly he had to *think* about what to do. His body had taken over for him until this moment, and now his mind had interceded, disrupting the purity and clarity of the experience.

He felt one ski begin to lose an edge as he carved a turn, and he compensated by digging in, knowing as he did that he would be losing hundredths of a second. He tried to block that thought but it was with him as he approached the next gate and he determined to make up the time. He came into the turn too fast, dug his edge, felt it catch, shifted his weight, knew that his balance was slipping away, tried desperately to right himself, using his pole for leverage but knowing all these efforts were fruitless.

He went down in a sprawl, flipping over in a drunken somersault while clawing at the snow for a grip to stop his downward tumble. His face scraped an icy outcropping and he felt the sudden warmth of blood, saw it fleck out behind him in a shower of pink on the snow. Down he tumbled, over and over, leaving a bloody smear behind him, feeling bones twist and muscles tear, and nothing, it seemed, would slow his ignominious descent.

And then, finally, he was able to clutch at the icy snow, digging in his hands, raking them through the snow pack, bringing his frantic tumble to an end. He lay there, staring up through immense treetops at a gray and rolling sky, unwilling to move for fear he wouldn't be able to. In seconds he was surrounded by teammates, medical personnel, and competition officials. When he demonstrated that he could move every part of him they asked, wasn't seeing double and could count backward, they did an emergency transport into the medical facility.

Before he dematerialized, he scanned the crowd for his father, but saw no one that resembled him even slightly.

That same night he was transported home, bones regenerated and muscle tears reknitted, still residually sore in places but essentially whole once more. He mother fretted over him and offered to bring him dinner in bed, on a tray, as she had when he was a child and was sick, but Tom wanted to be at the family table that night. Whatever his father thought of him for his mishap, he wanted to know what it was.

His sister Moira was with them that evening, home for the weekend from South Carolina, where she was in medical school. Moira had eschewed Starfleet Academy, as had his oldest sister, Kathleen, a fact that Tom had always appreciated, because both girls were brilliant students, and he had followed in their reflected glory during all of his school years. At least at the Academy he could chart his own course, unhampered by his sisters' reputations.

Moira was an elegantly beautiful woman, in Tom's opinion. She had classically delicate features, wide blue eyes set in an oval face, straight thin nose, lips a bit generous but not out of proportion. She pulled her dark hair back off her face in a severe fashion which seemed, on Moira, altogether fetching. She was straightforward and completely without guile, and Tom adored her.

"Didn't you race today?" she asked immediately, in her frank way. "How'd it go?"

Tom felt his eyes flicker to his father, who sat at the head of the table, eyes on a padd he was studying. Tom wasn't sure he had even heard the question.

"Not so well. I took a tumble in the middle of my run and lost my chance to compete."

"I'm sorry. It's a wonder to me everybody doesn't fall every time they go scooting down one of those mountains. I don't know how you do it, sliding around on those funny-looking slats. How can you control which way you go, anyway?"

"Practice" was Tom's laconic reply. He had no desire to get involved in a discussion of the techniques of skiing.

"Tom was actually doing well at the time," his mother added unhelpfully. His mother was a martial-arts instructor, in magnificent physical shape, and a paleontological scholar in her own right. She was also the most loving, warm, generous woman Tom had ever encountered. He had often wondered how she'd been attracted to his father.

Tom's eyes moved again to Admiral Paris, whose eyes had lifted from the padd, looking at his wife and children with the dispassionate look of someone who was running multiplication tables in his head. But, as Tom had suspected, he had registered every word that had been uttered.

"Hope you didn't hurt yourself," he said, his voice neutral, with no shading or inference of any kind. What kind of game was he playing? He had seen the fall, had seen people surrounding Tom, testing him, transporting him right from the slope to the medical facility. Why would Admiral Paris ask this curious question?

"I got pretty banged up," Tom replied, searching his father's face for reaction. "Broke some bones, tore some muscles and ligaments. But everything's been pretty well regenerated. I'm just a little sore."

"Glad it wasn't serious," his father intoned, then turned his eyes once more to the padd.

"Owen, Moira hasn't been home for three months. Don't you think you could put that padd away at the dinner table?"

Admiral Paris smiled good-naturedly and turned the padd off. "Sorry," he said. "The Ktarians have proposed an expedition into the Beta Quadrant. Just wanted to stay on top of it." He looked at Moira and smiled fondly. "What's new in South Carolina?"

Tom half listened as Moira launched into a rambling account of the miseries of medical school, a subject that seemed to absorb his father's attention completely. He was completely baffled by the admiral's behavior. Was his father so embarrassed by Tom's performance that he didn't even want to admit he'd seen it? Was he trying to spare Tom's feelings by pretending he hadn't been there?

Or was it—and this thought hit Tom like a fist in the stomach— that he *hadn't* been there?

Tom felt color rise unbidden in his face, shame greater than that he'd felt this morning in Switzerland undulating through him. His thoughts tumbled over each other, as though in homage to his spectacular plunge down the mountainside. Could he have imagined he'd seen his father? Or had he seen someone who bore him a vague resemblance and turned that person, in his mind's eye, into the admiral?

And if he'd done that—why? He didn't *expect* to see his father at a racing event, he didn't anticipate it; in fact, it was the furthest thing from his mind. That surprise was what had taken him out of the moment and caused him to stumble.

So if he didn't expect his father there, why would his mind have leapt to the instant conclusion that Admiral Paris was standing among the spectators on the icy slope?

The only answer Tom had for that one, he didn't want. Because the answer was that, deep down, Tom wanted his father to see him compete and so had imagined him there even when he wasn't. Tom's mind, given any fuel at all, would create his father's image and impose it on a stranger.

"Tom, you look a bit flushed. Are you feverish?" This from his mother, who was looking at him with concern. Tom shook his head, but couldn't speak. His father and Moira stopped their conversation and looked at him, Moira's eyes suddenly worried, the admiral's opaque and unreadable.

Ask him, said the voice inside Tom's mind. And the voice was right. Just speak up, ask if he was there; if he wasn't, Tom could simply say there was someone who looked a lot like him, make a joke of it. And if he was there—well, it'd be his father who'd look foolish for not having said so in the first place.

Tom felt three pairs of eyes trained on him, waiting for him to speak. When he did, his voice rang hollow in his ears. "Maybe I'll turn in early. It's been a long day. May I be excused?"

And with that unremarkable statement, he rose and exited the room, leaving his family staring after him.

Skiing gave Tom an immediate, visceral sense of speed and danger, but of course it paled next to the sensations produced by piloting a starship.

Tom had been piloting since he was small, first on the simulators to which his father had access, then on small but (to him) clunky youth vessels that had to fly at certain prescribed altitudes over certain prescribed routes. More than once, he was censured and even punished for violating those careful rules. He won several shuttle derbies as an adolescent, always pushing at the boundaries of the rules.

But not until Starfleet Academy did he come to appreciate what it was like to be at the helm of a ship flying at warp speed. Not the physical sensations, of course—inertial dampers buffered the impact to the body that would accrue from achieving such incredible velocity. But what it did to the emotions was, to Tom, almost indescribable.

It had to do with control. A few delicate movements of his fingers, dancing gracefully over the controls, and massive forces began to respond—and all because of instructions from him, Tom Paris, cadet. It was heady, intoxicating.

He couldn't resist demonstrating this prowess to Odile. She wouldn't begin pilot's training until next year, not having had Tom's prior experience, and she was eager for the demonstration. But she was more of a rule-follower than Tom, and was puzzled about their middle-of-the-night excursion as they walked silently through the darkened halls of Breyer's Hall, one of the classroom buildings.

"You do have the permission for this flight, *n'est-ce pas?*"

"Of course. I cleared it with Commander Barns, my flight instructor."

"Then why are we going at this hour?"

"Because this is when the shuttles aren't being used."

"It feels like we're sneaking."

"What's sneaky? We're going to a transporter pad."

"It's dark, we're whispering, and there's nobody here. It feels . . . illicit. Like we're going to get in trouble."

He glanced over at her, went momentarily weak at the sight of her profile, and resisted the very strong impulse to pull her to him and taste those full pink lips. He sighed.

"It's very simple. We transport to a shuttle. I take you out of the solar system and demonstrate the leap to warp speed. Then we come back. That's it."

There was silence as her eyes flicked over the deserted corridor. "It still feels sneaky," she insisted, and he laughed at her stubbornness.

Minutes later they were inside one of the shuttles that the Academy kept in synchronous orbit for instructional purposes. It was a craft Tom knew well, and had piloted on many occasions. He had even, in strict violation of the rules, given it a female nickname—privately, of course, so as not to offend the female cadets, who resented the practice of referring to flying craft as "she." He understood their feelings, and wasn't unsympathetic, but it was an ancient and proud tradition, and in following it Tom felt part of a long line of pilots and captains stretching back, he was sure, to the most primitive canoes and barges.

The name he had chosen was Tess. This was the name of a young woman he had adored during his first year in high school, albeit from afar. She was dazzlingly beautiful, intimidatingly brilliant, and wildly popular. Tom fantasized endlessly about asking her out, even going to the lengths of writing out the dialogue he might use, and practicing it so he would sound fluid and spontaneous. But he could never summon the courage to approach her.

And so it gave him perverse pleasure to name the shuttle after her, and to feel "her" respond to his commands, docile and compliant.

Of course he would never tell this to Odile.

She took the seat next to him, staring in fascination at the cockpit. "I can't wait to start my training," she breathed. "I've wanted to fly since I was a small child."

"Me, too. I just had more access to shuttles because of my father."

"It was very generous of your father to help you learn."

This caught Tom by surprise. Generous? It was hardly a word he'd use to describe the admiral. He wasn't sure how to respond, and when he did, he could hear his voice in his ears.

"I've never thought of it that way. Maybe you're right."

He could feel her gaze on him, and resisted turning toward her. He was going through the prelaunch check, and forced himself to concentrate on the routine. He didn't like conversations like this.

"My father and mother weren't particularly interested in what I wanted to do," she continued. "They wanted me to do what they considered important. That was to ski."

"And look at the result. You're a terrific skier."

"But could I have been a splendid artist by now? Or a poet? Or a pilot?"

"Are those what you'd rather be?"

He heard her heavy sigh next to him. "I don't know. I'm not really trying to find fault with my parents—they did so much for me. I wouldn't be at the Academy now if they hadn't given me such support." There was a small silence, no more than a second or two. "But I can't help but wonder what might have happened . . . if they'd been more like your father."

Something ugly rose in Tom's throat. The retort was on his tongue: *You'd have ended up believing you weren't good enough.* But he squelched it, and focused instead on the prelaunch. "All systems online. You ready?"

If she was surprised at his sudden shift of subject, she didn't reveal it. "Anytime" was her reply, and if anything, what he heard in her voice was eagerness.

Tom maneuvered the shuttle out of orbit, moved as always by the sight of Earth receding from them, then set a course out of the Sol system and in the direction of the Alpha Centauri system.

"We're ready to go to warp," he announced presently. "I'm only taking us to warp one this time. I warn you, it can be disorienting at first."

"I thought inertial dampers prevented any g forces," she commented.

"They do. But seeing the distortion of the stars . . . well, you'll see what I mean. Unless you don't want to look."

"I wouldn't miss it," she replied firmly.

And so he entered the commands, delicately as always, because a woman liked to be treated delicately, and then felt the palpable thrill as the shuttle responded, creating the warp bubble which cushioned it in a pocket of subspace, and then bursting forward into a speed faster than that of light.

He had gone through this process many times, of course, the first when he was only nine, but he never ceased to thrill at the sensation. The stars seemed to elongate, stretching as though they were rubber bands, further and further until it seemed they must snap and disintegrate before his eyes. When it looked as though they could protract no further, they blurred slightly. Then there was a brief moment of total silence, a vacuumlike stillness that seemed to pull at one's stomach, which churned briefly, and finally the moment eclipsed into the smooth subspace currents of warp speed.

Transfixed as always by the experience, he almost didn't hear the small groan from Odile. He glanced over and found her looking pale, her fingers clutching the edge of the seat, eyes filmy as she drew ragged breaths.

"Put your head between your legs," he ordered, and she complied instantly. She sat like that, head down so the blood would flow toward it, for several moments. Then, gingerly, tentatively, she lifted herself upright again, but was careful not to look out the windows.

"I didn't realize . . ." she said, still shaky. "You said disorienting. It's more than that."

"I guess I don't remember how it was the first time. It's all in what the eyes are telling the brain."

"My brain was talking to my eyes . . . telling them not to look. But by then, it was too late."

"You'll get used to it. After a while, it's almost narcotic."

Gradually, she lifted her eyes again to the windows, where the stars now looked like luminous streaks of light. "Now it's all right," she murmured. "It doesn't bother me."

"It's just the moment of going to warp that creates the sensation. For me it's almost . . . holy."

She looked at him pensively. He'd never shared a revelation so personal with anyone, and he found himself apprehensive. Would she laugh at him?

"I can understand why" was her reply, and Tom felt an enormous surge of gratitude.

They flew like that for a long time, not speaking, basking in the hauntingly beautiful sight of the stars streaking around them.

The week they taught Charlie Day to ski was the same week Tom decided to defy his father once more. This time, had the admiral asked him if a young woman were involved, he would have had to admit yes, there most definitely was, but his father didn't ask the question and Tom never volunteered the information.

It all happened at Lake Tahoe, where Tom, Odile, and Bruno had gone over the New Year's holiday to get some ski time in and to celebrate the passing of the old year. It was a ritual Tom had always found satisfying, the bidding farewell to the year past and the greeting of the new one. It was a time that seemed fraught with possibility, with hope and potential. He was invariably cheered by the prospect of the chronograph hitting twenty-four hundred hours and then beginning to count the first minute of the new year.

Starfleet Academy had acquired a building in the mountains surrounding the lake, and had turned it into a dormitory, largely for use by the ski team, which had grown in just two years to twenty-six people. Tom, Bruno, and Odile had planned to spend the whole New Year's break there, and Charlie was added to the mix when Tom found that his family would be off-world for a month.

Tom had been visiting the crystal blue lake in the Sierras since he was a small child, and it held a special place in his heart. It was surely one of nature's miracles, a vast basin atop a mountain range, breathtakingly spectacular whether viewed from the air or the ground. From lakeside, one saw 484 square kilometers of the purest blue water, ringed with majestic, rugged mountains. A forest of green clung to those mountain slopes, and the confluence of color—blue, green, white, slate—was powerful.

Nearby was another, equally pristine lake, smaller, which would forever remain linked with the tragic fate of the family that gave it its name: Donner. Even now, five hundred years later, the tale of the pioneers who had suffered so cruelly the ravages of nature and of each other had the ability to tantalize the imagination. There was still a shrine to the intrepid wagon train of long ago: a huge boulder had served as a cabin wall for one family, the Breens, and a plaque there commemorated their travails during the bitter winter of 1846.

Tom was the only one of the group who knew of that ancient catastrophe. To Odile and Bruno it was an obscure event in the history of another country; Charlie was more interested in science than in minutiae of the past. Tom was pleased, as they stood by the huge boulder, that they seemed moved by his reverential account of the Donners, the Reeds, the Breens, and the others of that ill-fated group.

"I'm not sure I could eat human flesh, even if it were the only way to survive," Bruno commented. Odile fixed him with a penetrating eye.

"Of course you could. If you got hungry enough, you'd eat anything. The organism is developed that way—it's in our genetic structure to survive."

"But it's in our cultural conditioning not to eat our own species. It's a deeply entrenched taboo."

"Deeply entrenched or not, I'm sure I'd do it if it were necessary."

"I'll keep that in mind if we ever go camping together," observed Charlie mildly, bringing smiles to the group.

"Let's go," suggested Tom. "We can still get in a few more runs today." In seconds they had transported back to the mountain range once known as Squaw Valley, now renamed for a branch of the indigenous Washo people: Wel Mel Ti. They took Charlie down the intermediate runs, giving him pointers as they went.

Charlie had amazed them all by taking to skiing with alacrity. In two days he was able to keep up with them on all but the most difficult runs, although he couldn't match their speed. He took the slopes at his own pace, measured and stately, but he was unafraid of steeps and moguls.

He had no interest in racing, even though they urged him to give it a try. Charlie wasn't a driven person, and seemed to feel no need to prove anything to anyone. Tom envied him.

On New Year's Eve they gathered in the dormitory's large common room with other students who were there for the holiday. The structure was several hundred years old, though it had been remodeled recently, and boasted a feature few of them had ever used: a fireplace. Even Bruno, whose parents had raised him in the woods and made him ski to and from school, had only heard about this ancient custom. But he knew enough to be able to pile some wood and pinecones they collected into the rectangular opening in the wall, and to ignite the mass with the intense beam of a tricorder.

The delight the group took in this ancient practice was instant and intoxicating. There was an appeal to the flames that was entirely lacking in microfusion energy systems, and the young people found themselves gathering round the burning logs, staring at the flickering flames as though mesmerized. The crackle of the pitch pine and the heady aroma of the woodsmoke were more beguiling than they could have imagined.

Someone had made thick, fragrant soup, and Bruno replicated a hot Scandinavian drink, *glugg,* which warmed them from within even as the fire warmed their skin. Odile began singing, sweet, plaintive love songs from the past, and then they all sang, old songs, new songs, raising their young voices in friendship and joy, and Tom thought he'd never felt more at peace, more hopeful about the future. As the chronograph turned to twenty-four hundred hours, a great cheer broke from the group, and Tom drew Odile to him and kissed her, gently, feeling the moment freeze in time as the sounds from the others faded and there were only the two of them, locked in tender embrace, each completing the other, a union as old as eternity.

The next day, Odile told him she would be staying in France for her junior year.

Tom thought she was teasing him, and entered into what he assumed was a charade. "Good idea. I think I'll just drop the junior year entirely. Commandeer a shuttle and chart planets where we can do some off-world skiing."

Her emerald eyes were fixed firmly on his. "This is not a joke, Tommy. I am quite serious. My mama has asked it of me and I have agreed. I will study at the Academy campus in Marseilles, which is close to Beziers."

"But . . . what about the ski team? What about your pilot's training? What . . . about me?"

She reached out and took his hand; her fingers felt like liquid silver. "I will not compete next year. But I'll continue my pilot's training. And we will see each other. It's not as though there aren't transporters."

What she was saying was true, but every part of him rejected it. It wouldn't be the same. He wouldn't run into her on campus, her red-blond hair flying behind her as she raced to class, never allowing even a minute's leeway, always cutting it right to the second. He wouldn't have lunch with her every Thursday, when their class schedules gave them a free hour at the same time. He wouldn't walk under her dormitory window at night and look up, imagining her there, lying in bed, asleep in the pale moonlight.

"Why? Why is your mother asking you to do this? It isn't fair." He heard the petulant tone in his voice and stopped, swallowing, trying not to behave like a spoiled child.

Odile hesitated before answering. "I believe . . . that my father is not well. She has not come out and said so, but I have seen him. He has become thin."

This blew away the head of steam Tom was developing. "Not well? What does that mean?"

"I don't know. It's just my instinct."

"That's an archaic way of dealing with a problem. Why don't they come out and talk about it? Why the mystery?"

"I think . . . they want to protect me."

"That's ridiculous. You suspect something anyway, only now you can't get it out in the open."

"That's the way my parents are."

Tom fumed to himself for a few moments, angry and frustrated, wanting to find someone to blame but knowing it mustn't be Odile's parents. This left precious few candidates, and Tom soon gave up and acknowledged the truth.

"I'm sorry, Odile, I'm selfish. I can't stand the thought of your being that far away for a year. I don't know what I'll do."

She picked up his hand and pressed her lips to it. "You are so sweet," she murmured, and Tom vowed that he would not, under any circumstances, lose next year with Odile.

"Does the campus at Marseilles specialize in any particular area of study?" he asked, mind already nibbling at a solution.

"It offers all the course work of the Academy. But if there's a strength, I would say it's exophilosophy."

This gave Tom pause. If she'd said any of the sciences, he'd be on firmer ground. On the other hand . . .

He put his arm around her, drawing her close as they gazed into the fire. "This is going to work," he promised her. "We won't be apart."

And so it was that Tom Paris spent his junior year in Marseilles, concentrating on the study of exophilosophies, an area of his education in which, as he'd explained to his faculty advisor and his parents, he was woefully lacking.

No one was particularly fooled by this sudden interest in alien philosophies, but no one thought it could do any harm, either, and all remembered young love and how searing it could be. If these two wanted to be together, why not let them?

Tom hadn't been in Marseilles a week when he discovered Sandrine's, a waterfront bar and pool establishment which had been in continuous operation for almost three hundred years. It was an eclectic blend of the ancient and the modern, and populated with a colorful assortment of the town's denizens.

Most enchanting, to Tom, was Sandrine herself. That wasn't her real name, of course—every proprietor of Sandrine's for the past three hundred years had taken the honorary name of its legendary founder, Sandrine Normand, who had established the bar in the troubled twenty-first century. She had created an environment that was clean, safe, and quintessentially French, in an era when those qualities were hard to come by. She was revered by her patrons, lived well over one hundred years, and died at work, making an aperitif for a wealthy horse breeder half her age who found her the most vital and appealing woman in all of France. She had presented him the drink, smiled and said, *"A votre sante, mon cher,"* and then keeled over behind the bar. The end was swift, painless, and elegant, characterizing Sandrine accurately.

Since then, each of the proprietresses had taken the honorary name of Sandrine. This one was sleek and blond, in her forties, with a worldly air that Tom found provocative. She was sexually bold to a degree that startled, but also tantalized, the younger man.

"You are *tres beau,* Thomas," she would purr to him. "Those eyes . . . *alors,* you know how to make a woman weak, *non?"*

Tom found this flirtation great fun, gradually lost his embarrassment, and entered into the teasing with complete enthusiasm. He assumed it was understood by all parties that it was nothing more than a harmless game. That's when he learned something more about French women.

Odile had spent the weekend at her parents' in Beziers, but had promised to meet him at Sandrine's on Sunday evening, when she returned to school. Tom had passed the time in her absence at the library, studying Vulcan *cthia,* the stoic approach to emotion control that had been formulated centuries ago by Surak. He found it mildly interesting but not enthralling, and by Sunday afternoon he felt justified in taking a break and heading for Sandrine's just a little early.

He'd made some friends among the regulars there, particularly the pool players, with whom he felt an affinity. One of those, a grizzled, wizened man named Balzac, who claimed direct lineage with the ancient writer, was an astonishingly talented player who had taken Tom under his wing and coached him in the finer points of the game. Tom found himself a natural student, and became semi-addicted to pool. He arranged a system of "rewards": four hours in the classroom or the library netted him twenty minutes of nine-ball. Eight hours, forty minutes. It took all his discipline to stick to this arrangement, but he did it with surprisingly few lapses.

Having spent all of Saturday, Saturday night, Sunday morning, and most of Sunday afternoon in the library had earned him an entire hour and a half of nine-ball. Since he was meeting Odile there later that night, he decided to collect his reward before that.

He arrived about six, before the place was too crowded. He eyed Sandrine behind the bar, exchanged a few ribald pleasantries with her, and then sought out Balzac. They'd been playing for about ten minutes when Sandrine brought them both a covered soup dish which contained a heavenly fragrant stew.

"It is venison, *cheri,*" she whispered in her husky voice. "I think you are a man who needs meat, eh?"

"There's no such thing as meat, Sandrine. It's all replicated."

"C'est vrai, but this is a special replication formula derived by my father. He claimed to have eaten the real thing, and said this was the closest version he'd ever tasted."

"Interesting." Tom took a healthy spoonful of the stew, which was rich with garlic and sage. It was a powerful taste, ripe and gamy, but not unpleasant. He smiled appreciatively at Sandrine. "Not bad."

She sidled closer to him, pressing one leg against his, and he was immediately conscious of the heat rising from her. She looked up at him through lowered lashes. "It is a wild meat," she murmured. "I think it is the right choice for a man like you."

Heat began rising from Tom, too. She was wearing a faint fragrance, something so subtle one was drawn closer in order to detect it, not cloying, not overly musky, but a hint of something delicate, delectable, sensual. He became aware of Balzac's bemused presence and backed away slightly, spooning more of the stew into his mouth, but keeping his eye contact with Sandrine. "I think you're right," he said right to her, not looking away. Her smile was hooded, mysterious.

"Are we going to play or are you two going off together?" asked Balzac with good humor. Tom put down the stew and picked up his cue. "To leave a game in the middle isn't honorable," he announced, enjoying this flirtation. It didn't seem dangerous to him, not yet.

Later Sandrine approached him again, carrying a crystal goblet. *"C'est un vin vrai,"* she said throatily, handing him the beautifully carved glass. "Not the wretched synthehol." She pronounced it "seen-tha-hol," which he found enchanting. When he tasted it, it was elixir. He never had real wine before, and now began to understand the French obsession.

Two glasses later he was flushed and exhilarated. He had beaten Balzac in the last three games, a unique experience. He had long since abandoned his reward system, having exceeded his hour-and-a-half limit, but it didn't seem a major transgression. He had to wait here for Odile, anyway, and had to pass the time somehow . . .

Never had the room seemed so inviting, never had pool been so effortless. And never had the extraordinary Sandrine been more desirable. Not that he intended to act on anything, but the delectable dance they were creating between them was too seductive to end just now.

"Thomas," she cooed, taking the pool cue from him, "help me with my technique. I think I'm not getting the stability I need for a strong shot." She bent over the table, positioning the cue, forming the fingers of her left hand into a "bridge" upon which the cue rested. She was stretched over the table like a supple lioness, blond hair sprawling, lithe body straining against her tightly fitting bodysuit. Tom wiped a bead of perspiration from his forehead.

He bent himself over her, stretching his arms to encompass hers, taking her fingers in his to reposition them. *"Zut alors,"* said Balzac, and wandered off to a less exclusive situation. Sandrine turned her head to look at him, her mouth only inches from his. "Do what you must, *cheri,* I am a very good student."

They were just like that, Sandrine stretched over the pool table, Tom virtually on top of her, faces only inches apart, when Odile walked in.

Balzac tried a discreet cough as a warning, but it was too little too late. Odile sized up the situation in an instant and strode to the pool table, directly across from Tom and Sandrine, and began speaking in rapid-fire French that Tom, though fluent, couldn't begin to follow. He leapt up, too late realizing how compromising the pose looked, and tried to babble some lame excuse. He knew, whatever he was saying, it didn't quite make sense, and he realized how the wine had garbled his thoughts. Odile paid him no attention and continued her diatribe toward Sandrine.

Whatever she said, it produced an instant, electric response from the older woman, who rose in response to the challenge, circled the table toward Odile, and began her own ardent harangue.

Tom had the sense that things were roiling out of his control, but he gave his best effort to contain the damage. "Odile," he said heartily, "I'm glad you're here. I was just giving Sandrine some tips about her bridge." It sounded inane, even to him, and he saw Balzac in his peripheral vision passing his hands over his eyes in mock despair, but the two women paid him no attention whatsoever, and continued their vicious tirades, which were growing in intensity and volume.

Tom found them both frightening. Odile's green eyes had changed from emerald to a deep, sea green that looked decidedly menacing, and her hair seemed to have lost its blondness and was the red of fire, almost giving off sparks.

He had never seen her like this, but he was equally unprepared for Sandrine's transformation, from sleek and voluptuous feline to a forceful predator. It had to be his imagination, but her fingernails seemed to have grown long and razor-sharp in the last minute. Maybe that's because she held them, curled as though for attack, just in front of Odile's face.

That's when Tom became really frightened, not for Odile, but for Sandrine. Odile was a fourth-degree black belt, and if she went for Sandrine, no sharp fingernails would stop her from inflicting real damage. Of course, one of the most formidable principles of martial arts was to avoid physical combat if at all possible, but the way Odile was behaving, he wasn't sure if pacifistic teachings would endure.

"Ladies, please, there's no need for this," he tried again, just as ineffectually. "Let's all cool down and talk this over like civilized—"

It was all he got out before Odile turned to him, and he suddenly realized her venom was about to be directed toward him, a prospect that struck dread in his heart. Far better that she and her country-woman continue whatever ancient ritual they were observing. They seemed to know the rules, but he didn't even know the game.

He stood, stock-still, as Odile hurled Gaelic invective at him, trying to follow any train of what she was saying, which seemed mostly to involve his ancestry. "Odile," he said, trying to put on his most charming smile, "you don't understand—"

"Putain!" she hurled at him, and then spun around and marched out the door. Tom felt as though he had been drawn into an antimatter chamber during the annihilation process, churned about by forces he didn't understand and couldn't control, and then spat out again after the reaction had consumed every atom.

Every eye in the room was on him. Most, he realized subliminally, were amused and tolerant, but that only made the experience more humiliating to him. He was aware of Sandrine next to him, breathing deeply, moist with unfulfilled anger, still muttering small invectives under her breath.

"I'm sorry," stammered Tom, and Sandrine immediately came to him and wrapped her arms around his neck. *"Mon cher, pauvre petit,* how awful for you. She is a vicious cat, this Odile—you are well rid of her."

Tom carefully untwined her arms from him, shock now sobering him, knowing he had to get to Odile quickly. "Thank you for everything, Sandrine, I mean it, you're terrific. And the stew was great. Loved it." He babbled like this as he backed toward the door, then was out into the raw waterfront night, where a cold rain drizzled down, and began calling for Odile. Passersby gave him curious looks, but paid no other attention. A man calling out a woman's name along the passageways of the waterfront bespoke a timeworn drama that was all too familiar to them.

He found her twenty minutes later, sitting on one of the antiquated docks that still lined the seawall, even though they hadn't been used by ships for a hundred years. She was huddled miserably, arms around her knees, sodden with the rain, hair matted wetly around her face, and sobbing pitifully.

He approached her gingerly. "Odile . . ." he began, and she turned her tear-streaked face toward him.

"Go away. I don't want you to see me like this."

Instinct told him she didn't mean that, and he walked slowly toward her, as though she were a volatile compound that might explode if he made any unexpected move. Presently he was at her side, and sat down beside her, not touching her, taking it one step at a time.

"Odile, I swear, it wasn't what you think . . . ."

He thought he'd blown the moment already, because her head snapped toward him and her eyes blazed once more. "Oh? Be honest, Tommy—it was exactly what I think, wasn't it?"

He tried to confront the question honestly and, yes, he had to agree. It was.

"It was flirtation, yes. Sandrine is very . . . alluring. But it was nothing more."

"How do you think that made me feel, to come in and see you draped over her like that? With everyone in the room watching you?"

He burned with embarrassment. He blamed the wine, which had effectively removed his inhibitions and his awareness that the spectacle he had participated in was public. The twenty-minute hunt in the rain had sobered him somewhat, and he now saw the entire incident with other eyes.

"It must have been awful. I'm so sorry." He put his hand tentatively on her shoulder, and was gratified when she turned to him and put her arms around his neck.

"If I didn't love you so much, it wouldn't hurt," she cried, and he whispered and murmured tenderly to her, reassuring her, rubbing her back and her wet hair until she was calm again. Then, she began shuddering from the cold.

He took her back to his quarters, which were part of the old city and boasted a bathtub. He bathed her gently in warm water until she stopped shaking, and then he carried her to bed, where their bodies continued to warm each other, sweetly.

In their senior year, Tom, Odile, Bruno, and Charlie Day competed for, and won, many different honors. Odile and Bruno won sports awards for their contributions to making the ski team a viable contender after just three years of existence. Charlie Day won top honors for his independent engineering project, to which Tom was a close second. Tom and Charlie vied for the highly prized positions on the Grissom aerial squad, the highest pinnacle to which pilots could strive. Odile and Bruno distinguished themselves as pilots, as well. The four friends went through the year like this, working hard, excelling and achieving, enjoying life and the camaraderie that came from richly nurtured friendships.

One of their favorite pastimes was off-world skiing. Charlie, though still not at a competitive level, was more than up to deep powder runs, and it became a game with them to seek out the freshest and most pristine snows on the most obscure planets. The Academy would have frowned on such extracurricular activity, of course, but the officers didn't think to scrutinize too carefully the behavior of four of its most stellar students.

Each was laying plans for the future, which seemed limitless. On a crisp and sparkling day in early spring, one in which San Francisco relented and allowed the sun to shine, the four sprawled in Tom and Charlie's quarters, munching apples and anticipating graduation.

"Guess I'm a glutton for school," mused Bruno. "I figure I'm looking at three more years for a graduate degree in astrophysics. But I'll get more piloting experience at the same time, and then be qualified for deep-space exploration."

"I'm hoping for a posting to a ship right away," said Odile. "Any ship, big or small, just as long as I get into space and have the opportunity to fly."

Tom's heart constricted a bit. They'd definitely be going separate ways in a few months and he wasn't sure how he'd stand it. But they had realized their careers might keep them apart for a while, and agreed that each must do what would best advance those careers. In a few years they'd reevaluate the situation and see if they wanted to change it. Tom believed that Odile was actually more comfortable with those arrangements than he was, which made him vaguely uneasy.

"Tommy and I are going head-to-head for the same post. May the best man win," said Charlie with a grin.

"What's that?" asked Bruno with curiosity, chewing the last fleck of fruit from an apple eaten nearly to the core.

"The *Enterprise,*" replied Charlie, casting a glance at Tom, who smiled in return.

"The *Enterprise?* You think the flagship will take on an ensign right out of the Academy?"

"They've been known to take one. They've never taken two," explained Tom.

"Since Tom is more qualified than I am, I'm counting on his family name to work against him," said Charlie affably. "Starfleet wouldn't want to be accused of favoritism."

Tom cuffed Charlie good-naturedly, but secretly thought his friend was absolutely right. The illustrious name of Paris mustn't be thought to be an influence in garnering a plum assignment aboard Starfleet's flagship. He would have to be such an outstanding candidate that his name wouldn't get in his way.

Of course, Charlie was as qualified as he was. Tom was the more experienced pilot, but Charlie had the edge in engineering. Tom often found himself overcome with self-doubt, able only to see Charlie's excellent qualifications and his own abundant failings. He worked consciously at purging those doubts.

This discussion was making him uncomfortable, and he looked to change the subject. "I heard of a great new planet for skiing," he told the group.

"What is it?" queried Bruno, eyeing another apple from the nearly depleted bowl.

"It's in the Epsilon Eridani system, twelve light-years away. It'd take us three or four days to get there, so we'd need a couple of weeks to do it right."

"Isn't that system under some dispute now?" asked Odile.

"That's been resolved," replied Tom. "I heard about it from one of my father's attachés." This wasn't precisely true. The Epsilon Eridani system was at the moment unofficially "off limits" to Starfleet. Apparently this was because of some obscure and poorly understood situation that had occurred in the last century, and Tom frankly felt this wasn't reason enough to pass up good skiing. But he didn't want to make the others wary, so he coated his reasoning just slightly.

"It's the eighth planet of the system, with weather conditions perfect for producing snow. And not just any snow—pure crystallized water vapor, free of mineral contaminants, powdery and pristine."

All the others were intrigued, as Tom knew they would be. They'd become almost addicted to the hunt for new ski worlds, spending every moment they could flying to planets where snow conditions prevailed. Nothing was as exhilarating as careering down a mountain of fresh powder no one had ever skied before.

Two months later, the four sat in a shuttlecraft, flashing toward the Epsilon Eridani system, three of them anticipating the thrill of the ski quest, Tom churning inside from playing and replaying the recent discussion he'd had with his father.

"You did *what?*" he'd asked the admiral, incredulous.

His father had regarded him with firm determination from behind his desk—the picture of authority—while the wall of pictures of the Paris lineage seemed to watch as well, mocking. "I asked that your name be removed from consideration for a posting to the *Enterprise.*"

Tom had flushed with anger and surprise; his throat had constricted as though a band encircled it, tightening. He drew a breath before he spoke. "May I ask why?"

"I'm very much afraid that, if you were chosen, there would be the appearance of favoritism."

"Starfleet doesn't operate like that."

"You know that, and I know that. We're talking about appearances. It would be unseemly for you to receive such a privilege."

"You don't receive a posting like that—you have to earn it. And that's what I would have done."

Admiral Paris looked pained. "Tom, I'm not trying to denigrate your efforts. I'm terribly proud of your accomplishments in the Academy. Your mother and I know how hard you've worked. And in a few years, with some experience on another starship, posting you to the *Enterprise* wouldn't cause a ripple. It just looks suspect to go there directly from the Academy."

Tom had glared at him, furious but impotent. A dozen retorts swirled in his mind, each more bitter than the other, their venom seductive, tantalizing. But he knew such utterances wouldn't prove satisfying in the long run; his father would be lordly and condescending, chastising him for losing control.

So without a word, he turned on his heel and left, not even nodding to Commander Klenman on the way out.

Now, as his friends chattered animatedly, Tom sat enveloped in gloom, constructing alternate endings for the encounter, each of which was predicated on a brilliant argument he might have made, something so incisive and scathing that his father, taken aback, would have seen the muddiness of his own thinking and rescinded his judgment.

But he hadn't done that. He'd let his father overpower him again, and gone creeping away like a chastised toddler instead of facing the admiral like a man. Self-loathing rose in Tom like a miasma, acid and vaporous. He was tempted to turn the shuttle around and return to San Francisco, but that wouldn't be fair to the others, who'd looked forward to this outing, their final trip together before separating.

Odile was the most jubilant of the group. Tom's black mood lifted a bit when he tuned in to her excitement.

"I couldn't find out much about the ship before we left, but Commander Harrison said the *Hera* is the perfect ship for me. Captain La Forge is well respected and apparently a wonderful officer for a new ensign to serve under."

"Her son's on the *Enterprise*," offered Charlie, who was still hoping for that post.

"Right. And the size of the ship is ideal, too—big enough to draw deep-space assignments, but not huge and impersonal. Like the *Enterprise*," she added with a sidelong glance at Tom. She was the only one he'd told of his father's interference in his plans, and he believed she was trying to make him feel better.

Which only made him feel worse, reminded again of his lost opportunity. He had a sudden picture of himself standing on skis at the top of a tall and dangerous mountain, flinging himself into the powder, headlong and reckless, heart pounding and legs churning, racing breakneck all the way to the bottom.

It seemed the only thing that might clear his mind of his noxious disposition, and he reached for the controls to put the shuttle into highest warp. It was suddenly important to get to Epsilon Eridani IV as soon as possible.

They achieved orbit four hours later, and spent two more studying the planet, its weather conditions, and topography. They determined a location for their first day's outing, and then settled in for a night's sleep until daylight came to the mountain they'd chosen.

But sleep was hard for Tom to come by, his mind smoldering like a volcano that was nearing eruption. Again and again he told himself there was no point in dwelling on the disappointment, that he should let it go and move ahead. But it was as though a tiny black hole had lodged in his mind, dense and powerful, pulling every stray thought into its event horizon.

It was his father's voice that rumbled through his mind, strident, determined. It was a voice that had the power to flay him, strip him of every shred of dignity and leave him emotionally naked and shivering.

How had it come to this? He was twenty-two years old, ready to graduate from Starfleet Academy, an outstanding student and pilot, and yet his father had this capacity to make him feel helpless and unworthy. How could he continue to let it happen?

Even as he vowed not to grant the admiral this crippling power, his mind churned with fury and resentment, and he didn't fall asleep until it was nearly time to get up.

The morning on Epsilon Eridani IV dawned crisp and golden. The foursome transported down to a mountain that was part of a large transverse range. Pure powder snow lay silken on the undulating slopes, inviting them to plunge into their untrammeled depths.

They stood for several moments, drawing in the cold, sweet air, reveling in the majestic sight of the endless mountain range that lay before them. "This is incredible," breathed Odile, her voice tinged with awe. "And just think—no one has ever skied this snow before."

Tom couldn't fully appreciate the grandeur of the moment. He was edgy from lack of sleep, and his eyes felt welded to millions of tiny grains of sand. His throat ached vaguely and he realized with irritation that he might be catching a cold and hadn't brought any antivirals along. He'd made coffee before they left the shuttle, which rested securely in synchronous orbit some thirty thousand kilometers above the planet, but it had had an acrid, sour taste and he didn't finish it. He hadn't been hungry when the others had breakfast, but now his stomach was rumbling to protest its emptiness.

All in all, not a great way to start the day they'd looked forward to for so long. Yesterday he had longed to throw himself full speed down the mountain, but today it hardly seemed to matter. Nothing was going to make him lose this black mood.

Charlie was scanning the slopes with a tricorder, a safety precaution they always took, scanning the snow pack for instabilities that might indicate the threat of avalanche. "Looks good," he announced finally, and snapped it shut.

"Let me check it out," Tom said, and he realized his voice was harsh. Charlie's eyes betrayed the slightest surprise at his friend's surly tone, but he handed over the tricorder. Tom scanned swiftly, verifying what Charlie had said: he could detect no instabilities. Stuffing the tricorder in his pack, he nodded his approval. The four made final checks of their skis, goggles, and poles. When they were ready, they turned to Bruno, who would lead the first descent, a task they rotated among themselves.

Bruno drove forward with a whoop that echoed endlessly through the mountains, skis plunging into the deep powder, snow spray kicking up around his body. Odile followed, then Charlie, and finally Tom.

Within minutes his mood began to lighten. The raptures of the day were irresistible—cobalt sky, virgin snow, the glorious sensation of plunging headlong down the slopes, powder spraying a fine exhaust, the exquisite silence of the mountains—and for the first time in days his mind began to quiet and its dark bile subside. He relaxed into the particular pleasure of powder skiing, which required one to navigate by feel since skis disappeared into the powder and couldn't be seen. It was perfect for focusing the mind, for squeezing out all thoughts of his father.

Fifteen minutes into the run, Charlie, ahead of him, caught the edge of his shoe and went sprawling; Tom braked but couldn't avoid him, and together they tumbled into the soft pack of snow. Neither took a bad fall, and they laughed like children, Tom grabbing a handful of snow and washing Charlie's face with it as they wrestled, cublike, the way they had when they were four or five. Odile and Bruno waited patiently for them a little farther down the mountain, and soon they collected themselves, found their poles, and started off again.

Another half hour passed and Tom realized Bruno and Odile had pulled up adjacent to a bowl-shaped formation. Clearly they were concerned about the possibility of avalanche, and as he and Charlie pulled up to them, he reached for his pack.

Reacting to the expression on his face, Odile asked, "What's wrong?"

"My pack is gone. I must have lost it when Charlie and I tumbled." He peered back up the slopes, from whence they'd come, and decided there was no way he could backtrack. And he had no coordinates to give the transporter to put him back at the site of the fall.

"I'm a little worried about this formation," said Bruno. "If the snow is unstable, we could be asking for trouble."

"Well, way back when they didn't have tricorders, people were still able to avoid instabilities," offered Tom. He was determined not to stop now, not when he was feeling buoyed for the first time in days. The exhilarating plummet down the mountain had whipped him clean of rage, and even now, confronting the possibility of truncating their expedition, he could feel it bubbling back. He was damned if he was going to stop now.

"Give me your shovel," he said to Bruno, who handed him the compact, short-handled digging implement. Tom began shoveling out a snow pit, working steadily until it was about a meter and a half deep and a meter wide. Then he used the shovel to shave the uphill wall until it was smooth and vertical. He blew gently to clear away loose particles, and then began to study the snow pack. This was something Henri Islicker had taught him to do long ago. "You might not have fancy technology to help you," the old man had stated firmly. "You have to be able to rely on yourself."

The layers of snow, always present in a terrain that has repeated snowfall, were readily apparent. Tom used his gloved hands to push on the pit wall to test the relative hardness of each layer. So far, so good. None of them seemed terribly soft, and all were well bonded together. He noted the top of what looked like a layer of hoarfrost at the bottom of his pit, and grabbed a handful. Its grains were reasonably cohesive, a good sign. Something in his mind nagged him to dig a little deeper and check that layer out more thoroughly, but he decided on a shear test instead.

Using the shovel, he carved a column of snow from the wall of the pit, about a shovel head's width on all sides. Then, he inserted the shovel at the back of the column and tugged gently. He was already encouraged because the column didn't collapse when he was cutting it, which would have indicated a weak layer that might give way. He was pleased when the gentle tug had no effect on the column, either. He increased the force of the pull and, finally, the column fractured at the level of the hoarfrost. But it had taken a solid tug to make it happen, which indicated a relatively stable snow pack.

Bolstered, he climbed out of the pit and reported the good news to the others. But instead of sharing his relief, they seemed to be troubled.

"We should call it a day for now, Tom," said Odile. "We had a good run and there's no point in risking avalanche. We can plot another course when we get back to the shuttle."

"But—I tested the snow layers. They're stable. There's no need to stop."

"Odile's right," chimed in Bruno. "The smart thing is to find another course." Tom felt anger rising in him as he turned to Charlie, who, somewhat abashedly, shrugged at him. "We really don't have enough information about this environment to be relying on old-fashioned tests. I'm with the others."

Tom took a breath, trying to still the fury he could feel overtaking him. These cowardly quitters were going to cost him his feeling of well-being and plunge him back into the well of despair he'd been in for so long. How could they do that to him? Indignation flanked anger and they began to fuel each other.

"I can't believe this. You call yourselves Starfleet cadets? I thought courage was one of the attributes we're supposed to have."

"Common sense is another," said Bruno, unfazed by Tom's sarcasm. His unruffled demeanor provoked Tom even more.

"I call it cowardice. I wouldn't want anyone flying next to me who was going to back off because they *imagined* there might be danger ahead."

Even good-natured Charlie took affront at that. "I guess I wouldn't want someone flying next to me that was going to put us at unnecessary risk."

The fact that Charlie, his friend since childhood, sided against him cut Tom to the quick. His fury returned in full force, and his voice was venomous when he spoke. "Then go on back. I'll finish the run by myself."

"Tom," he heard Odile say, imploringly, as he carved into the snow, but he neither answered nor looked back. He'd made one turn when the snow suddenly seemed to settle, a dusting of white rising from its surface. Startled, he came to a stop and looked back up the slope.

The snow had fractured fifteen meters below Odile, Charlie, and Bruno, who had realized it and were staring at him. "Move!" yelled Tom, and turned to ski out of the path of the descending slab of snow.

The sound was terrifying, a massive rumble like a thousand volcanoes erupting. Tom's heart pounded heavily in his chest, but he thought there was a good chance he could get to the side of the avalanche and avoid it.

A second later, the full impact of the descending snow slammed into him, upending and completely engulfing him. His poles were ripped from his hands as he was tossed about like a dandelion puff in the thundering snow, and the noise level suddenly subsided: all he could hear was a surprisingly gentle *whoosh*.

As the snow enveloped him, it took his breath away and he gulped for air, a mistake he instantly regretted, for his mouth immediately filled with snow, a phenomenon he'd read about and remembered now he should have avoided by keeping his mouth closed. His mind raced to recall the other survival techniques associated with avalanches.

Swim, he thought, and began moving his arms and legs as best he could while being carried down the mountainside by what had to be kilotons of snow. The sensation of speed was incredible, and the realization that he could be slammed into a rock, or a tree, and broken like a piece of balsa threatened to panic him once more. The snow in his mouth had quickly condensed into a hard ball that he couldn't expel, and he felt as though he were drowning.

But he kept his legs and arms moving as best he could, flailing at the snow as though it were a flume of water, and he felt himself rise in the rushing snow and managed to get himself into a kind of sitting position, legs in front of him.

He had no idea how long the headlong plummet down the mountain would last—not until the slab of snow reached a leveling of the ground—nor whether its breakneck descent might carry it, and him, over a cliff, plunging him to his death.

But he must be ready to thrust for the surface the second he sensed the snow slowing, because once it slowed and stopped, the weight of the snow would become like concrete, packing him in, unable to move. He would have just a few seconds to try to get his head above the snow pack so he could breathe, or an arm free so he could dig out.

Down, down he plunged, for what seemed endless minutes. He paddled furiously in the snow, trying to swim up, where it was lighter, for that way lay air, and freedom.

The mass began to slow almost imperceptibly, and Tom redoubled his efforts, thrusting upward, straining toward the surface, for he knew in just seconds the avalanche would run out and the massive weight of the snow would bury him solidly. He strained like a swimmer streaking for the surface and thought for an instant he was going to make it when suddenly he slammed into something unyielding. Darkness overwhelmed him.

Tom, Tom, the piper's son, kissed the girls and made them run . . .
It was Charlie, chanting the old rhyme and laughing with glee as he did, running ahead of a hard-charging Tom, who was running full speed to catch him and throw him onto the grass, making him stop.

They were five years old and the world was new. The hills of the Portola Valley stretched for kilometers, green from the winter rains, a vast playground for the two best friends, who'd first encountered each other when they were six months old and just crawling. Their mothers had described the first visit, when the babies, plopped down on the floor, had first stared in some amazement at each other, unable to categorize this creature who, unlike everyone else in their lives, was not a giant.

Baby Tom had extended a tentative hand to Charlie's plump cheek and touched it, as though to verify the reality of this vision. Then he'd let out a whoop and started crawling away, immediately followed by a smiling and chirping Charlie.

They'd been friends ever since. They'd played, fought, teased, nagged, defended, and trusted each other for over twenty years. Charlie and Tom, Tom, the piper's son . . .

His head hurt and his throat burned. Why was Charlie teasing him?

His eyes fluttered open and he looked into Charlie's eyes. Odile and Bruno also hovered over him, looking pale and concerned. He struggled to orient himself, but it was hard to shake off his vision of childhood.

Odile was passing a medical device over him, and gradually his head cleared. Now he realized he was lying on the floor of the shuttle, and he remembered everything, his anger at his friends, his determination to traverse the snowfield, the avalanche . . .

Shame and embarrassment welled in him, but he subverted those vulnerable feelings into hostility. "Let's get out of here," he snapped, and those were the last words he spoke to them on the journey home.

A week later, Tom's black mood hadn't dissipated, but lay lodged in him like a heavy meal he couldn't digest. He knew he was acting like a surly child, but the worse he behaved, the more tenacious the angry feelings became, until he was a seething mass of resentment and fury.

It was in this mood that he took his team of small attack vehicles—piloted by himself, Odile, Charlie, and Bruno—to practice strafing runs in the Vega system's asteroid belt.

The exercise, developed for the purpose of dislodging comets, planetoids, or asteroids on a possible collision course with Earth, was a routine one. The lead pilot dived toward the chosen asteroid and fired a glancing phaser shot at one edge of the target, then pulled up and out, to be followed in succession by each of the others. The successive impact of the four shots would nudge the asteroid off its previous path. This maneuver would be performed as many times as necessary to deflect the object from an Earth-bound trajectory.

In reality, there were easier ways of dealing with errant asteroids, and the exercise was merely a structured method of taking target practice. Timing was critical to its success, and the maneuver was considered valuable in terms of strengthening coordination among the four-vessel teams.

"Paris to SAV team beta-nine. We're approaching the target."

"Aye, aye, *sir,*" came Charlie's response, tinged with sarcasm in reply to the formality of Tom's announcement. They'd flown together for a long time, and were accustomed to more easygoing communications, but Tom hadn't felt particularly friendly ever since the botched ski trip the week before, and had reverted to by-the-book procedures.

"Disengage automated systems." The highly sophisticated attack vessels could of course perform this maneuver and many others without intervention from the pilots, but in keeping with Starfleet's rigorous insistence on self-reliance, pilots were taught to be able to function without their vaunted technology. In the event of a systems failure, pilots had to be prepared to go to manual controls and follow visual flight rules.

"Check two."

"Check three."

"Check four."

Charlie, Odile, and Bruno in succession reported that they were now in manual control of their vessels. Tom could see the asteroid field looming ahead, and at its periphery, the intended target, a huge chunk of rock some six kilometers in diameter.

"Target at heading three-four-one mark two-nine-zero." Again, the others signaled their acknowledgments. "We'll take an echelon formation for the approach." In this formation, a part of aerial combat for hundreds of years, the ships deployed in a diagonal behind the leader, each of the following planes stepped slightly down from its predecessor. This allowed all the pilots to observe the target, and the vessel immediately in front.

Trust and cooperation were at the heart of this maneuver. Each pilot kept eyes glued to the ship immediately ahead of him, depending on that vessel for timing. In a well-coordinated run, the lead ship would fire and pull up, the next ship wouldn't fire until the first ship had pulled away, and so on.

Tom felt energized by the prospect of combat practice. This was where a pilot's skills were honed; this was where expertise counted. Anyone could pilot a ship intent on exploration and scientific inquiry; it took genuine skill to go up against an experienced adversary. Tom secretly regretted having missed the Cardassian conflict, where he was sure his abilities would have been tested and proven in heroic style. But those hostilities were over. And he wasn't going to be posted to the *Enterprise*. He'd likely pull duty on a science vessel and spend his career chasing nothing more exciting than a dust nebula.

So he created a small fantasy, hoping to channel his venomous mood into a diverting exercise. He wasn't performing a routine maneuver on an asteroid; he was in a strafing run against a Cardassian warship, one that could blast him and his team into bloody bits. They'd have one chance to destroy it, only one, so each part of the maneuver had to be performed with precision timing.

Tom felt his mind focus, like a crystalline lens, and for the first time in days he felt in control of his destiny. Ahead of him lay the dangerous Cardassian warship, coiled like a rattlesnake, ready to annihilate him. He glanced to his left and saw Charlie's ship, just behind and below him, ready to follow him in.

"Let's do it," he said to the comm, and nosed the ship in a dive toward the asteroid/enemy.

In his mind's eye, he saw the Cardassian ship open fire, hitting his shields, continuing the barrage. He kept his nose down, judging the speed of the target and the angle of his deflection, in order to gauge his one shot. One shot, right at the warp nacelle. This was one Cardassian ship that wouldn't attack Federation borders again.

Down he plummeted, eyeing the nacelle, waiting until the last possible second so his shot would be as accurate as he could make it, so it would have maximum impact. Wait . . . wait . . . wait . . .

Now! Tom unleashed his phaser volley and then pulled up. Only then did he realize he'd taken the formation too low, held the dive too long, caught up in his fantasy, determined to score against the Cardassian ship. He barely escaped slamming into the asteroid.

Charlie, following him, was doomed. He had only Tom's example to go by, Tom's timing determining his own. The margin of error increased with each following vessel, and the precious second that allowed Tom to escape impact was lost to Charlie.

And to Odile, whose ship plunged into the asteroid right behind Charlie's. Bruno, the final ship, stood some chance of pulling out in time, but was caught in the violence of the antimatter explosions that the other two ships produced, and his ship cartwheeled out of control until it, too, erupted in a massive detonation.

In horror, Tom turned his ship back to the point of impact. "Paris to SAV team . . . Charlie . . . Odile . . . Bruno . . ."

No response, as he'd known there couldn't be. A burning debris field clustered just over the surface of the asteroid, no chunk of which was more than a meter long. There was no sign of his friends, who would have incinerated in the violent explosion.

A terrifying silence enveloped him as he stared at the drifting remnants of the SAV ships, already spreading into space, dispersing among the asteroid field that had become his friends' graveyard. For a moment nausea enveloped him and he thought he would throw up, but he took some deep breaths and regained control.

Tom wondered what their last thoughts had been. Were they of betrayal, of the awful perfidy of their friend? Did they die hating Tom for what he'd done?

These were the questions that ate at Tom as he flew his lone ship back to Earth. He didn't sleep, couldn't sleep, couldn't eat. He sat at the controls, frozen in place, imagining the last moments of Charlie, Bruno, and Odile. He fantasized every possible emotion, felt the panic and the terror they must have experienced as they realized they were going to die, the anger they must have felt that Tom Paris had been the cause.

By the time he got to Earth he felt like a dead man himself. He was gaunt and hollow-eyed, devoid of emotion, unable to feel anything. He thought he would probably never sleep again, and that seemed entirely reasonable. He was in a state of suspension, almost noncorporeal, a consciousness in near total shutdown.

He could live like that.

The faces of his family swam before him, his mother radiating concern, holding him tightly, crying with relief that he was alive. His father was pale and quiet, his eyes reflecting a pain Tom had never seen there before. The admiral put his arms around Tom, enveloping him, squeezing hard as though to make absolutely certain he was there. His sisters couldn't keep their hands off him, tears in their eyes, love and empathy shining from them.

But Tom himself felt nothing.

"So this was nothing more than routine target practice?"

"Yes, sir. There was nothing extraordinary about it at all."

Tom's jaw was beginning to ache. He'd held it so tightly clamped since the hearing began that little rivulets of pain were spreading from the hinge of his jaw toward his ears. In a way, the pain was comforting. It gave him something to anchor himself to this reality, because otherwise, he might believe himself to be in an alternate dimension.

Admiral Brand sat at a table before him, flanked by Admiral Finnegan and Captain Satelk. Aides to the admirals sat to one side of the small, windowless room, paneled in old wood from another era, a close, boxy room that reminded Tom of a cell. It felt difficult to breathe, as though the air weren't being circulated.

Tom sat alone, on a chair facing the array of admirals. The room was stark and unadorned, devoid of any humanizing touch, its walls gunmetal gray, the carpet a similarly neutral hue. Tom imagined that a tomb might look like this on the inside.

Behind him sat his father, Admiral Owen Paris, the sole spectator. Tom couldn't see him, but his presence was charged, as though he emanated some kind of potent forcefield, his eyes drilling into Tom's back like tiny phaser beams.

They'd been here for about twenty minutes so far. Tom had given a painstakingly detailed description of the relationships between himself, Odile, Charlie, and Bruno. The latter three had been solemnly remembered in services at the Academy and then privately in their home cities. Their bodies were now among the stars, whose exploration they would never experience.

"If you were the team leader, why was Cadet Katajavuori leading the strafing run?" This from Admiral Finnegan, a friendly-looking man with once-red hair now shot with gray, and kindly blue eyes.

Tom clamped his jaw together once again and took a deep breath. He would tell them what he had told everyone informally, what he had told his family, Charlie's family, and Odile's and Bruno's, what he was almost coming to believe himself was the truth.

"We frequently switched roles. I thought it was important that each member of the team have the opportunity to take charge, to get experience in the leadership position. And this was a routine exercise, one we'd performed many times. It seemed the perfect time to let Bruno—Cadet Katajavuori—head up the team."

"And what, in your mind, was the cause for the accident?"

"For some reason, Bruno held his dive a few seconds longer than he should. I can't explain it. He must've misjudged his distance somehow. The second and third ships in the echelon—Cadets Day and

223

Launay—didn't have enough time to react, and impacted with the asteroid."

"But you didn't."

"As the trailing vessel, I had a second or so to realize what had happened. My ship got tossed pretty badly by the shock wave from the explosions, but I was able to avoid hitting the asteroid."

"I would imagine your piloting skills helped you there."

"Maybe so. I think I was just lucky."

There was a brief pause as the admirals reviewed their notes. "Tactical logs indicate you did fire your phasers. How did you manage that in the middle of this catastrophe?"

"I honestly don't know. I don't have any memory of it. I was ready to fire, of course, ready to follow Odile in as soon as she pulled up. I must have done it instinctively."

The admirals exchanged looks. "Is there anything else you think might be pertinent, Cadet?"

"No, sir, I think that covers it. But I would like to say, for the record, that Cadets Day, Katajavuori, and Launay were three of the best that Starfleet will ever encounter. It was my honor to be their friend. I don't believe Cadet Katajavuori's mishap should in any way be held against him. We all make mistakes. I also accept responsibility for the fact that assigning him to be team leader was my idea. If I hadn't done that, they might be alive today."

There was silence then, a sudden vacuum that left Tom light-headed. He could feel his heart slamming in his chest, and wondered if the others could hear it.

Finally, Admiral Brand spoke. "Cadet Paris, this has been a tragedy of terrible proportions. The loss of three young lives, lives with such great potential, has left their families bereft and all of us at Starfleet sobered.

"But we are aware that it has been a terrible loss for you, as well. It is not our desire to make you suffer any more than you have already."

Brand paused and glanced briefly at Admiral Paris. "You come of a long line of Starfleet luminaries. Any one of them would tell you that losing those you've worked with closely is devastating. But we've all been through it. If there is any good to come of this catastrophe, it may be in serving to help you become a better officer in the future, knowing as you do the awful penalty for error. Dismissed."

Tom felt his muscles release so suddenly that he was afraid he was going to collapse to the floor. He clutched the sides of the chair and then, as the room began to swim, lowered his head so blood could run into it. Presently he felt stable enough to lift his head, and when he did, his father was kneeling in front of him. Wordlessly, Owen Paris put his hands on the sides of Tom's face, and gazed at him with unabashed concern. "All right," he said softly, "all right. It'll be all right." And at that, Tom burst into tears.

"Set a course, Ensign. Warp six."

"Aye, sir," said Tom, now Ensign Thomas Paris, as he keyed in controls that would guide the *U.S.S. Copernicus* to Betazed. He was eight months into his posting to this Oberth-class ship, a science vessel assigned to collect data on solar winds and magnetic fields in several Alpha Quadrant systems. It wasn't the most thrilling mission in the world, but that was all right with Tom. He wasn't looking for excitement and he wasn't looking for challenges. He put in his duty shift each day, spent several hours in the gym keeping himself in shape, unwound with a few synthehol ales in the evening, spent a night of dreamless sleep, then got up and did the same thing all over again.

The only variation to this routine came with shore leave on the various planets they visited. During those days and nights, Tom occupied himself exclusively with one activity: the pursuit of women.

Until his graduation from the Academy, Tom had tended toward stable, long-term relationships, like that with Odile. Since then, he had begun to find women a narcotic, something he craved insatiably, without reason. Sleep came most easily in the entwining arms of a lissome young woman or, lacking that, in fantasies of such a woman.

It was never difficult to find a willing partner. He was attractive and charming, and he seemed to exude pheromones that left no doubt about his intent. He found most women were attracted to this candidness, almost in proportion to its outrageousness.

His goal was to keep the dreams at bay.

One or more of his dead comrades had begun to crop up in his dreams soon after he graduated and received his commission. Almost always, they were re-creations of the good times they'd shared, and Tom found these reminders unbearable. The first time he spent a night with a woman, he didn't dream at all, and he became determined to repeat this pattern as often as possible.

Now the *Copernicus* was on its way to Betazed, a visit Tom

anticipated with lustful eagerness. The women of Betazed were known to be both beautiful and liberated, a combination that tantalized him no end.

And which, as he discovered soon after their arrival at Betazed, was not exaggerated.

Lissine had hair so dark it seemed almost to shine blue, skin pale as cotton blossoms, and the characteristic black eyes of all Betazoids. She was a civilian scientist in the cosmochemistry lab, with a mind as nimble as a gazelle and a sensuality ripe as a bursting plum. The minute Tom spotted her, he wanted her, and he pursued her with practiced zeal. By nightfall, they were strolling through a lush garden, one of many that dotted the communities of Betazed, whose inhabitants prided themselves on their pastoral settings. Blossoms quivered on their stems at the caress of the night breeze, and flung perfume into the night like fragrant ribbons of silk, wooing the gentle winds. Somewhere in the distance, a woman's voice sang an achingly beautiful melody, which danced on those same winds, haunting and poignant.

Tom drew Lissine to a seat on the ground, where a soft pillow of moss nestled them. He was almost giddy from the powerful fragrance of the flowers, the plaintive faraway song, and Lissine's lush presence. There seemed no need for words. He bent to her, touched her full lips with his, and felt her tremble in excitement. His hands trailed her arms, feeling heat rising from them, and her breath quickened. He kissed her again, more hungrily, aching for her now and knowing she was as eager as he.

He was light-headed, all but drunk with the moment. The perfume of the flowers overwhelmed him, penetrated him, and the far-off song drilled into his mind. He gasped and inhaled even more deeply, and suddenly the world began to spin. He pulled his hands from Lissine's willing flesh and held his head as though to steady it.

"Tom . . ." breathed Lissine, her voice a throaty growl, urgent and needful.

"What's happening . . . ?" he stammered, as the dizziness began to pass.

"I'm touching you . . . your mind . . . with mine. Please . . . don't shut me out."

He had forgotten Betazoid telepathy. He looked at her, saw eyes glistening darkly, mouth parted, imploring. "That's never happened to me before," he said, wanting her but wary of this new sensation. She bent toward him.

"Let go of your apprehensions. It will be wonderful, I promise. The union of our minds will only enhance the pleasure of our bodies." Her eyes burned in the darkness. "Close your eyes . . . let me touch you . . ."

Tom hesitated for no more than a second, then closed his eyes. Immediately the intoxicating symptoms returned, but this time he didn't fight them, and yielded to a sensuality so powerful it took his breath away. His mind went racing through the dark garden, skimmed over treetops, ascended into the night sky and then danced among the stars, which streaked in a multicolored profusion, a kaleidoscope of patterns and mazes, ribbons of silk, a paradise where every sense became mingled and he could taste the colors, see the fragrant breeze, touch it all, everything part of him, spinning in rapture, exquisite, exquisite, until the stars exploded for hours and he undulated among their ecstatic outpourings until later, much later, he fluttered gently to earth, dying star-embers drifting with him, falling softly until the mossy ground received him and nestled him warmly.

Tom opened his eyes. Lissine lay beside him, breathing softly, body moist with bliss. She turned toward him, satiated, and took his hand. "Well?" she asked.

"That was amazing."

She lifted herself on one elbow and looked down at him solemnly. "Tom, there's something dark inside your mind. Something you've locked away so it won't hurt you. It frightened me."

He was silent. He hadn't anticipated that an erotic telepathic intrusion into his mind might also graze on the secrets held there. "I'm sorry," he said sincerely. "I guess we all have a few demons inside us. But it's nothing that could ever hurt you, I swear."

Her black eyes burned into him. "It hurts you terribly," she said simply. "I must warn you—after this, you might not be able to keep it shut away so easily."

A cold lancet of fear pierced him. What did she mean? Would his awful secret now rise up like a serpent, coiled and ready to strike? His stomach tensed and nausea flooded his throat with bile. He couldn't talk.

"If you'd let me, I might be able to help. But first we'd have to talk about it." Her voice was warm, nurturing. She was offering to be his friend. For a moment he wanted desperately to clutch at this proffered intimacy, hold on to its calm steadiness, pour out everything, all the black truth, and feel the sweet balm of relief soothe his tortured soul. All he had to do was tell her.

"There's nothing to talk about, really," he heard himself saying, and he forced a casual smile. "Maybe you're seeing monsters where they don't exist."

She didn't answer, but put her hand on his cheek, staring into his eyes. Fearful that she was trying to invade his mind again, he focused on shutting her out. After a moment, she dropped her hand and looked away. "I'm sorry for you, Tom," she said in a whisper so soft he could hardly hear her. "I'm so sorry."

And then she was moving away, a rustle of clothing brushing through the flowers, until she was gone and he could hear nothing.

The distant song had ceased. A stillness pervaded the garden, a silence as vast as the reaches of space. He felt more alone than he had ever felt in his life.

They came to him in his quarters aboard the *Copernicus*. He had followed his usual routine, serving his watch, working out in the gym, and then stopping by the officers' mess for a few bottles of ale, finally returning to his quarters and falling into bed. He had eschewed synthehol for genuine alcohol, finding that he fell asleep more easily if his senses were truly deadened.

The sleep hadn't been dreamless lately, which bothered him. He had succumbed to a kind of nocturnal mania, pursued by dreams that were vivid and charged. He would wake with his heart thudding in his chest, gasping for breath, flooded with some anchorless anxiety whose underpinnings had vaporized the instant he woke up. He knew he had dreamed, but he couldn't remember what. He considered going to the ship's physician, but didn't want to undergo questioning as to the possible causes of his anxiety.

It had been like this since his experience with Lissine, and her ominous portent echoed in his mind. She was right: some sleeping giant had been wakened in his mind, and was stirring restlessly, massive limbs flexing, preparing to break free. The thought filled him with dread.

On this particular night he had drunk enough that he fell asleep—passed out—as soon as he lay down. Later he would realize that he hadn't dreamed before he woke, the first such occasion in many nights. But what greeted him instead was far worse.

His eyes snapped open suddenly in the darkness at an imagined sound—at least he thought it must be imagined, because he couldn't account for it otherwise. It was a faint sigh, as though wind were slipping through an abandoned attic, but of course there was no wind on a starship.

A motion caught at the corner of his eye and he swung his head toward the window, which looked onto space. A dark silhouette stood there, rimmed by the streak of warp stars. The features were dark and indistinguishable, but from the tuft of hair that protruded from the top of the head, there was no mistaking who it was.

It was Charlie.

Terror clutched at him and his hands began to shake violently. He clawed awkwardly toward the control pad at his bedside, desperate to turn the lights on and banish this unwelcome visitor. In his panic he couldn't find the pad in the dark, and he began pushing frantically at all the controls, hoping to find the lights at random. Nothing happened. He was afraid to glance back over his shoulder toward the window, for fear Charlie's figure would be moving toward him, ready to reach out and seize his shoulder. Frenzied, he pounded his fist on the controls—

Light erupted into his eyes, blinding him briefly, and then he forced himself to look back toward the window to verify that the apparition had vanished.

Charlie stood there, silent, pale skin etched with blood, staring at him not in accusation, but in wistful sadness.

And flanking him were Odile and Bruno.

Tom's body jerked in a violent spasm, and he hoped he was having a heart attack, that death and oblivion would overtake him swiftly and he could be free forever of these awful specters. But he remained conscious, chest squeezed in a vise, perspiration spilling from his pores, eyes locked on the frightful visages before him. Their sadness was far worse than anything else he could imagine—if they were angry, or threatening, he could almost bear it, but this awful melancholy was terrible to behold. Through his panic, the thought occurred to him that they were sorry for him, but that didn't make any sense, because he had cheated death and they had died at his hand.

He tried to scrabble backward on the bed, to get away from them, to get to the door, but his body wouldn't obey his commands. It was like the dream everyone has had when they are trying to run from a monster, but the limbs are agonizingly slow, trapped in molasses, and instead of running one can only move in frustrating slow motion. He felt himself inch across the bed, kicking at the blanket, terrified that they would try to move toward him, would overtake and overwhelm him, smothering him in the putrefaction of the grave.

He tumbled onto the floor and could only scoot backward across it, for what seemed long minutes, eyes still firmly locked on the three apparitions, finally bumping into the door of his quarters, which opened automatically at his touch and closed behind him. Once in the corridor, he tried to get to his feet, but his legs seemed boneless, and he collapsed again to the floor. All he could do was to crawl on his hands and knees, which he did, like a demented six-month-old, all the way to sickbay.

The next several days passed in a haze. He had medical evaluations, psychological evaluations, medications, interviews. Through it all, he insisted he had to return to Starfleet Headquarters as soon as possible, an unacceptable demand from a junior officer, even one whose mental stability the captain of the *Copernicus* had begun to question. Finally it was the name of Paris that prevailed, Tom in his desperation invoking his father and imploring the captain to respect the line that had served Starfleet so well for so long.

And so it was that Tom was returned to San Francisco by shuttle, piloted by a lieutenant whose orders were never to leave Tom unattended because there was genuine concern about the possibility of his doing damage to himself.

That was fine with Tom, who more than anything else wanted to avoid being alone. He forced himself to stay awake as much as possible, only occasionally dozing off and then jerking awake in terror, afraid of another visitation from three people he knew couldn't really be visiting him. But each time his head snapped up in fright, he saw only Lieutenant Pierson glancing over at him to make sure he was all right.

The second hearing in the windowless room was much briefer than the first. The same three admirals were there, with their aides, as he confessed to his awful lie and correctly assumed responsibility for the terrible tragedy in the Vega system's asteroid belt.

His father wasn't there this time. In the end, only his mother stood with him, misery etched on her face but love ultimately stronger than pain. Head erect, proud, she stood next to him as he was officially cashiered out of Starfleet, not for the deed, but for the lie, the damning, dishonorable lie which wrongly cast blame on one of his fellows, a betrayal so heinous and unthinkable he would carry it with him the rest of his life.

Even his mother's forgiveness, vast and all-encompassing, couldn't lighten that burden.

For a period of time, he drifted. Long accustomed to the vastness of space, he discovered the immensity of Earth, transporting variously to places with names he'd never heard, much less contemplated visiting. Bamako . . . Mopti . . . Ende . . . Telde . . . He stared, unmoved, at cliff dwellings that perched precariously atop a sandstone escarpment and that had been in continuous use for almost fifteen centuries. Vibrant desert life swirled around him in cacophonous symphony: the beating of a ritual drum, crying infants, a donkey braying, the heated voices of Elders in argument, laughter, and the strange melodic piping of a wooden whistle. It was a magical concoction, historic and vital, but Tom found nothing remarkable there and moved on.

Ihlara . . . the Peristrema Gorge, where ancient Byzantine churches were carved into canyon walls, replete with crumbling frescoes of various saints and religious figures, a holy place of the long past. Tom looked, and felt nothing.

Lahore, and the famed Shalimar gardens . . . Kathmandu and the temple of Pashupatinath, dedicated to Shiva, the awesome creator/destroyer god . . . Songpan and the habitat where giant pandas were rescued from extinction three hundred years before and now thrived in roly-poly fecundity . . . Tom searched desperately for the experience that would reawaken something in him, *anything* that would stir his deadened spirit.

Nothing did. On he pressed: Tobago . . . Petra . . . Turnapuna . . . Baruta . . . Caesaros . . . Beausoleil . . . Göteborg . . . Alicante . . . Skopje . . . He saw communities he could not have imagined, pockets of cultural diversity, villages that had steadfastly preserved rituals and traditions from their past. He walked through crowded marketplaces, some of which displayed the only sight in all his wanderings that gave him pause—the display of pieces of meat, haunches, shoulders, ribs, making him realize that there were places on Earth where people still hunted, and who ate genuine, rather than replicated, flesh. The thought made him queasy, and he moved away, shrouded once more in numbness.

After that, his appetite disappeared along with his emotions, and he had to force himself to eat. Pounds dropped away, leaving him gaunt and drawn, yet with a curious lightness of spirit. This new, leaner person didn't seem to carry such heavy burdens. Yet this person was also wearier, sapped of energy. He began to sleep more, sometimes all day long. He found, upon waking, that a drink of alcohol revived him, at least briefly, and so it became a ritual.

He didn't go near North America, and communicated only with his mother, sporadic messages that assured her of his health and well-being, and promised a visit soon.

Time became meaningless, and he rarely knew if days, or weeks, or months had passed. He moved through this quasi life in a miasma, rootless and torpid.

Later he would wonder what instinct drove him to the location where he settled for almost a year, but at the time he lacked the awareness to question motivation. It seemed as good a place as any, and so it was that he returned to Marseilles.

A woman whose name he had already forgotten twined her arms around Tom's neck, murmuring softly in his ear. It wasn't a particularly erotic sensation, but it wasn't unpleasant, and he allowed her to cling to him as he sipped his drink and eyed his opponent.

That was a blue-skinned Bolian whose name he had also forgotten, but whose prowess at pool was impressive. The vague thought came to him that there was a time when that challenge might have invigorated him, sending adrenaline coursing and pulse quickening, pushing him to marshal all his skills to best his adversary. But that time was long ago, and receding quickly in the alcohol-shrouded mists of faint memory.

The past didn't matter anymore. In fact, the present didn't matter so much, either. And the future was a void, so it warranted no concern.

So there was really nothing to worry about.

He took another sip of his drink, and reflected briefly on the glories of single-malt Scotch whiskey. He anticipated the first drink of the day with a reverence that was almost holy. The initial taste on the tongue, smooth as liquid velvet but burning with an intense heat . . . the course of the whiskey down his throat and into his stomach . . . and then its plunge into his bloodstream, warming him, smoothing the mild shake in his hands, blunting the ache in his head.

It was enough to get up for.

"Tommy . . . come on . . . we've been here long enough . . . can't we go?"

The woman was beginning to irritate him. He unwrapped her arms from his neck and held her away from him. "If you want to go—go," he said. "I'm busy."

He was aware that she went into a pout but he didn't really give a damn. He was more concerned that the Bolian was running the table. That was—what? The fourth time tonight? Well, it didn't matter. There was no wager. There was nothing worth wagering. If the Bolian had his ego gratified with the victory, that was fine with Tom. He threw up his hands and headed for the bar. His glass was empty.

Sandrine was behind the bar. She was the same one who had befriended him when he spent a semester in Marseilles during his stint at the Academy. That was—a long time ago. He tried briefly to remember if it was five or six years, but couldn't, but that was all right because it didn't matter.

Sandrine was eyeing him in clear disapproval. "Go home, Tom," she said in French. "You've had enough."

"One more, my love. Can't quite embrace the arms of Morpheus without a dollop more," he replied in English. It was a game he played with her, because he knew it annoyed her that, even though he was fluent in French, he refused to speak in anything but English. These days, one took one's victories where one could.

She poured the drink, as he knew she would. He took it neat—the need for ice or water had long since passed. As she tipped the bottle over his glass, he put his fingers over hers, coaxing out another inch of the liquid. Sandrine pursed her lips and turned her back on him. He laughed.

He sat alone at a table, aware that the woman who'd been draped over him was standing against the wall, arms crossed and lips pursed in a telegraphed snit. He wondered if she really thought that was going to make him come over to her, to grovel and let her lead him around like a poodle. Well, she could stand there till she turned to granite for all he cared.

"You alone?" The voice came from someone who'd approached from behind him. He turned and looked up to see a tall, strapping human with short black hair and a strange tattoo on his temple. His voice was quiet but commanding, with a timbre that made even Tom, in a whiskey daze, take notice.

"Yeah, as a matter of fact. By choice."

"Mind if I sit down? I have a proposition for you."

"Not interested."

"I think you might be if you hear what it is."

Tom had gotten into fistfights with people less pushy than this. But something in this man's voice, his very presence, exuded a power that was compelling. Tom allowed his eyes to flicker to the adjoining chair, and the man pulled it out and sat.

"My name's Chakotay," he began, but Tom waved a hand at him blearily. He wouldn't remember the name, so there was no need for formalities. He didn't offer his in return.

"I understand you're a pilot," Chakotay continued. "We might be able to help each other out."

Tom was silent, not encouraging the man, but finding himself unaccountably curious. He felt Chakotay assessing him, and for the first time in a long time, he wondered if he was measuring up.

"I'm part of a group that's always looking for good pilots."

"What kind of group is this?" The whole thing had a suspect quality to it. Federation planets weren't known to be home to groups who solicited pilots in waterfront bars.

Chakotay's eyes flickered around the room, checking on their privacy. Tom noted briefly that the woman had disappeared, and felt a sense of relief. "Do you know what's happening in the demilitarized zone near the Cardassian border?" asked the man.

Tom shrugged. He'd heard muttered comments here and there, but had no real interest in events that were so far away. Now, he found himself wishing he'd paid more attention; something made him want to impress this man as a knowledgeable person.

He struggled to follow as Chakotay unfolded the tale, and wished he'd had less to drink that day. He forced himself to concentrate as the man told him of an abortive treaty the Federation had made with Cardassia, effectively putting a long conflict to an end, but stranding a number of colonists in the newly created demilitarized zone between the two areas of space. The colonists were supposed to evacuate, but many of them—Chakotay's people included—refused to abandon their homes, and opted to remain in the zone without the promise of Federation protection.

And of course the Cardassians were exploiting that fact, harassing them, raiding them, hoping to make things so miserable they'd leave their colonies to the Cardassians.

A growing number of people—humans, Vulcans, Bolians, Ktarians, a virtual melting pot of Federation species—were banding together in a loosely knit group to protect themselves. They called themselves Maquis, after ancient Earth freedom fighters of the twentieth century. Chakotay was part of that group, and had heard that a skilled Starfleet pilot was unoccupied at the moment, spending his days in drinking and playing pool in Marseilles.

"We could use you," he said simply. "And you'd get to fly again."

Something vaguely remembered began to stir in Tom, a quickening, a response that he'd thought dead. Suddenly he wanted nothing more in the world than to fly again, to serve with this powerful man whose sense of purpose was so profound. Chakotay cared deeply, passionately for his cause, and that fervor had touched Tom. For the first time in years, he wanted to care about something—anything—and feel alive again.

He started to speak, felt his voice catch as it did long ago whenever he feared his father, and coughed. He pushed the glass of whiskey away from him and looked into Chakotay's eyes, which were black and impenetrable. "Count me in," he said, trying for a studied nonchalance that he didn't feel. A silence fell between them, and Tom spoke once more, this time with sincerity. "Thanks," he said, and felt like a small child once more when Chakotay smiled in response.

Flying again gave him more satisfaction than he would ever admit. His fingers were awkward at first; they had lost their alacrity. But the skills came back rapidly, and he felt a resuscitation of purpose that made him feel almost giddy.

As his former self was revived, however, so were his former demons. He hadn't hit it off well with their chief engineer, a half-human Klingon woman named Torres. She struck him as a passionate, driven woman, completely focused on her work and uninterested in developing friendships. It was exactly the assessment he would want people to make of him, but something in Torres's rejection of him had piqued him and left him somewhat unsettled. His response was to keep baiting her.

In general, he treated the women on the Maquis ship as sexual objects, a behavior that effectively irritated them. With the men he adopted a confrontational attitude, which gained him no popularity but insured that no one could get close enough to hurt him.

But when it came to Chakotay, things were more complicated. Tom found that he wanted this captain's approval, yet he hated that neediness in himself, hated the childlike stirrings it created, and so he constantly sabotaged the relationship. He was flip and disrespectful; smart-mouthed retorts slipped out before he could stop them. Chakotay responded in the beginning with patience and courtesy, but that only confused Tom, and he felt pushed to further disparagement.

Finally they fell into a strained, silent relationship, Tom being careful to do his job as best he could so as not to be banished completely, but unable to surmount the craggy barriers he had erected between them. Chakotay, for his part, seemed to ignore Tom, devoting himself instead to their primary purpose: deviling the Cardassians.

"Evasive action!"

Chakotay's shout was accurate but unnecessary; Tom had already entered a pattern into the controls as soon as he'd spotted the Cardassian attack vessels leaving the orbit of Dorvan, one of the planets in the demilitarized zone. There were two of them, heavily armed, and they were a lot more maneuverable than the three-decade-old Antares-class ship he was piloting. Chakotay had warned him that the Maquis had to get ships as they could, and up-to-date technology was a luxury they rarely had. That was fine by Tom, who was familiar with the Antares ships, and who could coax every bit of performance from them that they could deliver, and sometimes more.

Now was a time when he needed more, or his career with the Maquis would be short-lived. They, for that matter, would be short-lived, dying in a fiery explosion in the dangerous space of the demilitarized zone.

"They're powering weapons!" This from Torres, who was on the bridge. The first barrage of shots from the fighters struck them squarely, in spite of Tom's maneuvers. The impact was considerable, and knocked them around the small bridge.

"Shields at eighty-four percent," shouted Torres, just before they took another volley, and Chakotay called out, "Returning fire!"

Their phaser volley hit a glancing blow to one of the fighters but missed the other entirely. Tom made an instant decision.

"I'm taking the controls off line. I can do this better if I do it manually." He didn't wait for Chakotay to respond, but quickly keyed the console and began to maneuver the ship without controls.

He was able to maneuver more deftly that way—at least, he was convinced he could—and he worked not only to evade the two ships but to give Chakotay good firing positions. "Firing," yelled Chakotay, and sent off a volley that caught one of the Cardassian ships in its weapons system.

It exploded in a cascade of light and matter, and Tom had to handle the *Liberty* nimbly in order to avoid being hit by the debris. Without making a conscious decision, he maneuvered the ship directly toward the other enemy vessel.

Chakotay launched one of their precious photon torpedoes, which scored a direct hit on one of its warp nacelles.

Ship number two was reduced to flaming fragments, but not before they fired off a death rattle. The *Liberty* was jolted by a massive hit, Tom felt his eardrums vibrate painfully from percussive impact, and then, somehow, he was on the deck of the bridge as chaos erupted around him.

Tom picked himself up and struggled back to his post. Acrid smoke filled the compartment and stung his eyes and throat, and he heard the sizzle and pop of a console in its death throes. Through the haze he could see Chakotay moving toward a dark shape on the deck, bending over it in concern. Torres, he realized, and hoped she wasn't badly injured. She'd already cheated death once, on a planetoid in the Badlands they had visited, and would need the lives of a cat if she stayed much longer with the Maquis.

He swiftly checked the ship's systems and realized they were in worse shape than he'd thought. The comm was down completely, weapons were off line, propulsion showed thrusters only, and life-support was minimal. He turned toward Chakotay and was relieved to see Torres sitting up now, holding her head.

"We've taken a lot of damage," he reported tersely, running down the dead and failing systems. Chakotay nodded, arm around Torres, who looked dazed. Suddenly another figure rushed onto the cramped bridge, breathless and urgent.

"Are you all right?" The concern in her voice was palpable, but Tom was aware she spoke only to Chakotay. She was Bajoran, and her name was Seska. He hadn't felt good about that one from the moment he set foot on the *Liberty,* and had not even bothered flirting with her.

Now Seska witnessed the tableau in front of her—Chakotay kneeling protectively next to B'Elanna, arm around her supportively—and she stiffened perceptibly. Tom was instantly aware of powerful feelings of possession and jealousy from Seska, feelings she immediately suppressed and replaced with concern. It was a brief moment, but a chilling one.

"B'Elanna has a head wound—maybe a concussion," said Chakotay.

"I'll get the med kit," replied Seska immediately, and disappeared again. Chakotay turned to Yuri Terikof, their navigator.

"There's a colony on Selka that's sympathetic to us. Take the shuttle and tell them we need help."

Tom was out of his seat immediately. "I'll do it," he blurted, and headed for the exit, but Chakotay put out a restraining hand.

"I told Yuri to go," he said quietly. Tom held his look steadily.

"Pardon my frankness, but it'll take a better pilot than Yuri to get through the debris of those Cardassian ships. Your only chance is to let me do it."

Chakotay hesitated, and Tom realized with a sinking feeling that his captain didn't trust him. "I'll do it," he promised. "I'll get through and I'll bring help."

"If you run out on us, I swear I'll hunt you down," Chakotay said, then jerked his head toward the portal, tacitly giving the order.

As Tom exited the compartment, he caught a brief glimpse of Torres, face wet with blood, eyes black and unyielding, and determined that he'd do whatever he could to bring help for her, then quickly squelched the thought. It had made him unaccountably fearful, and he didn't like the sensation.

He launched the shuttle and weaved his way through the debris of the two Cardassian ships until he was in clear space, then set a course for Selka and jumped to warp speed. With luck, he'd have help on the way within hours.

Two hours later he detected the approaching Starfleet vessel and realized it was coming to investigate the massive explosions that had taken place in the demilitarized zone. It would discover the wreckage of the Cardassian ships and, hovering nearby, helpless, Chakotay's wounded craft. Starfleet considered the Maquis little more than outlaws, and would undoubtedly bring Chakotay and his crew before a tribunal.

The Starfleet ship hailed him.

"*U.S.S. Bradbury* to unidentified shuttle. Please respond." The disembodied voice over his comm system reverberated slightly, giving it a faintly mystical quality. Tom's mind began to churn. The hail presented him with options, the most appealing of which was to pass himself off as a colonist of the zone, ignorant of any recent battle with the Cardassians. He was near enough to Selka that it was a plausible story. He could be quaffing an ale that very evening in a friendly bar, arms around a supple and eager playmate.

"*U.S.S. Bradbury* to unidentified shuttle. Respond or we will take you in tow."

Once, a lie had come easily to him. He had looked Admiral Brand in the eye and, with voice unquavering, placed the blame for the asteroid disaster on Bruno Katajavuori. But the price he had paid was too great.

He punched a control to open the comm, carving his mind into halves as he spoke to the *Bradbury* while simultaneously entering a complex series of instructions into his console.

"This is Tom Piper, piloting the shuttle *Equality.*" He wasn't about to use the now infamous name of Paris when addressing Starfleet personnel. He knew how he was regarded among his former colleagues. "Sorry, my comm system is malfunctioning and I'm not getting a clear transmission. Could you repeat?"

"This is the *U.S.S. Bradbury.* State your purpose in this space."

"My purpose?" Tom chuckled audibly, as he continued to enter commands. "I'm on my way to visit a lovely woman on Selka. My purpose, frankly, is—well, let's just say it's my own business. But you might wish me luck."

"We're investigating a series of explosions we detected about one light-year from here. Did you get any readings on them?"

"Sorry, *Bradbury.* I took off from Kripkin a couple of hours ago and came directly here. Haven't detected any explosions. Frankly, my sensors are in about as good shape as my comm system."

"We're having no trouble hearing you."

"Pardon? Repeat that?" Tom had completed his task—entering a deeply encrypted message to the colonists on Selka, giving them the location of the damaged *Liberty* and requesting immediate assistance. He now entered the transmission command, piggybacking the message onto thermal emissions from the nacelles, which would probably not get the attention of the Starfleet ship. The encryption would also make the source of the message undetectable, meaning Chakotay would never know that Tom had done what he said he would. He would be accused once more of betrayal and Chakotay would undoubtedly, as he had promised, hunt him down.

But he couldn't worry about that. The ship was visible now, looming before him. He turned the nose of the shuttle directly toward the Starfleet vessel. The faceless voice was still barking at him, asking questions, demanding answers. "Sorry, *Bradbury,* you're still garbled," Tom muttered, gauging the distance between them carefully.

Finally within range. *"Bradbury,* this isn't working. Let's do this face-to-face. If you'll drop your shields, I'll transport on board."

There was a hesitation, and Tom knew they had detected him power his phaser array. Oh, well—shields or not, the result would be the same. He fired a volley directly at the Starfleet ship and then veered sharply away from it.

The phasers impacted the *Bradbury*'s shields, jolting it but inflicting no real damage. Nonetheless, it behaved as Tom had anticipated: it changed course to pursue him.

He pushed the shuttle's warp engines to their maximum, which was just over warp four. It wouldn't take long for the Starfleet ship to overtake him. But he was leading it *away* from the destroyed Cardassian ships, and away from Chakotay's helpless craft. The colonists of Selka would have time to rescue the Maquis and they would survive to continue their zealots' cause.

Tom Paris, on the other hand, would probably be spending time in a Federation Rehabilitation Colony. What do you think of that, Dad? The plummet continues. Not only was your only son drummed out of Starfleet in disgrace, he now has a criminal record. Maybe you'd like a picture of him in a prison jumpsuit to include in your array of family pictures.

Tom uttered a mirthless laugh, and put the shuttle into a series of evasive maneuvers. He'd prolong the inevitable as long as possible, sending a clear message to the Starfleet officers on the *Bradbury* that Tom Paris could fly a ship with the best of them. And with that thought buoying him, he plunged into the black void of space.

New Zealand wasn't the worst of places to serve out a sentence. The work was hard—restoring ancient ruins for a historical project—but Tom found the physical labor satisfying, especially in that it allowed him to sleep at night. That hadn't been the case between the time he was taken in custody by the *Bradbury* and his eventual sentencing to the Federation Rehabilitation Colony. Those were the nights when he lay awake, imagining what his mother was going through as her only son was processed through the judicial system.

He didn't wonder about his father; he could hear the admiral in his head, resounding like tympani. But he ached for the pain his mother must be experiencing now, and he fell into a dreadful self-loathing that was worse than any punishment Starfleet could mete out.

When he was transported to Auckland and began working for long hours on the restoration project, his mood improved. But the burden of his indiscretions was constant. He formulated in his mind a chart of his assets and deficits. Deficits: poor impulse control, manipulating others, self-involvement, recklessness, and of course the granddaddy of them all—the ability to lie. There were others that sprang to mind; the deficit list could go on and on. But when he took stock of his assets, the list was short: he was a damn good pilot.

Pathetic, if that's what his life amounted to. Something in him wanted to turn that all around, to formulate a plan that would redeem him; another, elusive part of him sabotaged those instincts and told him he should just serve out his time and then see what happened.

And so he continued to drift.

He'd been at the Colony for seven months, and was focused on a new welding technique he'd been taught. The day was warm and humid, but the air was sweet and he could hear wild birdsong in the woods around the ruins. He was so intent on the job he was doing that he didn't hear anyone approach, and jumped slightly when he heard a woman's voice: "Tom Paris?"

He looked up to see standing above him a trim, petite woman in a Starfleet uniform, wearing a captain's pips. She looked cool and composed even in the sweltering sun, and something about her made him wish he weren't sweating like a boar.

"Kathryn Janeway. I served with your father . . ."

And with those words his life was changed forever.

CHAPTER
9

WHEN TOM STOPPED TALKING, HE REALIZED HE HAD BEEN SPEAKING SO softly that everyone had craned closer to him in order to hear. He was surprised to realize that his eyes were wet, and he jabbed at them with his fists, embarrassed. But he didn't sense disdain or scorn from his comrades; rather, there seemed to be an outpouring of support. B'Elanna's hand was on his arm, and every eye that he met returned friendship.

"Well," he said after a few deep breaths. "I didn't realize how cathartic that was going to be." He shook his head, trying to come back into the present. "Wish I'd done that a long time ago."

"That was very courageous, Tom," said B'Elanna, and he heard sincerity in her voice. He felt a lightness of spirit that was completely unfamiliar to him.

"I believe we should go to sleep now," said Tuvok in his perfunctory way, and Tom was glad to have this fragile mood broken. "Tomorrow will be arduous."

They all rose and filed into the shelter, but Neelix hung back for a moment with Tom. "Tom," he said hesitantly, "thank you."

"For what?"

"You've given me the heart to do something I should've done a long time ago." And then Neelix turned and went into the shelter.

Tom wondered for a moment what he was talking about, but then B'Elanna took his arm and pulled him inside, then down, and they fell asleep in each other's arms.

Neelix woke the next morning with a sense of purpose. His belly rumbled with hunger, but he knew everyone else's did, too, and he tried simply to ignore the pangs. Today he would scour the camp, wouldn't stop until he'd found some of the components they needed to create their makeshift transporter.

He ate his morning meal—by now, they were all forcing themselves to save a portion of their rations until the next day, even though they were hungry enough to devour it all as soon as they got it—as slowly as he could, chewing each small bite in order to savor it as long as possible. He believed that process filled him slightly fuller.

As he chewed, Neelix surveyed the scene before him: the camp, never wholly asleep, never truly quiet, was stirring slowly, like an old dray horse huffing in the early-morning mists, lumbering to its feet and snuffling for its feed. A layer of fog still hung on the tops of the trees that surrounded the camp, but soon it would burn off under the merciless glare of the sun.

The Rai' were rising and moving about in resolute activity. Neelix watched them, admiring their discipline, their sense of duty. Those people would persevere, he told himself. Then he realized they were preparing a meal, stirring something into a pot of water heated over a fire. What could it be? How did they get food? If he could tap into a food source, he could greatly increase his group's chances of survival.

He chewed pensively, slowly, enjoying the taste of the fibrous root, wishing the chunk he had saved were just a little larger. He thought about the *Voyager* crew on the other side of the camp and wondered how they were faring. He disliked having the group split up like this and would have far preferred they all be together. But he recognized the necessity of the choice.

Thoughts of absent comrades drew him inevitably to thoughts of Kes. Dangerous territory. The beautiful Ocampan had been gone from *Voyager* for almost a year now, but she still haunted Neelix's mind. Her going had been so sudden—in a mysterious transformation that caused her to vanish—that it left everyone unprepared and sorrowful, even if she herself believed she was going to something better, greater, higher. None of that helped Neelix. To him, she was just gone.

His pain lay in him like a heavy stone, not severe but constant. Her absence was a palpable thing, the opposite of a vacuum, a dark but invisible actuality that shrouded him like a cloak.

Neelix rose abruptly, shaking off those thoughts, which, if allowed to gain momentum, would take him to a gloomy place that was difficult to leave. He drew a breath of the damp morning air and then adopted as jovial a manner as he could. He strolled over to the Rai' complex, where one of the tall aliens was stirring whatever was cooking in his pot.

"Good morning, my friend," Neelix called out. "I trust you slept well?"

The coal-colored man towered over Neelix, shocking white hair ringing his head like a halo. He gazed down at the Talaxian in mild curiosity.

"Well enough. And you?"

"As well as one can in a place like this."

That seemed to exhaust the small talk. They stood in silence for a moment, the Rai' stirring assiduously, Neelix savoring the aroma that wafted from the pot. "May I ask, friend, what it is you're cooking there?"

"Beans," said the Rai' tersely, no doubt thinking Neelix was there to beg some.

"And where does one get beans in such a wretched place?"

"There's a mining detail which leaves the compound every day. If you draw a pass to work, it's possible to gather edibles from the forest."

"I see. Very interesting." Neelix watched the stirring for a moment more. "What does the mining work involve?"

"The usual. Scanning for underground mineral deposits. Drilling ore from the veins. Loading it onto antigravity carts."

Neelix's mind was racing with the possibilities. A scanning device might be of value to B'Elanna and Harry. And if the miners used matter-displacement drills for deep digging, they might have phase-transition coils. Things were beginning to look up.

"Just how does one get such a job?"

The huge man scrutinized Neelix for a full moment before answering, as though trying to ascertain his motive in asking the question. When he spoke, it was straightforward, as though Neelix had passed some kind of muster.

"The Rai' receive work passes. In the event we are exchanged for Subu prisoners, they want us to report that we were treated fairly."

"And do you ever include others in this fortunate situation?"

There was another slight pause before the huge man answered. "It has been known to happen."

"Perhaps we could arrange a trade. There are a number of ways in which I could be valuable to you."

"I would be willing to consider such a proposal."

Neelix was feeling quite encouraged by this conversation, and was ready to begin offering his services, when a commotion rumbled through the camp, distracting them both.

One of the doors in the far wall was opening, and several figures had emerged. Neelix moved back to his group, and saw Tuvok staring into the distance, tensed and alert. "Vorik," he said quietly to the young Vulcan next to him, "go at once to Commander Chakotay's group."

"What is it? What do you see?" asked Neelix, who didn't possess the superior eyesight of the Vulcans.

Tuvok turned to him and said something that so stunned Neelix that he thought he must have misheard. For what Tuvok said was "I believe Captain Janeway has entered the camp."

Chakotay had become aware of the shift in attitude among the prisoners which always heralded the arrival of guards, and like the others, he and his group busied themselves with mindless activity in order to stay anonymous. He caught in the corner of his eye a brief flash of color, and realized someone was with the Subu guards, but it wasn't until the contingent was almost on top of them that he realized who it was. He heard a woman's voice saying, "With all these laborers, I'm surprised the price for your psilminite is so high."

Reigning in his shock, Chakotay allowed his eyes to flicker upward, and when they did, his heart suddenly constricted.

Kathryn was walking next to the commandant, old whalehead himself, who strutted officiously in his three-legged gait. She was dressed in a kind of robe of blue and purple, with heavy earrings dangling from her lobes and ornate rings on several fingers. She looked, to Chakotay, like a goddess.

"Not all may work," whalehead growled. "Only the trusted ones."

Suddenly Kathryn came to a stop, looked directly at Chakotay, and pointed. "Who are those people?" she demanded.

"I don't know what they call themselves. They were discovered invading one of our small planets. Undoubtedly they're mercenaries working for the Rai'."

Kathryn's eyes narrowed and she walked closer to Chakotay. "They're human," she said angrily, "or at least some of them are. I've run into them before. They're mercenaries, all right. They attacked my holdings on Grivus and killed members of my family."

She was right in front of Chakotay now, staring at him with furious eyes. He had no idea just what was happening, but he trusted her enough to go with her game.

"Sorry I missed them all," he said casually.

Her hand exploded across his cheek, backhand, and he recoiled at the blow. Kathryn had a mean punch. He touched his cheek and felt dampness, and saw that his fingers were red with blood. One of her rings had ripped the skin of his cheek.

"Commandant, I would hate to think these wicked beings could escape to kill others."

"No danger. Many security measures."

"I certainly hope so." She gave Chakotay one last angry glance, then walked on. "Let's finalize the price, shall we? I've lost interest in this filthy place."

The small entourage moved back toward the wall from which they had emerged, the prisoners still occupied with busywork. Chakotay and the others stared after them.

"What was that all about?" wondered Harry.

Chakotay, still putting pressure on the cut in his cheek, let his mind consider all the possibilities. "She's in disguise for a reason. Probably to see if we're here, and what our situation is. Trying to figure out some way to get us out."

"But what could that be? And why did she hit you?"

"I guess to put on a good show." He looked around at the others. His cheek had stopped bleeding. "Let's get moving. We have work to do." And once again they spread out to see if they could find what they needed.

Neelix spent the day on a work detail with the Rai', and returned from the experience exhausted but ebullient. "The guards pay no attention to the workers at all. They don't seem to be worried about anyone trying to escape, and they don't seem to care much about the mining operation. Mostly they sit around eating some kind of cane plant and yammering at each other."

The group was gathered round him, eager to hear about this new development in their lives. Neelix, who enjoyed being the center of attention, was orchestrating this tale with an idea toward saving the best for last. "And so," he said provocatively, "that allowed me the opportunity to liberate any number of items from the equipment there."

He reached into his abundant jacket and began extracting his booty. "To start with, a high-frequency tomographic scanner," he began, indicating a device similar to a Federation tricorder. B'Elanna immediately snatched it and pried it open. Inside, there was a maze of components.

"This looks good, Neelix," she said as she inspected it. "These chips look like integrated photonic circuits . . . and there are transtators . . . optical couplers . . . and coherent microwave emitters. It's a treasure!"

Neelix beamed his pride, then reached under his coat, behind his back, and with some difficulty pulled out a large disk made of composite alloy coils that were embedded in a cocoon of circuitry. B'Elanna grabbed this as well.

"Phase-transition coils—and sarium kelleride power cells. This is wonderful!"

"I got them from the matter-displacement drills. The miners use them to destabilize and displace cores of matter beneath the surface." Neelix looked at the smiles on the faces of his colleagues and basked in the joyfulness he saw there.

Even Tuvok seemed impressed. "Nicely done, Mr. Neelix," he said, and Neelix was sure he even heard some note of appreciation there. "Vorik, take the news to Commander Chakotay at once."

Vorik nodded and departed with several containers under the pretense of going for water. B'Elanna continued to inspect the contraband Neelix had provided, and her enthusiasm was palpable. "I can work with these things," she said eagerly. "This tomographic scanner produces three-dimensional maps of the planet's interior. If I can combine its capabilities with the phase-transition coils, I think I can fashion a transporter. A crude one, but it should work."

Tuvok, as usual, wanted more information. "Explain your theory, Lieutenant."

"First, I think I can use the tuning circuits from our commbadges to modulate and control the transporter beam. The scanner could be modified to read our molecular structure—and the phase-transition coils would be used to convert our molecules into energy. Then the coils would have to be field-reversed to turn that energy back into matter."

Tuvok nodded gravely. "Are there any contraindications?"

B'Elanna hesitated. She was so excited about the prospects that she hated to diminish them. But there was no getting around it. "There's one big drawback. There's no way to construct a pattern buffer. In a starship transporter, the buffer stores the pattern of the person for a few microseconds while the computer makes sure all the other system components are functioning properly. It's a valuable safety measure." She looked around at the solemn eyes of her comrades. "Without it, transporting is risky. It's like being on the high wire without a safety net."

That statement hung heavily in the air until Neelix chimed in. "Staying here in Hellhole has perils, too. I'd rather take my chances with B'Elanna's transporter." From their reactions, the others clearly shared this opinion, and B'Elanna smiled at the vote of confidence and sat down to begin fiddling with the stolen components.

Neelix then shared his dinner ration with the others, because, as he told them, "I've had my fill of food. On the work detail there's plenty to eat. Today my pockets were full of contraband, but tomorrow I'll bring more food."

This prospect, added to the now very real possibility of creating a transporter, made the small group almost heady with excitement. They became a little silly, laughing and joking like small children, then sank into a contented silence.

Neelix waited for a moment, then spoke quietly. "If no one objects . . . I'd like to add my story to those that've been told."

"I'd like that, Neelix," said Tom sincerely.

"There are things about myself I've never told anyone. Not even Kes. I've never wanted people to know." He hesitated, looking pensively at Tom. "I told you last night you gave me courage. I don't think I could have done this without your example."

Tom gave him a brotherly pat on the shoulder. "I feel a lot better for it," he said encouragingly.

Neelix was quiet for a moment. "I don't know how to start," he admitted.

"Start with the easy things," Tom suggested. "Your childhood, your family . . . the things you enjoyed."

Neelix considered this briefly and then smiled. "Thanks," he said. "I know exactly where to begin."

CHAPTER 10

SINCE HE WAS A SMALL BOY, NEELIX HAD LOVED THE HOLIDAY OF PRIXIN more than any other. His sisters, all five of them, spoiled him shamelessly, baking his favorite dishes and giving him extravagant gifts on each of the five nights of the celebration.

The year he was fifteen was the most memorable festival ever. For weeks the people of Rinax, the moon of Talax where Neelix's family lived, had scoured the woods to find the most fragrant branches of the fellin bush with which to bedeck their homes. For at least that long, the heady aroma of moolt spices filled the air as the inhabitants made fruit compotes that would age in the moolt nectar until the first night of Prixin. Then they would become the ceremonial elixirs consumed in the Feast of the First Night.

Neelix had suspected his family had planned a great surprise for that night. On several occasions, he had come into a room to find his sisters or his parents engaged in covert whispering, which stopped immediately upon his entrance. He had taken note of strange sly smiles among his sisters when the plans for Prixin were being discussed.

He hoped he knew what all the secrecy was about. He had been longing for a hover vehicle ever since his spots came in a year and a half ago. He desperately craved the freedom it would bring him to roam the hills of their verdant moon.

All his life, he had loved to wander. When he was a toddler, he was notorious for slipping away from the family on their frequent outings, oblivious of the consternation these peregrinations caused. By the time he was eight, he had explored as much of the woods as he was allowed, and begging to push the boundaries even farther.

Only his sister Alixia shared his wanderlust. Six years older than he, she volunteered to take him on overnight camping trips into the hills and the deeper parts of the woods.

Neelix adored her for it. She would pack wonderful treats for them, knapsacks full of brillin, and trove bars, and frosty containers of iced neth. They would hike for hours, deep into the woods, Alixia pointing out unusual plants and trees that grew only in the dark and shaded moistness of the forest depths. Finally they reached the secret place Alixia had found several years before: a clearing that contained, magically, an abandoned hut. Alixia believed it had belonged to a woodsman many years before, but if so, no one knew who he was or where he had gone.

It was a simple affair, one room with a door and a window; no furnishings, and one cupboard, which was empty. But it became Neelix's castle. He swept it clean of dust and insect webs, and began furnishing it with objects he found discarded in the affluent neighborhoods of Rinax. Many long treks through the woods were required to carry in the belongings: pillows, a cot, lamps, window coverings. Alixia helped him each time, portaging the heavier items for him.

No one knew of the place except for himself and Alixia. He shared the secret with neither his friends nor the rest of his family. Alixia seemed to recognize the importance of this private domain, and as far as he knew, she kept the secret as well.

He spent hours there, his activities changing as he grew older. As a youngster, he dwelt for long periods in fantasy, imagining himself to be Prince Morax, who drove the evil Krebe creatures from Talax so many eons ago, thereby insuring lasting peace. He portrayed each of the legendary battles, from the first infamous debacle at Xelon shores, to the final near-miraculous triumph on the plains of Talax. He, Prince Morax, slew the grotesque Krebe monster Lothal, lopping off his head with the curved blade of Simus, ending the threat forever.

He envisioned the victory procession, which legend said lasted fourteen days, during which Morax neither slept, ate, nor drank, having been sustained by eating the heart of the monster Lothal. Neelix usually skipped over that part, not able—or willing—to let his vivid imagination conjure up the sensation of eating a raw heart.

But he soaked in the adulation of the illusory people. Massive crowds cheered him, their delirious gratitude transporting them into a mass rapture. They wouldn't stop screaming their praise, couldn't contain their adoration. For fourteen mythic days Morax was saturated in the bliss of his people.

That fantasy began to play itself out when he was ten or eleven, to be replaced by a fascination for weaponry. His household provided no role models for him in this intrigue: his father was a bookish man who found nightly entertainment in a game of Threx with his wife; his sisters were bright, studious girls who excelled in school and whose spare time seemed to be devoted to flirtatious games with young men.

No one cared about weapons.

Neelix's interest was piqued when, in picking through the trash a wealthy family had discarded, he discovered an ancient energy weapon. It was big and clumsy, and had long ago ceased to function, but there was something about it—the heavy weight, solid in the hand, the spare, functional design—that appealed to Neelix. He carried it to his woodland hut and took it apart, carefully aligning each piece as he removed it, so he could put it together again.

He did that four or five times until he understood the principles of the particle-beam generator, and then he set about finding out how to repair it. He found old books which gave some rudimentary instruction in weapons repair and he studied them painstakingly. He realized there was only one way to activate the weapon he had found, and that was to procure some radiogenic isotopes.

How could a twelve-year-old get such a substance? What possible reason could he concoct to persuade someone to give him some? He had no doubt that if anyone suspected he was trying to create a working weapon, the uproar would be enough to bring his parents and perhaps the authorities to his hut, ending his secret world forever.

Alixia was his only hope. He found her one evening sitting by the stream that ran through their property, cooling herself in the warm summer night. Above them, the planet of Talax loomed huge, casting a brilliant light on the inhabitants of its moon.

"Alixia, I've been given an honors project in school. I need to find some radiogenic isotopes." Alixia had just entered Level Ten School, and Neelix knew she might have access to the wealth of supplies this advanced institution provided.

Alixia looked up at him with immediate suspicion. "Radiogenic isotopes? Whatever could you be doing that would require a dangerous substance?"

"It's for nuclear chemistry. I'm building a charged-particle analyzer."

"If it's for class, won't your instructor provide the necessary supplies?"

Neelix was ready for that one. "Part of the idea is that we have to build our projects from scratch, providing all the elements ourselves. It's to develop self-reliance."

That was a perfectly reasonable statement, which derived naturally from the Talaxian system of education, which fostered independent thinking and self-sufficiency. Alixia seemed to accept it. "I'm taking a laboratory course in bionuclear medicine. There might be some isotopes available. I'll find out."

Neelix's spirits soared. He knew he could count on Alixia. And, sure enough, in a few days she gave him a small vial that was carefully wrapped in a protective batting. "Be careful," she warned him. "It's awfully volatile."

He knew that, and felt proud that Alixia would trust him to handle it responsibly, even though it was dangerous and he was only twelve. Almost immediately, he was on his way through the woods.

The infusion of the isotopes into the prefire chamber of the energy weapon caused an amazing transformation. One minute he had an inert and useless piece of technology; the next he had a potent weapon which hummed with a pulsating power. Trembling with excitement, he stepped from his hut and into the clearing.

He had prepared his test firing carefully, constructing three cutout targets, which he'd drawn to resemble Krebe warriors, with frightening, snarling faces, and placed them in the woods. The Krebe were a guileful species known for their treacherous ways. They were his adversaries, threatening to attack his domain. They must be routed.

He held the throbbing weapon at his side, walking with calculated nonchalance in the direction of the first target. Neelix was no longer Neelix; he was Xebot, master spy, behind enemy lines in the heart of Krebe territory. So far he had not been detected. But he had learned that several of the Krebe were suspicious of him and were planning to execute him. He must act first.

When he was about seven meters away, he suddenly lifted the weapon, whirled in the direction of the Krebe, and fired.

The cutout shimmered briefly as it absorbed the energy charge, then burst into plasma flame. Within seconds it was consumed. Neelix continued his slow, calculated ambling, tacking indirectly toward the second cutout. As he seemed to pass by it, he turned suddenly and fired at the third one, some twenty meters away, because that one had spotted him and was ready to fire.

But Neelix was quicker. The Krebe took the impact right in his chest and, like his recently departed colleague, burst into plasma flame.

Now Neelix spun back to the second attacker, who was rushing toward him, weapon drawn, and fired for the third time.

The weapon exploded in his hand.

Neelix screamed. The remnants of the weapon went flying and scattered on the ground, sizzling in their death throes. His hand was raw and pulpy, burning with a pain unlike any he'd ever imagined. He stared at it, panic overwhelming him. Was he going to die? He had to get to a doctor. How could he get home through the woods in this much pain? His hand would have to be amputated.

Nausea began to rise in him, and he grew light-headed. He was vaguely aware of the two destroyed cutouts, and of the third, which still stood, triumphant, mocking him. If they'd been real he'd be dead by now. He suddenly felt cold, racked with chills, and the world of his imagination, which had been his fantasy playground for so long, now seemed a hostile and uninviting landscape. He turned in a circle in the clearing, trying to clear his head, trying to wish away the pain, and longing for his mother's warm embrace.

He had to sit down for a few minutes. He was, after all, just a small boy, and he didn't know how to handle problems like this. What was he to do? He began shaking violently, watching as his hand began to turn from red to purple.

How long he sat, he didn't know. He had fixated on his hand, and now it was all he could see. His vision, he realized, had darkened at the edges. If he stayed very still, maybe the darkness would simply close in farther and farther into the center, until the sight of his grotesquely burned hand was eliminated.

He could die here. Never again would he sit in the loving embrace of his family, never join his sisters at the table while Papa patiently lectured them about the events of the day, never wake to the smell of freshly baked trove bars. He would die alone and uncomforted. How long would it be before they found his body? Alixia would know to look here, so maybe they'd find him before the insects had invaded his body and rendered it a disgusting, spongy mass, like the dead animals he saw from time to time in the woods.

How could this be happening? It wasn't fair—he was only twelve years old. There was so much he'd planned to do, there were so many things to learn, so many adventures to have. How could he die now? Where was Alixia?

He looked up and his eye fell on the one remaining cutout Krebe. The terrifying face he'd drawn glowered at him, eyes boring into him, teeth bared in a vicious sneer. It seemed to mock him, celebrating its triumph and the vanquishing of its enemy.

The fearful visage galvanized him. I have to get out of here, he thought. Home.

He managed to get to his feet without touching his injured hand to the ground. The clearing swam viciously, and for a moment he thought he might pitch over. But gradually the world settled into its proper position and his vision cleared somewhat.

He took one step, and then another, toward home. Each step fired a jolt of intense pain into his hand and the nausea returned, sending acid bile into his throat. He forced himself to keep going, a third step, a fourth, a fifth. Just one more step, he told himself each time. Just one more step.

He invoked no gods, for he'd never believed in an unseen and unknowable supreme being, but he made promises to each of his loved ones that if he could just make it home, he would never disappoint any of them again. He would excel in school. He would be helpful to his parents. He would never argue with his sisters again. If he could just make it home.

One more step . . . one more step . . . one more step . . .

Some twenty thousand steps later, well after dark, he stumbled, barely conscious, into his yard, where he collapsed. Even the agony as he fell on his roasted hand wasn't enough to ward off oblivion. His last thoughts were of Alixia.

It was she who was standing over him when he woke in the hospital, hand swathed in bandages and mind groggy from pain-relieving drugs. Her kind eyes swam into view, and her familiar smile brightened her face. "Oh, Neelix . . . you scared us all so badly. What would we do without our baby brother?"

It took months for his hand to heal. He had a number of surgeries in order to repair nerves and tendons, and then further operations to do a series of skin grafts. During all this time, no one in his family berated him for playing with a weapon.

When healing was complete and he was back in school, Papa approached him one night with a stack of reading material. "If you're going to learn about weapons, Neelix, you're going to do it the right way." And his father proceeded to sit with him as they read the manuals, discussed types of weaponry, and generally researched the topic from the ground level up.

Weeks later, when the research phase of the project was over, his father presented him with a new, low-energy weapon, along with a maintenance kit. When Neelix had demonstrated his ability to dismantle, clean, and repair the weapon, Papa announced that the time for target practice had arrived. They went to a place Neelix had never known existed: a broad grassy plain dotted with targets of all shapes and sizes, upon which some twenty Talaxians took aim.

"Well, Eximar . . . we never thought we'd see you on the weapons range." This from a tall, stout man whose spots were almost black with age. His eyes glittered, and his tufts of hair were combed and fluffed into an elaborate arrangement.

"The boy wants to learn how to shoot, Uxxin," said Neelix's father. "I'm making sure he does it properly."

"Good," said the first man. "We'll need an armed citizenry the way things are going."

Neelix noticed that his father frowned a bit at this statement, and moved him away from the speaker, to a place where he could stand by himself to practice firing the weapon. They stayed for over two hours, and by the time they left, Neelix's accuracy had improved vastly.

When Neelix had mastered that first weapon, Papa procured a second, more sophisticated one, and the process was repeated. And in this studious, scholarly way, Neelix gradually became proficient in any number of weapons, from personal armaments to starship disruptor cannons.

Only once did his father ask him why he was so intrigued with these devices, why he wanted to master them. Neelix couldn't answer. Then Papa said something very peculiar: "Are you worried about the Haakonians?"

Neelix was puzzled by this. He'd heard of the Haakonians, but couldn't remember in what context. "Should I be?" he queried.

His father looked worried, and that wasn't like him. Neelix felt a little squirm of fear in his stomach, an unpleasant sensation. "There are rumors," Papa said vaguely. "Our ruling body, I fear, isn't comprised of the most diplomatically proficient. They may offend the Haakonians."

"What does that mean? What's going to happen?"

Papa reached out and clapped Neelix on the shoulder, smiling reassuringly. "Nothing, nothing. I'm sorry if I alarmed you. You'll always be safe here, with your family, on Rinax. Any problems that may occur will be localized to Talax."

But Neelix wasn't reassured. The vague ominousness was more unsettling than hard information would have been. What did his father mean, "Any problems will be localized to Talax"? What problems? How could anyone be sure they'd be neatly contained on Talax? Was this what the man at the practice range had been talking about when he said they'd need an armed citizenry? Neelix, who had never known anything but comfort and security, now saw a fearful uncertainty inform his days.

He increased his target practice and kept his weapons scrupulously clean. If there were an emergency, he would be ready.

But gradually the months wore on, and the murky sense of threat began to fade. And when his spots came in, when he was just shy of fourteen, all other thoughts were eclipsed.

He had suspected he was transitioning when he began to feel a slight burning on his face and neck, and for weeks he peered at himself in a reflector, looking for the first hint of spots. Finally, he saw them—a faint, hazy series of halos that dotted his head, neck, back, and extremities.

At last, he was a man.

As the weeks passed, the spots darkened, becoming more and more prominent. He felt a new spring in his step as he walked the corridors of his school, feeling his kinship with those who had already transitioned, and faintly sorry for the boys his age who were still spotless.

And, inexorably, he found his eye being drawn to females.

He'd heard of this powerful lure, but it had always sounded faintly silly to him. Taking pleasure in the sheer act of *looking* at a female? It was absurd. But now he found that this simple act produced sensations he could not have imagined before. He was bewildered, beguiled, and frightened. Every opposing emotion conceivable seemed to be occurring simultaneously within his young frame.

His schoolwork suffered as a result of his new preoccupation. At night, he found himself recollecting Bibixen's lustrous tufts or Xela's bewitching yellow eyes. He heard Uxana's silvery laughter, smelled the dusky, alluring scent of Maxis's perfume. His studies lay open, undone, as he indulged these agreeable reveries. His weapons collection, once his pride, was stored away unused.

The only thing that rivaled young women in his thoughts was his desire for a hover vehicle. He hadn't visited the hut in the woods for many months, preferring to stay closer to home on the chance he might spot his neighbor Vaxi swimming in the pond that separated their yards. But if he had a vehicle . . . he could invite her on rides through the woods. He might even show her the hut, the only person besides his sister who would know of its existence.

And so, as he awaited the Feast of the First Night in the year he was fifteen, Neelix went to sleep each night thinking of whisking through the woods with Vaxi at his side, frightening her a little, perhaps, with his daring maneuvers, whipping around trees and skimming over rocky streams. She would squeal and shiver and cover her eyes, but he would be in sure control, and gradually she would relax, realizing his mastery of the vehicle, and admire his skills. She might even take his arm as he threw her off balance by careering around a particularly sharp curve. He imagined her hand on his arm, clutching it, feeling her exquisite fingertips like hot little brands on his skin.

Finally, the Feast of the First Night arrived. Neelix was in a paroxysm of anticipation. He had prepared all the gifts he was giving his family: lockets he had carved for his sisters, a delicate keepsakes box he had made for his mother, and a strong joiner tool for his father.

But his thoughts—for which he felt only mildly guilty—were all about his own longed-for gift.

"Children, come to the table." That was the traditional opening statement for the Feast of the First Night. Neelix and his sisters trooped eagerly to their dining table, which had been festooned with garlands of fellin branches. Scented candles cast off the aroma of testle blossoms, a heady fragrance that Neelix associated with the most joyous childhood memories. On this night, he found that he wasn't experiencing the feelings of his newly acquired manhood, but rather those of the small boy whose eyes had widened at the sight of the gifts of Prixin and whose stomach was sated with the delicious foodstuffs.

He and his sisters took their places, and their father led them in singing the hymn of Prixin, which was an expression of gratitude for peace, for food, and for shelter, but which also spoke of the virtues of the family, and the importance of the bonds of love. Neelix loved this song, which never failed to comfort and inspire him.

"Join our loving hearts together . . . we are not afraid. Join our hands in strong communion . . . we are not afraid. We are blessed to have each other . . . alone we do not stand . . . loving hearts will stay the nightfall . . . loving hands will keep us strong."

Then it was time for the revelation of the food. His mother, Axa, lifted the coverings from bowl after bowl of the traditional dishes: roast game, dusky tubers, trove bars of course—but best of all, the fruit compotes, soaked in moolt, which even children were allowed to eat because it was Prixin. Neelix ate several bowlfuls, and enjoyed the slightly light-headed sensation that came from the moolt.

"Now it is time for the gifts," announced his father. Neelix's heart quickened. He saw his sisters exchanging sly glances, and he was more certain than ever that a vehicle awaited him.

He forced himself to be patient while he and his sisters exchanged their gifts; they were delighted with his lockets, which pleased him, and he appreciated the assortment of games and tools they had given him.

Next came the presentation of the children's gifts to their parents, which took a very long time because his parents insisted on going on and on about each gift, praising its virtues and thanking the giver at great length. Neelix vowed that when he had a family, he wouldn't torture his children by making them wait so long for their parental gifts.

Finally, it was time. The parental gifts were given to each child in order of their births. This meant Neelix was last, and he summoned all his patience in order to be properly happy for his sisters as they were given their major gifts.

His parents were generous, and each of the girls received a substantial gift: a flawless gemstone for Raxel, a vacation trip to Talax for Mixin, a valuable piece of sculpture for Alixia, a rare perfume for Xepha, and silk clothing for Melorix.

Finally, it was time for Neelix. His mother and father exchanged a smile and announced that they must all go outside in order to see Neelix's gift. His heart hammered—he was right. A hover vehicle waited outside. He would ride it this very night to Vaxi's house.

His father opened the door and all of them trooped out. It took a few minutes for Neelix's eyes to accustom to the darkness, and at first all he could see was a dark shape in the yard. He moved toward it, realizing that his parents and sisters all hung back, letting him approach it alone.

It wasn't a vehicle.

It was a large old cannon, of the sort he knew had been used over a hundred years ago. These antiques were highly prized, and he knew his parents must have gone to a great deal of trouble to find it.

But it wasn't a hover vehicle. And he could hardly expect Vaxi to be enchanted by it.

He forced a smile on his face and turned to face his family. "I'm overwhelmed," he said honestly. "It's too much . . ."

He father was beaming. "It's been fully restored, to mint condition. Except for its firing ability, of course. That cannon is much too powerful to be activated."

"Of course." There was a pause as Neelix sought something more to say. "It's beautiful. I've read all about these Xeno-class cannons. They were technological marvels in their time." Another pause. "I can't thank you enough."

"We knew you'd be thrilled," said his mother. "Your father spent months looking for this."

"You shouldn't have gone to so much trouble. I don't deserve such a remarkable gift."

"We're proud of you, Neelix," said his father, his plump cheeks widening in a smile. "We wanted to show you how much."

"I'm honored. I'll try to live up to your expectations." The words sounded hollow in his ears. The conversation was losing all spontaneity and deteriorating into a series of platitudes. He wanted to get away from all of them. He went to his father and laid his head on Papa's chest in a traditional Talaxian gesture. He did the same to his mother, and she caressed his tufts gently.

"My baby," she murmured. He shut his eyes, miserable. They did love him, and had gone out of their way to present him with a remarkable gift. He tried to summon genuine gratitude, but he was empty. He pulled away from his mother and smiled as warmly as he could.

"I'm going to my room. I'd like to look up some of the reading I did on Xeno-class cannons. Thank you so much. I love you."

He retreated awkwardly, smiling and waving until he was inside the house. Then he fled to his room, conflicting emotions roiling within him. How dare he be disappointed? He was one of the most fortunate people alive. His family adored him and showered him with love. He was smart, and healthy, and capable. The future was limitless. He should be rejoicing every day of his life.

But bitter disappointment was like an insidious acid, oozing its way through him, eroding any sense of well-being and leaving him bereft and miserable. His fantasies of Vaxi had cracked and shattered like a reflector that was dropped. He shut his eyes and imagined Vaxi, whose spots were the most delicate shade of beige, pale and dainty. Her eyes were the lightest yellow, almost a white, giving her a mystic look. Her voice was like the purr of a kimcat, a husky, tender cascade of music.

Vaxi, Vaxi . . .

"Neelix . . . Neelix . . ."

His head jerked up. Was he hearing things? Was someone calling his name? There it was again, coming from outside his window. "Neelix . . . open the window."

Puzzled, he moved to the window and peered out. Then almost jumped backward in shock.

Vaxi was there, just outside, calling to him. "Neelix, I have to talk to you. Please open the window."

In his haste, he fumbled with the lock, fingers shaking from the surprise of seeing her in his yard. Finally, he managed to get the window open. A sweet, warm breeze caressed him as he leaned out and stared at Vaxi. "What's wrong? Is there a problem?"

"Neelix, could you come outside? I need your help."

His heart began pumping harder. Sweet Vaxi needed his help? Had she had an argument with her parents? Was she in some kind of trouble—or danger? He immediately swung his leg over the sill and scrambled out, a maneuver he'd made many times in his life.

Vaxi was standing near a small grove of fern trees at the back of the property. She was wearing a pale, filmy dress which caught the breeze, shimmering in the light of Talax above; its golden hue brought out the yellow of her beautiful eyes. Neelix thought he had never seen anyone so lovely, and his throat caught unexpectedly.

"Vaxi, what is it? What's happened?"

She didn't look worried, he realized. She looked—what? Eager? Expectant? His mind raced around itself, trying to understand this strange unfolding of events. He thought he heard a small rustling within the fern trees, but he could see nothing.

Incredibly, Vaxi was extending her hand to him. He hesitated, but she beckoned insistently toward him. "Come here, Neelix. I have to show you something."

He approached her carefully, still off balance and wary. This was the most curious behavior he'd ever seen in Vaxi, who was ordinarily a quiet, retiring young woman. She took his hand and immediately turned, pulling him into the grove of fern trees. Bushy fronds immediately surrounded them, and Neelix lifted his other arm to ward them off, but Vaxi marched unerringly forward.

Neelix was palpably uneasy. It was all too bizarre to comprehend, this mysterious plunge into the fern grove. Should he stop and refuse to take another step until Vaxi explained her strange behavior? A large part of him wanted to do just that.

Yet he was forced to admit that he was peculiarly titillated by this odd jaunt, and by the touch of Vaxi's soft hand tugging at him. He was close enough to inhale her fragrance, a faint scent of sweet grasses which quickened his heart as much as their brisk pace. He decided he would enjoy this unusual closeness regardless of what awaited them at the end of their outing.

What was that? A branch snapping? He jerked his head to the side, peering through the gloom. Was someone else in the grove with them? His feelings of well-being dissolved immediately, and the night was once again filled with ominous portents.

He heard a quiet cough from somewhere ahead. Instinctively, he slowed down, but Vaxi turned and pulled at him. "Come *on,*" she whispered hoarsely, moving inexorably forward.

A dark shape loomed ahead of them. This time Neelix stopped short. He wasn't going a step toward that shape. The time had come for answers.

But Vaxi wasn't pulling him forward anymore. She had stopped, too, and turned toward him, exuding anticipation. He heard sounds of movement off to his side, and a sharp intake of breath, as though someone were containing a laugh.

Then floodlights suddenly snapped on, illuminating the shadowy depths of the fern grove. Neelix squinted, almost blinded by the intrusion of intense light. He shaded his eyes, peering ahead at the now illuminated shape.

It was a hover vehicle.

Simultaneous with that realization came a whoop of laughter, and then there were a lot of people emerging from the ferns—his parents, his sisters, Vaxi's parents and brother. The scene seemed unreal, incomprehensible. What was happening? His mind struggled to find a context for these inexplicable events.

Alixia's laughter centered him once more. His eyes were pulled toward the sound, and he saw her approaching him, ebullient. "Oh, Neelix, you should see your face!"

He turned from her to Vaxi, and saw Vaxi, too, giggling uncontrollably, turned back to see his parents almost beside themselves with delight, his father's tufts bobbing in the harsh white light, his mother's eyes gleaming golden.

His astonishment wasn't lessened as he realized what was happening and how elaborate the plan had been. He stared at his father, speechless.

"Well, Neelix, I can tell you're surprised, all right. I guess we pulled it off."

"We've planned this for *weeks,*" said Alixia merrily. "Everyone's been a part of it. I don't know how we managed to keep the secret so long."

Neelix, still reeling, turned back toward the hovercraft.

He thought he'd never seen such a magnificent vehicle. It was a two-seated pod, sleek and racy. It wasn't new, of course, but it was in excellent condition, its diburnium chassis smooth and undented. Well, maybe a small dent on its underbelly, but it was hardly noticeable. It was a deep shade of burgundy, so dark it was almost black, and was trimmed with burnished steel.

"You . . . this . . . is . . . for . . . me?" His voice stammered and shook, a fact that seemed to produce a new round of mirth in the onlookers, his sisters all but squealing in glee.

"Maybe it was a bit cruel, pretending the cannon was your only gift," said his father. "But these malicious women," and at that he gestured good-naturedly toward his wife and daughters, "would hear of nothing else."

Neelix's legs felt shaky. He had to draw a few breaths of air as he assimilated the enormity of what had happened.

He'd been given a hovercraft!

He looked from one to the other of his family and friends. He felt a giant lump forming in his throat, which deep breaths did nothing to dissolve. "I . . . don't know what to say. Thank you . . . I'm . . . I'm . . . in shock . . ."

"You tried so hard to convince us you weren't disappointed with the cannon," giggled Alixia. "You were so sweet . . . but you looked as though someone had killed your pet kimcat."

"You . . . you planned all this? The cannon . . . the vehicle . . . ?" Neelix felt himself babbling, but he was still trying to comprehend this extraordinary event.

His mother smiled. "The girls convinced me you would appreciate a hovercraft more if you thought you weren't getting one. They knew you expected it. So they evolved this whole scheme, and persuaded Vaxi to be a part of it."

"We knew you'd never guess what was happening if she was involved." Mixin grinned.

"But I was so nervous," breathed Vaxi. "My heart was pounding—I was sure I'd mess everything up somehow, and you'd guess what was going on."

Neelix walked toward the vehicle and ran his hand softly over the finish. "It's beautiful," he said. "I couldn't have imagined anything better." He turned to his family, to his neighbors, and his eyes began to sting. He felt surrounded, enveloped by love. How did he deserve such happiness? "Thank you," he breathed. "I'll always try to . . . to . . . I'll try never to disappoint you. Any of you."

It was an odd little speech, and he didn't quite know where it came from, but his father embraced him strongly and his mother hugged him; Vaxi's father clapped him on the back, and—bliss of blisses—Vaxi planted a delicate kiss on his cheek. His skin flushed and his stomach twitched in an unfamiliar but decidedly pleasurable way.

He was happier than he'd ever been in his life, happier than he would ever be. He couldn't imagine ever being unhappy again.

Four years later, just twelve days before his nineteenth birthday, he stood, terrified, stricken by catastrophe, in the yard of a hidden compound on Talax. The world as he knew it was over, and misery was the most positive emotion he could summon.

How had it come to this? How could everything have crumbled so completely, so dreadfully? Was life truly so unpredictable, so uncontrollable? And could he hope that, someday, it might reverse itself as completely and render him happy again?

And, most important: Was there anything he could have done that might have altered this unspeakable course of events?

And as he asked himself this fateful question, he realized the answer. Yes, things might have been different. He would be dead now, of course. But at this point that seemed a far more comforting possibility than the life to which he was now consigned.

In a strange way, it had all happened as a result of his Prixin gift four years ago. His hovercraft. His liberation.

His fantasies had come true. He mastered the craft quickly, and became a skilled pilot. He took Vaxi for long and exhilarating rides over the countryside of Rinax, and she squealed at his bold maneuvers. She even clung to him, as he had imagined her doing, and her dainty hands were indeed like pinpoints of fire, burning into his skin.

They began studying together every night, a practice which immeasurably improved Neelix's grades. They swam in the pond between their homes, and went to concerts together or in the company of their parents.

His father had acquired a small, knowing smile which appeared whenever Vaxi's name was mentioned, and his mother seemed serenely happy about the relationship. He knew they were anticipating the eventual acquisition of yet another daughter into their large and loving family.

He never got around to taking Vaxi to his hut in the woods.

He never even mentioned it. It seemed childish now, and he was embarrassed to reveal the detritus of his youth to her. She would undoubtedly think it was foolish and immature behavior, this retreat to an isolated hut for the purpose of living a fantasy life. She would find it strange, aberrant. He couldn't risk that.

Yet he felt vaguely guilty, as though he'd abandoned a childhood friend without ever saying good-bye. He pictured his hut, standing alone and forlorn in the woods, insects once again draping it with webs, voracious undergrowth creeping toward it across the clearing, vines climbing its walls and obscuring its windows.

These thoughts made him disturbingly uncomfortable, and each night he vowed he'd go tomorrow and clean the place up, restoring it to its pristine state.

And each day he'd spend every moment he could with Vaxi.

It was also during this time that the dark specter of conflict began rumbling through Talax. People began speaking more and more about the Haakonians. Neelix had learned that the Talaxians had successfully battled this warlike species more than a century before. The rulers of Haakon, after a decades-long attempt to subjugate Talax and its moon, had withdrawn in ignominy and chosen to vent their aggressions against other, less tenacious people. For generations, Talax had known only peace.

Now there were disquieting rumors that Haakon planned to move once again against Talax. Neelix had heard these murmurings for the first time when his father had taken him to the weapons range three years before; now, the murmurs had become a constant babble. Haakon was arming a huge fleet. Haakon would mount a surprise attack against Rinax. Haakon wanted to turn Talax into a huge penal colony. The specifics differed, but no one seemed to disagree that something dire was looming.

What to do about that something dire was another matter entirely. There was sharp disagreement among the members of government—and among the citizenry—about the proper way to deal with the prospect of invasion. Some favored an immediate aggressive stance, the creation of armed forces, and the conversion to a military society.

Others felt that only the maintenance of a peaceful and nonthreatening posture could dissuade the Haakonians. And there were moderates—among whom was Neelix's father—who felt that Talax should adopt no overt or militant strategy, but must quietly develop armed forces for defensive purposes.

Neelix found the entire prospect unsavory. He knew he should take a position, as a man was expected to do, but he found himself recoiling from the hideous idea of war. He had never experienced it, but in his readings on weaponry he had learned enough about it to know he wanted no part of it. And yet, if Talax were invaded, would it not be his responsibility to help defend their way of life?

He thought longingly of his childhood, when such decisions weren't called for and his fantasies of the exploits of Prince Morax were as close as he ever needed to come to warfarc. He began to wish he were still a child, protected from harsh reality and nestled in the bosom of love.

He decided to visit his hut.

He packed a hamper with trove bars and iced neth, recalling wistfully the excursions he used to take with Alixia. Alixia was mated now, as were Raxel and Mixin; all three had chosen partners within the same year, and then decided to join in a triple mating ceremony. He missed Alixia deeply, but when he thought of Vaxi, he understood her happiness and didn't begrudge her.

He took his hovercraft into the woods and immediately felt a sense of well-being settle over him. The dusky aroma of damp leaves was perfume to him, and made him feel eight years old again, tagging along behind Alixia as they explored.

He drove slowly, savoring the woodlands, the hovercraft skimming silently over the forest floor, a moist breeze cooling his skin. He would refurbish the hut and begin visiting it once more. Next year he would have to attend school on Talax, so he'd best get some use out of his old retreat before then. The prospect was calming.

In his vehicle, he covered the terrain quickly. Why hadn't he bothered to come here since he'd gotten the craft? Neelix shook his head ruefully. As soon as he had the means to travel swiftly—which was why he'd wanted the vehicle in the first place—he'd stopped exploring.

He'd begun exploring Vaxi, instead, and while he certainly had no regrets about that adventure, he was sorry he'd given up his sorties into the woods. There was continuity here, a pattern that comforted. These woods were devoid of uncertainty.

Ahead, he spotted the clearing. As he neared it, he realized his vision of the neglected hut was accurate: brushy growth had overtaken the clearing and surrounded the small structure; copious vines had crept up its walls and laced an errant design on the roof. The windows were all but covered with leafy shades, and a mossy fungus encrusted any exposed surface.

It looked as a structure would that had been unused for three years.

And yet—something was off. He couldn't decide quite what it was . . . certainly nothing that caught the eye. But something, *something,* didn't feel right.

Neelix climbed out of the vehicle carefully, senses alert, fingertips tingling with wariness. Someone had been here, been here recently. But how did he know that?

He inspected the hut from a distance. The undergrowth looked undisturbed, and he could hear nothing except for the hum of insects and the occasional call of a yute bird.

Quietly, slowly, he approached the door. He could almost hear his heart pounding in his chest and his breathing sounded loud and raspy. What was causing this apprehension?

He was only a few steps from the door when he realized it was something he smelled. The scent of the forest was strong and familiar, a combination of decaying leaves, wild blossoms, and dank moistness. But there was a tiny vein of something else lacing that pungent odor, no more than a hint of something, so subtle it might have gone unnoticed. But to Neelix, the fragrance of the forest was a part of him. He could detect any deviant element.

Something had burned. He couldn't be sure what, but the whiff of acridity seemed to become more pronounced as he identified it. He glanced around the clearing for signs of a cooking fire, but saw none. He turned back toward the hut, realizing that the odor must be coming from inside.

He could turn around, walk back to his craft, and return to the sanctuary of home. It would have been easy. And, in retrospect, the wise thing to do.

But he felt an ineffable sense of violation. Someone had been using his hut, his retreat. He knew he had no legitimate claim of ownership to it, but his proprietary feelings were no less intense because of that. He'd put hours of work into this place. He'd invested it with literally years of his young life. It *belonged* to him, and he deeply resented anyone else using it.

So it was with indignation that he opened the door.

And with horror and revulsion that he recoiled at what he saw.

A man—something like a man—was sitting on a chair . . . his chair . . . slumped over. He was prevented from falling because he was tied into the chair.

His face, if it could be called that, was a pulpy mass, purple and bloated. It had distended into a grotesque mask, like the ones children wore on the Day of the Specters. Neelix could barely see the eyes, which had swollen closed.

Someone had beaten him hideously.

Neelix stood at the door, transfixed, uncertain what to do. He didn't want to walk closer to this monstrosity, but he felt compelled to determine whether the man was alive.

He hoped he was not.

Forcing a calm he didn't feel, Neelix stepped toward the man, and realized his chest was rising and falling imperceptibly. He was alive.

But then Neelix made another, more horrible observation: the source of the burnt odor.

Beating was not the only thing this man had endured. Parts of him were charred and black . . . feet, ankles, legs . . . He had been cruelly used, flesh roasted from the bottom up. Neelix began shuddering, and was afraid for a moment he would throw up. The smell had become powerful, assaulting his nostrils and lungs until he felt he couldn't breathe.

He stood frozen for what seemed like hours, trying to control himself. Finally he gasped as he realized the man's eyes were open, looking right at him.

Open, that is, as far as they could in that puffy face. Dreadful, milky eyes, shot with blood, staring dully at Neelix.

"I'll . . . I'll . . . I'm . . . going to get you out of here," stammered Neelix. He hadn't intended to say that; the words came out unbidden.

267

A husky rasp emerged from the bound man's throat, but Neelix had no idea what he was trying to say, and he didn't want to draw nearer in order to hear him. But the man rasped at him again, more urgently.

"What? I can't hear you . . ." said Neelix. His mind was trying to figure out how he could get this horribly injured man into his vehicle. He couldn't walk, not on those charred feet. And he was too heavy for Neelix to carry. How was he to accomplish his promised act of rescue?

The hoarse whisper escaped the man's lips once more, lips that were caked with dried blood. Neelix watched in horrible fascination as flakes of the brown crust fell from his tumid lips and onto the floor, where they settled softly onto the dust that had accumulated there. The sound was more urgent still, and Neelix realized he would have to move closer to this monstrosity if he were to hear.

He forced himself to take a few steps forward, then leaned down and looked away from the man's face, placing his ear close to the bloated brown mouth. This time the words took a crude shape. "They . . . will . . . find . . . you . . ."

The horror this struck in Neelix was unimaginable. What did this mean? Who? Would they do to him what they'd done to this wretched man? He fought panic, and turned to face the hideous face once more. "I can't get you out alone. I'm going for help. I promise I'll get back as soon as I can."

There was no response. The man's chin had fallen once more onto his chest, as though uttering those few words had drained every vestige of energy he had left.

Neelix backed away, toward the door, and then sprinted across the clearing toward the hovercraft. Later, as he sped through the forest, he wondered if he should have taken steps to erase evidence of his visit. He hadn't even closed the door. Then he realized there could have been someone in the woods, watching him, someone who saw him enter the hut and then come dashing out.

Someone who could identify him.

Shaking off these terrifying feelings, Neelix raced into his house calling for his father. And not an hour later they were both with a kindly civil defender named Tixil, and several of his men, plunging in an official vehicle through the forest. It didn't matter that the hut's existence would no longer be a secret. His sanctuary had been violated in an unspeakable manner already.

He led the group to the clearing, and emerged from the hovercraft in dread. He didn't want to see the man again. He'd already described him to the authorities, and he wanted them to take over now, so he could go about the business of trying to erase the awful sight from his memory.

But the first thing he noticed was that the door to the hut was closed.

He'd left it open, he was sure of that. He had worried about it during his headlong flight through the woods. That meant someone had been here after he left, and closed it.

He stopped short. Tixil looked at him. "What is it, Neelix?" he asked.

"The door was open when I left. Someone's been here."

Tixil nodded and drew his weapon. The sight of it comforted Neelix. Here was a person in authority, a powerful person with a powerful weapon. He would restore stability to Neelix's world, would somehow right this distorted, careening reality.

Tixil paused at the door, then flung it open and stepped in, weapon trained before him. After he'd scanned the room, he turned and beckoned to the others.

Neelix and his father walked into the hut, Neelix just behind his father, hoping his tall presence would shield him from the sight of the tortured man.

He wasn't there.

The chair he'd sat in was back in its usual place near the small table. The room looked as though no one had been there in years. Dust covered the floor, and there were no footprints, no markings in the dust, no indication that a chair had been dragged across the room.

No flakes of crusted blood on the floor.

Neelix realized that several pairs of eyes were fastened on him, including his father's and Tixil's. They were silent.

"I . . . I . . ." Neelix heard his voice crack, and took a breath. "He was here. Right here. Tied into that chair, only the chair was here, in the middle of the floor." His voice sounded hollow in his own ears.

Tixil inspected the room carefully, looking at windows and cupboards, scrutinizing the dust-laden floor. Neelix realized miserably that their own presence had made indelible prints on the floor. It was impossible that someone could have been here and not disturbed this layer of dust.

Neelix glanced up at his father, who was watching carefully as Tixil completed his examination of the room. Finally Tixil turned toward them, eyes troubled. When he spoke, his voice was gentle. "I don't know what to say, Neelix. I can't see any indication that anyone's been here in a long time." He paused uncomfortably. "I don't know if you're a young man with a vivid imagination——"

"I saw him. He was here," retorted Neelix firmly. Tixil nodded as though trying to give credence to this improbable statement. He glanced at Neelix's father, then looked down at the floor, with some embarrassment.

"I apologize for bringing this up," he began, clearly uneasy with the topic, "but I feel I must." He hesitated, then continued. "Rhuludian crystals have become popular with a number of young people these days . . ."

Neelix heard his father gasp, and hated Tixil for raising this awful possibility. He stepped right toward his father. "I have never . . . *never* . . . touched those things. And I never would."

Papa nodded solemnly, and looked up at Tixil in vindication, but Tixil made no comment. Finally he drew a deep breath. "I'll have my men make a thorough search of the woods. See if they can turn up anything. I promise we'll let you know the results."

Neelix's father nodded as though that were acceptable, but Neelix felt betrayed. "You don't believe me," he accused Tixil. "You think I imagined it, or hallucinated. But I didn't. There was a man here, who'd been tortured. Whoever did that is still . . . out there. Somewhere." He felt a chill at that last statement. The tortured man's hoarse prophecy seared his mind. Someone was out there who would find him. He swallowed and took a deep breath.

And smelled the tiniest whiff of burnt meat.

"There—do you smell that?" Tixil and his father looked somewhat startled. "It's like something burnt. That's what they did to him, to his feet and legs."

Tixil and his father obligingly turned their noses upward, sniffing carefully. But clearly they didn't detect the acrid odor. Neelix wasn't sure if he would've, either, had he not smelled it so strongly when he was here before. Both men looked somewhat embarrassed, and acknowledged that they smelled nothing.

His father put an arm around his shoulder and led him from the hut. Tixil followed, eyes carefully sweeping the room one last time.

It was in complete silence that they made their way back through the woods to home.

Tixil deposited them at their door and promised to contact them tomorrow. Neelix stared after him, as his power and authority receded in the distance.

Neelix felt alone and vulnerable. He had no appetite for dinner, and excused himself. He went to his room and got in bed, where he huddled like a small child, fearful of unknown monsters in the dark.

The smell of burnt flesh assailed him. He knew it wasn't really there, that he was simply remembering its awful odor—he *did* know the difference between imagination and reality—but it made him faintly queasy nonetheless. Even here, in the bed of his childhood, there was no sanctuary.

He had no idea how long he'd been there when he heard a tap at his door. Night had fallen, and he was in some indistinct stage between sleep and wakefulness. At the sound of the knock, he was alert and tense.

"Neelix?" It was his father's voice. Neelix got out of bed and padded to the door, opening it.

His father stood there with a man who looked vaguely familiar, but whom he couldn't immediately identify.

"Do you remember Uxxin?" asked his father. "You met him at the weapons range the first time we went there."

The memory registered in Neelix's mind. The tall, erect man, spots black with age, tufts elaborately arranged. He was the one who'd spoken of the need for an armed citizenry.

But the tale he brought tonight was far more frightening than the as-yet-unfounded threat of the Haakonians.

Neelix sat with the two of them at their dining table—the scene of so much mirth and pleasure over the years. It would never recall good times again; from this night on, the dining table would remind him only of the awful things Uxxin was telling them.

"The boy must leave Rinax tonight. If he's here tomorrow when Tixil comes back, you'll never see him again. I've made arrangements to get him to Talax, where we have friends who will hide him."

Neelix's head was spinning with disbelief. What was Uxxin talking about? Why did he have to leave his home?

His father looked at him solemnly. "Uxxin is part of a group who are trying to avoid war with Haakon. But there are strong factions that want the war, and who consider the moderates a threat. The whole thing has turned ugly."

"I believe the man in the hut was one of our group who disappeared several days ago. I have no doubt that Tixil and his men tortured him for information about us."

"*Tixil?*" Neelix couldn't believe what he was hearing. "Tixil the civil defender?"

"I'm afraid the authorities are riddled with people like him—who want war and who will do anything to suppress opposition to it."

The room began to swim. What was life coming to if one couldn't trust the civil authorities? Those sworn to protect and defend?

"Tixil knows you saw someone who'd been tortured. He can't afford to let you spread that around. It's a wonder he didn't take you in for questioning right away." Tixil paused portentously. "You'd never have survived."

Visions of the man's burned feet danced in Neelix's vision, and he tried to blink them away. Was this the fate that awaited him? Cold terror began to creep from his belly, radiating outward to his extremities. His father wouldn't let this happen. His father was wise, and strong. He would protect him.

But his father was talking to Uxxin, making the plans for his clandestine trip to Talax. Neelix was told to pack quickly, taking only necessities. Within fifteen minutes after Uxxin had arrived, Neelix was standing with his mother and father and his sisters Xepha and Melorix, the only two left at home. Tears were streaming down their faces, and while crying was exactly what Neelix felt like doing, he forced himself to appear confident, for their sake. "I'll be back as soon as I can," he promised, kissing the briny tears on their cheeks. They cried even harder.

His mother embraced him, her eyes moist as well, but she was stalwart and refused to give in to grief. And finally Papa held him strongly, briefly, unspeaking. And then Neelix was gone, off in the night like a felon on the run.

He never saw any of his family again.

Inevitably, war broke out. Talax actually made the first strike, the warlike faction of their race having predominated. But after that, it hardly mattered who had started things. It was brutal and relentless, fought on many fronts: in space, on the Haakonian homeworld, and on Talax. Losses on both sides were staggering. The economy was devoted entirely to the war effort, and food shortages abounded. Winters were devastating, because fuel was in short supply. Medical centers were overrun with the war wounded.

Haakon suffered just as harshly. Resources were dwindling and riots had broken out on Haakonian outposts everywhere. Their government was under great pressure from the citizenry to end the devastating conflict.

Neelix spent two years helping to run a sanctuary for deserters from the military. He had never acquired the zealousness of his fellow pacifists, and from time to time considered coming forth and offering to join the military. But he knew the time had passed. He was a deserter, having never shown up for obligatory service, and would be executed summarily.

And so he protected those who had fled the fighting, those who were convinced the authorities wanted to protract the war for their own financial gain. These hardened veterans told tales of unimaginable horror about the battle fronts, and spoke with loathing of the venality of the government that would perpetuate this evil.

In the end, Neelix didn't know what to believe. He had come to his situation not through ideology, or passion, or even choice. Fate had placed him squarely on one side of the argument whether he liked it or not. He was as helpless as a leaf blown before the wind. He reasoned that he should eschew philosophical musing and simply do the best he could for the cause that had protected him, snatching him from Tixil's grasp and keeping him safe for over two years.

He had to admit that when he heard the heartrending tales from the front, he felt relieved not to be a part of it. It all sounded so futile, so needless—fighting for weeks over a kilometer-wide strip of land, taking and retaking it countless times, back and forth until the corpses were stacked like deadwood and no one could even remember why that strip of land was so important.

They heard rumors that the Haakonian populace was out of control, threatening to storm the governmental buildings unless the war was terminated. Hope sprang in many hearts that, soon, it would all be over.

And so it was.

The end of the war occurred on a warm spring night, and the terminus took no more than four minutes.

Neelix was sitting outside, in the walled compound of their hideaway. A wild yute bird sounded, reminding him of home, and somewhere someone was playing a gentle melody on the ixxel. For a moment, it was possible to believe that, soon, life would become normal once more, that love and joy would return to their hearts, that bellies would be full and spirits nourished. That he would see his family again.

He inhaled the spring air deeply, and gazed up at Rinax, luminous in the night sky, half in shadow at this time of the month. He imagined his parents and his sisters, and hoped they weren't suffering too badly from the war. He'd supposed his sisters' husbands had been pressed into service, unless they were protestors and avoided conscription. He had had no contact with any of them for two years, since he'd been taken off Rinax crammed in a cargo container loaded onto a freighter piloted by a friend of Uxxin.

As he stared upward, a curious brightness illuminated Rinax, turning its whiteness briefly to a cold blue.

Then it began to disappear.

Neelix stared upward, trying to reconcile the puzzling sight with some understandable phenomenon.

He couldn't do it.

It was as though dark fingers began to obscure the moon, creeping swiftly over the surface, occluding it completely. Dust clouds, he thought, or some unusual space storm. But a coldness in his heart told him this was something far worse than a storm.

As he stared upward, the call of the yute bird still wafting through the night air—and forever afterward, he would associate that sound with the catastrophe that had struck—Rinax disappeared completely. He knew it was there; he could see its faint outline, as one does in an eclipse, but it was a dark disk in the sky.

It hadn't been an eclipse. It didn't behave like one. What were those strange fingers of darkness that clawed at his home, like bony talons of death?

He wasn't sure how long he stood staring up at the darkness where Rinax had been, but after a time he heard a commotion inside. People were shouting. Then he heard an unearthly wailing.

Lixxisa, a good friend, came running toward him. Her eyes were wide, and her face was pale in the darkness. "Neelix . . ." she began; then her knees buckled and she sank to the ground. Alarmed, he crouched beside her. "What is it? What's happened?"

"Unthinkable . . . unthinkable . . ."

"Lixxisa, tell me!"

"Rinax . . . destroyed . . ."

Neelix's mind froze, and he willed time to reverse itself, to return him to the pleasant reverie of mere minutes ago. If he could back up just those few minutes in time, all would be righted. Rinax would still gleam in the night sky, and this time, events would proceed differently. It would not disappear before his eyes, Lixxisa would not come running, pallid, from the house and crumple at his feet. She would not say the awful words she had just spoken.

But his will wasn't strong enough. Time pressed inexorably on.

Lixxisa gasped for air, as though she'd been hit in the abdomen. "A weapon . . . horrible weapon . . . a cascade . . . every village on Rinax is gone . . . everyone dead . . ."

This litany of horror droned on, but Neelix tuned it out. He couldn't listen. If he refused to hear it, it would be robbed of validity. What one doesn't hear cannot have happened.

But once again his determination was thwarted. Lixxisa kept on, and on. "Massive fireballs . . . the atmosphere nearly consumed . . . no one's ever heard of anything like this . . . what kind of animals are they who'd develop a weapon like that?"

Aghast, Neelix stared upward at his home. Now, through the dark clouds, streaks of light were visible. Orange flickers, licking at the darkness. Flames. Massive fireballs.

Rinax had been attacked with weaponry so strong that the smoke from the explosions had completely obscured it. And now the fireballs were blazing. If they could be seen from Talax, they must be immense. No one could possibly survive.

Pictures of his beloved family seared his mind. His father and mother, entwined in each other's arms as they were incinerated. His sisters, writhing in agony as flames burned the flesh from their bones. Sweet Alixia screaming and screaming and screaming . . .

He could smell the odor of burned flesh.

A hot coal formed in his belly. He couldn't identify it; it was completely foreign to him. It hurt, and yet it was somehow satisfying. It grew steadily, burning him from within, taking him over completely, overwhelming, igniting his brain, boiling his heart.

It was rage.

Rage sustained him for weeks after the disaster. The war had ended summarily, with Talax surrendering immediately and becoming in essence a Haakonian outpost. The weapon, they learned, was called the Metreon Cascade, and had been developed in order to bring the war to a swift and certain conclusion.

Neelix volunteered to be part of a rescue mission to Rinax, and was among the first to set foot on the devastated landscape. Fires still burned there, and the smell was something that would haunt his dreams for years: the same odor of roasted flesh that had permeated his hut after he had found the tortured man. Clouds of rancid smoke and dust billowed placidly, like a meadow of dark flowers, their gentle swaying a grotesque counterpart to the horror they manifested.

No one could be alive in this place.

He and his friends forced themselves forward, steeling themselves to the awful sights, breathing through moistened handkerchiefs to quench the noxious odor. They soon realized this search would not be lengthy, because almost nothing was left of Rinax.

His house was gone. Not even the foundation was left, just a large black spot indicating that something had burned. Vaxi's house, too, was obliterated, and the pond the children had frolicked in was nothing more than a dry pit in the ground.

Someone observed that they must be very near a "ground zero" point—where the weapon had made its initial contact. That was the first heartening news Neelix had heard in days. That meant it was very likely that his family had been annihilated on the spot, instantly vaporized and suffering no pain. They would now be united in the afterlife, where one day he would join them. He tried to remind himself of this faintly comforting fact as they continued to prowl the smoldering ruins.

It was he who first detected the faint sound that emanated from the undulating clouds of smoke. At first he thought it might be a bird, and wondered how a bird had survived this devastation.

Then he saw figures moving toward them with maddening sluggishness, each step taken as though through heavy mud.

They were monsters.

Charred skin, the color of shale, hung from their torsos and extremities. The pulpy flesh underneath, swollen to bursting, dripped with watery fluids. The monsters had no faces, just a mask of spongy tissue, swirled as though someone had stirred a thick batch of red and black pudding.

Vague orifices emerged from the pudding, distorted beyond any identification as eyes or mouth. Yet somehow from the misshapen gullets a sound emanated, a keening, a bestial moaning, that made the tufts on Neelix's head stiffen.

One of the monsters moved in his direction, hearing rather than seeing the members of his group because its eyes were obliterated, its hideous limbs outstretched, scorched skin dangling. Terrified that the thing would touch him, he turned away.

"Wahhhh . . . wahhh . . ."

The thing spoke with what could clearly be identified—even though the words were distorted by the monstrous mingling of lips, teeth, and tongue—as a child's voice. Appalled, Neelix turned back.

The child was pointing toward its grotesque mouth. "Wahhh . . . wahhh . . ." it repeated, and suddenly Neelix realized the poor creature was asking for water. He reached for his container, uncapped it, and held it out. The child couldn't see it.

Neelix held the container to what had once been lips and tipped the liquid into the ravaged mouth. The child managed a few sips but then began choking from the pain of swallowing through such damaged tissue. Neelix felt himself begin to tremble. What was he to do for this creature? This was beyond his experience.

He glanced around and saw the members of the team busy with others of the unfortunate survivors. They seemed to know what they were doing, and he wondered briefly how they could function so calmly when presented with a calamity of this magnitude.

He remembered that he had a pain medication in his medical container, and reached in for it. But before he could administer it, the child tumbled into his arms, unconscious, leaving hunks of burnt matter on his clothing. Revulsion threw gorge into his throat, but then it subsided, and Neelix felt the tiny weight of the child, the frantic beating of its heart. He picked it up effortlessly and moved toward the others. He made a determination that this child would live.

Thirty-seven people survived the Metreon Cascade, all that remained of a population of more than two hundred thousand. Those thirty-seven were alive only because they were in an underground recreational facility miles from ground zero. They were taken to medical facilities on Talax, where doctors were stupefied by their condition. Traditional burn treatments were simply ineffective, and gradually, one by one, the survivors began to die.

The child's name, Neelix learned, was Palaxia. Though badly disfigured, she had suffered less damage to her internal organs than some of the others, and the doctors believed she had a chance to survive. She was resilient, they said, and possessed a will to live. That was often the factor that made the difference.

Neelix spent weeks by her side. She was blind, eyeballs having melted in the blast, and so he read to her for hours at a time— inspirational stories of Talaxian heroes who had overcome difficult circumstances, hoping that she would be heartened by the examples. He had no way of knowing if this was so, of course, as Palaxia had lost the power of articulate speech, scar tissue having occluded her larynx. But she could hear, and he imagined that the sound of his voice, hour upon hour, was comforting to her.

Skin grafts were applied and quickly sloughed off. This process was repeated three times before doctors began shaking their heads and admitting that they didn't know what to do next.

Palaxia was kept on powerful pain medications. Without them, she would have been in constant agony. With them, she still suffered, but at what the doctors called a "tolerable level." Neelix wondered how they managed to determine this, or even how they assessed the level at which she hurt, but was glad something was being done for her.

Palaxia, for her part, lay quietly on the bed, tiny chest rising and falling, face and body swathed in dressings, enduring her agony privately, in a world she could share with no one.

And Neelix sat with her day after day, reading, talking, even singing some of his favorite songs from Prixin, although he usually couldn't finish them because his own grief would overcome him.

Palaxia lived five and one half weeks, three weeks longer than any of the other survivors. Neelix was with her as her breathing became more ragged; she stopped and then started breathing four separate times, as though her will refused to let her die. He spoke to her throughout, words of comfort and solace, telling her that she would soon be reunited with her family, who had been waiting for her.

Finally her chest rose and fell no more. Neelix quietly gathered his things and left the medical facility, saying good-bye to no one. He shed no tears for Palaxia, or for his vanished family and friends. He did not mourn them at all. It would have destroyed him.

He met Wix two years after that, while he was in a prolonged euphoria caused by inhaling the smoke of burning Rhuludian crystals.

They weren't really crystals, of course, but dried and ground herbs with a potent narcotic effect. The term "crystals" had been coined because of the amazing clarity one felt after inhaling the smoke. Neelix had first started using crystals after Palaxia died. He knew others in his group often partook of them, but he never had. After the Metreon Cascade, he couldn't remember why it had seemed so important to abjure their use.

And when he first inhaled the fragrant smoke, he was sorry he'd waited so long.

Why were there such dire warnings about using crystals? Why had his parents and every other adult he knew cautioned him never to consider inhaling them? They'd made a huge furor over nothing. The crystal fumes didn't make him disoriented, or dizzy, or out of control. Quite the opposite: his mind was never sharper, never more focused than when he'd lit the tightly packed taper and drawn the sweet smoke into his lungs. He gained clarity and insight that were unachievable otherwise.

But most important of all, he could forget what he had seen on Rinax. The dreadful sights that he had thought were permanently etched into memory faded into obscurity. The queasiness in his stomach—a constant since the Metreon Cascade—disappeared. Well-being returned, and he could plan for a future once more.

Why would one not partake of such a therapeutic substance?

He had to be careful not to become addicted, of course. He had to monitor his usage, not let it get out of hand. But that wasn't a problem. He didn't *have* to use the crystals; he could stop whenever he wanted to. He simply chose to use them in order to lessen his pain. Once his life was in order again, he'd quit entirely.

Until then, he had to continue finding a supply. That had become more difficult since Haakon had won the war. They took a rigidly negative view of crystal use, and set out to eliminate the trade on Talax.

And so it was that Neelix left the planet, one of several passengers on a cargo freighter, mind humming with possibility after inhaling a few sniffs of smoke, ready to seek fate and fortune among the stars.

Among the passengers was Wixiban, a young man near his age, who was witty and clever, who spoke beguilingly about the possibilities of scavenging as a career, and who had a copious supply of crystals, which he was willing to share. For a price, of course.

"I have friends who've done very well for themselves," said Wix ebulliently, "by collecting discarded items, refurbishing them, and then selling them or trading upward. It's honest work, and even helps the environment by recycling items which would otherwise molder as trash."

Neelix nodded his agreement. He found Wix impressive— enlightened and persuasive. "I've often been surprised at the things people throw away," he added. "It's shamefully wasteful, especially when someone else might get years of use from such a discard." This statement seemed to Neelix, in his heightened awareness, suffused with profundity.

"We'll need a ship, of course," Wix continued. "Nothing big, nothing up-to-date . . . just an old runabout. We can probably find one in a ships' graveyard. People discard old vessels as casually as they throw out last night's garbage."

"We can fix it up, make it good as new." Neelix was already looking forward to this project, his mind conceiving all the components he'd want on his very own ship: hypercharged engine power, of course, and chairs lined in tanned libbit skin, the most supple of upholstery. And a communications system with isoacoustic speakers. Nothing like loud, lively music to make the vast distances of space collapse a bit.

That and Rhuludian crystals, of course.

Neelix realized that as his mind had wandered, Wix had continued to speak. Neither seemed aware that the other was essentially communing with himself, a fact which Neelix found amusing. He chuckled a bit.

The more he thought about it, the funnier it seemed, and soon he was laughing out loud, drawing curious stares not only from Wix but from the other passengers as well. He clapped Wix on the shoulder in a gesture of goodwill and solidarity, and was gratified when Wix threw his arm around him in a brotherly hug.

A brother. That's what Wix would become to him. Neelix felt tears of happiness sting his eyes as he realized the pain of the past was no more, and that he had a family once again. He probably wouldn't even need the crystals anymore.

They found their ship, a battered but serviceable scout vessel, in a vast graveyard overseen by a huge Wellyump, one of a beastlike species with a reputation for being hard bargainers—a reputation Neelix and Wix soon found to be accurate. In the end, they had to relieve the mountainous, hirsute creature of the battered vessel they wanted through subterfuge: after giving him a few drinks of sokrit, a potent liquor, Neelix engaged him in a game of cards, which Neelix managed to win because he had inhaled crystals and his mind was nimble. The Wellyump's senses, on the other hand, were muddied by the sokrit, and he couldn't remember to count his cards. Neelix won game after game, each time collecting a precious gemstone from his opponent's gradually shrinking pile.

The danger in all this was triggering the Wellyump's legendary temper, but Neelix wasn't worried. He was capable of controlling the situation until Wix had made off with the ship. He knew the big behemoth would keep playing, desperate to regain his jewels.

"I'm a fair man, sir, and I offer you the chance to recoup these splendid gems. How about this: one game in which you stand to gain much, and lose little. If I lose—and surely I'm due, don't you think?—you recover everything." Neelix spread the sparkling jewels on the table, the light catching their luster. "And if you lose—you owe me only one more."

The big creature opposite him settled in his chair with a grunt. Rolls of fur-covered fat undulated around his body, quivering. He reached again for the sokrit cup and swigged deeply. Finally he looked up at Neelix through drooping eyes. He nodded.

The sad thing was, Neelix thought, it wasn't even a challenge. The Wellyump was so besotted he could hardly see the cards, much less play them with any precision. That's what drunkenness did to you, and he thanked the fates that he didn't partake of such destructive substances.

He won the game easily, and his opponent sagged in his chair, inebriated and defeated. A wheezing gurgle emitted from deep in his throat, and Neelix wondered if this was a warning. He decided to be politic, and sacrifice some of his gains in order to insure his safe departure from this potentially dangerous being.

"Sir, you've been a challenging opponent, and I enjoy a game well played. Because of my respect for you, I'll share these winnings with you." He scooped up roughly half of the jewels and shoved them across the table to the Wellyump, who seemed dazed and uncomprehending, but who nonetheless put out a hairy claw to receive the proffered booty. Little grunts emanated from him, though what their interpretation was Neelix didn't know. Shoveling his gems into his sack, he pretended to quaff a drink from his cup and rose. He backed toward the door, smiling genially and waving.

The Wellyump had passed out, collapsing on top of his recovered jewels, which he cradled to him like a litter of babies.

Neelix moved through a passageway in the station, and saw through an airlock that Wix had the decrepit-looking ship docked and ready, and in minutes they had departed the graveyard, laughing at how easy it had all been, euphoric about the adventure, and eager to continue this unique partnership. It was easy, it was fun, and their future was limitless.

"Where are they? Tell me where they are, you moldering pile of fecal matter, or I'm going to roast you alive! I swear I will!"

Neelix held his hands around Wix's throat, driven by outrage, shaking his partner with a fury that fed itself and mounted still higher. Wix struggled in his grip, trying to loose the hands that were tightening on his trachea, but he was unable to pry off even a finger. Neelix's ferocity gave him inconceivable strength, and it wouldn't be long before Wix blacked out.

Wix pointed toward the weapons locker of the ship, and Neelix's response was instantaneous. He released his grip and dashed to the locker, threw it open, and began rummaging through it in a frenzy, throwing out weapons and ammunition in his hunt.

When the locker was empty and he realized he'd been tricked, he whirled on Wix, who was standing at a distance with an electrokinetic pistol pointed at him.

"You've got to stop using the crystals, Neelix. We can't keep going through this."

"You tricked me! You unmitigated piece of slime! I'm going to kill you!"

"I'm trying to help you. The crystals are destroying you."

Neelix's eyes narrowed and he stared at Wix with unconcealed indignation. "I know why you're saying that. You want them for yourself."

"Neelix—"

"I'm hardly being destroyed. The crystals are no problem to me. You're inventing that so you can hoard them all yourself. Well, I'm too clever for you, Wix. And I intend to find your cache."

The weariness in Wix's voice was evident. "There's no cache, Neelix. We don't have any crystals left. You've inhaled them all."

"Liar!" Neelix's ferocity returned twelvefold. Did Wix think he was a blind fool? A naive child? It was perfectly clear to him what his supposed friend was up to, and he deeply resented the thought that Wix believed he could be so easily fooled. He flung himself toward Wix in a frenzy, saw the weapon raised, heard the distinctive buzz of an energy discharge, and then blackness enveloped him.

He ached. Every muscle in his body felt as though it had been shredded with a hasp. His whole body hurt except for his feet, which he couldn't feel at all.

He tried to turn over, to see if that would alleviate the stiffness, but found that he couldn't. He opened his eyes to discover the reason for this immobility, and realized he was bound at the wrists and the ankles, tied to his bunk in the ship he and Wix had stolen from the Wellyump. It had been a sorry piece of trash, to be sure, but Wix knew that although it looked like a rusting chunk of space flotsam, its engines were sound. They had restored a portion of the exterior and were eagerly making plans for their salvage business. Then what?

Ah. Wix had hidden the last of the crystals and tried to convince Neelix there were no more. Treachery and betrayal. And now, what was this crude imprisonment? What was happening to him?

He looked around the cramped quarters and saw Wix sitting nearby, staring balefully at him. "I'm sorry, Neelix. But I had no choice. You were out of your mind."

Neelix stared at him, uncomprehending. What was he talking about? Why had he tied Neelix up? Nothing made sense to him, none of these ever more preposterous events. Why was Wix behaving in this bizarre fashion, turning on him, making ridiculous accusations, and now holding him captive—

Then he realized with awful clarity what a serious predicament he was in. Wix was crazy. He wasn't the friendly, easygoing scamp he pretended to be, that was all a ruse, a façade created to draw in unsuspecting strangers like Neelix. How could he have let himself be fooled like that? And how dangerous, exactly, was Wix?

He looked at the man sitting on the stool near the door. He was good, Neelix granted him that. He appeared to be genuinely concerned, brow furrowed and shoulders slumped, but of course that was part of the ruse. In fact, this man had no real hold on reality, had slipped into some kind of psychosis, and made Neelix a prisoner of his mad fantasy. Neelix knew he had to be very, very careful or he wouldn't come out of this alive.

"I see," he extemporized. "Why exactly do you think I'm out of my mind?"

Wix gave a short snort of frustration. "Are you kidding me? Any time you're not inhaling crystal smoke, you're out of control. You're rabid until you get your next batch. It's got a dangerous hold on you, Neelix, and I've got to do something to help you."

Neelix considered this. It was clear that Wix was unaware of his insanity, and that made him hazardous. Neelix would have to be careful, and clever, to get out of this one. If only he'd realized Wix was this unstable when he met him, he would never have ended up in this perilous situation.

"Let me see if I understand. You're helping me . . . by tying me up like this?"

Wix nodded. "I'm going to keep you there where you're safe until the crystals are purged from your system. It won't be easy. I'm told it's a painful process. But it's the only way. I'll be here with you, and I'll take care of you."

Neelix's mind was racing, trying to come up with a plan, a way to get Wix to untie him. But his mind didn't seem to be responding; he felt edgy, and nervous. Fear began to invade him, and he felt a cold fist clutching at his stomach. Well, who wouldn't be frightened to be in the hands of a madman? He tried to reposition himself on the bunk, because his muscles were beginning to ache even more, and he had to move around somehow, get rid of the stiffness.

"Wix, you have to loosen these ties. They're too tight. I can't feel my feet."

"That's not the ties. It's your body's response to the fact that your system doesn't have a fresh supply of crystals."

"How do you know so much about this? You inhale as much as I do. You're the one with the problem." Neelix was finding it difficult to speak; he could hear his voice ringing in his ears with a surreal quality.

"No one inhales as much as you. I've never known anyone who needed the crystals so often. I enjoy them as much as the next person, but I've kept it in moderation. You haven't."

Neelix could feel himself beginning to get desperate. This was impossible. He couldn't lie here like a trussed gotha hog while his muscles began to inflame and his mind scramble. Wix had to understand that, he had to find a way to reach this madman.

"Let me go, Wix. If you untie me now, there'll be no hard feelings. If you don't, I'll put a blade in your guts and rip them out of your body."

Wix's sad eyes held his. "It'll be over in a few days. I'll be here, and I'll do my best to take care of you."

Panic clutched at Neelix. He had to get up. He had to move his arms and legs and stop the burning in his muscles. He strained against his bonds and pulled as hard as he could. They didn't yield.

"Wix, let me inhale just a little, one more time. To ease off. That couldn't hurt, you've got me where you want, I can't go anyplace. Just one little sniff, to take the edge off, that's all, and I won't ask again, I promise."

Wix shook his head forlornly. "Would you like some water? You mustn't get dehydrated."

Disbelief rattled through Neelix's fragmenting mind. Wix wasn't going to listen to reason. He was absolutely, unequivocally a raging lunatic, and he was going to sit there and mouth his ridiculous theories while Neelix died slowly in front of him.

"Wix . . . just untie one arm. Let me move it around for a while. Then you can retie it and loose the other one. What harm can that do?"

"It isn't going to help you to move your arm around. And I can't risk your finding a way to get loose."

Neelix screamed, a sudden, violent howling, intended to startle Wix and impress on him how determined Neelix was, and Wix certainly did react, jumping off his stool and backing against the wall in alarm. But after that initial reaction he seemed to stiffen his resolve, and sat down once more.

The screaming hadn't helped Neelix's burning muscles, either. Now they hurt even more, as though they were being grated with sand. Hot sand. Sand that had been roasted over flames, tiny pinpoints of fire rubbed into his insides, burning and burning . . .

He burst into tears. He didn't see how he could bear even another minute of this pain, much less—what had Wix said?—days. *Days!* He'd never make it, he'd die, he'd *rather* die than go through this. Tears coursed down his face, and he was sure (well, not sure, not sure of anything anymore, but hopeful) that Wix in seeing his misery would relent and free him. He'd find some crystals, not many, just enough to ease the pain, and then he'd do this his way. He'd break the habit, he just had to do it slowly, gradually, not in this sudden violent way that was such a shock to his body.

But Wix made no move to help him, just sat there on his stool and stared at him with limpid orange eyes.

It was a three-day descent into hell. Looking back, something he tried not to do but couldn't always avoid, he didn't know how he survived. He hadn't wanted to survive. Again and again he'd begged Wix to kill him, to put a weapon against his head and put him out of his misery, but that plea met with no more success than any other.

Every minute was hours long, and the hours lasted for days, nightmares of pain and hallucination, a kaleidoscopic fantasy of demon images shot with blood, punctuated with the sounds of his own screams. He saw ghastly tableaux of wretched souls undergoing every dreadful form of torture imaginable. He saw the poor man he'd found in his hut, an eternity ago, feet being burned with hot coals, shrieking in agony. He saw his family at the moment of vaporization, bodies rent apart at the molecular level, then held there at that moment, in eternal anguish, piteous cries of suffering unheard.

Time did not pass. There was nothing, no reality, no ship, no universe, nothing except pain, which consumed him but would not kill him. He wanted death, wanted oblivion, wanted a nothingness that would spare him this unbearable affliction, but only the pain was constant, ageless and eternal.

He thrashed in his bonds like a fish flopping on dry land, drowning in oxygen. His throat was hoarse from screaming. He was wet from perspiration and urine, alternately trembling with cold and then raging with fever. If he could go mad perhaps the brain would find a way to deal with his horror, but a psychotic snap did not occur. He was Neelix, he was pain.

Occasionally he was aware that Wix was still nearby, sometimes wiping his face with a damp towel, sometimes spooning a bit of cold liquid between his parched lips. At one point he tasted something acrid, burning, which revolted when it hit his stomach and came churning back up his throat in a stream of bile. Blood dripped from his palms, where he'd dug his nails into the flesh as deeply as he could, an instinctual effort to shift the focus of pain, but nothing could get in the way of the burning of his body from the inside out.

All of these moments were fleeting, fragmentary, grace notes to the symphony of pain he was enduring. The agony was a totality, an inevitability, a blinding, searing colossus that obliterated everything else. He knew no hunger, no thirst, no fatigue. He was spitted on a skewer of fire, burning, burning.

He had no memory of lapsing into unconsciousness.

He became aware, gradually, that Wix was speaking to him, calling his name. "Neelix . . . Neelix . . . open your eyes . . . Neelix . . ."

Neelix didn't want to open his eyes. They felt welded shut, crusted with dried matter. He ached miserably, and smelled the stench of his own body. He tried to go back to sleep.

"Neelix! Listen to me—open your eyes." Neelix felt a warm, moist cloth sponging his eyelids, loosening the crusts, soothing his skin. His lids quivered for a moment, then opened, closed almost immediately as light flooded into widened pupils.

"I think you've done it. How are you feeling?"

What an odd question. And an odd statement—what had he done? He remembered nothing . . . but wait, wait . . . that was Wix speaking to him, Wix, his newfound friend, his partner in a salvage business . . .

He opened his eyes again and blinked at the brightness, but saw Wix's face peering down at him in concern. Neelix struggled to sit up, but every movement brought a protest of pain from his body—what had happened? He felt as though he'd been beaten with boards.

And then he remembered. He propped himself up against the wall and stared at Wix, recalling the horror of the ordeal he'd been through, his rage at Wix and his conviction that Wix was insane . . .

Wix continued to bathe his face with the warm towel as he chattered. "I know it was awful, but you're through with it. It's over. We'll see about getting you bathed and finding some clean clothes . . ."

At last, Neelix understood the extent of the great gift Wix had given him. He had been addicted to the crystals—their withdrawal wouldn't have been so devastating to him had he not—and Wix had forced him to cleanse his system, had sat patiently and taken care of him, had endured his abuse and his threats, and was there to revive him when the ordeal was over.

It was a gift he could never repay. Tears of gratitude welled in his eyes, and he put out a hand and clutched Wix's arm, squeezing it tightly, all he could manage because at this point he didn't trust himself to talk.

Wix smiled, and cuffed him gently on the temple. "We have to get you up and moving, Neelix. You and I have a business to run."

And they did, for almost a year. Gone were the Rhuludian crystals, to be replaced by hard work, long hours, occasional chicanery, and a lot of laughter. They didn't become wealthy, but they always ate well, and if they had to keep moving because sometimes there were disgruntled customers left behind—well, they had no burdens to keep them tied to any one place. All of space was their home, and they enjoyed forging new trails, heading into the unknown, surviving by their wits.

Their once-dilapidated vessel had been refitted and now was tidy and trim. The quarters had been personalized and made into small, cozy havens where they would sit and plan and scheme. Neelix felt, for the first time since the Metreon Cascade, a measure of peace, and the challenges of survival kept him keen and buoyed.

The Ubean incident, which was to put an end to all this, was never anticipated as more than a routine trade negotiation. The Ubeans did have a fearsome reputation, that much they had gleaned from stops at stations along the way, but Neelix and Wix had met menacing species before and discovered that everyone has basic needs: clothing, shelter, food, and the ability to travel through space. They were scrupulous about staying well out of political discussion and maintaining neutrality above all else. In this way they were even able to travel among warring species without being put in harm's way.

The Ubeans should have been no different. And when Neelix and Wix first met with a scouting party from their homeworld, they were encouraged by the stiff formality of this quadrupedal race, with their long snouts and their small, curious eyes. Although bristling with weaponry, the Ubeans maintained a polite dignity, and Neelix soon discovered that they had a pressing need for microarc thrusters, for which they were more than happy to provide pure tantalum ingots.

Perhaps it was their reserve, their seeming courtesy, that lulled the duo into taking a risk that was perfectly unnecessary but, in their minds, quite acceptable. Neelix and Wix had assembled several crates of microarc thrusters, but didn't have enough of the necessary magnetic pumps to render the units functional. They could have traded only for the complete thruster assemblies, but they knew the tantalum the Ubeans would be giving them was highly prized in the sector, and they hated to see their profit margin slashed. So they reasoned that they could stack the functional units on the top layer of each crate, so when the Ubeans inspected the merchandise, they'd encounter the complete units and not bother checking the rest.

A bit risky, perhaps, but then all business requires a certain amount of risk, and theirs perhaps more than some. They were confident they'd be collecting their tantalum ingots and speeding off to find a buyer.

The Ubeans insisted that one of them accompany the crates to the surface of their homeworld while the other waited in orbit. Neelix and Wix tossed stones to see who would do what; Wix drew the one marked for the planet.

"No worries, Neelix," said Wix confidently. "I'll be back within the hour and we'll be off for deeper space before they've even unpacked the crates."

Neelix had clapped his hand on Wix's shoulder, with more certainty than he actually felt. Shameful, he admitted to himself that he was relieved Wix had drawn the colored stone, for he wouldn't have relished the idea of traveling alone to their fearful planet.

But Wix seemed nonchalant, and grinned as he departed for the Ubean ship. Neelix forced himself to smile in return.

Seven hours later, he was in a paroxysm of indecision. Something must have gone wrong, or Wix would have been back. Prudence dictated that he get out of there before he, too, was taken into custody. But how could he abandon Wix?

Summoning his waning courage, he hailed the planet. Almost instantly, the face of a Ubean official came onto his small screen.

"What is your business with us?" the Ubean asked in a none too friendly tone.

"I'm inquiring about an associate of mine, who delivered some microarc thrusters to your colony several hours ago. He's late returning, and—"

"The Talaxian is in custody. He's been convicted of fraud and will be serving time in prison."

"But—"

"Don't bother asking to talk to him. He won't be receiving messages." The Ubean glared at him, then added, "And I'd advise you to leave our space immediately. There are those who want to imprison anyone who had a hand in this distasteful affair. But I'm willing to give you an hour's lead."

Neelix felt his stomach constrict. He had a chance to save himself, but that would mean leaving Wix to bear the punishment for their indiscretion by himself. And yet—what could he do to help him? The Ubeans would simply throw him in prison as well.

Anguished, ambivalent, guts churning, Neelix finally broke orbit and headed away from Ubea, flying blindly into deep space, terrified that he would be pursued and hunted like an animal, sick with guilt over leaving Wix behind.

He didn't stop for six days. At that point, he had to refuel and find supplies, as the stores on board were dwindling rapidly. He found a friendly outpost manned by the Neklos, where he was able to trade for food, water, and fuel, and then he continued his headlong flight, stopping only when necessary.

Six months later he found himself in the realm of the Kazon.

He hadn't realized at first that he was entering a part of space dominated by one species. The Kazon, he would later learn, consisted of many sects, or factions, many of them different enough that he was unaware they were biologically related.

Neelix found them vainglorious, strutting popinjays lacking rigorous intellect, moral imperative, or even base cunning. They thought well of themselves but hadn't even developed their own technology,

289

having acquired it from the Trabe, a race that formerly held them in bondage. Their ships were inadequately maintained, their outposts shoddily constructed. They lacked the resources to improve their lot, and seemed barely to eke out an existence; as such, they provided prime opportunities for barter, because they always needed something to keep ships in repair or to upgrade defensive systems.

Neelix moved with relative ease among the various sects, observing their protocols carefully, wary of creating some unintentional slight, watching his back at all times. And so it was that he came to the planet of the Kazon-Ogla miners.

He had learned that water was more prized than gemstones in this realm. The planet the Ogla inhabited was a vast desert, arid and sere. But it was also a repository for cormaline ore, for which other sects were willing to trade water. Neelix felt this situation of mutual need was an opportunity he must not ignore.

His plan was to insert himself into the midst of this trading opportunity as a middleman. He went first to the Kazon-Sara and offered to ferry water to the Ogla in return for a percentage of the liquid. The Sara, whose ships were in disrepair, accepted—perhaps not eagerly, but not reluctantly, either.

Then Neelix went to the Ogla, armed with tanks of water—including his own reserve supply. He offered to trade for cormaline, returning it to the Sara in return for a percentage of the mineral. After a few loops like this, he had built up a tidy supply of both water and cormaline ore.

He might have become reasonably well off from the Kazon if something completely unexpected hadn't insinuated itself into his life. He had never counted on falling in love.

He saw her first on a typical visit to the Ogla. He had barrels of water from the Sara, which the Kazon miners needed desperately, as he hadn't paid them a visit in several weeks. He landed his small vessel near their mining colony, a crude affair set not far from some crumbling ruins that had belonged to prior inhabitants of the planet.

Neelix entered the stone structure the Ogla had built to ward off the cruel desert sun, and immediately felt the temperature drop by twenty degrees. It was also blessedly dark inside, a relief from the unremitting glare outside. Odd bits of furniture dotted the room, homemade or cast off, and mismatched crates were stacked against the walls. In spite of its respite from the heat, it was a joyless place, and Neelix was glad he had to spend little time there.

He saw Jabin, the powerful and mean-spirited Maje of the mining faction, sprawled in a chair, sweating, every millimeter of his massive body covered with a fine white dust. His matted hair was dotted with what looked like chunks of debris; all the Kazon decorated their hair like this, but Neelix had never wanted to ask if it represented anything more than crude fashion. He tried not to wrinkle his nose at the odor Jabin exuded.

"Did you bring water?" the hulking man growled as soon as Neelix entered.

"Indeed, my good friend, I have seven barrels—cool and pure. It should slake your thirst handsomely."

Jabin bellowed some unintelligible order at an aide, and Neelix felt, rather than saw, a flurry of activity in the dark room. Almost immediately, one of Neelix's barrels was carried in and set next to Jabin, who called out yet something else.

There was a brief silence, and then someone emerged from the deep gloom of the chamber, moving quietly toward them. Neelix squinted, for this figure was one he'd not seen before, dainty and petite.

She was a young sprite, a nymph, a vision of ethereal loveliness. Pale wisps of hair curled, unkempt, on her head, framing a face that would cause any man to catch his breath. Large blue eyes, roughly the color of the sky on a spring morning, gazed sadly at nothing. In spite of her breathtaking beauty, she was forlorn, wreathed in melancholy. As she turned her head, Neelix saw delicate, wing-like ears, the mark of a species with which he was unfamiliar. They were unusual, but only added to her fragile beauty.

As she neared, Neelix also saw the unmistakable purpling of bruises on her ivory skin, and his heart constricted. She had been mistreated.

The waif seemed to know her duty: she took cups from a nearby table and, kneeling in front of the water barrel, drew several fingers of the precious liquid into each cup and presented them to Jabin and Neelix.

Neelix realized he was staring at her, but she kept her eyes lowered, deferential. Or—and he thought this was more likely the case— fearful, unwilling to provoke an outburst of wrath from Jabin for even the most imagined slight.

Jabin chuckled, a low, throaty growl that caught Neelix's attention and made him jerk his head away from the girl and back to the hefty Kazon Maje. Jabin was eyeing him with sardonic amusement, and Neelix felt himself color in embarrassment.

"Quite a beauty, isn't she? But that's where her assets end. She's all but worthless as a slave. Tires easily, wilts in the heat, no strength at all."

A spark flicked in Neelix's mind and he tried to appear casual. "I can see that," he said with what he hoped was indifference. "She's frail. Probably sickly." He paused, letting that assessment sink in. "I might find household work for her, if you'd be interested in trading. She'd bring a number of water barrels."

Jabin's eyes narrowed and he peered at Neelix through the darkness. "If you're thinking what I suspect, don't bother. She's a cold one as well."

Neelix shrugged. "I was thinking more of what I could get for her in return. I know some families that would be interested in having a serving girl."

Jabin snorted and took a sip of the water, a surprisingly delicate gesture from such a brutish man, but the Kazon had learned to ration their water carefully, and to savor each small swallow. "She's worth nothing to me as a worker, but she has information I'm determined to get. She's proved recalcitrant so far, but I'm ready to move to more persuasive methods."

Neelix felt his stomach clutch. The maggot intended to torture this poor child! He had to prevent that somehow. His mind scurried to find a way, even as he bought time by chatting with Jabin. "Information? What kind of information could be so valuable as to bother with a wretched thing like this?"

"Her people live underground, protected by an entity that sends them energy for all their needs. If I knew how to get down there, the Ogla would have that energy. And then, little man, I wouldn't have need for avaricious barterers like you."

What Jabin had said seemed quite remarkable. An entire species that dwelt underground? He'd never known of such a thing. And what was this entity that protected them? This tale was becoming altogether fascinating. "If they live beneath the surface, how did you find this one?" he inquired.

Jabin cackled. "She's too curious for her own good. She wanted to see what was up here. She'd no more stopped squinting at the sun than we had her, and I'm keeping her until she tells me what I want to know."

Despair clutched at Neelix. He couldn't let this happen. He couldn't bear to think of this lovely being suffering at Jabin's hands. He glanced over at her and found her looking at him for the first time, blue eyes fixed on him in a kind of desperation. He felt a thought stirring in his head, then realized it was more than a thought, it was a sound. *"Please . . . help me . . ."*

Startled, he realized she was communicating with him telepathically. He blinked, hoping this would tell her that he had received her thought, but kept his face impassive, as though he were simply assessing her.

"Send her away, Jabin," he said suddenly. "I'd like to talk to you alone."

Jabin jerked his head and the nymph exited the chamber. Neelix looked at him with a sly confidence. "Let me spend some time with her. By myself. I think I can get the information you want."

The big man exhaled explosively, a grunt of derision. "How could you possibly do that, Talaxian?" he queried.

"My people have a saying: Sweetness brings the tillah birds, tartness leaves them wanting. You haven't been able to get anything from her with brute force—why not let me try to win her over? Become her confidant. Her friend. Before she knows it, she'll be telling me anything I want."

Jabin was silent, staring down at the floor. Neelix was heartened that he hadn't negated the idea right away. A moment passed, then Jabin looked up. "How long do you think this effort would take?"

"A few weeks, perhaps. It depends on how quickly I can establish a relationship with her. But I warn you—this information won't come cheaply."

Another long silence. Neelix concentrated on looking unconcerned, as though this were nothing more than a typical bartering situation. It wouldn't do for Jabin to know how important it was to him that he be able to protect this girl, to keep her safe until he'd figured out a way to rescue her.

Finally Jabin stirred, then touched his tongue once more to the cup of water. "All right, then, we'll try it. But if nothing is accomplished within four weeks, the arrangement is canceled and I'll resort to my own methods."

"That's fine with me. I don't want to make this my life's work, after all. I'm willing to try it in hopes of getting a tidy amount of cormaline."

Jabin seemed to lose interest in him then. He took a swallow of water, and proceeded to swirl it around in his mouth, eyes closed in private ecstasy as he savored the precious liquid.

Neelix walked out to find the pale girl.

She stood quietly in the shade of a stone column, studiously ignoring the taunts and jeers of the lascivious Ogla miners, staring out at the vast desert as though willing herself into its searing depths. Neelix stood at a distance, uncertain about interrupting her intense reverie. But then he heard a husky voice in his head. *"I feel I can trust you."*

He approached her, feeling as bumbling as an adolescent. "You can," he stated simply. "I'm your friend."

And so it was that Neelix came to know the Ocampan known as Kes, and heard the remarkable story of her climb to freedom and swift capture, of the entity known as the Caretaker, and of Kes's own indomitable spirit, her intellectual curiosity, her sweetness of manner.

They were able to keep Jabin at bay for several weeks, Neelix faithfully reporting to the Maje that Kes was beginning to share some secrets of her underground world and that the location of the tunnel to the Ocampan city would undoubtedly be revealed soon.

But Neelix made an error, one that threatened to bring their subterfuge crumbling down, sending Kes back into Jabin's hands for interrogation.

He stole water.

He did it for Kes, of course, and he thought he'd gotten away with it, but one of Jabin's men discovered the theft and Neelix had ended up running to his ship just ahead of the Kazon pursuers, yelling at Kes that he'd be back for her.

How he intended to do that, he had no idea. He had located the mighty Array that supplied the Ocampa with energy, and he tried to communicate with the entity that Jabin said controlled it, but to no avail.

He tried not to think what Kes might be undergoing at Jabin's hands, and racked his brains to come up with a rescue plan. But he was one man, alone, in a ship with pitiful weapons. What hope did he have?

He decided to revisit a debris field he'd encountered some time back but had never explored. Maybe luck would be with him, and he'd find something he could trade for weapons. He was trawling through the space rubbish when he spotted a ship of a sort he'd never encountered before. Alarm gripped him—this ship was much bigger than his, and undoubtedly intended to collect the most valuable detritus for itself. It wasn't fair!

His communication system was activated and he sprinted to the small screen, having first to uncover it and then set it at the proper angle. It wouldn't hold, so Neelix cocked his head and assumed the most confrontational pose he could muster. "Whoever you are, I found this waste zone first," he said imperiously.

A woman stared back at him. She was small-boned, dressed in what looked like some kind of uniform. Her hair was swept back off her face and her eyes blazed with intelligence. "We're not interested in this debris, Mister . . ."

Her trailing voice indicated that she wanted an introduction. Neelix, more at ease now that she had indicated no interest in the waste field, adopted his most gracious mien. "Neelix. And since you aren't interested in my debris, I am delighted to meet you . . ."

His inflection indicated that he wanted her name, too. The woman smiled, and even from a screen Neelix could feel her warmth. "Captain Kathryn Janeway of the Federation starship *Voyager*," she said, in a voice husky as old velvet. Neelix had no way of knowing that that voice would change his entire life.

CHAPTER

11

Neelix found that he couldn't look up at his fellows when he'd finished. He was exhausted with the emotion of reliving his past, and somewhat uncertain as to how the others would respond. He, after all, was not really one of them, not an Alpha Quadrant, Starfleet-trained person. Would they judge him differently?

Finally he raised his eyes. Tom moved to him and again clapped him on the shoulder in a brotherly fashion. He had just opened his mouth to speak when Harry Kim burst into the shelter.

"Seven," he said breathlessly, "you've got to come quickly. Something's wrong with Chakotay."

This sinister statement alarmed them all. "What is it? What's wrong?" asked Neelix.

"He's sick or something. We don't exactly know."

"Why would you ask for me?" inquired Seven. "I don't possess medical expertise."

"He keeps asking for you. I think we have to risk it."

Seven looked toward Tuvok, who nodded acquiescence. "Go to him," said the Vulcan. "Later we will send Vorik to take a report."

Seven and Harry immediately departed, leaving behind the others, whose mood had changed abruptly from expectation to apprehension.

Vorik had reported to Tuvok's group the story of Captain Janeway's unusual visit, which had heartened them all. But now it seemed that her blow to Chakotay might have unexpected and disastrous results.

"I think the cut in his cheek is infected," Harry speculated as they walked back through the fetid air to Chakotay's shelter, trying to appear nonchalant so as not to draw attention to them. "First he said he was sick to his stomach; then the cut started to get inflamed. A little while later he said his head felt like it was caught in a vise. And finally he collapsed, moaning . . . kept saying your name. I don't know if he's just delirious or if he thinks there's something you can do."

Seven made no comment, but seemed to be musing on what he said. They walked in silence until they reached the shelter, eyes straight ahead, shutting out the misery of the beings that surrounded them.

When they entered, Harry saw that Chakotay's infection was worse. His cheek was swollen, and red striations streaked under the skin like angry snakes. The commander was twisting on the ground in agony, trying to muffle his groans, fists clenching and unclenching as he struggled. Noah Mannick was sitting next to him, putting a wet compress on his forehead, looking frustrated by his helplessness to do anything more.

Seven went immediately to him and knelt down. "Commander, how can I help you?" she said.

At this, Chakotay's eyes flickered open, and Harry saw they were dull with pain. "Seven," he breathed, clearly with difficulty, and pointed to the wound on his cheek. "What is this?"

Seven frowned and looked carefully at the distorted flesh. Then a strange look came over her face and she glanced up at Harry. "Did you say the captain struck Chakotay on the face?"

"Right. Backhanded him. She had a bunch of rings on her fingers and one of them slashed him."

A small smile played on Seven's lips, much to Harry's surprise. "Why? What is it?"

"If I'm correct, the captain has implanted a Borg nodule in him."

This was astonishing to Harry. "A Borg implant? Why?"

"I do not know. But I recognize the pattern of the striations. I would estimate that it will fully erupt within minutes."

And so it did. With Chakotay writhing in anguish, biting the back of his hand to keep from screaming, a gray metallic node distended the skin until it burst through and spread over his cheek with tentacles like an octopus. Then the tips embedded themselves back in his flesh. Harry, Brad, and Noah watched in horrified fascination.

"He'll feel better now," said Seven, and she was right. In a few minutes the commander seemed to relax somewhat, stopped his agonized writhing, and opened his eyes. He drew several breaths and then sat up.

"What happened?" he asked, voice still weak from his ordeal.

Harry was so relieved he felt his knees go weak. He hadn't realized how frightened he was until the crisis was over. Or at least he hoped it was.

"You have something in common with Seven now," he said. "You've grown a Borg implant."

Chakotay touched his cheek gingerly, confirming that there was in fact a strange metallic object there.

"I suspect the captain has found a way to send us a message," said Seven, but then Chakotay suddenly fell back on the ground, arms upraised, eyes wide in terror.

"Falling . . ." he yelled, and then he slumped, staring off at nothing. He lay like that for a moment, then looked up at them. "I had the strongest sensation I was falling . . . falling a long way. Very odd. And now . . . now . . ." He looked up at Seven, with a puzzled expression on his face. "What's happening?" he asked.

"I don't know, Commander. If the captain has sent you a message, I fail to understand why it would be about falling. Are you aware of other sensations? Images?"

Chakotay seemed to test this thought for a moment. "I feel . . . pulled somehow."

"Pulled?" asked Harry. "What does that mean?"

"It's hard to describe. As though . . ." He trailed off, unable to complete the thought.

"As though you want to follow something?" asked Seven.

"Yes. But there's nothing to follow."

"It's a homing pattern, carried by the nanoprobes the implant has deposited in your bloodstream. It will lead you toward a signal which is emanated. You may remember that I responded to such a signal when I rediscovered my parents' ship."

Harry remembered this well. Seven had suddenly and inexplicably bolted from the ship, certain she was being called by the Borg. But at the end of her journey was the *Raven,* the small vessel the Borg had assimilated many years before, when she was just a child.

"The captain's trying to tell us where to come," said Chakotay.

"Then B'Elanna had better keep working on that transporter," said Harry. "We aren't going anywhere without it." From Harry's tone, it was clear that he was frustrated not to be able to help in the process. "Commander, can't I go to the other shelter? I'm sure B'Elanna's doing all she can, but I'd sure feel better if I could pitch in."

Chakotay shook his head. "There's been too much coming and going between the shelters as it is. I know it's unlikely that our every movement is being watched—but we'd be better off to pretend that it is. Let's not make careless mistakes now when we have a plan that seems to be working."

Harry nodded glumly and subsided, while Chakotay turned to Seven. "For the same reason, I think you should stay here. Minimize the movement between the two groups."

"Very well." Seven gazed at him imperturbably. "In the meantime, please describe to me any sensations, any images you feel as a result of the nodule. I might be able to interpret them and add to our understanding of Captain Janeway's plan."

"In the first place, it hurts like hell." Some of the twinkle was coming back to Chakotay's eyes. "Is this how it feels to be a Borg?"

"If assimilation is complete, there is no further sensation of pain."

"Great. Either I become a Borg or I feel like my face is on fire."

"It might be helpful to move beyond this point," said Seven neutrally. "Is there any sensation other than pain?"

"You're all heart, Sev," said Chakotay, clinging to quips in order to help combat the discomfort he was feeling. But he closed his eyes as though to concentrate on whatever sensations he might be experiencing. "There's nothing strong now . . . not like before, when I was falling . . . I still feel like something's calling me, pulling me . . . but it's a less intense feeling now."

Seven made no comment to this, merely nodding as though storing his statement in a database. Eventually, Chakotay fell into a troubled sleep peppered with dreams about falling endlessly through space.

In spite of the fact that B'Elanna was making real progress with the portable transporter, and the mood of the crew was generally positive, Neelix found himself inexplicably saddened. He continued to accompany the Rai' on their mining passes, in return for which he prepared an evening meal to be shared by them and the *Voyager* group, and he was grateful for the activity.

But at odd moments of the day he found himself thinking wistfully about Kes. Telling the others about meeting her had stirred memories that he thought were long buried, and he had to admit that he missed her more than he might have imagined.

When he returned from the work detail that night, his pockets full of food, he made a stew which the Rai' seemed to enjoy and the *Voyager* crew devoured hungrily. Neelix put a portion for Chakotay's group into water containers to be taken to them by Vorik.

But before the young Vulcan could start out, Neelix looked up to see a surprising sight: Chakotay and the others of his group straggling along the pathway carrying their meager belongings, and looking as though they'd been in a brawl. They were bruised and bleeding, uniforms ripped and dirty. But in spite of that, they seemed cheerful.

"You look like you just did ten rounds with a wildcat, Commander," said Tom, "or maybe with a Borg." This was the first the others had seen of Chakotay's newly erupted implant.

"Not far from it. We were attacked by some behemoths who thought they were tougher than they were and wanted our rations. We fought them off—but we figured we could use the fracas as an excuse to get out of there and back with you."

"Well done," said Tuvok approvingly. "This will greatly simplify our plans."

They fell to and quickly erected the second shelter as the Rai' watched somewhat warily. Neelix realized they may perceive the added group as a threat and he sauntered over to Tassot Bnay, who had provided the work pass for him.

"No need to worry, my friend. These are our fellows and they're as peaceful and likable as we are. They'll cause you no trouble."

"They've been fighting."

"Yes, they certainly have. They were set upon, it seems, and had to defend themselves. That's why they left the spot they'd settled in."

Bnay looked for a while longer at the newly arrived group and then seemed to accept Neelix's explanation. He turned away without another word and began talking softly with the other Rai'. Neelix returned to his friends to find them all gathered in one shelter.

A sense of expectation electrified the air. Harry was kneeling beside B'Elanna, fiddling and tinkering with two strange-looking contraptions, a cobbled arrangement of the components B'Elanna had been working with. Harry's face shone with anticipation and with the relief of finally being able to serve a function.

"I think we're ready to give it a try," said B'Elanna. "I won't make any promises . . . these can only be described as primitive."

"That's why we're only going to try it on the psilminite ore now. We'll set it to dematerialize a spot below ten kilometers. That's how far down the Subu sensor net goes." Harry had a split lip and a welt on his temple, but he was obviously elated. Neelix began to feel a lift in his spirits as well.

"Do you have the coordinates set, Harry?" asked B'Elanna.

"Ready to go."

"All right. Let's do it." B'Elanna took a breath and a charged silence fell on the group. She manipulated a part of the device and then waited, anxious.

"I think we've got the annular confinement beam established," said Harry. "Let's dematerialize the ore, then transport it as powder."

Another tense moment passed . . . and then a fine shower of white dust materialized in the air and sifted down to the ground.

"It worked!" yelped Harry, and the others erupted into a spontaneous shout of joy, only to be silenced by Tuvok.

"We must not call attention to ourselves in that way," he cautioned, and the group was silent once more.

"Here's the plan," said B'Elanna. "I built two of these, because we'll need them to get us out of here. One transporter alone doesn't have the power to dematerialize something as complex as a biological organism and transport them as far as we need to."

"So we'll have to leapfrog our way out," chimed in Harry. "We're going to hollow out a chamber, fifteen kilometers down and right under the wall that surrounds this place. I'll beam into it with the second transporter, and then B'Elanna will beam someone else to me and I'll put them on the surface, in the woods outside the sensor net."

"Then we keep it up until everyone's out."

"And after that?" asked Neelix, amazed as always at the ingenuity of these people.

"Then Commander Chakotay will lead us," said Seven. "We must trust that the captain has implanted our escape route in him."

"It's going to take a while to carve out the chamber. The underlying rock strata are incredibly dense—we can only take out a little bit at a time."

"Is it a good idea to keep dumping it here, in the shelter?" asked Harry.

"I don't think so. It's going to get all over us, and that might be noticed."

"Where, then?" queried B'Elanna. "We can't do it where someone might see it. And the transporters don't have enough power to take it very far."

"I know a place," said Neelix. "Why not beam it right into the ore quarries? There's plenty of dust there already. There's an area behind the antigrav storage units where the guards never go. They'll never see it."

"Good idea, Neelix," said Chakotay. "Can you give them coordinates?"

Neelix did so and Harry continued with the process as the others disbanded. Neelix saw Tuvok leave the shelter, and he followed.

Tuvok was sitting on the ground, eyeing the denizens of the camp with a wary eye. The scuffle with Chakotay's group was a reminder that no one was truly safe in this place, and one had to be alert at all times.

Neelix took a seat next to Tuvok. He hoped the Vulcan would make some comment about his story, but a long silence ensued. Neelix found himself feeling unaccountably nervous, reading into Tuvok's silence a general disapproval—and yet, what could he expect? From the moment they first met, Tuvok had been aloof and judgmental.

Nonetheless, his opinion mattered to Neelix, and so, inwardly chastising himself for doing so, he turned to the somber man.

"So, Mr. Vulcan . . . what did you think of my story?"

Another silence. Neelix felt himself begin to perspire. Why wasn't Tuvok answering him? Had he embarrassed himself that fully? He felt his heart beating in his chest.

"I know I've done some awful things in my life," he stammered, "but I've tried to make up for them. I hope you won't hold what I've told you against me . . ." He trailed off lamely, his words sounding hollow.

Tuvok turned slowly to look at him, his dark visage glistening in the heat of the setting sun. His eyes seemed to pierce Neelix's brain. He stared like that for a full moment before he spoke.

"I found it an exceptional story. You have complexities, and courage, I would never have imagined."

Neelix couldn't believe what he was hearing—Tuvok was actually complimenting him! He felt a little shiver of pleasure, but he couldn't for the life of him think of anything to say in return. He suddenly wished that Kes were here, and could hear what Tuvok had to say. She would have been proud.

Suddenly, before he had a chance to think about it, he was talking about her. "I still miss Kes," he said in a rush of emotion. "Sometimes during the night I think I hear her voice, and I sit up and look around. But of course she's not there."

Tuvok looked at him once more with those intensely focused eyes. "But she is," he said simply.

"What?" asked Neelix, confused.

"She is with us still," continued Tuvok. "Her going was a transcendence, not a death. She is connected to all of us."

"How do you know this?" asked Neelix. It was comforting to think it might be true, that Kes hovered somewhere, perhaps on another plane but aware of her friends, able to see and hear them and feel a part of their life.

"Our minds were meshed on many occasions. I possess her katra within me."

"That's amazing."

"And I sense her presence from time to time. So it's no surprise that you might have done the same."

"I have no telepathic powers."

"But your emotional connection to her was quite strong. I'm sure she has kept that bond."

Neelix was torn between feelings of pleasure and sorrow: he enjoyed the thought that Kes was still bound to him in some way, however ephemeral; but he couldn't avoid regret for all that was lost.

"I know it's a cliché, but it's true that you never realize what you have until it's gone. There's so much I don't know about Kes . . . our life together started when I met her in that Kazon encampment. I didn't want her to know some of the things I'd done before that, so I never brought up the past."

Neelix stared down at the dirt for a moment, collecting the thoughts that would communicate his turbulent feelings. "I regret that now. There's so much of her that I never shared."

"Regret accomplishes nothing."

"I'm sure you're right. But some of us can't turn off our feelings on command."

Tuvok was silent once more, and Neelix felt they had exhausted the moment. Feeling no better than he had when he started the conversation, he returned to the shelter and lay down. Maybe, if he was lucky, he could at least dream about her.

He wasn't sure how long he'd been asleep when he heard her voice. In fact, when it was all over, he wasn't sure that he'd ever woken up. But, sleeping or waking, he heard her. It seemed to him that his eyes opened to the darkness of the shelter, saw the slumbering forms of his crewmates, and then stared into blackness for a long time.

But that might have been a dream.

If so, it was a dream unlike any he'd ever had. The sound of Kes's voice in his mind was palpable, and he had to resist the urge to answer her out loud. He lay quietly, letting happen whatever was happening, feeling borne along on a series of images like a toy boat bobbing on the waves of a fast-rushing stream.

He saw, in his mind's eye, the underground city of the Ocampa, that wondrous creation he had visited just after he'd met Kes. It seemed that he were flying through the city, dazzled by the immensity and beauty of the buildings that stretched for many kilometers throughout the deep caverns of the planet.

And all the while, her voice in his mind . . . soothing, mellifluous . . . he couldn't really hear words, couldn't assign them meaning, but somehow the voice was communicating to him nonetheless.

His flight came to an end in the great Assembly of the Ocampa, where he stared down at a small child, long blond hair trailing down her back, staring up at an Ocampan man who looked, if anything, beleaguered.

Kes.

CHAPTER

12

"WHY?"

Kes was staring up at her father, feet spread, fists planted firmly on hips, small mouth pursed in determination. She'd asked a question and so far she hadn't received a satisfactory answer, and she wasn't going to move an inch until she did.

Her father gazed back at her, his face a mixture of bafflement, frustration, and adoration. Kes didn't identify them as such, for she was too young yet to comprehend the complex network of emotions that can exist at once in people. She was less than halfway through her growth cycle, a period of time that she would later come to identify in human terms as nine months, and still focused on herself: her needs, her perceptions, her questions.

"Kes," her father began in a tone of voice that was becoming familiar to her, "you have to accept the fact that there simply aren't answers to every question."

"Why?" Somehow everything Benaren said led to a new question, and more often than not, it was "why?"

Her father drew a breath, looking around for someone who might rescue him. They were standing in the courtyard of the Assembly, the soaring, magnificent structure built for them by the Caretaker so many generations before, which was the focal point of Ocampan life. Here daily rations were dispensed; entertainment was provided; social groups gathered. It was always full, but there was never a sense of congestion. The rhythms of Ocampan life were leisurely, ordered. No one rushed, no one pushed or shoved, no one exerted any more energy than was absolutely necessary.

That sense of enervation was one of the first things Kes had questioned, as her own restless spirit began to manifest itself. "Why does everyone sit around so much?" she had queried, on one of her early visits to the Assembly. "They just do," replied her father, and was duly introduced to Kes's relentless tenacity.

"That's not a reason," she stated with conviction, looking at her father with full expectation that a more satisfying answer would be forthcoming.

It was not. Every attempt he made to answer her in a convincing way was met with another question.

"This is our way of life, Kes. This is how people behave."

"How did it get to be our way of life? Who said it should be?"

"No one said anything, it's just always been that way."

"But how did it start in the first place? Who were the first people who acted that way?"

"No one knows. It was a very long time ago."

"Then how do you know that's the way it happened?"

The first of many long sighs issued from Benaren. "We assume that's how it was. It makes sense."

"But maybe there are other things that could make sense, too. Maybe people were different a long time ago, and something happened to change them."

"Like what?"

Kes had bit her lip, mind struggling to comprehend something she had no reason to believe was so but which she nonetheless instinctively knew was the truth.

"I don't know. Something . . . that made them not care anymore."

That had been the first of her inquiries, some months ago, and they hadn't abated. Now, she was pursuing a line of questioning that she found infinitely fascinating: the Caretaker.

She'd asked many questions in her short life about this mysterious being, to whom most Ocampans were so reverential, and none had ever been answered persuasively. Today, as she and her father stood in line to receive their rations, she had introduced the subject again.

"If the Caretaker built our home for us, under the ground, he must have had a reason to do it. Doesn't anyone ever wonder what it is?"

"Most people are grateful for his generosity. He gave us our home, food, energy, water—we owe everything to him."

"Why do we owe anything to him? He chose to do this. He must have wanted to."

"I've told you—no one knows why he did it. But it would be wrong not to be grateful for our good fortune."

Kes pondered that for a moment as they moved—slowly—toward the head of the line. She was impatient, as always. It always took so long to wend one's way to the front, where the rations were doled out. Surely there was a better way to handle this process, one that wouldn't waste so much time, time that could be devoted to . . . to other things. More interesting things.

And that certainly didn't include, for instance, sitting in front of the entertainment screens, those massive plates which displayed continuous imagery of a calming, tranquil kind. Most people seemed content to sit for much of the day, gazing in a kind of stupor at the placid images, but Kes found it intolerable, becoming bored within minutes and jumping from her recliner to dash across the floor of the Assembly, much to the consternation of the others.

Now, as she and Benaren inched their way toward the head of the line, another line of questioning occurred to her. "Father, why did the Caretaker build our home here, underground?"

"This is where it is safe."

"Safe from what?"

"From our enemies."

"Who are those?"

"We don't know their name. But they would take our energy, and our water."

"Why?"

"Because they need it."

"Why?"

"They don't have as much as we do."

"Why?"

"Just because they don't."

"Why?"

"That's not for someone your age to worry about."

That is when Kes planted her fists on her hips and refused to budge until she got an answer.

"Kes, move along. Others are in line behind us."

"I'm not moving until you answer me."

"You have to accept the fact that you're too young to know some things."

"No, I don't have to accept that. I want to know."

And at that, Benaren gestured to the people in line behind them. "Step around her," he told them. "She doesn't want to move." To Kes's irritation, the line wound around her and her father moved with them, leaving her behind.

He expected that she'd follow him, she knew, and that realization stiffened her resolve. She stood resolutely, immobile, refusing to budge as the long line snaked around her in its slow progress toward the food stations.

When Benaren had received his allotment, he came back to Kes, still standing where he had left her. "Come along, Kes. Your mother will be waiting for us."

"I told you I'm not moving until you answer me," she replied firmly.

"I've answered you as best I can. I won't be manipulated to do more."

"Fine. I'll stay here forever."

Benaren sighed and started away. "When you get hungry, come home."

Kes stood in the Assembly for a very long time, how long she wasn't sure. The entertainment screens droned on, people collected their rations, and eventually the crowds began to thin out, which meant the time of rest was drawing near. Any number of people had stopped to ask if Kes had needed help; each time, she shook her head and replied that she was waiting for her father.

As time wore on, she began to grow weary, and decided that it wasn't really violating her resolve if she sat down. She did, watching as more and more people left the Assembly. She was beginning to feel somewhat forlorn as she realized her father wasn't going to yield to her determination, but she was utterly unable to swallow her pride and return home.

One minute she was sitting on the floor of the Assembly, feeling somewhat drowsy, and the next she was waking up in her bed at home. It took her a brief moment to realize where she was and then she looked up to see her mother, Martis, sitting by the bed.

"How did I get here? I didn't want to move from the Assembly," said Kes.

"You fell asleep and one of the Elders, Toscat, carried you back here."

"No! He should have left me there!" Kes felt her eyes begin to burn and then grow moist.

"He knew you should be at home in your bed."

"I said I wouldn't move until Father had answered my questions."

Martis leaned forward and stroked an errant lock of hair away from her daughter's face. "Kes, you're a bright and beautiful child, and your father and I love you very much. But you're also willful and stubborn, and that concerns us. We don't want you to grow up to be spoiled and arrogant, and so we're not going to allow you to decide what will and will not happen in this family. Benaren and I are the adults, and you are the child. We'll make the decisions that determine your behavior until you're an adult and can make wiser choices."

Kes didn't like being chastised. It made her feel funny inside, queasy. She idolized her beautiful mother, and didn't like the thought she had disappointed the woman who had always given her such loving care. She hung her head, unable to look up.

"It grieves your father if he thinks he hasn't been able to give you the information you want. But you ask questions that can't be answered."

"I don't understand why not. I don't understand why these aren't questions that everyone asks."

"Darling child," said her mother, "you can't begin to believe how unique you are. I've known that since you were born. I told your father that I thought someday you would see the sun."

This aroused Kes's curiosity instantly. "What does that mean? What's the sun? Why would it be special to see it?"

Martis smiled. "We've decided it's time for you to hear about the surface. Usually parents wait until a child has finished the growth cycle, but you are precocious, and can probably understand the story now."

Kes sat up in bed, eager to hear about the "surface." This was more like it. Now maybe some of her questions would finally be answered.

"Long ago our people lived on the surface. A giant orb in the sky, called the sun, provided light and heat. The Ocampa were a happy, peaceful race with an affinity for the arts. Then for reasons no one knows, or remembers, a disaster befell the planet, and climatic conditions changed. Drought ensued, and water became more valuable than gems. A people called the Kazon began to raid the

Ocampan settlements and steal their water. Our people were in danger of dying out."

Kes listened in fascination to this story. She already had a dozen questions about what her mother had said so far, but she knew she should wait and hear everything before interrupting.

"That's when the Caretaker presented himself to us. No one knows in what way, but somehow he made it clear that he would protect us from the Kazon. It was a promise. He built this magnificent city for us, under the ground, and supplied us with endless amounts of energy and water. That was long ago, and he has kept his promise ever since."

Kes was bubbling with questions, but wanted to make sure there wasn't more to the story. "Is that all?" she asked, breathless with excitement.

Her mother nodded, and Kes leapt in. "Where did the Caretaker come from? What was the disaster that happened to change the climate? How long did all this take? Why are the Kazon so mean? What happened to them? How did we get down here? Has anybody ever been back?" She took a breath, more questions forming even as she'd asked these. Her mother smiled and held up a hand.

"Everything we know, I've told you. If I knew the answers to those questions, I'd give them to you. But all that was lost over the time we've been here. We just know that the energy keeps coming and the Kazon have never bothered us here."

Kes sat back, mind racing, turning over these astonishing details in her mind. It was maddening—each element of the story led to a set of endless, and apparently unanswerable, questions. She probably had enough questions for the rest of her life, but there weren't any answers. Or were there?

"Aren't there any records, any writings about all this? Why wouldn't we know about our own history?"

"I don't know of any writings. The story has been handed down from generation to generation."

"That's unbelievable. Why wouldn't someone record all this?"

"I don't know. They just didn't."

It was the kind of answer Kes hated most. It wasn't really an answer, just saying "because because." It was frustrating.

"Has anyone ever tried to go to the surface and see what's there now? Do we even know if the Kazon are still up there? Maybe we could go back now."

"Why risk it? We're safe here, and we have everything we need."

Her mother rose, signaling an end to the discussion. "I would think you'd be hungry. We saved you some rations from yesterday. Come along."

Kes rose and followed, but she knew somehow that things would never be the same. She had tasted knowledge, and it was intoxicating. She had to learn more.

Kes met Daggin soon after she'd completed her growth cycle. He was a sweet-faced boy just slightly older than she, with a quick mind and a ready smile. She'd noticed him looking at her in the Assembly, and she returned his smile. That apparently worked as some kind of signal, because Daggin hurried to her and introduced himself.

That was the first thing she noticed about him: he hurried. She was immediately intrigued that someone besides herself moved to quicker rhythms than most Ocampans. Soon she would learn that Daggin was unusual in many ways, and he was to be a formative influence on her young life.

"Would you like to see the farm?" he asked as soon as she'd told him her name. She was curious—what was a farm? She'd never heard the word.

In reply, Daggin led her out of the Assembly, and then, to her vast surprise, out of the well-traveled confines of the city. Her breath caught as she realized they were past the boundaries, moving through unfamiliar parts of the underground space.

"Where is this? How long have you been coming here? How did you know about it?"

"These tunnels go on and on, all around the periphery of the city. I started coming out here shortly before I finished my growth cycle, when my mother brought me. She has friends who decided to cultivate the farm."

Kes was fascinated. Daggin had actually answered her questions, and although more had immediately formed, she was content to be silent and see where they were going, trusting that any questions she had would be responded to.

Shortly they emerged into a natural chamber which Kes found astonishingly beautiful. Terraces had been carved into the walls of stone, and green plants grew in abundance on each of the terraces. Lights were suspended above them, casting a warm glow throughout the chamber. There was an unusual aroma, something fresh and clean, that Kes found exhilarating. She turned in wonder to Daggin.

"Tell me about this place. Whose idea was it to build it? What are the green plants? Why are they here?"

Daggin smiled but it was a smile of comradeship. "My mother and her friends created this farm. They believe we shouldn't just sit around all the time, waiting for rations to be handed to us. They've begun growing plants for food. We work to tend the farm, and we eat the fruits of our labor. We're active, we have more energy than the others, and our minds are being used."

Kes stared at him. Everything he said was resonating deeply within her, as though a powerful bell were pealing in her mind. A sense of wonder and joy enveloped her, for she knew she had found kindred souls, that she wasn't unique and alone after all. There were others who questioned their existence, and challenged it. Her heart was pounding in excitement and anticipation.

"Can I do this, too?"

"Of course. I thought you might feel that way."

"Why is that?"

He smiled and his eyes sparkled as he did so. "I saw you the night you stayed in the Assembly until you fell asleep. I knew you were someone with a questing mind, someone who didn't accept this docile life of ours. But I waited until you'd finished your growth cycle before approaching you."

Kes reached out and fingered one of the plants. The leaves were silky and inviting, and she looked forward to nurturing them. For once her mind was quiet, satisfied for now, knowing she had found a place, a niche, where she could be who she was, among others who would understand her and who would answer her questions. She felt a peace she had never in her short life known before.

It wasn't long after that she found the access tunnels. Once she realized the boundaries of the city weren't the boundaries of their underground space, she became a relentless explorer. Deeper and deeper into the caves she ventured, always careful to leave markers so she could find her way back, but pressing ever forward, away from the city.

Even Daggin became concerned. "You mustn't go on these expeditions alone," he warned. "You could fall, and no one would know. I'll go with you any time you want."

But Kes preferred the thrill of exploring on her own. She knew it might be dangerous, but that was part of what tantalized her, and she didn't want to give it up. If she wanted safety she'd go back to standing in line for food rations.

It had been an accident that she found the tunnel. She certainly hadn't been looking for one, since she didn't know they existed, and almost passed by the opening without realizing what was there.

It was the color that caught her eye. The stone of the caves was gray-white and striated in a horizontal pattern, without variation. As she moved through a particular passageway, magnasite lamp in her hand, she swept the beam over the walls that surrounded her.

A dark, orangish streak, faint and dimmed with time, intersected the gray striations of the stone. She'd never seen a mark like that, and she stopped to stare up at it.

It seemed to emanate from a crack in the stone about a meter above her head. As she played the light over that crack, it seemed that she could discern a pattern in the fracture that made it seem planned rather than random. Curiosity began to burn in her.

She looked around for a boulder to roll against the wall so she could climb on it and reach the strange stain and the unusual fracture, but there was nothing except a large and imposing stone that she couldn't possibly move by herself. She would need help.

A short while later, she was back with Daggin, who was as excited as she by her find. Together they were able to roll the boulder into place, and Kes started to climb onto it. Daggin put a hand on her shoulder, restraining her.

"I'll go first," he cautioned, and Kes rankled at the implication he would be better qualified to deal with whatever surprises their find might lead to. She started to protest, but Daggin was already on the boulder and shining his lamp onto the stain.

"It's rust," he announced, tapping on the stone face with a small tool he'd brought from the farm.

"Then there must be something metal behind that rockface," said Kes, becoming more excited every second.

"Let me see if I can pry this section of the rock out," replied Daggin, inserting the flat end of the tool into the crack and wedging it back and forth. Slowly, gradually, a piece of stone was worked from the casing into which it had been placed.

"Watch out—as soon as it's out far enough, I'm going to let it fall onto the ground." Kes backed away. The stone would be dangerously heavy.

Another few minutes of wedging each side of the stone and it came tumbling out of its housing, crashing heavily to the ground and throwing up plumes of dust. Kes waved her hand to dispel them as Daggin moved close to the opening he'd created and shined his lamp into it.

"What is it? What do you see?" Kes asked, almost dancing with impatience.

His smile was eager, excited. "Come up here."

She scrambled up beside him and stood on tiptoe to peer into the opening.

She could see before her a round, darkened chamber, symmetrical to a degree that told her it had to have been constructed. She shone her lamp carefully around the periphery, and soon it revealed a long-unused control panel of some kind. And immediately adjacent to the panel was one of the most remarkable things Kes had ever seen: a staircase, old, rusting, dilapidated, leading upward.

Kes and Daggin exchanged glances, amazed. What could this be? Daggin extended his arm and ran his hand around the periphery of the opening on the inside of the chamber wall.

"There's hardware on this wall. That's what caused the rust stain."

"What is this, Daggin? What are those stairs for?"

He looked down at the stone plug, now lying on the bottom of the cave floor. "We have to figure a way to put that back," he said, and Kes was frustrated again.

"Why? Why can't we go in there, see where those stairs lead?"

"Because they lead up—and up is where the surface is. And if we can come up those stairs, the Kazon can come down them."

The Kazon again. Why was everyone so frightened of these mythical monsters? Who was to say they'd ever existed, much less lurked on the surface after so long a time? Wouldn't it be better to find out if they were still a threat than to live one's life in fear of the unknown?

But Daggin, for all his enlightened attitudes, apparently was just as cowed by the Kazon as everyone else. He was testing the weight of the stone that he'd pried out of its housing, and apparently found it daunting. "We'll have to get some help with this. It will take three or four of us, at least."

"Do we want others to know about this? Is that wise?"

Daggin pondered. She knew he realized she had a point. A discovery like this wasn't the kind of thing one wanted to be general knowledge. Soon word of it would get to the Elders, and who knew what they'd make of it?

Kes decided to press the point. "Why not just leave it? It's not likely that anyone's going to wander this far from the city. In all this time, no one's found it before—I think it's safe to say no one else will."

"It leaves us vulnerable if anyone were to come down that staircase," mused Daggin, but she knew he was ambivalent.

"If anyone got that far, one small stone wouldn't provide much protection. If the enemy comes for us, we'll just have to fight."

He glanced quickly at her, hearing the steely tone in her voice. He looked back at the fallen stone, then up at the opening in the wall. "All right," he said uneasily. "But I want you to promise you won't come back here by yourself."

She hesitated. She had every intention of doing just that, and of climbing at least a little way up the staircase. But she couldn't lie to Daggin, couldn't make a false promise.

"I thought so," he said knowingly. "Kes, what am I to do with you? Curiosity is one thing, and courage is certainly a virtue—but together they can easily turn to foolhardiness. You have to learn to temper your impulses. That's what true wisdom is all about."

Silently, Kes simmered, and blocked her mind so he wouldn't sense her attitude. Who was Daggin to be lecturing her? Had he developed "true wisdom"? He was barely older than she.

He drew near her and took hold of her arms just at the shoulders, looking down at her with concern. "Please promise," he said softly, and something in his voice caught her attention. "I couldn't stand it if anything were to happen to you."

An unaccustomed feeling began to stir in her, a sensation she'd never felt. It was strangely pleasant, like a piece of odd music that haunts the mind. She felt Daggin's eyes on her, peering through the darkness, and she looked up at him. "I won't promise not to come here again, but I'll tell you before I do."

He nodded, and they held a look for a moment; then Kes turned and started back down the passageway.

Kes's first run-in with the Elder known as Toscat came shortly before she cut off her hair. Whether one precipitated the other was a matter of concern to her parents, but not, frankly, to Kes.

It was unusual for someone to request an appointment with an Elder before they were three or four, and there were lifted eyebrows when Kes spoke to his aide, Marlath, about an interview. Bemused by the thought of a child seeking audience with an Elder, Marlath arranged the meeting with a manner that Kes found condescending.

But she didn't say anything. She was trying to learn to control her tongue, realizing as she grew older that it often created difficulties for her. She had a goal in mind now, and was determined not to sabotage her own efforts.

The afternoon she met with Toscat, she dressed carefully, choosing a sober, conservative outfit—something she thought an Elder would approve of. It was so neutral in color and style that it called no attention to itself. Kes thought it was boring, but knew she wasn't dressing to please herself. She vowed that when her growth cycle was complete, she would never adopt the bland dress style of the Ocampan women. She'd find some way to be different.

She brushed her long golden hair thoroughly, until it shone. She tied it back in a modest style and assessed herself. She looked colorless and dreary, probably just right for a meeting with Toscat. But as she gazed at herself in the glass, the thought came to her that she was very nearly grown. She looked almost as mature as she would for the next seven or eight years, at which point she would enter the morilogium, or final phase of existence. Then, aging would be rapid, leading within months to the end of life.

All the Elders had offices in the Assembly building, and Kes waited in the stark white anteroom while Toscat, in his office, finished a conversation with another Elder. She wondered what they talked about, how they occupied their days. There really was nothing for them to do: the Caretaker provided for everything, and most of Ocampan society had become serene and complacent, so there were never any problems. Yet the Elders always seemed to think they were very important.

She looked up to see Marlath eyeing her. He was probably only a year older than she, but acted as though he were an Elder himself. She found him arrogant.

"Tell me, Kes," he intoned telepathically, *"just what do you want to discuss with Toscat?"*

"I have some questions for him about our past," she answered frankly, out loud, then frowned with irritation as she saw him erupt into a smug grin.

"I see. And what could a little girl who's barely finished her growth cycle possibly want to know about our past?"

"A great deal. Everything. No one seems to know the details and I thought if anyone did, it would be an Elder. So here I am." Marlath's smile only grew larger, and Kes felt anger beginning to stir in her. That wouldn't do. She couldn't allow this petty aide to annoy her; she had to keep herself composed for Toscat. So she forced herself to smile back at him, her mouth feeling like a frozen slit on her face.

Fortunately at this point the doors to Toscat's office opened and he strolled out, arm around another of the Elders, chortling at some shared witticism. The men said their telepathic farewells and then Toscat turned to Kes. His face was pudgy, the skin of his cheeks stretched taut below eyes that were small and vacuous.

"Well, Kes, there you are—and looking more grown-up by the minute. You must be nearly at the end of your cycle."

"I'm already finished." She insisted on speaking out loud, even if no one else did.

"Well, come in, come in. I've been looking forward to this." He gestured toward his office and Kes preceded him inside. It was a spacious room, pale and unadorned, with windows that looked down onto the floor of the Assembly. Kes could see throngs of Ocampa below them, standing around, staring at the entertainment screens, standing in the food lines. She shivered slightly.

"Are you cold? I can warm up the room if you like."

"No, thank you. I'm fine."

Toscat smiled and gestured to a large black sofa. Kes sat on it, sinking into soft cushions and feeling quite small in their vast depths. Toscat sat opposite her, in a large chair with a high back and rolled arms. It was quite imposing, and Kes was feeling smaller all the while.

"Well, then," Toscat said, beaming, *"to what do I owe this visit from such a pretty little girl?"*

Kes's cheeks burned. He was treating her like an infant, like a worthless tot good for nothing more than minding her manners and looking pretty. He was speaking telepathically even though she continued to speak aloud. It was all so irritating. She took a breath to calm herself, then looked directly into Toscat's eyes. "I want to know if there are any written records from our ancestors."

The look on the Elder's face was worth the indignities she had suffered. It was at once perplexed, surprised, and wary—a panoply of emotions that rolled around his plump face like the light patterns on the entertainment screens. Kes felt a tiny twinge of triumph.

"Written records . . . ?" extemporized the older man.

"Yes. I can't believe there aren't writings of some kind. We had an extraordinary past, and it doesn't stand to reason no one would have recorded it."

She held his look firmly, unwilling to look away or do anything that might make her appear weak in his eyes. Finally it was he who broke contact, who rose and strolled to the window that overlooked the Assembly floor. *"Why are you asking about this?"* he asked, still not speaking aloud.

"I'm curious. I think we should know as much as possible about our true origins. How can we know what we're meant to be if we don't know what we came from?"

Toscat turned slowly and stared at her, as though he were inspecting an alien insect, something quaintly repulsive. He sighed, and the sigh rippled through her mind like wind on water. *"Kes, Kes, Kes . . . you're much too young to be troubling your mind with thoughts like these."* He smiled avuncularly. *"You're going to etch worry lines on that beautiful forehead if you try to think so deeply. Why not get your food rations and spend some time in front of the entertainment screens? That should settle those restless thoughts."*

She felt anger stirring in her again, and this time she wasn't so quick to suppress it. She rose to her feet, and her voice, when she spoke, had taken on a certain edge.

"I don't want to settle them down. I want to keep them churning. I have a lot of questions, and no one seems to have answers, so I came to you because you're an Elder and you should be showing us guidance but you won't help me, either. I'm quite serious, Toscat—I want to know if there are any written records and where they are and why no one knows about them and most of all, I want to read them."

He blinked in what seemed to be stupefaction, and Kes realized he was completely unaccustomed to being addressed like that. Probably it was the first time anyone had challenged him, much less a child barely through her cycle. She kept her eyes fixed on him.

His voice in her head had hints of steel to it. *"Be careful, young lady—I won't be threatened. You mind yourself or I'll take you back to your parents and tell them what a rude girl you've been."*

With a great struggle, Kes calmed herself. She wanted answers and this man might be able to provide them. It wouldn't do to alienate him. She lowered her eyelids in a docile gesture and spoke to him with her mind, like a good girl would. *"I'm sorry, Toscat. I meant no disrespect. I'm just burning with questions and I knew someone as wise as you would have answers. You're an Elder because you have great wisdom, and I only wanted to have the benefit of your knowledge."*

She looked up at him through her lashes, and saw him soften perceptibly. He walked toward her, arm extended in an ameliorative gesture. *"There, that's better, now you sound like a proper Ocampan child."*

It made her queasy that he was so easily manipulated. How could this man be an object of respect? He was a narrow-minded fool. She carefully closed her mind so he wouldn't intercept her thoughts. He moved toward her and stroked her hair, and she forced herself not to wince under his touch.

"Such beautiful hair . . . and your ears—so delicate. You've gotten those from your mother, I'm sure. Benaren's are thick-tipped."

Kes was confused and uneasy. She didn't know why he was suddenly assessing her physical qualities. It made her decidedly uncomfortable, but more to the point, it had nothing to do with the reason she'd come here. She eased herself away from him. *"You must know so much, Toscat. I can't imagine all the knowledge you possess. Please tell me . . . are there ancient writings? Is that how you became so wise?"*

Toscat's face was wreathed in a smile. Flattery had oiled his mind so that the information she wanted came slipping out. *"There are indeed. Only the Elders are allowed to peruse them. Frankly, I don't think you'd find them to be particularly interesting, or of any use to us now."*

Kes couldn't believe what he was saying. Not interesting? The records of their ancestors and the tale of their diaspora underground not *interesting?* What could he be thinking? She tried to still her hammering heart so that she could continue to question him. *"Do they tell of the Caretaker? And why he decided to protect us? And what it was like on the surface? Did they talk about the sun?"*

But Toscat had apparently offered up as much as he intended to. He patted her hair again, his fingers lingering to stroke the silken strands. *"None of this is of any value to you. Before you know it, you'll find a mate, and go through the elogium. You'll have your child and, believe me, there won't be time to be asking yourself these pointless questions."*

He stepped back as though to signal that the interview was over. *"This has been most pleasant. My door is open to you at any time, as it is to all of Ocampa. Please give Martis and Benaren my best wishes."* And he gestured toward the door.

Kes hesitated for a heartbeat, knowing the next seconds would be perhaps the most important in her life so far. She could do as she should—bid good-bye to Toscat and go sit in front of the screens—or she could do the unthinkable, and defy him. It took only seconds.

"Where are they?" she demanded, feet planted squarely, hands on her hips. "They belong to all of us, and I demand to see them."

Toscat's face took on a decidedly purplish hue, and his cheeks quivered. He opened his mouth and spoke aloud to her. "I'll let your parents know about this insolence, you can be sure of that. *Marlath!*" He yelled out a call for his aide, who instantly opened the door, amazement etched on his face. "Escort the young woman to her home and tell her parents to expect a visit from me."

Marlath nodded, clearly caught unawares by these events, and held the door open for Kes. She turned directly to Toscat and, quite calmly, said to him, "I got you to speak out loud, Toscat. That's a step in the right direction. Maybe there's hope for your lazy mind yet."

And she swept past him, head erect, with as much dignity as she could muster.

When she arrived home, she immediately took off her drab outfit, loosened her hair, and bathed in a tub of warm, fragrant water. It was as though she needed to wash away any reminder of her encounter with Toscat. She soaked for a long time, washing every part of her and rinsing her hair over and over. But when she dried herself and donned fresh clothing, she could still feel the touch of Toscat's hand on her hair.

She found a sharp blade among her father's possessions, and began to sever chunks of her long curls, cutting them close to the scalp in ragged layers. Only when most of her tresses lay on the floor did she feel cleansed of Toscat's plump hands. She carefully gathered the cut hair and took it outside the periphery of the city, into a passageway, where she found a rounded indentation in one of the stones. She placed the hair there and burned it, finding a soothing catharsis in watching the curls of smoke dissipate in the cool, dark air, as though dissolving Toscat into nothingness.

That night, she sat at the table with her parents, who apparently couldn't decide which shocked them most: her misbehavior with Toscat, or her self-induced hairstyle. She could see her father struggling with feelings of outrage, shame, and compassion.

"I thought I'd taught you there are ways to achieve your goals," said Benaren aloud, genuinely trying to understand his daughter's aberrant behavior. Kes was grateful that her parents, at least, avoided the slothful temptation to speak only telepathically. "If you approach someone with courtesy and reasonableness, if you treat them politely, with respect—you're a lot more likely to get what you want."

"I tried that. He was stubborn and insufferable."

"So you succumbed immediately—and brought yourself to his level."

Kes dropped her eyes. It was a fact, she'd lost control in an instant. Her father's chastisement rang true. "You're right. But I honestly believe that the outcome would have been the same no matter how self-possessed I was. He just wasn't going to tell me about the ancient records."

"He's under no compunction to do so," offered her mother. "There are rules which govern a society. Here, the Elders decide those rules, and it isn't up to a child to question them."

Kes's head snapped toward her mother. "Why not? Why isn't it all right for *anyone* to question authority? Even a child. If the authority is valid, it should stand up to examination."

She saw her mother and father exchange a glance, but she couldn't read what was communicated there. She thought, however, that she detected a hint of pride.

"Tell me this," continued Benaren, "what made you do that to your hair? Did it have anything to do with Toscat?"

"I'm not sure," replied Kes, and at this point that was true. Surely the fact that the Elder had touched her hair wasn't reason enough to cut it off, even though it had seemed so at the time. "I think I just wanted to be different."

From the corner of her eye, she saw a twist of a smile appear on her mother's lips, then as quickly disappear. "It will grow," said Martis philosophically, and that was the end of the discussion of her hair.

A month later, Kes stood in the middle of the Assembly floor. Her hair was somewhat neater than it had been after her impromptu styling, as her mother had sat her down and trimmed the uneven parts so it looked purposeful, rather than as though she'd been attacked by someone with a dull knife. She was wearing a new outfit, one Daggin's sister had made for her. It consisted of soft leggings and a tunic over that, and Kes was more comfortable in it than she'd ever been in any clothing. There was an ease to the outfit, a freedom of movement, that she found liberating. But there, on the floor of the Assembly, she was an oddly incongruous sight.

She was nervous about what she planned to do, but she'd discussed it with Daggin and the others in the farming group, and they all agreed it was a necessary step—and that Kes was unquestionably the one to take it.

"Citizens of Ocampa," she called out in a clear, confident voice. "Please listen to me. I want to let you know of something extraordinary that's happening in our society. There are records—written records—that tell of our past. We could all know the circumstances which brought us to live here, beneath the surface. We could learn about the Caretaker, and why he put us here, and why he provides for us. We could know these things—but our Elders won't give us access to those records. They insist the writings are for their eyes only, and they withhold these ancient truths from the public. Is this fair? Do they have that right? Shouldn't we all be allowed access to our history?"

She noted that a small group of people had gathered round, but realized it was primarily Daggin and their friends. Most of the Ocampa were transfixed by the entertainment screens, and couldn't stir themselves enough to pay attention to this minor insurrection that was occurring in front of them. Kes kept going.

"Knowledge shouldn't be hidden away from the people, it should be given freely to anyone who requests it. Knowledge itself isn't dangerous—but lack of it can be devastating. Wouldn't we be better off as a people if we had *more* knowledge, rather than less? These writings of our ancestors contain a gift more valuable even than energy and water—they contain *truth.* That's a quality that is valuable in and of itself. All people should seek the truth, and those who govern should have that same quest. But we're being denied the truth, because of a small group of people who have decided on our behalf that truth and knowledge are better off kept secret. Do you see any wisdom in that kind of thinking?"

She glanced up at the glass-front façade of the structure that contained the Elders' offices. She was fairly sure she saw Toscat's squat shape standing at his window, peering down. The sight gave her a rush of vindication, and she turned to the small group that had gathered around her. She was gratified to see that it had grown somewhat; some of the citizenry had apparently developed curiosity about what was happening.

"She's right," called Daggin from the periphery. "We ought to be able to study our own past. Why are these documents being kept from us? Is there some ulterior purpose? We should hold the Elders accountable for their actions!"

A lusty cheer arose from the small band of their supporters, but the other Ocampans merely looked perplexed. This was a singularly unconventional event, one outside their ken, and they had no idea how to respond. The pacifying influence of the screens was more familiar, and some of them wandered back.

"Who will go with me to the Elders?" called Kes. "Who will join in our demand to find the truth of our past?" Again, Daggin and the others pressed forward, calling, "We will!" But most of the citizens began to drift away, unable to absorb what Kes was proposing. She watched them melt back into the milling crowds, and for the first time began to feel doubt. These people were too far gone, too docile, too drained of initiative. They would never challenge the Elders.

Then Kes saw a familiar figure standing near one of the columns. It was Martis, her mother, and she was smiling at Kes with what could only be called unabashed pride. Their eyes locked, Kes felt a surge of love pass between them, and her courage returned. She turned back to the crowd. "Come with me," she rang out, "let's go right now. They can't refuse us."

She began to stride toward the office structure, followed by Daggin and their friends. She noticed that a few other Ocampans fell in behind them, though more from an instinct to follow than from revolutionary zeal. So be it, at least their numbers had swelled.

Marlath's face was startled when they burst into the anteroom and demanded to see Toscat. He was clearly disquieted by the appearance of this unruly group, for nothing like this had ever happened, so far as he knew. He stammered as he spoke.

"I . . . I don't know if he's here. He may have . . . have gone to . . . to . . ."

"Don't bother, Marlath. I know he's here. I could see him from the Assembly floor," challenged Kes. At that point the door to Toscat's office opened and he appeared, summoning as much mastery of the situation as he could.

"Citizens, how can I help you?" he asked, and Kes was intrigued that he chose to speak out loud. They'd had an effect on him, after all.

"We want the right to review the records our ancestors kept," announced Daggin firmly. Toscat's eyes swept the group and stopped on Kes.

"I see you've been busy, Kes," he said, with a hint of disappointment in his voice, as though she had somehow personally betrayed him.

"We all feel alike, Toscat, and we feel very strongly. What is your response?"

Toscat surveyed the group for a moment, then threw open his hands. "I can't make this decision myself. I must convene all the Elders. It must be discussed thoroughly before we find the true course."

"When will you convene?"

"I'm not certain. I'll have to discuss scheduling with the others."

"It's not as though you have a great deal to do," said Kes, unwilling to let him procrastinate indefinitely. Toscat drew his breath in sharply and glared at her.

"How would a child like you know what responsibilities we must shoulder? You have no idea what our days are like—"

"When, Toscat?"

He drew a breath and sighed wearily. "I'll try to convene everyone tomorrow."

"We'll call on you before nightly rations, then."

He nodded and disappeared back into his office, shutting the door firmly. Kes, Daggin, and the others exchanged a triumphant look. "See you tomorrow, Marlath," said Kes, and they all filed out with feelings of great victory.

Of course, the Elders didn't convene the next day, nor the next, nor the next. And when they finally did, under great pressure from the militant and tenacious group of farmers, they didn't make a decision. They kept this delaying tactic up for days, and would probably have continued it indefinitely, if something extraordinary hadn't happened, something so bizarre and unexplainable that even the Elders became worried.

One afternoon, as Kes, Daggin, and the others sat in the Assembly hall, discussing what further measures to try to bring pressure on the Elders, there was a sudden and unusual sound, a ringing, a shimmering, that seemed to come from nowhere and which became almost painfully loud. People covered their ears in discomfort, and gradually, the ringing faded away.

When it was over, two alien beings lay on the floor of the hall.

Awed, wary, a few of the braver souls crept toward the beings, who were clearly of a species unlike theirs. Their skin was covered with a thick white fur, they were much taller than Ocampans, and their heads were elongated into a spherical shape. They were quite the strangest beings Kes had ever imagined.

"Where did they come from?" someone asked, but received no answer. People moved closer, and noticed that there were what appeared to be sores dotted on the arms and shoulders of both aliens. Glances were exchanged and shoulders shrugged as no one knew what to do next.

Kes moved through the group to stand over the alien beings. "They're sick," she announced. "We have to help them." She knelt down and ascertained that both were breathing, but apparently unconscious. "Daggin, get the medical service." Daggin hurried off, and Kes was glad there was someone there who wasn't stupefied into immobility by this amazing appearance.

Within minutes, Toscat and two of the other Elders had arrived, followed shortly by physicians from the medical service. Toscat surveyed the situation, and the unconscious aliens, and made a pronouncement: "The Caretaker has sent these beings to us. It is our duty to care for them."

How he had arrived at this conclusion was a question Kes would like to have asked, but she didn't want to ruffle Toscat any more than she already had. She still had hopes that the Elders would relent and grant access to the historical writings. Besides, she agreed that they had a responsibility to help these aliens, regardless of where they had come from or how they had gotten there.

The two large, furry beings were carried off to the central clinic, after which no news of them was forthcoming.

However, within days, two more arrived in the same manner.

These beings more closely resembled the Ocampa, except that their ears were tiny and unembellished, and their skin was a dark red color. They had no hair on their heads. They, too, had the sores which had appeared on the first pair, and like those first arrivals, they were carried off to the medical center.

These strange visitations became a regular occurrence, every several days witnessing the advent of two more sick beings, all of them different from the Ocampa, all of them unconscious and ridden with sores of unknown origin.

The Elders seemed flummoxed by the events. They convened regularly, often staying up well into the night cycle, the lights from their offices the only lights seen in the Assembly hall. It was after two weeks of this that Toscat summoned Kes.

This time she stayed on her feet rather than get swallowed into the voluptuous cushions of Toscat's couch. The plump little man looked haggard; the jowls of his cheeks seemed to sag a little more than before, and the skin beneath his eyes was yellowish, signifying a lack of sleep.

"We know the Caretaker is sending us these aliens for a purpose, but we are unable to comprehend what that purpose might be. We have cared for them to the best of our ability, but so far, every one of them has died. We are failing the Caretaker." This was interesting news, but didn't explain just why he had summoned Kes. She held her tongue and waited. Toscat paced away from her, hands clasped behind his back.

The next seemed difficult for him to say; she was sure she heard his voice catch a few times. But it didn't matter, because what he said was so exciting that she scarcely cared what he sounded like. "It has occurred to us . . . that is, the possibility has been broached . . . that the Caretaker was for some reason unhappy that you were not granted permission to read the old texts. Not that I give this theory any credence, mind you, but others have posited it, and it's been agreed that we dare not risk offending the Caretaker, even unintentionally." He paused, gazing out the window. They both heard the characteristic shimmery ringing which had become so familiar, and knew that more aliens had arrived.

"The Elders have decided that you may study the writings. Perhaps that will appease the Caretaker. Perhaps you will find in those texts some revelation that will explain why he is sending these beings to us."

Kes's heart was pounding so loudly that her ears were pulsating. She was going to be able to read about their past! For once she felt a twinge of gratitude toward the Caretaker, whoever or whatever he was, for having such a profound influence on the Elders. If they hadn't been so nervous about him, she might never have won the right to read the ancient records.

"Come with me," continued Toscat, "and you can begin immediately." He turned and walked from the room, followed closely by Kes. They proceeded down the corridor to a tiny room Kes had never realized was there, as it was hidden by a door that had been made to resemble the wall. They entered the room, the doors closed—and then Kes's stomach almost jumped into her throat as the little room began to descend!

She turned to Toscat, eyes wide with surprise. "It's a conveyance chamber," he explained. "The only one in the city. It leads to the vaults."

This adventure was becoming more intriguing all the time. Vaults! Buried deep below the Assembly hall—who would have thought it?

Kes took several deep breaths to calm herself, but she couldn't quell the excitement that possessed her.

They exited the chamber and walked down a long, dimly lit hallway until they reached its terminus. There Toscat put his hand on the wall in a particular location and the wall swung open—another concealed door. Toscat stepped through and gestured for Kes to follow him.

The room had an unusual smell to it, a mustiness that Kes found appealing. It was the scent of history, and its odor was intoxicating. She looked around her to see the walls of the room lined with bookshelves, all of which contained bound books of various sizes and thicknesses. Some looked relatively new and unused; others were clearly ancient, the covers cracked and shriveled from age. In the center of the room stood a square table with two chairs precisely placed at either end, suggesting that they were rarely, if ever, used. Kes walked immediately to the section containing what she perceived to be the oldest of the books.

"Those are the earliest of the writings," said Toscat without emotion, which was surprising to Kes, who was so excited to be here that she felt sick to her stomach. "They were composed by our forefathers soon after the Caretaker created our home here. A history was kept for many generations . . ." Toscat walked from one side of the room to the other, where the newer books were shelved, and gestured. ". . . until several generations ago, when the histories gradually dwindled out."

"You mean—people stopped writing about us? We've lost part of the past?"

Toscat looked impatient. "What good was it doing us? Nothing ever changed, and fewer people knew how to read or write." He turned to her and gave her a skeptical look. "I trust you can read. No one's going to do it for you if you can't."

Kes lifted her chin proudly. "Of course I can read. And write. My father and mother made sure of that."

Toscat made a funny sound in his throat, a cross between a grunt and a chuckle, which irritated Kes even more. She turned away from him. "Can I start now?" she asked coolly.

The man shrugged. "As you like. The door will lock behind you automatically, so if you leave and want to return, you'll have to contact me."

"It will take me days to go through all these books."

"I would imagine so. I'll arrange to have food and drink brought to you."

He turned to go, but she was compelled to make one last effort to reach out to him, to share this remarkable experience. "Toscat . . . the first time you read these writings, weren't you excited? Didn't it *inspire* you?"

He stared at her with a curious expression on his face. "I've never read any of these old tomes," he said dismissively. "I've never had time—and I can't imagine what good would come of it anyway."

He turned and went out the door, which closed behind him. Kes stared after him in amazement. Ocampan history was here, at his fingertips, and he'd ignored it. Something was very, very wrong with their people if they could purposely ignore the precious connection to their past. She went to the first book on the top shelf in the oldest section and pulled it out, releasing a small dust cloud as she did. She carried it to the table, opened it to the first scrawled page of writing, and began, in rapt absorption, to read.

"They called it the warming. Gradually the climate got hotter and hotter, until the water on the surface was almost dried up and the whole planet was a desert. The Caretaker opened a deep chasm in the ground and led our people here to the city he'd created. Then he erected a special energy barrier that would keep the Kazon from following. He promised to take care of us forever."

Kes spoke with breathless excitement to her friends, who listened with hushed, eager attention. They were as avid as she to hear the details of their past, and had sat quietly, listening, as Kes chronicled their origins.

"And this is the most exciting part," she continued. "I think our ancestors could do things with their minds that we're no longer aware of. They make reference to some extraordinary abilities—like moving objects with their minds—but after eighty or ninety generations, there's no more mention of such things."

"What could've happened?" mused Daggin. He had gathered the group, which Kes was gratified to see now numbered about forty people. The farmers' ranks were swelling.

"I think we lost those abilities because we stopped using them. The Caretaker provides everything. We've become lazy because we don't have to work to survive. Our mind is like a muscle that's atrophied from disuse."

"But what does any of this have to do with the diseased people the

Caretaker is sending us?" This was from Allia, a nurse that worked at the central clinic, and a new face in the group. She had burnished auburn hair and a kind, compassionate voice. Kes imagined she would be a very good nurse indeed. "And why has he increased the amount of energy he sends?"

No one had an answer for this, though everyone was aware that the pulses which signaled the delivery of energy had increased as of late.

"Something has changed," said Kes. "Something is different from what it's been for almost five hundred generations. And I think we should find out."

She saw Daggin's startled look, but pressed on. "Daggin and I have found an ancient access tunnel that I think leads to the surface. I intend to go see what's happening up there."

There was absolute and stunned silence at this announcement. Even these forward-thinking young people were apprehensive about the boldness of such a plan.

"Our enemies are up there," said Allia tentatively, but Kes didn't let her get any further.

"How do we know? Why should we think things are exactly as they were so long ago? It's foolish and ignorant of us to assume that. Maybe it's time for us to leave the underground and live in the sun once more."

There were some uneasy stirrings in the group and Kes could tell that they weren't ready to support this radical idea. "Let's think about it," said Daggin, ever the diplomat. "Maybe there are ways to make such a journey safely."

Privately, she scoffed at him. Sometimes there just weren't ways to do things safely. Sometimes you had to make up your mind that something was worth doing and then do it, no matter what the consequences. But she didn't say this, and was careful to block her mind so the others wouldn't know what she was thinking.

"Have you finished all the journals?" asked Allia.

"Almost. But after a while they all begin to sound alike. You can chart the course of our apathy. The tone of the writing becomes more and more dispirited as time goes by, until finally it's without vitality, without curiosity. It sounds just like our Elders sound now—dreary."

She looked around the group, friends she loved dearly and acquaintances she barely knew. An overwhelming urgency rose in her. "Do we want to become like that? Or do we want to fight against that tedium?"

"You know the answer to that, Kes," said Daggin. "Why else would we be growing our food? We're using our minds, we're working to take care of ourselves."

"Maybe that's not enough. Maybe we have to push ourselves even further."

"By doing what?" queried Allia.

"I'm not sure. I just think we can accomplish more."

No one had a reply for that because suddenly they heard a voice in their minds. *"There you are, Kes,"* intoned Toscat, and they all looked up to see the portly Elder moving toward their botanical setting. He looked at the rows of green plants, some thick with fruit or vegetables, with feigned interest.

"So this is your famous farm," he said genially, and, thought Kes, falsely. "Very interesting. I suppose young people need amusements like these."

Daggin stepped forward. "What can we do for you, Toscat? I can't believe you're truly interested in our farm."

"Of course I am. I've been meaning to come out here for some time. Of course, I suspected I might find Kes here, as well. How are you, my dear? And how is your little project coming?"

Kes stopped herself from making a retort to his condescending questions, remembering her father and mother's remonstrations about not sinking to his level. "It's coming very well. I've read nearly all the journals. They're fascinating."

"I'm sure, I'm sure. I was hoping you'd let me know what you've found out." His eye swept over the assembled group, as though committing to memory the faces he saw there. "I assigned you to that reading for a purpose, if you remember."

"I remember very well. I haven't reported to you because I found absolutely no information which would suggest why the Caretaker is sending us those sick aliens. If in fact he's doing that at all."

Toscat purpled slightly. "Of course he's doing it. Who else would?"

"I have no idea," said Kes, a bit wearily. She simply had no impetus for a fight with Toscat. It was a waste of energy. "All I can tell you is there's simply no clue in the books as to what's happening to us now."

Toscat's face dimpled with concern. "I see," he said ineffectually, then looked around at the group once more. "Well, the Caretaker has his reasons, and if we can't interpret them it is our failing rather than his." Having made this pronouncement, he nodded curtly and moved away from the group once more. They were silent until he was far enough from them not to hear them, and then they all burst forth with laughter. It was a moment of shared warmth, and the last one Kes would know for a long, long time.

Getting through the portal to the access tunnel wasn't difficult, but the drop to the floor on the other side was a long one, and Kes felt the impact in one of her ankles. She sat for a while, rubbing it, until it stopped throbbing.

She was inside a stone-lined shaft, around which wound an old and dilapidated metal stairway. Light stanchions were embedded in the walls at regular intervals, but most of them were dark, and those that weren't provided only a fading, flickering light. She peered up the shaft, trying to see where it led, but the stairs disappeared into darkness within a few meters.

She glanced once at the opening she'd come through and realized that even if she changed her mind, she wouldn't be able to scale the wall to get back through it. Of course, if she simply waited here, Daggin would realize where she'd gone and come looking for her, and would help her climb out. That was why she had to move quickly, why she couldn't afford this last-minute hesitation. She drew a deep breath, trying to quell the nervousness that tickled her belly, and put her foot on the first step upward. It wobbled somewhat precariously, but successfully bore her weight.

Slowly she climbed, so as not to tire herself early. She had no idea how far she had to go, but suspected it was a long way. She would need all her energy. And as she climbed, she focused on these last remarkable, painful weeks.

Her father had entered the morilogium just over a month ago, and began the swift aging process that signaled the end of life. Gradually he became weaker and weaker, until finally he was confined to bed, where Kes and her mother stayed by his side as was the custom among their people, sharing memories and remembering the loving moments of their family life. It was a process which helped the waning person to move gently into the next stage of existence, and helped the surviving family members to accept their loss.

Except that it didn't work that way. Kes was grief-stricken, devastated, although she worked very hard not to let either Benaren or Martis know that. But they were too wise, and knew her too well, to be fooled. The process of leave-taking became much more about helping Kes to mourn, until finally she was able to accept, as her father clearly did, the inevitability of his death. His last words to her and her mother were of love, and he closed his eyes peacefully before breathing his last.

When that happened, Kes felt a huge stillness, a void, settle within her. As though recognizing that, her mother turned to her, took her by the shoulders, and said, "You must see the sun."

The black void dissipated, and a lightness of being overtook her. Her mother's generosity was astonishing, for she was giving Kes permission to do something that would possibly take her away forever, leaving Martis alone—and yet she knew it was what Kes must do.

And so Kes found herself now, climbing ever upward, into the unknown. She alternated between moments of exhilaration and terror. It was entirely possible the Kazon still existed on the surface, and that she was walking into terrible danger.

On the other hand, they might have departed long ago. All the water on the surface had been burned away, and the terrain was anything but inviting—at least, that's what the most ancient journals indicated. Why would people remain in such a hostile environment?

But what impelled her upward most of all was her mother's simple pronouncement: She had to see the sun. She had to know its light, to feel its radiant warmth on her skin. Why that was so important she wasn't sure, but it was a vision that kept her climbing, even when her legs began to ache and quiver from the thousands of steps she'd taken.

She stopped to rest periodically, eating some food rations and drinking the water she'd brought along. Then she would rise and begin climbing again, sometimes holding the deteriorating handrail, sometimes having to climb over stair slats which had pulled away from their fastenings. The stairway never felt completely sturdy, and she began to fear that it might at any time collapse under her weight, sending her plummeting down hundreds of meters to her death.

But still she climbed. She lost track of time, and moved in a near-stupor, her only reality the step of her feet on the stairs, the flickering lights on the walls. Her mind drifted, remembering her father, his wisdom, his gentleness. What she was doing now she was doing in his honor, because she knew he would have been as supportive of this quest as her mother.

A twinge of regret nipped at her as she thought of Martis. Maybe she should have waited for a while before leaving. She could have spent some time with her mother, helping both of them to adjust to life without Benaren. And yet she knew her mother was strong, strong enough to urge Kes to take the gift of freedom.

She wasn't sure how long she'd been hearing the strange buzzing noise. It was something she became aware of gradually, then realized she must have been hearing it faintly for some time. It was a sound she'd never heard before, and she paused briefly on the steps, trying to assess it.

Her mind ran down what she'd read in the journals about the journey underground. There had been no mention of a sound like this, and yet it was unmistakably there, growing louder the higher she climbed. Her hands became moist in apprehension.

And then, a significant goal: The stairway ended, leading into a tunnel not unlike those that surrounded their underground city. She was in a cave, but one much, much closer to the surface. Cautiously, she made her way through the passageway toward the buzzing sound.

A faint glow began to emanate from somewhere deep within the tunnel, a glow which intensified as she drew nearer. Finally, she stood before the phenomenon that produced both the glow and the humming noise: a crackling green energy barrier that stretched from one side of the cave wall to the other. It danced and sizzled before her, looking perilous, even lethal, and gave off a faint odor of energized atoms, an acrid odor that intensified its aura of danger.

This must be the barrier the Caretaker had erected to keep out the Kazon. It was still in place, still working, even after all these generations. Did that mean there were still Kazon on the surface? Would the Caretaker keep the barrier in place if there were no longer any need to do so?

But, more importantly, how was she to get through it? She certainly had no intention of quitting now, when she had climbed so far. But this hissing energy field was intimidating. She picked up a stone from the ground and flung it toward the barrier. It hit the grid and clung there, sizzling, for a brief instant, then burst into flame and fell to the ground, rendered instantly into a fine ashy powder.

She sat down on the floor of the cave and stared at the barrier, refusing to admit defeat, studying the crackling grid carefully, trying to figure out a way through. Her eyes roamed over every millimeter of it, and gradually she realized something interesting: The energy emanations seemed to be unevenly distributed through the grid. There were patches of yellow in the green, suggesting a temperature variance that might denote weaker energy. Along the right side of the grid there was a long strip of pale yellow. If that was a weak part of the grid, was there something she could do to attack it, weaken it further?

She found more stones, larger ones this time, and hurled them against the yellow strip on the right side. The stones were vaporized, but each time, the strip became a paler yellow. The impact was having some kind of effect.

She found more stones, and kept up her assault, until finally a gap in the grid developed. Along the side of the cave wall, there was a space where the grid was not functioning at all. If she could widen that space . . .

Some time and many stones later, there was an opening in the energy barrier that she thought she could slide through. She approached the grid, which she now thought of as a malevolent entity, hissing in fury at the abuse it had endured, and flattened herself sideways to it, back against the cave wall.

Gently, slowly, she squeezed herself through the opening. The heat from the barrier threatened to singe her skin, and the acrid smell nauseated her, but little by little, millimeter by millimeter, she was passing through it.

And then she was on the other side! She felt a tremor of thrill, and instinct told her that her quest was nearly at an end. She moved quickly through the remaining part of the tunnel, where at one point she saw light coming through a few cracks in the wall. It was an opening, she knew, and in moments she was there, pushing at rock and earth that had piled up in front of it. In a few moments she had cleared a space large enough to crawl through . . .

. . . and she emerged into the sunlight.

Unimaginable brightness assaulted her, pierced her eyes painfully. Involuntarily she covered them, then opened them just a crack because she had to see what it looked like on the surface.

Ahead of her stretched a vast plain, a desert of red-hued dirt, studded in the distance with rock outcroppings. Gradually her eyes adjusted to the sunlight and she opened them further, turning in place to absorb the immensity of this astonishing place. Never in her life had she seen such a vista, such a distance. Above her, not the rock and stone of the underground cave, but a broad expanse of blue which she knew to be "sky," and which held, glowing too brightly for her to look at directly, the blazing orb which provided the golden light of this planet—the sun. There was another wondrous sight as well: huge, brilliant flashes that arced through the sky toward a distant mountaintop. These, she knew, were the energy transports from the Caretaker, which she had known in the nearly twelve months of her life as muffled thumps, constant and reassuring.

Her eye caught the opening through which she had emerged, the stones shoved aside, and an instinct so strong it was almost like a voice in her mind told her to conceal that opening. She moved the stones back in place and dusted her footprints away. She knew exactly where the spot was, but no one else could tell. Somehow, she knew that was important. Then she looked around again at the magnificence of open space that stretched before her.

Even though it was hot, very hot, Kes felt a slight chill ripple through her. She had done it: she had overcome fear and ignorance and done what everyone else she knew was afraid to do—left the security of their underground womb and flung herself into the unknown.

But now what? If there was truly no one left on this planet, what was she to do for food? And water? She had only a little left of the supply she'd brought along, and clearly the climate of the planet hadn't recovered from the warming of long ago. Everywhere she looked she saw only sere, scrubby vegetation, and the endless expanse of dry red dirt.

And if she were to return to her underground city and tell everyone what she'd seen, what would be the reaction? No one would want to leave their cool and beautiful home, where there was abundant water and energy, and relocate to this arid desert.

So what, in the long run, had she accomplished?

I saw the sun, she reminded herself. That was reason enough to have made this journey, something that could never be taken from her. So perhaps the thing to do was go home, share this remarkable experience with her mother, and her friends, and work to make the Ocampan people less complacent, more independent, more like they had been before the Caretaker started protecting them.

She realized she had moved quite a ways from the opening in a small rocky outcropping through which she had emerged, and in fact wasn't quite sure where it was. She had started back toward where she thought it was when she heard the pounding.

This was different from the sound of the energy flashes. It was low and muted, a vibration that she seemed to feel, rather than hear. Instinctively she lay on the ground and put her ear on the red dirt; now she heard the noise distinctly, a drumming as though many

335

objects were being pounded on the ground. Never had she experienced such a sound, and she rose, puzzled, trying to see where it came from.

Across the desert she saw two figures moving rapidly toward her, more rapidly than anyone could run—at least, anyone she'd ever seen. She shielded her eyes from the sun and squinted, trying to make out the figures. As they came nearer, she realized there were actually four figures racing toward her, two beasts that were running on four legs, while simultaneously supporting two men on their backs. The beasts had long tails of hair which streamed out behind them as they ran, and they struck Kes as incredibly beautiful. She stared at them, fascinated, as they bore down on her.

The men atop the beasts were very large, and wore an elaborate headdress which was wild and unkempt, giving them a fierce appearance that once more brought a chill to Kes.

Were these Kazon?

The beasts charged hard until they were almost upon her; she stood, immobile, frozen by apprehension, afraid to move and knowing there was no place to hide, anyway. The beasts pulled up suddenly, apparently at some command by the men astride them, and stood pawing and snorting, eager to run again.

Kes looked up at the riders, who loomed over her, backlit by the sun so their faces were shadowed, presenting only their unruly silhouette. A low, growling voice emerged from one of the figures.

"What's this? A little mole that's come creeping into the light?"

"Maybe we should just squash it and let the insects eat it clean." Both men laughed as though this were the height of hilarity.

"Who are you? Where do you come from?" Kes intended her voice to sound strong and determined, but she was dismayed to hear a slight quaver in it. But the men seemed delighted that she had said anything at all.

"Listen! It talks! Maybe we should allow it to live . . ." One of the men suddenly leapt off his beast and peered down at Kes. She could see his face now, which was the color of old leather and about as worn. His eyes were small and ringed with lines, the kind that only appeared on Ocampan people when they had entered the morilogium. Perhaps that's what happened to people who lived their lives in this bright sunlight.

"Where did you come from, little thing?" A foul odor emanated from the man, and when he spoke, a further nasty smell came from his mouth, causing Kes instinctively to turn her head away. Suddenly she felt a rough hand on her chin and her head was snapped back in the direction of the speaker. "I asked you a question," he said harshly, still holding her chin in his grip.

"I asked you a question first. Answer mine and I'll answer yours." She said this with all the courage she could muster.

He stared at her for a brief moment, then burst out laughing again. "She's a spunky little thing. Jabin will be intrigued with her. Let's get her back to camp."

And Kes felt herself suddenly lifted into the air and flung across the huge beast, which whuffed and snorted until the man climbed on behind her. Then they were racing across the desert floor, hot wind on her face, teeth rattled by the pounding of the animal's feet as it flung itself into the distance. Even though she was frightened, she was also exhilarated; the sensation of dashing across the desert on top of this powerful four-legged creature was remarkably exciting, no matter what awaited her at the end of the ride.

In a scant few minutes, Kes could see what appeared to be structures rising from the desert floor, but which, upon closer inspection, were only partial structures—ruins of edifices that had crumbled from age or attack. Nearby was a cluster of makeshift buildings around which stood more of the wild-looking men with their bizarre headdresses.

Their headlong ride over, the men jumped off the beasts and roughly pulled Kes down as well. They half-dragged, half-carried her inside one of the structures and she instantly felt a drop in temperature. It seemed too dark to see at first, but gradually it seemed to grow lighter, and Kes decided her eyes must have the ability to adjust to varying degrees of light intake. She saw at the opposite end of the room another of the rough-looking men, sitting in a chair, one leg over the armrest in an indolent, arrogant pose. He smelled no better than the others.

Her two captors—for that is what they must surely be—scuttled her toward the man and then let go of her arms. The hulking man in the chair sat up in curiosity and peered at her. Kes decided once more to go on the offensive.

"I'd like to know who you are and why you've brought me here," she said, and was glad that this time her voice held steady. The man smiled, but it was not a smile of warmth or friendliness.

"By all means, plucky one. I am Jabin. These are the men that work in the mines under my command. And they wisely brought you here because they realized you can be of great service to us."

"Are you Kazon?"

The man smiled again, and this time Kes noticed that his teeth were stained in ugly brown blotches. "We are indeed. Kazon-Ogla, the strongest and most courageous of all the sects."

Kes's stomach clutched slightly. Everyone else had been right—the Kazon still loomed on the surface. Did they still consider the Ocampa their enemy? "What do you mean," she asked, "by being 'of great service'?"

Jabin reached out and put his fingers on her face, turning it first one way and then the other. "I mean it literally. You will make a lovely serving girl."

Kes jerked her chin out of his grasp. "I have no intention of becoming your servant," she said hotly, deciding that the time had come to let them know she wouldn't be taken advantage of.

But immediately she felt a stinging blow to the side of her head and she went sprawling heavily to the floor, her ear ringing as though it were on fire. She clutched at it, trying to stifle the pain, as Jabin stood over her. "Let's be clear on this. Everyone in this camp does exactly as I tell them. You are certainly no exception. Do you understand?"

Kes managed to nod, but Jabin drew back his boot and kicked her viciously in her shin. She screamed and grabbed at it, the pain eclipsing that in her ear. "When I ask you a question, answer me. Like this: 'Yes, Maje.' That's all I ever want to hear from you. 'Yes, Maje.' Do you understand?"

"Yes, Maje," whispered Kes, who could barely make herself form the words as she battled to combat the pain in her leg and her ear. She was suddenly jerked to her feet and she struggled to stand alone.

"That's much better. You're a pretty little thing and I'd rather not deface you. If you behave, we can get along very nicely. Don't you think?"

He looked piercingly at her and Kes knew what he was waiting for. "Yes, Maje," she said hoarsely. He positively beamed.

"Very good. Very good. Bring me some of the bread from that table, and then we can have a nice, long conversation. I want to know all about you—and I particularly want to know how you got to the surface. You, my little Ocampa, will be the means of our regaining the water that is rightfully ours."

Kes went to the table with dread in her heart, and for the first time in her life she wished devoutly that she had listened to others instead of following her own youthful impulses.

* * *

Three weeks later, Kes could barely remember anything of her life underground. Only the now, the miserable present, was with her. She spent long days waiting on Jabin, preparing and serving him meals which he consumed rapidly and messily, all but destroying her own appetite. When she wasn't busy tending to his needs, he made her chip cormaline nuggets, a hateful job that left her hands splintered with shards of the ore, nasty little cuts that took forever to heal. He never told her why she was doing it, and she suspected it was for no purpose other than to make her do a mind-numbing task.

Sometimes at night, when she was finally allowed to crawl to a crude mat in a small outbuilding and sleep for a few hours, she would try to summon up the memory of her mother and father, but they seemed like dream figures, vaporous and fleeting.

She had lost the ability to cry. At first she wept constantly, until Jabin's vicious slaps conditioned her not to, and eventually, even when she was alone, she couldn't summon tears as a release for her misery. It was as though she were inert, not dead but not living either, a husk that moved through the parching days by rote, trying not to do anything that might ignite Jabin's temper.

Only one triumph was hers, and she clung to it desperately, determined not to relinquish it for it had cost her a great deal of pain and she refused to have suffered like that for nothing.

She had not revealed the place of her emergence from underground.

Jabin had taken her to the place where his men had discovered her, and she poked in a desultory fashion around the rocks, but insisted to the Maje that everything all looked alike to her and she didn't know where the entrance to the tunnel was. She was thankful she had thought to conceal it when she first stepped out into the desert.

Jabin beat her then, assuming she was lying, but even then she insisted she didn't know where it was. Jabin's men didn't find it either, for all the searching and kicking and jabbing with sticks they did. It occurred to Kes at one point that perhaps it didn't exist, that the dimly remembered past was a fantasy and that she had lived in this hard servitude forever.

Finally, Jabin gave up the search, but denied her food and water for the rest of the day.

She was constantly thirsty. Water was doled out by the tiniest of cupfuls, and she was the last to drink; often there were only drops left for her. She tried to remember the gushing waterfalls that ringed her city, as though the thought might quench her thirst, but they, too, seemed impossibly unreal.

But the worst of times came when Jabin indulged in a drink called gannit, a strong, foul-smelling liquor that he fortunately didn't imbibe often, as it dried the mouth and produced a thirst which couldn't be quenched with limited water supplies. He'd have been better off to leave it alone entirely, but he couldn't seem to do that.

The first time she saw him drink gannit was a week after she arrived in the Ogla camp. She was lying, exhausted, on her pallet when she heard him bellowing her name. She jumped up and ran into the room that served as his "office."

"Yes, Maje?" she offered as she entered the room. He was standing up, but he seemed uncertain on his feet. His eyes were red-rimmed and when he spoke, he words weren't uttered crisply.

"Little Ocampa," he began, and then seemed to lose track of what he wanted to say next. He sat down heavily on a long, low bench that stood against one wall of the cluttered room. He raised one hand and gestured vaguely with it, and she surmised that he was telling her to sit opposite him. She did.

"Didn't . . . feel like being . . . alone. Tonight." His words were halting and slurred. She was astonished; she had never seen him—never seen anyone—behave like this. Was he ill?

"A woman . . . understands. You understand. Don't you?" He sounded like a confused child, and had she not hated him so much she might have felt sorry for him.

"I hope so, Maje," she said neutrally. She hoped only to escape this encounter without his hitting her, and carefully edited her words and her demeanor not to set off his volatile temper.

But Jabin was in another mood entirely, morose and self-pitying. "Should have . . . been the most powerful of Majes . . . why am I here, on this cursed planet with no water . . . no family . . . I had a family once . . . did you know that?"

"No, Maje."

"A woman . . . two sons . . . killed by the Nistrim. Butchered. I still dream of them."

"I'm sorry."

He grunted at this and rose, proceeded unsteadily to a table that was piled with various artifacts, and picked up a dark glass bottle. He drank from it briefly, then stoppered it and put it down again. He looked at her with a rueful smile. "I'll pay for this tomorrow. My mouth . . . will be drier than the sands . . . but sometimes . . ." He trailed off and went back to the bench, where he lay down. Kes sat very still as she watched his eyelids droop closed, but only when he was snoring strongly did she feel safe in leaving.

The next morning Jabin was in a terrible temper, and even his men did their best to stay out of his sight. He took the water rations of several people, including Kes, to slake his heightened thirst.

The second time he became intoxicated—for she now knew this is what was happening to him—was not so easy. He summoned her well before he was ready to pass out and indicated that she should sit next to him on the bench. He had a cup of gannit from which he sipped as he told her long, rambling tales of his valor and cunning.

"One day the Ogla will achieve supremacy over all the Kazon," he declared emphatically. He seemed agitated, bursting with energy, and Kes was fearful; these were the moods in which he was most volatile. "We have the only supply of cormaline, and if I manipulate the market properly, they'll all have to come begging to me." He took a healthy swig of the drink, then put one hand on her thigh as he continued to rant.

"I'll get off this planet, as soon as the mines are barren, and trade the cormaline for more ships, warships, stocked with weaponry. And then I'll make my move." As he spoke, he punctuated his words by squeezing her thigh. Kes felt bile rising in her throat and her mind searched desperately for a way to get away from him.

"You're very clever, Maje," she said, sliding off the couch and reaching for his cup. "Let me get you a little more." She went to the table and poured more of the liquor into his cup, then returned it to him, forcing herself to smile at him. He took the cup and drank, but before she could back away, his hand snaked out and grabbed her arm, pulling her back down on the bench.

"I do get lonely," he continued. "I had a family once . . . a woman, two sons . . ."

"I know." He turned abruptly to look at her, puzzled.

"How could you know? I've never mentioned it before."

"Forgive me, Maje, but on another lonely night you told me about them. They were killed by the Nistrim."

He stared, utterly perplexed. "That's right," he said finally, "but I have no memory of having told you. I rarely mention them."

"I was honored that you would share it with me." His hand was on her thigh again, squeezing aimlessly.

"Little Ocampa," he murmured, now trailing his hand up and down her leg, "you're nothing like her. She was a big woman, strong and passionate. She always told me I was the only man who could satisfy her. You're such a pallid little thing, it's hard to imagine you in lust." His other hand was now on her cheek, her shoulder, her upper arm. His liquor-laden breath stifled her and for a moment she thought she might be sick at her stomach. It occurred to her that a beating might be preferable to this.

He spent some minutes fondling her body, telling her erotic stories about his amorous wife. Kes sat quietly, enduring it, refusing to look him in the eye. Finally he uttered an oath of disgust, shoved her aside, and returned to his cup. "Icy little bird. It would take the heat of a thousand suns to warm you up."

He took the cup and walked out into the hot desert night; Kes waited for a long time before she dared to venture back to her pallet, where, in spite of the heat, she shivered uncontrollably.

Two weeks after that, Neelix came into her life.

She'd been aware that someone new had visited their camp, a man of a species unlike the Kazon, who brought water in return for cormaline. She had watched from the recesses of Jabin's room as the two men talked and negotiated, but she kept to her usual practice of staying out of sight unless called for.

She liked the voice of the visitor; there was a kindness to it that Kes hadn't heard in a long time, and after the man had visited, she was able to conjure visions of home, where compassion and tenderness were so widespread. She found herself looking forward to this stranger's visits, so she could sit in the darkness in a corner of the room and listen to his gentle voice.

One night Jabin summoned her to his room and when she entered she realized with dread that he had been drinking gannit again.

This time, he was neither melancholy nor amorous. His eyes flickered hotly and he paced from one end of the crowded room to the other. "You know how to get back to your underground city. Did you think I believed your lie? I'd hoped you would reward my generosity to you by giving me the information, but I can see you're entirely too selfish to do that. I'll get it out of you, don't think I won't."

Fear nibbled at her belly. He hadn't mentioned the tunnel in quite a while, and she'd hoped he'd given it up as a lost cause. Now, in his liquor-induced madness, it became a dangerous subject.

"Do you think it's painful when I beat you? You have no idea what real pain can be. I promise you, it won't be long before you'll be promising me anything if I will just stop hurting you."

"Maje, I've served you faithfully. Please believe me when I tell you I couldn't find the tunnel again—"

"Quiet!" His voice was an explosion that reverberated through the night. He leaned across the table toward her, eyes glittering, frenzied. "Think about it all night, little Ocampa. That frail body of yours won't stand much, I promise you. Go. We'll see if you're more cooperative tomorrow morning."

He turned away from her and drained the last of his cup of gannit. Kes scurried away and huddled on her pallet, terrified, afraid for the sun to rise again.

But morning brought no mention of the tunnel, or of his threats of hideous torture. She stayed out of sight at the back of the room, hoping the liquor had clouded his memory. Then a figure entered the room and she heard Jabin say, "Did you bring water?"

The visitor whose voice she cherished replied, "Indeed, my good friend, I have seven barrels—cool and pure. It should slake your thirst handsomely."

Jabin called out an order and almost instantly a water barrel was brought before him. "Ocampa!" he yelled, and Kes quailed. He'd not forgotten about her. She walked out of the protective darkness and toward the two men, hoping to escape this encounter without being hurt.

This was the first time she had seen the visitor closely. He wasn't nearly as large as the Kazon, and had a series of spots patterned on his head and hands. A fine ruff of hair protruded from the top of his head and spilled down his back, and his eyes, a yellow-orange, were as kind as his voice. A feeling of peace came over her when she looked at him, and she decided that was because he was an innately good man.

Jabin jerked his head toward the water barrel and Kes understood that he wanted her to serve them. She drew cups of water for both, then withdrew slightly, hoping to stay out of Jabin's vision.

But she was intensely aware that the other man was staring at her, as though transfixed. Jabin laughed. "Quite a beauty, isn't she? But that's where her assets end. She's all but worthless as a slave. Tires easily, wilts in the heat, no strength at all."

"I can see that," said the visitor. "She's frail. Probably sickly. I might find household work for her, if you'd be interested in trading."

Kes could hardly contain herself at this statement. Was it possible this man might get her out of the Kazon encampment? Would Jabin be willing to trade her for water? She didn't quite hear what they were

343

saying next, she was so excited. But when she tuned back in, that excitement shattered, to be replaced by despair.

"She's worth nothing to me as a worker," Jabin was saying. "But she has information I'm determined to get. She's proved recalcitrant so far, but I'm ready to move to more persuasive methods."

He hadn't forgotten the night before. He intended to do terrible things to her, to force her to reveal the hiding place of the tunnel opening. What could she do? Panic rose and she tried to will it away, tried to keep her mind composed so she could devise a plan. In desperation, she felt her mind reaching out to the kind stranger, the man who had suggested taking her away. *"Please . . . help me . . ."*

The visitor turned toward her and blinked. She knew he had received her thought, and was comforted by that. "Send her away, Jabin," he was saying. "I'd like to talk to you alone."

Jabin jerked his head and Kes hurried from the room into the white glare of the sun. She was grateful to be out of Jabin's presence, if even for a moment. What were they talking about? Why did the stranger have her sent from the room? Was it possible he wasn't as kind as she thought, and was even helping Jabin prepare torments for her?

No. He was a good man, she was sure of that. Her mind had told her that immediately, and she trusted the instinct. She could only hope that he had some kind of plan that would spare her from torture, even if he couldn't get her off the planet. She comforted herself with that thought as the Ogla miners gathered round, making lewd remarks about her as was their wont.

Presently, the visitor came out of the stone structure, squinting in the brightness of the day, searching till he found her. His sweet eyes locked on to her, and she felt her mind reaching out once more. *"I feel I can trust you."*

The man walked toward her. "You can," he said with sincerity. "I am your friend. Come walk with me, and let's talk." When they had moved out of earshot of the miners, he said, "I've convinced Jabin to let me try to befriend you, so that you'll reveal the opening of the tunnel to your city. We can keep him at a distance for a while, until I can figure out a way to get you off the planet."

Kes was so relieved she almost stumbled, her legs suddenly without bone and muscle to support her. The man held tightly to her arm until she steadied herself. "Thank you," she breathed. "He was going to torture me."

"I know. I couldn't let that happen."

She clutched his arm as though afraid ever to let go. "I don't know what to call you," she said.

"I'm Neelix."

"I'm Kes. What a good man you are."

"I wish that were true."

"It is. I knew it the first time I heard you speak. You're the first good person I've met since I came from underground."

"Tell me about your city. You've lived underground all your life? You've never been in space?"

Kes hesitated. She felt suddenly foolish when she thought of all the circumstances that had brought her to this wretched pass. She wanted this man to care about her, not to discover what a rash and impetuous child she'd been. So she gave the briefest of accounts, ending with the acknowledgment that coming to the surface was a foolhardy thing to do.

But Neelix patted her hand affectionately. "I think it was courageous of you. And you're not to worry about it anymore, because together we'll come up with a way to rescue you."

For almost two weeks, Neelix visited the encampment frequently, spending long hours with Kes. He told her about himself, and she ached with sorrow when she heard of the horrendous loss of his family. He talked about being addicted to something horrible called "Rhuludian crystals," and how painful the process was when he was forced off them by a friend—a friend who was now languishing in prison on an alien world.

Kes was happier than she'd ever been, and was only vaguely aware of Jabin, who largely left them alone, though he lurked on the periphery. From time to time Neelix would visit him, reporting the "progress" he was making in winning Kes's confidence.

Then he told her he had a plan. "It's risky, sweeting," he admitted, "but all of life is a risk. I think we can do this."

"Tell me."

They were sitting on the remains of an ancient wall, part of the Ocampan city that had been here so many generations ago. Kes liked to prowl among the ruins, imagining what it had been like for her ancestors, when the planet was green and cool, and all of life was lived in the sunlight. There was time for such exploration since Neelix had concocted his plan; Jabin was only too eager to give them time alone. Of course, he found other ways to make Kes's life a torment: he had taken away her water rations that day, and her mouth was parched, her lips cracked and sore.

"Tomorrow I'll tell him you've agreed to show me the opening— but only me," Neelix said. "I'll offer to go with you to the site and memorize its location. What he won't know is that my little ship will be parked not far from there, so that you and I can run for it and leave the planet before he realizes we're not coming back."

Kes pondered this. It sounded possible. Dangerous, but possible. "But what then? Won't he try to follow us?"

Neelix smiled and patted her hand lovingly. "Don't you worry about that. I know this part of space better than I know my own spots. I know hiding places. I have friends. And I can always whip up a little bad blood between the Ogla and the Sara, which will give Jabin more to worry about than one escaped serving girl."

Kes nodded. She was feeling weak from dehydration, and the heat of the sun was making her light-headed. She covered her eyes briefly.

"What is it? What's wrong?" The concern in Neelix's voice was palpable.

"Jabin took away my water rations. I'm a little dizzy . . ."

"That monster. I'll go speak to him." He rose and was starting back toward the camp, but she grabbed his sleeve.

"No, don't do anything to provoke him. He's leaving us alone, let's keep it that way. It's only one more day."

She saw Neelix squeeze his lips together, as though trying hard not to say something that wanted to come out. Finally he nodded, though his eyes were clouded with misgiving.

That night, as she lay on her pallet, thirsty and unable to sleep, full of anticipation for the escape attempt tomorrow, she heard a whispered voice call her name. She raised up, and saw Neelix moving toward her in the darkness. He put a finger over his lips to keep her from speaking aloud, then he gave her a canister.

It was water. Joyfully she clutched it, and reached out a hand to touch his cheek in gratitude. Then he slipped away in the darkness once more. Kes opened the canister and drank greedily, experiencing a euphoria that she thought must be more powerful than that produced by gannit or even Rhuludian crystals. The canister was still at her lips when she heard the muffled shouts from outside.

Quickly she hid the water container and moved to the doorway. Angry shouts carried easily through the night air, and with a chill she realized the Kazon had discovered that Neelix had stolen water, and were chasing him.

She drew back into the room, panicked. She had to find a better hiding place for the water, for if Jabin knew Neelix had brought it to her, he would punish both of them severely. She retrieved the canister from beneath her pallet and stood holding it in two hands, turning in the room, trying to think of a place to secrete it.

That was when Jabin came to the door. He lunged at her, grabbing the canister and jerking her arm so hard she feared he was pulling it from the socket. He dragged her like that into his squalid chamber, where a solitary light burned. "Did you put him up to this?" Jabin demanded, shaking her roughly.

"Yes," she chattered, "it was my idea. Don't blame him—I couldn't help it, I was so thirsty. I begged him. He was just being kind."

"Do you know what happens to those who steal water?" he challenged, shaking her even more viciously. Kes felt as though her eyes were banging against her brain.

This couldn't be happening, not on the eve of their escape. Kes tried desperately to think of a way to placate Jabin, to preserve their plan for tomorrow. "It's all my fault. Please, it wouldn't be right to punish Neelix. You and he are friends—"

"No longer!" snapped Jabin. "I've been waiting weeks for him to provide me with certain information, but all I've gotten are excuses. Now he betrays me by stealing the most important resource I possess. He'll discover what betrayal costs a man." Jabin was interrupted at this point by one of his men, who entered the room breathless from running.

"Well?" the Maje barked.

"He got to his ship and was gone before we reached him," gasped the Kazon.

Jabin brought down a burly fist onto the table, knocking over several glasses. He turned toward Kes, fury distending the ridges in his forehead. "Tomorrow we begin. I think very shortly you'll be telling me the information I've wasted two weeks waiting for. Go to bed."

Kes exited as quickly as she could. Desperate thoughts swarmed through her mind: Could she try to slip away under cover of night? Could she find a place to hide, to elude Jabin? Might she even find the opening to the tunnel in the dark and somehow get back to her home? But none of those seemed like viable options. She had no idea how to find the rock outcropping that contained the tunnel; the desert was black at night and she'd have no sense of direction.

Could she find a weapon and take her own life before morning? It would be preferable to what Jabin had in store, she was certain. But the Kazon didn't leave energy weapons lying around for anyone to pick up. And the thought of something crude and uncertain, like a knife, made her queasy enough to know she could never bring herself to use it.

She lay on the rough mat, trying to think of other possibilities. Finally, she decided that she wouldn't simply submit to Jabin's torture without a fight. She might hesitate to use a knife on herself, but she'd use one on him in a second. She rose and moved in the darkness to a nearby table, where she knew a knife was used for cutting bread. She fumbled for it, finally felt its sheath, and, running her finger along its jagged blade, wondered how she could hide it on herself until she could use it on Jabin.

It was at that moment that she heard the first explosion.

The outbuilding trembled, and the night air was lit by an orange flash as a thunderous sound impacted painfully on her eardrums. Immediately she heard men shouting, running, calling for help. Frightened but curious, she ran to the window and looked out.

One of the ruins nearby was ablaze. With as little water as was in this encampment, it was unlikely any of it would be used for fire suppression, and the vestige of the ancient Ocampan city would be left to burn to the ground. She felt a small twinge of regret that part of her past would be incinerated in such a fashion. What had caused this conflagration?

No sooner had that question come to mind than she saw an amazing sight: a small alien ship, similar to those of the Ogla, was swooping through the night, weapons firing steadily, yellow beams of energy lancing from ship to ground, producing explosions and fire everywhere. Jabin's men were running in all directions, shouting at each other, disorganized, trying to evade the brutal weapons fire.

Some of them had reached their own ships, and soon she saw several of them rise from the desert floor and quickly engage the enemy fighter ships. The dark night was now brilliantly alight with the incandescent glow of the weapons fire, and Kes could see well across the floor of the desert.

What she saw was an army of men approaching, running toward their encampment, hand weapons drawn. A loose phalanx of Ogla had drawn a defensive line to meet them, and soon both sides were engaged in fire, and, quickly, hand-to-hand combat.

Kes drew back into the recesses of the small building, trying to grasp the meaning of this turn of events. Who were these attackers? Would they consider her part of the Ogla camp and kill her, too? Or would Jabin's forces be strong enough to withstand the onslaught and fight them off?

The noise level was escalating, as weapons fire erupted in an endless concatenation, and the shouts and screams of men in battle rose in cacophonous counterpoint. It was worse, somehow, to hear the sounds of the melee without seeing it, and she started to move again to the window when the door burst open and a dark figure exploded into the room.

It was Jabin. He was looking for something, pawing through the detritus on the table, pulling items out of cupboards. Kes shrank back into the corner as far as she could, curling herself into a tight ball so as to be as hard to see as possible.

Jabin finally found what he was looking for—a small hand weapon. No sooner did he have it in hand than another figure hurled itself into the room and directly at Jabin, who grunted under the impact and lost the weapon, which went skidding across the room directly toward Kes.

"I don't need a weapon, you Sara offal," growled Jabin as the two men scuffled. "I'll enjoy killing you with my bare hands."

"You'll need four or five others to do that, Ogla scum," snarled the other man, who Kes decided was a Kazon, but of another sect. He looked not unlike Jabin, but his headdress was somewhat different, though equally outlandish. The two were crouching, circling, looking for an opening, and continuing to hurl epithets at each other.

"My sister could dispatch you, vermin."

"Your sister is only good for one thing—every man in my squad can attest to that."

"Your mother spreads her legs in hell."

Kes found these interchanges extremely odd. What purpose could it serve to insult each other's relatives? What did that have to do with anything? If these men had a dispute, why didn't they resolve it by discussing it; or, if they felt combat was absolutely necessary, why not just get on with it? What sort of strange ritual was involved with these perverse denunciations?

But it seemed to whip both men into some greater lather, and suddenly they sprang toward each other, collided heavily, and then went sprawling onto the floor, grappling, fists pounding, boots digging into the floor for traction, grunting and swearing and clawing at each other.

It was quite remarkable, and had she not been so vulnerable she might have found it interesting to observe. But no matter what the outcome of this brutal duel, her situation was precarious. She half-hoped it would go on and on, because as soon as there was a winner, she would be in danger once more.

Then her eye fell on the weapon which Jabin had lost, and which lay within easy reach of her now. She snaked out a hand and grabbed it, feeling its cold metal in her hand like a balm. Suddenly her situation had reversed itself: not only was she not vulnerable, she held the upper hand. The realization was heady, intoxicating, until she realized she had uneasy choices. Should she wait until this primal struggle was over and there was a clear winner—and kill him? Kill both of them right now? Would that do any good when there were dozens of other combatants outside, still fighting, the outcome of the overall battle still in doubt?

Questions, questions. Why did her mind work like that? Why couldn't things ever present themselves simply, with obvious answers?

Then she realized that Jabin was taking the worse of it; the other man was seated astride him, one hand around Jabin's throat, the other holding one of Jabin's arms away from him. Jabin was choking, clawing at the man's hand, trying to pry it from his throat.

"You're breathing your last, Ogla," gasped the other man. "You're heading for hell and it won't be my mother that greets you there."

Suddenly the choice was clear. Kes raised the weapon and, without hesitating, fired it at the back of the man who was choking Jabin. His body jerked spasmodically and he released his hold on his captive, sprawling sideways and onto the floor. Jabin stared at him for a moment, then climbed out from under the inert body and stood, looking in astonishment at Kes.

She kept the weapon trained on him. "Is he dead?" she asked unflinchingly.

"He's just stunned. But you can be sure I'll take care of that." He took a step toward her but she raised the weapon slightly to affirm her intent.

"I didn't hesitate to use this on him and I won't spare you either, Jabin."

Jabin stopped. "If the Kazon-Sara defeat us and you've injured one of them, it will go hard on you. And if my men are victorious and you've injured me, it will be worse. Give me the weapon."

Kes pondered his words. They made a certain perverse sense, and suddenly she wasn't so confident anymore. As she hesitated, he suddenly sprang at her and wrested the weapon from her grasp.

"That's better. I must go help my men." He turned to the door only to be greeted by one of his aides, out of breath and bleeding from a head wound.

"They've turned tail, Maje," the man gasped. "We've routed them."

Jabin clapped the man on the shoulder. "Water rations for all," he announced, then turned back to Kes, who shrank miserably back against the wall. He stared at her for a moment, then regarded the figure on the floor. He made an adjustment to the weapon and then fired once toward the fallen man.

He vaporized.

Kes drew a shocked breath, then shut her eyes, believing that the same fate awaited her. At least she would be spared the promised torture. But only silence prevailed, and she opened her eyes again to see Jabin looking at her with what might almost pass as gratitude.

"My life is yours, Ocampa. That's a debt no Kazon would fail to honor. I'll keep you here because I enjoy you, but you have my word I won't hurt you again."

And with that he walked out of the room. Kes sank onto the floor and, for the first time in weeks, began to cry.

Two days later there were no signs of the battle. The one Ocampa ruin was destroyed, of course, but that was hardly remarkable. Jabin's men had buried their dead and tossed the bodies of the Sara victims into the desert as feast for the insects—the only life-form to have survived the intense heat of the last millennium.

Kes had a black eye and a split lip from the last time Jabin had smashed her face, but he had kept his word and not laid a hand on her since the night of the attack. The work, however, was as punishing as ever, the rations as meager, and the heat as stifling. She was torn between trying to escape back to her underground city, and waiting to see if, somehow, Neelix might still be able to take her away from this awful place.

She knew, of course, that the likelihood of that was slim. He had angered Jabin, and the Maje wasn't one to forgive easily. Neelix was but one man, in a dilapidated starship, who couldn't possibly hope to take on this well-armed contingent of Kazon warriors.

Finding the access tunnel that would take her home again seemed like the only viable option. She began laying plans to escape, noting

Jabin's schedule, the times when most of the men were in the mines, secreting scraps of food and droplets of water to sustain her in her walk across the desert floor.

She was sitting in the shade, chipping cormaline, pondering the best time to make her escape, when she heard a great outcry of voices. The Kazon were shouting angrily, and her heart constricted with fear as she thought they were coming for her.

Tentatively, she rose and crept toward a space between two of the compound's buildings, edging close enough to be able to hear what was happening. She had deduced that the Kazon had taken a captive and were threatening to execute him, when suddenly she heard Neelix's voice! He was the one they were about to dispatch. Paralyzed, she listened as his dear voice called out, imploring them.

"Jabin! My old friend."

A silence followed. Then Neelix again: "Water! I have water to replace all that I borrowed!"

Her breath caught sharply. If he could bring them water, they might forgive him, and he might then be able to get her off this wretched planet. She eased forward, closer and closer.

"Their ship has technology that can make water out of thin air," Neelix was saying.

There was another silence, then Jabin spoke. "You have more?"

And then a woman's voice, strong and commanding, completely unafraid: "Janeway to *Voyager*. Energize."

Something in the woman's voice compelled her to move forward, to hear better and even to see who possessed this confident manner. She heard complexities in the voice, richness and compassion and wisdom. And in that moment, she knew it was a voice she would instinctively follow, no matter where it led.

CHAPTER

13

NEELIX DIDN'T KNOW WHEN SLEEP RECLAIMED HIM—IF, IN FACT, HE'D EVER been awake—but he opened his eyes in the morning feeling more peaceful than he had in some time.

And closer to Kes than ever.

There was solace in understanding what had brought her above ground, what had precipitated her great adventure. He believed, though he would never say this to anyone, that she had heard his story, and decided to share hers with him. It was an extraordinary gesture, and it buoyed him, draining anxiety and coating him in a balm of well-being. Because now he knew that Tuvok was right: she was still with them.

The hollowing out of the underground chamber was a slow process. Harry and B'Elanna worked in shifts, patiently beaming out pulverized psilminite and depositing it in silty layers behind the storage facility in the quarries. Neelix was able to check the progress several times the next day and, just as he'd thought, the guards didn't suspect a thing. The dust from the ore materialized in the air and filtered to the ground in a fine mist, adding to the layers of dust that had already accumulated.

The quarries were hot, and dirty, and the work, though not physically demanding, wasn't pleasant. There was no shade from the unrelenting sun, and the clouds of dust from the ore settled on the workers, clogging pores, irritating the nose and lungs, and leaving a bitter, alkaline taste in the mouth.

Neelix tended to work with Tassot Bnay, whose generosity with the work passes had allowed the Talaxian to escape the camp and take advantage of the food—and of course the duotronic components—available to the work detail.

But although the tall and elegant Rai' had befriended him, Neelix didn't reveal to him the elaborate escape plans of his group. He could trust no one in a place like this.

"Do you think you'll ever get out of here, see your home again?" he asked Bnay as they toiled to load the antigrav sleds.

"There have been prisoner exchanges in the past. But none for a long time. I don't know why."

Neelix was impressed by the composure of this man, who always seemed to rise above the indignities of his situation, his bearing erect, his demeanor calm. He personified a quality Neelix had long sought, and that was dignity.

"Will the war ever end, do you think?" Neelix inquired.

Bnay shrugged. "My father fought in this war. And his father before him."

Neelix was amazed. His own experience with war had been horrendous, but short-lived. He couldn't imagine a strife that endured for generations. "Is there no end in sight? Aren't there those who are working for peace?"

Bnay looked at him with mild astonishment. "Peace? It's a concept that has lost all meaning among our people. The war defines us. We are instructed in battle from childhood, and every Rai' is prepared to endure the prisoner camps, to survive them in hopes of being exchanged."

"But . . . if you are exchanged . . . will you go right back to war?"

"Of course."

Neelix pondered this diffident statement. He was often bemused by the behavior of the Federations, who possessed an ethic that he couldn't quite grasp—though he was trying—but one thing he respected about them was their abhorrence of violence. Oh, they'd fight when they had to, but they clearly preferred to avoid armed conflict, and worked to find nonviolent solutions to problems. Neelix was convinced this was the way to conduct oneself, war having taken from him what he held most dear, and so it was difficult to accept Bnay's calm acceptance of an enduring state of battle.

The guards, as usual, were lolling about in the only area of the quarries that afforded shade, a rocky overhang that jutted from the side of the hill into which the quarries were dug. They all chewed on a fibrous root which Neelix was beginning to suspect had narcotic qualities, as the guards became first jovial, then relaxed and sleepy as the day wore on. By the end of the day they were short-tempered and irritable, as though the euphoric sensations they had experienced were wearing off. Memories of his days on Rhuludian crystals made him shiver with distaste, and he thought once again of Wix and the loyalty he had demonstrated in forcing Neelix off that pernicious drug.

"I'm going to exchange this antigrav sled," Neelix announced to Bnay in midafternoon. "It's a little sluggish."

Bnay nodded and Neelix guided the sled around the periphery of the quarries to the storage area. It abutted both the hill and the adjacent forest, into which Neelix now peered. If their plan worked, they would have to plunge into that foreboding dark woods, with nothing more to guide them than Chakotay's instincts. It was a sobering thought.

Neelix saw that the process of transporting ore from underground was continuing. Even as he approached, a cloud of powdery dust materialized in the air and then sifted quietly to the ground, indistinguishable from the silt that was already there. It was a good plan.

He guided the antigrav sled to the end of a row of several others, then spent a moment selecting a replacement. As his eyes swept the row of sleds, he noticed the footprints he had left in the white dust, and then their gentle disappearance as another load of transported ore dust materialized and settled to the ground. He felt a moment of pride as he reflected on the ingenuity of his comrades, and a lifting of the spirits as he sensed that this escape plan, which had sounded so tenuous at first, was proceeding flawlessly.

He guided the second sled out of the storage area, leaving more footprints behind, and taking odd comfort in the knowledge that they would soon be covered over.

That night, after a meal supplemented by the rations Neelix had managed to smuggle from the quarries, B'Elanna made a portentous announcement.

"We have to find out whether these units will transport a person."

This statement brought an energized silence to the group, all of whom were jammed into one of the shelters. Everyone was keenly aware of the dangers of trying to transport anything as complex as a biological organism, especially without the safety factor of the pattern buffer. The units B'Elanna and Harry had created worked just fine on psilminite, but that was no guarantee they would be able to handle the infinitely more difficult process of dematerializing and rematerializing a living person. A moment passed before anyone spoke.

"It should be me," said Chakotay quietly. "I'm in command."

"That's exactly why it can't be you, Commander," said Tom. "We can't afford to lose you. Besides, you're the one with the captain's message implanted in you. We'll need that to complete the escape."

There was a murmuring of agreement with that statement. "I'll do it," said B'Elanna. "Harry can beam me." She smiled wryly. "I made these things. If anyone's the guinea pig, it should be me."

"You're another person we can't lose, B'Elanna," said Harry. "If something goes wrong, you'll need to modify the transporters. So you beam me, instead."

It went like this for a few minutes, with almost everyone volunteering to be the first transportee, when a deep and determined voice emerged from the back of the shelter.

"I shall go."

It was Vorik, and something in his voice made everyone stop and look at him. "It is the most logical decision. I am the least senior member of this party. Should a mishap occur, my presence will not be missed."

"That's not true, Vorik," said B'Elanna instantly. She had a fondness for the young Vulcan, even though he'd given her a world of trouble when he went through the Pon farr and declared his amorous intentions toward her. "We'd all miss you."

"Thank you, Lieutenant, but I meant the statement not in an emotional sense, rather in a practical one. I perform no essential service here and the group would not suffer my absence."

There was a quiet moment before Tuvok spoke. "My young counterpart's logic is unassailable." He walked to Vorik and put his hand on the young man's shoulder. "You do us proud, Ensign," he said somberly, and only a few blinks of the eye betrayed Vorik's pride in his mentor's statement.

"I'll want to check out all the components before we try it," said

B'Elanna, and bent to the task as Harry did the same on the second transporter. While they worked, each member of the group approached Vorik to offer words of encouragement and support. The young man accepted them stoically, but there were those who would swear they saw his eyes begin to shine wetly.

"All right, I think we're set. Harry?"

Harry looked up at B'Elanna and nodded.

"The question is—where do we beam him? We can't risk materializing him where he can be seen."

"Put him into the other shelter," suggested Chakotay.

"Good idea," agreed Harry. "I'll go over there with the second transporter, and be ready to send him back. That way we'll have a test of both units."

Minutes later, Harry left the shelter with the second transporter contained in a tarpaulin they'd acquired, his arm around Coris, whispering to her as though they were taking this opportunity to get some time alone.

B'Elanna positioned Vorik in the center of the shelter, directly in front of the transporter. "Ready?" she inquired, and Vorik, eyes straight ahead, nodded briskly.

Neelix realized that Vorik actually had his eyes fastened on Tuvok's, a gaze so strong it might have been a forcefield. He could almost sense the strength that Tuvok was willing to the young man.

"Okay. This is it." B'Elanna took one quick glance toward Vorik, drew a deep breath, and then said, "Energizing." And she pressed the controls.

It didn't look like a transport any of them had ever seen before. Vorik began to shimmer, which was expected, but then patches of him faded and vanished, only to reappear a second later. He became a strangely undulating figure, as his right thigh went, and then returned, then his left arm and shoulder, a shimmering, half-dematerializing presence that would neither disappear nor be restored to a whole.

Perspiration broke out on B'Elanna's forehead. "The annular confinement beam is destabilizing. I'm compensating."

Vorik's eyes, when they were visible, had gone wide with some unidentifiable emotion, but he kept them locked on Tuvok's. His jaws were tensed from clamping his teeth tightly together. He was clearly experiencing profound distress.

"All right, I'm reestablishing the confinement beam," said B'Elanna, trying to keep the emotion from her voice. Neelix himself felt as though a block of ice had settled in his stomach, and he realized he was digging his fingernails into his palms. It was harrowing, watching poor Vorik come apart in bits and clumps. He could only imagine what the young Vulcan was feeling.

B'Elanna pushed the controls again with fingers that were a little shaky. Then she looked up at Vorik.

Piece by piece, part by part, he was dematerializing, in a patchwork effect that reminded Neelix of the quilts his mother used to fashion. Foot, arm, eyes, belly—a grotesque, distorted image of a young man dissolving as though by the random splash of acid.

Finally, he was gone.

There was a mass exhalation of breath among the group. "Neelix," Chakotay said quickly, "go see if he made it."

Neelix hurried out of the shelter and into the chill night air, into the noisy, braying organism that was the prison camp, with its fetid smells and its fearful sounds, and raced the few steps to the second shelter, bursting in through the canvas that covered the entry.

Except for Harry and Coris, it was empty.

Neelix felt as though a fist had been driven into his abdomen, and reflexively, he bent over. "Isn't he here?" he asked unnecessarily, for it was apparent Vorik was not in the shelter.

Harry shook his head, looking pale.

Then, before them, an arm appeared.

Followed by a pair of feet, a midsection, part of a head.

It took an agonizing ten seconds longer, but finally, Vorik the Vulcan stood in front of them, fully materialized.

They stared at him, afraid to speak, afraid to move for fear he would vanish again. Vorik himself appeared to be in shock, and Neelix half expected him to fall unconscious—or dead—at their feet.

But finally Vorik drew a breath and gazed at them with eyes that were once more imperturbable. "That was a most unusual experience," he intoned, and then his legs began to wobble and give way.

Neelix and Harry caught him and helped him to sit, and only after ascertaining that, although somewhat shaken by the ordeal, Vorik was physically intact did Neelix leave to report the good news to B'Elanna and the others.

"Thank goodness," said B'Elanna when Neelix had finished. "I see now what the problem was—I'll have to compensate for the variance in our power supply. That should take care of the problem."

"I'll happily volunteer to let you test that theory," said Neelix. He felt that only exposing himself to the same ordeal would help to get rid of the icy knot in his stomach.

And when, minutes later, he was transported to the second shelter, the process was, if somewhat slower than the beam-outs he was accustomed to, reasonably smooth and comfortable. Harry's transporter was modified to make the corrections B'Elanna had ordered, and both Neelix and Vorik were beamed back to the first shelter without incident.

It was a unanimous decision that Vorik should get extra rations that night, but if Vorik was to be rewarded for his bravery, he had other ideas as to the compensation.

"It was you who gave me the courage, sir," said the young man to Tuvok. "I felt your strength sustaining me during the experience."

"If I was able to contribute to the success of the endeavor, then I am gratified," replied Tuvok with Vulcan modesty.

"I should like to ask you for something more," continued Vorik.

"What is that?"

"I would like to share in your wisdom and your experience. If you, like some of the others, would speak of your early years—"

That was as far as he got before Tuvok held up a restraining hand. "I do not care to expose my life in this public company."

"Hmmm," said Neelix with a sly twinkle. "Things in that shady past you're ashamed of?"

"Not at all. It is simply unseemly to disclose the intimate details of my life."

"That didn't stop Chakotay, or Harry, or Tom, or B'Elanna or Neelix," said Seven of Nine, and Neelix could have sworn he saw a glimmer of humor in her blue eyes.

"That's right," agreed Chakotay. "I doubt you could shock us after all we've heard already."

"I am not concerned about shocking you."

"Then what's the problem?" queried Tom. "Why not give us a peek into that Vulcan mind of yours?"

Tuvok was beginning to feel that a tide of determination had taken over the room. It was as though the collective energy of the group had been galvanized toward one purpose: convincing him to unveil the innermost secrets of his life.

But that, in his mind, was not good enough reason for him to agree to it. He felt quite capable of withstanding the most vigorous onslaught by his fellow crew.

What he wasn't prepared for was the unexpected plea that came from Vorik.

"Sir," said the young man with respect, but with an underlying urgency, "you have been my mentor. You assisted me in withstanding the rigors of the Pon farr. You have guided me in meditative techniques. You helped me endure the recent ordeal of transporting. Do you not think that there would be much I could gain from hearing of your own journey toward wisdom and enlightenment?"

Tuvok was silent for a moment, reflecting on what Vorik had said. It was true, he realized, that there were many of his life's experiences that might prove of value to a young man. He had, after all, done some things, and seen some things, that few Vulcans ever had. If Vorik were to become aware of them, the young man's moral fiber might be enhanced. For that matter, so might that of everyone else in the room. Perhaps they were right. Perhaps he had no right to withhold the events of his life from them.

And so he regarded the people in the room austerely, and said, simply, "Very well."

CHAPTER

14

"ARISE, TUVOK. THE MORNING IS HALF GONE."

Tuvok lifted his head from the pallet and squinted out the window. He saw T'Khut, Vulcan's sister planet, hanging just above the mountains, huge and ringed with red. Dawn was just beginning to break, and the desert floor was still dark. This didn't surprise him; his mother usually rose hours before the sun and considered sleeping until daybreak a wastrel's schedule. He put his head down again and closed his eyes, though reason told him there was no point in this delaying tactic: his mother would loom over him until he pulled himself from the pallet and stood before her, awake and alert.

But on this morning, reason failed to move him. He was fresh from rapturous dreams, and he craved their seductions. He sank again into drowsy mists, trying to recapture the delicious images. What was it that had been so pleasurable? A silken voice began singing in his head, a low and keening song, and he was inexorably drawn toward it. He found himself walking down a long and richly appointed corridor, following the siren song, which emanated from a door at the end, a door draped in rich brocades . . .

"Tuvok. Do not make me call you again." This voice was not

silken. It was hard and glittering as a diamond, slicing through the vaporous dream world as easily as a blade carves through ripe fruit.

"I am awake, Mother," said Tuvok, defying reason once again by hoping that this pronouncement would satisfy T'Meni and make her leave the room, allowing him to drift once more into that opulent corridor and move inevitably toward the singing voice.

"I did not tell thee to wake, I told thee to rise."

Tuvok's eyes snapped open and he sat up instantly. His mother's use of the formal mode was not to be ignored. The Eldest of a house could use it with any of her family, of course, but T'Meni was not the Eldest Mother—that honor fell to his great-aunt Elieth. Why had his mother chosen the formal mode at this hour of the morning?

He rose to his feet and peered at her in the darkness. One rosy finger of light had begun to snake its way down the mountains beyond the desert, and it cast some small illumination into Tuvok's room. The chamber was sparsely furnished, for he preferred a clean, uncluttered look, and did not wish to complicate his life with an accumulation of material objects.

His mother stood before him, tall and slender, head held erect, black eyes glinting beneath delicately upswept brows, dark skin shining in the growing light. It occurred to him—as it did almost every time he looked at her—that he resembled his mother more than he did his father, with chiseled features, finely tipped ears, and a rounded hairline. His mother at ninety-three was still a formidably handsome woman, and a formidably powerful one as well. Even though her aunt Elieth commanded the title, most people in the family accorded T'Meni all the respect of an Eldest Mother. Something about her seemed to demand it.

Tuvok regarded her curiously, reached out to touch her mind but found it sealed against his inquiry. *"No, Tuvok,"* he heard her chide. *"Thee wilt not probe for answers now. Dress and come to the table. Thy questions will be answered."*

He nodded briskly at her, though perplexity consumed him. This was most curious and inexplicable behavior on her part. What could it mean? His mind considered possibilities and rejected them instantaneously. Nothing in his twenty years' experience with his mother provided a satisfactory answer for this unusual conduct.

He bathed and dressed quickly, and by the time he had descended to the first level of their home, light from Vulcan's primary white star (its lesser stars, a white and a red dwarf, tumbled about the giant mother star like gemstones) had turned the desert into a blazon of red and illuminated the high-ceilinged, spacious rooms of the house.

His mother sat at the table, as did his father, Sunak, which was almost as surprising as the extraordinary beginnings of this day. His father was usually at the temple at this hour, meditating with the priests. In another year, Tuvok would be able to join him, for he would have passed the trial of his manhood and could retire with the adults to the temple sanctuary. It was a privilege he had been dreaming of for most of his life.

His mother nodded him into a chair and Tuvok sat, resting his hands on the polished marble of the tabletop. It was a rare, green-veined stone, much prized on Vulcan, an heirloom that had been in his family for at least eleven generations. Tuvok had always loved the feel of it, glacial, precise, and unyielding. As a small child he made almost a fetish of running his fingers over it, knowing that each time, it would feel exactly the same. Its immutability was soothing.

The cool touch of the marble helped settle the disquieting sense of puzzlement that had pervaded him since his mother's unexpected summons. The marble was as it always was, and therein lay assurance.

"Good morning, Tuvok," said his father, and Tuvok felt comforted by the gentleness in his father's voice. Sunak was not a typical Vulcan, though Tuvok would not come to realize that until he was much older. All he knew at this age was that his father's presence was calming, and, given the singular beginnings of this day, he was glad his father was not at the temple but here, at the table, kind eyes resting on his son.

Tuvok's eyes drifted to his mother's, and a unique sensation began to overtake him. How would it be described? A disquiet, perhaps, a lack of ease. Curiously, it manifested itself in his stomach, in the form of a tingling which he found thoroughly unpleasant. He made a mental note to describe the sensation in his journal, for the purpose of objectifying and then controlling it.

For now, there was no control. The sensation resided in his belly like a school of tiny fish, flickering this way and that.

He hoped his mother wouldn't continue to speak to him in the formal mode.

"Your initial schooling will be completed within four months," T'Meni announced without preamble. Tuvok nodded, this pronouncement being obvious and unremarkable. His mother hesitated before saying the next, but when she did, it was with firm conviction. "You will be going off-world at that time."

The school of fish reeled in his stomach as though they were trapped in a whirlpool. Going off-world? What was she saying? This had never been in his plans, never even been discussed.

His eyes swept toward his father, and he tried to interpret what he saw there: Pity? Compassion? Pain? None of it made sense. He drew a breath and turned toward his mother, whose elegant eyes immediately held him in her sway.

"Could you explain, Mother?" he asked in as calm a voice as he could muster. "I had never contemplated going off-world."

Something he'd never seen and couldn't identify flickered in his mother's eyes, and then was gone. "You have been accepted to Starfleet Academy, on Terra," she said quietly.

Tuvok pressed his fingers as hard as he could against the solidity of the marble; it held. There was stability in the universe. In his belly, the fish darted this way and that, careening into each other, colliding with his stomach wall. A faint taste of bile rose in his throat.

"I am entering the temple," he began, doing his best to eradicate the tiny quaver he noticed in his voice. "It's been planned for years. I will study the Disciplines, and become a priest, I've pledged myself to *cthia,* to the writings of Surak, it's all I've ever wanted . . ." He heard himself babbling, almost out of control, and closed his mouth before he embarrassed himself further.

His mother's eyes had become hard, like shale. "It is that desire which is unhealthy," she announced flintily. "It comes dangerously close to passion, which has the power to usurp reason. You must first cleanse the mind with science. Then, if passion recedes, we may reconsider."

"I have no need of science. The Disciplines will cleanse my mind. I am well on the way to achieving mastery of my volatile elements and believe I should be allowed to continue on my present course."

"The decision has been made, Tuvok."

Something hot and unpleasant burned in him. He realized the tiny fish had disappeared from his stomach, only to be replaced by a scalding ember. He drew a breath as though in physical pain, and felt his heart hammering against his ribs. Desperately, he repeated a prayer in his mind, striving for control. *Heya . . . heya . . . heya . . .* The image of Seleya, the sacred mountain, cooled his mind and his breathing became more regular.

"It is illogical to make this decision without me," he began, but his mother quickly snatched that line of defense from him.

"Do not invoke logic to support your desire. It is clear you are ruled by emotion in this matter. It must be purged, and the object of your desire denied you. Only in that way will you truly achieve *cthia.*"

Tuvok turned from his mother's implacability and sought his father's support. "Terra is a barbarous place," he pled, "and humans are intemperate and ungainly. Surely it is deleterious to spend time in such an undisciplined environment." Images of the temple crept into his mind, its vaulted ceilings and unadorned spaces, the absolute quiet, tranquil priests padding softly to their meditations. This was where he belonged.

"Have you ever been on Terra?" his father inquired mildly. "And have you ever met a human?"

Tuvok instantly regretted his rash statements, for they had led him into a corner from which there was no escape. Indeed, he had never visited Terra or met a human. He decided to make one final stabbing effort.

"I have never met an Underlier, either, but everyone knows they dwell beneath the sands of the desert. Would you suggest I deny their existence because I have never encountered one?"

Sunak turned his palms up in a gesture of diffidence. "What one has not experienced, one cannot know. What one accepts on faith is fraught with ambiguity. Once one accepts the ambiguous as truthful, one is doomed to ignorance."

Tuvok regarded his father with respect. His mother was all flinty strength, and the most powerful presence he had ever encountered; but his father for all his kindheartedness possessed a command of logic that was almost unbearably elegant. Sunak's mind could seize on a point and turn it and turn it, honing and polishing, then unspool the idea like silver wire into an argument that was tensile, incontrovertible.

Tuvok acquiesced, but allowed himself one last pettiness. "Am I at least able to choose my course of studies? Or has that been chosen for me as well?"

A lightning strike into his mind, instantaneous and searing. *"Thee will not speak with such insolence, child. Apologize at once."*

Tuvok suddenly felt like a small child again, remonstrated, powerless. Like a child's, his mind reached out to his parents', tentative and hopeful. *"I ask your forgiveness,"* he offered sincerely. *"I ask that you understand how unprepared I was for this decision. I am being unreasonable, which ill befits a person of my age. It will not happen again."*

The briskest nod from his mother, and a sweet, ineffable look from his father, ended the moment of mild rebellion. His mother plucked a crystal bell from the sideboard and rang it, summoning breakfast.

It was the last discussion they would ever have on the subject of his attending Starfleet Academy.

"Go, Tuvok, you pointy-eared wonder, go!" The howl from the sidelines carried easily to Tuvok's sensitive ears, but he hoped that for others, it would be lost in the tumult of the exuberant crowd that packed the Academy stadium. He didn't begrudge the enthusiasm of his roommate, Scott Hutchinson, but he did wish that the young man would rein in the excesses of his sobriquets. Pointy-eared wonder, indeed.

Tuvok was running the four-hundred-meter hurdle race in a track-and-field competition against their longtime foe, the University of California at Los Angeles. For generations, the "plucky little Bruins" had dominated collegiate sports in the western part of the country, until the advent of Starfleet Academy, in 2161. Gradually the Academy developed its sports program, highlighted by top-notch Parrises Squares teams, until the school rivaled mighty UCLA and the competition between them became ever more intense.

Vulcans weren't eligible for many sports because their superior physical strength gave them an unfair advantage over other species. Running, however, was open to them, and in his first year at the Academy, Tuvok had elected as his required sport to run the intermediate hurdles.

The whole emphasis on sports competition was one of the many strange anomalies he discovered when he arrived on Earth—the name by which humans referred to their world—four years ago. He was unable to understand fully the ardor with which humans treated their games. On Vulcan, games had two purposes: the dissipation of excess energy and the quieting of the mind. Neither purpose had anything to do with winning or losing, and Tuvok had never acquired the typical human determination to defeat anyone who challenged them.

Nonetheless, his natural physical prowess insured that he won most of his races, to the utter delight of his teammates and the student body, and particularly his irrepressible roommate. And he had to admit that he found running a particularly satisfying activity; now that he had adapted to the thicker and cooler air of Earth, it was bracing to sprint around the track, hurdling the barriers in a measured cadence. He found the layout of the track appealing; its symmetry pleased the eye, its neatly configured lanes with their precisely placed fences forming a unified pattern.

Tuvok and a human from UCLA had been neck-and-neck for most of the race and were heading for the last hurdles. A lusty roar from the crowd urged both runners on; Tuvok tried to shut out the din, which he found distracting, and to concentrate on his form, leaning forward as his first leg cleared the hurdle, his rear leg at nearly a right angle from his body. He worked to keep his body relaxed, the rhythm of his stride intact, the hurdle just a smooth part of the whole. Finally they were sprinting for the finish, the last forty-three meters, and Tuvok focused his mind, cleared it of everything except a tiny pinpoint of light and ran for that light, watched it get larger and larger and larger—

And he crossed the finish line one half step ahead of the UCLA runner.

The crowd erupted in a frenzy and Scott came tumbling out of the stands, orange hair falling in a mop over his freckled forehead, to fling himself on Tuvok in some kind of ecstasy, pounding him on the back and babbling almost incoherently.

"Tuvok, you did it, old pointy-ears did it, I knew you would, you're the best, Vulk, the best of the best of the best. Hey—this is my roommate! I taught him everything he knows!" This to the gathering crowd of well-wishers who pressed close to congratulate Tuvok.

"Hey, hey, roomie, give us a smile, what do you say? A great, big, toothy Vulcan smile—c'mon!" This was a frequent plea from Scott, a game which seemed to provide him never-ending amusement and which Tuvok frankly found baffling. Surely Scott knew that a smile would never be forthcoming, and consequently, what could be the continuing allure of this doomed request?

After four years, Tuvok still found humans puzzling in general. They were rambunctious, eager, generous, disorganized, unruly, passionate, argumentative, compassionate, ebullient—in other words, as far removed from the ideals of *cthia* as could possibly be imagined. On several occasions, he had been granted audience with Sarek, the Ambassador Extraordinary Emeritus of Vulcan to Earth (and the entire Federation of Planets), and had sought greater understanding of this puzzling species.

Sarek had been less than helpful. It was clear that he was comfortable among the Terrans, and had even taken one as his wife. Sarek had some affinity for these people, but he was never able to articulate it in a way that Tuvok could grasp.

"You cannot hold them to Vulcan standards," the venerable old man told Tuvok. "Of course by such measurements they will fail. You must see them only in relationship to each other."

"I think they must resemble Vulcans in the time before Surak."

"No, no, no, not so bad as that. They are exuberant, but not violent. They are undisciplined, but not chaotic. They have much to recommend them."

Tuvok decided to risk a query which was potentially embarrassing. "One thing I do not understand is what they call 'jokes.' By placing someone in a humiliating position, they seem to derive such pleasure that they laugh aloud. Can you explain that?"

"Give me an example."

"On the first night that I was here, I dressed for sleep and got into bed. As I put my legs under the sheets, my feet encountered a barrier, and I discovered that the bedclothes had been folded in such a way that it was impossible to extend my legs fully. This was an oddity, certainly—but then I witnessed my roommate doubled over with laughter, as if this were the most amusing thing he had ever seen." Tuvok paused a moment before continuing. "And the fact that I failed to understand the humor encouraged him to an even greater state of hilarity."

What was unmistakably a smile pulled at Sarek's mouth. "It's called 'short-sheeting,' Cadet," he said, and his wise eyes twinkled as he said it. "It's an ancient tradition on Earth and I wouldn't imagine it's going to go away any time soon. It's not meant as disrespect, just as a kind of irreverent fun."

Tuvok pondered this reply, but found no satisfaction in it. He decided to try another example. "I have found that, at least among the males of this species, there is endless delight taken in stories which involve the functions of the toilet. They will howl with laughter over a description of almost anything that is a bodily function. Does this not strike you as odd?"

The smile on Sarek's lips was even more pronounced this time—in fact, a gentle laugh was escaping them! Tuvok stared, fascinated. He couldn't ever remember having seen a Vulcan laugh.

"It seems that at approximately age four, human boys become

fascinated with bodily functions and deal with this fascination by making fun of these physiological necessities. It has a term—'bathroom humor'—and you are correct in your observation that the females seem not to share in it. Unless, of course, the female is like my wife, who is much saltier than most human females. At any rate, men seem not to outgrow this infantile behavior, and continue for most of their lives to find amusement in stories about the bodily functions.''

Tuvok had pondered statements like these for days afterward, hoping there would be contained within them something he could grasp, something that would help him to endure the beings with which he was now surrounded. But it seemed to come down to the fact that Sarek enjoyed humans, while he could summon no such response.

And then there were the women.

They had proven as astonishing as anything Tuvok had encountered on this singular world. He was accustomed on Vulcan to women of uncommon power, but Earth women were extraordinary in their brazenness. Audacious, forward, impertinent, bold—they struck him as not unlike hungry lematyas, the fearsome beasts of Vulcan who often hunted in packs.

It was not unusual for one or more human women to follow him across campus, striking up conversation for no apparent reason, or to sit themselves down with him at dinner and begin asking the most probing of personal questions. On several occasions he had returned to his dormitory to find one of them sitting on the floor outside his room, who would then follow him into his quarters unabashedly, as though this were commonplace and proper.

He had received from them countless invitations to dances, concerts, and lectures—and he had, at times, accepted, depending upon the appeal of the occasion. But he never failed to feel somewhat breathless and disoriented after an encounter with one of these frank and disarming creatures.

One of the most memorable of these adventures involved a young woman, Lily Astolat, whose name Tuvok found unremarkable, ignorant of its origin. She was delicate, with honey-golden curls and pale brown eyes, and skin that was so smooth and flawless it looked as though it had been replicated.

She sat next to him in his calculus class, and seemed to absorb the mysteries of calculus with an effortlessness he found intriguing. She also seemed less bold than some females, and he appreciated that. So it was that, after struggling for several days with a problem in metric differential geometry, he accepted her offer of help.

They met in one of the study rooms of the dormitory and found it, for once, empty. The fact that it was eight o'clock on a Saturday evening, a day and time when there seemed to be many social activities, undoubtedly accounted for the privacy they enjoyed now.

Lily proved an excellent tutor, and sorted through the intricacies of the problem with him. She clarified the rules of tensor-product formation, and once he had grasped those basic concepts, the rest fell into line. Inspired, he worked through the rest of the problems while she watched, smiling.

But then, as he finished, she rose and sat herself down in his lap, twining her arms around his neck! Tuvok was dumbfounded, and could only think to sit quietly, not encouraging her. She was murmuring to him as she stroked his head, mouth whispering the most outrageous suggestions into his ears.

Then her tongue snaked out and began dancing on his ear tips, a curious but not particularly pleasant sensation. It would never have occurred to him to lick parts of another's body, and he believed that Lily had taken leave of her senses.

Then her mouth was on his, kissing him deeply as she locked her hands around the back of his head, pulling him hard against her, tongue continuing its remarkable oscillations on his lips.

It was time to put an end to this.

Tuvok put his hands under her armpits and stood up, placing her firmly on the floor in front of him. She stared at him, wild-eyed, breathing hard. "What's the matter?" she murmured, coming at him again.

"Thank you for helping me with the differential geometry problem," he said calmly, all the while holding her at arm's length. "It was good of you to take the time. I shall see you in class on Monday."

"Tuvok, don't you find me attractive?"

The question was unbelievably forward. Tuvok drew himself to his full height and gazed down at the disheveled young woman. "You are a cadet of great intellectual prowess, particularly in the field of mathematics. I predict a long and successful career for you."

Her snort of disdain and frustration puzzled him, but he wanted nothing more than to remove himself from this disquieting situation and return to his room to meditate. Tentatively, he released her wrists and then began backing away from her, watching her carefully all the while.

"Again, thank you. You have great skill as a tutor. Have you considered a teaching career? It might suit you quite well."

And then he was at the door, which opened as he approached it, and then gone, hoping he had handled the situation with appropriate courtesy.

Tuvok had not yet experienced his first Pon farr, and consequently knew nothing about it, Vulcans being loath to discuss this most primal of their lives' milestones. It would not be until several years later that he passed through what was historically known as the Rapture, and be transformed. At that time, he remembered the incident with Lily, and for the first time, understood.

Now he stood on the infield of the stadium, breathing the chill April air, enduring the felicitations of his teammates and of Scott, who persisted in pounding him on the back in exultation. And Scott was saying something in his excitement that Tuvok hoped he was misunderstanding.

"She's dying to meet you, old Vulk. She has a thing for pointy ears, I guess, I don't get it myself. But she's primo, Tuvok, absolutely choice. We'll be waiting outside the locker room."

And Scott—who knew him only too well—disappeared before Tuvok could scotch this uninvited introduction.

Sure enough, when Tuvok ventured from the locker room, showered and dressed, Scott was standing there, a female cadet at his side. There was no escaping.

"Tuvok, this is your lucky day. May I present Sophie Timmins, of Somerset, England."

Tuvok looked into large, grave eyes, the color of a dusky pearl. They held his gaze solemnly, the most remarkable feature in a face that was defined by its symmetry and balance. A straight, unobtrusive nose divided the planes of the face and pointed to lips that outlined a somewhat small mouth. The woman was tall, almost as tall as Tuvok, slender and straight. Her hair, which seemed almost the same shade as her eyes, was pulled off her face and hung down her back in a plait.

There was a reserve to her that Tuvok found familiar and, consequently, comfortable. Nonetheless, he had no desire to spend time with this woman, and was determined to extricate himself from her as quickly as possible.

"I've made reservations at Momo's," Scott continued relentlessly.

"There's a Bolian singer there who's supposed to be amazing. A five-octave range."

"Thank you, but after a race, I always meditate. It's part of my training program."

"Since when—" Scott began, but the woman, pearly eyes fastened on Tuvok, cut him off.

"I've always found Vulcan meditation rituals more satisfying than any others when it comes to slowing the heart rate. But they seem to increase the activity of my mind, rather than reduce it."

Tuvok was curious in spite of himself. He appraised the poised young woman who held his gaze so unflinchingly. "How did you become familiar with Vulcan meditations?"

"My mother travels to Vulcan frequently as a cultural liaison. I began accompanying her when I was a small child. I've spent several summers studying at the Temple of Amonak."

Tuvok regarded her with bemusement. He had long wanted to study at the Temple of Amonak, a notion supported by his father but disapproved of by his mother, on the grounds that he needed more well-rounded activities. "He'd spend all his time in a temple if he were given the chance," he'd heard his mother say on more than one occasion. And now he was face-to-face with a human who had been able to accomplish what he had been denied.

"With whom did you study?"

"Primarily with the priestess M'Fau. She held special classes daily for young people. She was remarkable. I think she may be the reason I find it difficult to still the mind when I follow her meditations—I'm always reminded of her, and I begin thinking about how wise she was, how much I learned from her—and pretty soon my mind is a jumble of thoughts."

Curiosity was giving way to something else, something Tuvok had experienced before and which he strove rigorously to control. He had no words for these incipient feelings—for that is unmistakably what they were—but they had to do with this cool human woman and the fact that she had had experiences which he had been denied. He had a wish to hear of those experiences, and a sense that there was something wrong if a human could study with M'Fau and he could not . . .

Some of these sensations were unpleasant (those which others would identify as resentment and jealousy), and Tuvok used all the techniques at his disposal to suppress them. Another sensation was less bothersome, and seemed somehow less treacherous; it was like a curiosity but magnified a thousandfold. He allowed the sensation to roil within him for a moment, testing it, trying to decide if it had to be quelled or if he could act upon it. He decided he could.

"I would very much like to speak with you about your experiences at Amonak," he intoned. "It would be interesting to hear of your classes with M'Fau."

He was vaguely aware of Scott's surprised and elated expression, his quick good-bye and equally swift departure. Tuvok was completely focused on this provocative woman with the dusky gray eyes and the forthright manner that was so . . . so Vulcan.

He spent inordinate quantities of time with Sophie Timmins during the last months of his senior year at the Academy, discussing the teachings of M'Fau, meditating communally, and discussing the profundities of *cthia.* He discerned that Sophie's fascination for things Vulcan was not merely an intellectual curiosity; she seemed to want, on some deeply felt level, to *be* Vulcan. She pored over Vulcan history, and studied Surak's writings assiduously.

She was the first true friend Tuvok had made among humans, and that only because she did everything she could to disavow her humanity and to inculcate Vulcanism.

But in the end, she, too, wanted more. She was unable to free herself completely of human longings, unable to quell the fiercely passionate spirit that seemed to inhabit all Terrans. She wanted a physical intimacy that he could neither understand nor satisfy.

The end came during an evening in June, when the weather was uncharacteristically warm for San Francisco. Tuvok and Sophie sat in a gazebo situated on the grounds of the Academy, secluded within a grove of eucalyptus trees. They had been studying the tenets of *Kolinahr,* the most rigorous of the mental disciplines of Vulcan, when suddenly Tuvok heard a catch in Sophie's voice, and he turned to see tears falling from her eyes.

He had seen this phenomenon in humans before. Mostly in the females, although it was not uncommon for the males to indulge in this release of excessive emotion as well. He had observed a teammate, a pole vaulter, racked with sobs in the locker room after he failed for the third time to make his vault at a height of six and one half meters, a relatively easy height, thereby losing the match. Tuvok found it a disquieting experience, and worked the Disciplines for an extra hour after witnessing it.

Now as moisture overflowed from Sophie's eyes, he was similarly uneasy. Tears signified unhappiness so urgent that it couldn't be ignored, pain that could no longer be assuaged. These were situations which Tuvok was singularly ill equipped to handle, and at this moment, he didn't know how to proceed.

He simply waited, hoping the moment would pass, and indeed, he could see Sophie struggle to suppress this moist display. But each time he thought she had succeeded, a small choking gasp would emit from her throat and the tears would begin anew.

He had observed certain behaviors among humans when one of their kind shed tears. In the locker room, as the pole vaulter had held his head in his hands, sobbing, other humans had come by and patted him on the back, offering solicitations. The track coach had sat close to him, arm around his shoulder, murmuring comfort in quiet tones. And finally, when the distraught young man regained some control (to Tuvok's relief) and stood, a teammate enclosed him in what Tuvok knew to be a "hug," a commonly used gesture of succor.

Should he try one of these behaviors on Sophie? He wouldn't be able to whisper to her, because he had no idea what he should say. But if it would help to stroke her arm or pat her back, would that be appropriate?

His mind turned the question over, assessing its relative merits and defects. If it caused her to cease this display of emotion, his solicitude would be justified. On the other hand, it might be interpreted as sanctioning such overwrought demeanor, and that would surely be in error.

And while this internal debate unfolded, Sophie gradually regained control and wiped at her eyes, which, he noted, were now swollen and tinged with an unpleasant red.

"I'm sorry," she breathed. "It's just . . . getting more and more difficult . . ."

He was pleased that she was verbal once more, for that meant they could discuss the situation, resolve the problem, and return to the study of *Kolinahr.*

"What is becoming more difficult?" he asked pleasantly, hoping his attitude would neutralize the situation. It was, therefore, with some dismay that he observed that her response to his question was not an answer, but a fresh display of tears, seemingly more intense than before.

This time he decided on a course of action. It was only logical to emulate human behavior in a situation as out of control as this one seemed to be. Though he didn't understand why physical contact would be helpful, he had observed it to be so, and at this point he would frankly have done whatever was required in order to put an end to this inordinate exhibition of emotion.

He extended his arm and began to tap her softly on the back.

This gesture produced a remarkable result. Sophie wailed aloud and flung herself upon him, arms holding him close, head pressed against his chest, body shuddering violently in a fresh outburst of sobs. Startled, he held his arms away from her, afraid of what might happen if he touched her again.

She was clutching at his uniform, which was now damp from her tears, kneading at him in the way baby sehlats kneaded their mothers' underbellies as they suckled. "Sophie," he remonstrated, "strive to regain control. Remember the Disciplines, remember *cthia.*"

She wailed aloud and flung herself away from him, rising to move to the gazebo's entrance, where she clung to the wooden rail and drew three deep breaths, which was the prelude to the First Discipline. Gradually, the breathing calmed, Sophie pulled herself erect, and turned to face him. He was about to congratulate her for her mastery of her emotions, but when she spoke he realized she was still in some kind of anguish.

"I don't understand," she said, and her voice was hoarse from her crying. "Vulcans become intimate. They mate, and have children. Don't you ever . . . have such urges?"

He stared at her, uncertain how to answer the question. It was as though she were speaking in an alien language that the Universal Translator couldn't translate. "I have assumed," he stated carefully, "that one day I would have a wife and family. I have never associated that decision with . . . urges. I don't believe I can answer a question which I fundamentally don't understand."

Her hair was damp at her temples, and he noticed the tendrils had a tendency to curl, ringing her face in a delicate frame. She looked quite young and vulnerable in the growing dusk of the evening, and Tuvok was suddenly struck with insight into the inevitable outcome of this extraordinary situation. She was moving toward him through the growing shadows, fragile and ethereal. "I love you, Tuvok. I've never felt this way before. I want to be with you always . . . and . . . I want intimacy. It's part of life . . . can't we have that?"

A calm settled over Tuvok as he saw his course with clarity and precision. He experienced a gratitude for the teachings of Surak, for they always proved reliable, leading the way from any entangled situation into lucidity.

"Do you remember," he said firmly, "the initial notes Surak made as he was developing *cthia?*"

She looked at him, smoky eyes a deeper gray in the growing darkness. He could detect disappointment in them, but he continued nonetheless. *"Ideally, do no harm,"* he intoned, on surer ground now. *"Harm no one's internal, invisible integrities. Leave others the privacy of their minds and lives. Intimacy remains precious only insofar as it is inviolate: invading it turns it to torment."*

He looked at her, trying to discern what impact these words had on her. Would she understand what he was trying to say? "I wish you no harm, Sophie," he assured her, "and it becomes clear that our being together does you great harm. Surely that violates the integrities of both of us, and is therefore an intolerable situation."

"Don't leave me," she breathed, voice barely audible, as though the sound were dampened and absorbed by the evening shadows that were enveloping the gazebo. "Please."

To his satisfaction, he found he was not disquieted by what he could only describe as her unseemly groveling. The universe was ordered, and he had rediscovered order after having lost sight of it for a moment. That was the effect humans had had on him, and he must find a way to disengage that effect.

"If I am to follow Surak, I must be true to his teachings. I must not harm another, must not cause another pain, for such actions speed entropy, the heat death of the universe."

Her slender body began to tremble, and he sensed a fierce struggle within her, a concentrated effort to achieve mastery over her ragged emotions. Finally she drew three deep breaths and lifted her eyes to him.

"I offer you peace," she said, quoting Surak, *"and peace again until I die."*

"And in this way you will find peace," he intoned. Then he turned and left the gazebo, never looking back. It was his last encounter with her.

"I can no longer live among humans. They hasten the heat death of the universe."

Six years had passed since his graduation from the Academy, and he was standing in the formal room of his parents' home on Vulcan, feeling the comforting familiarity of the intense heat, and the lightness of spirit that came from returning to one's origins. T'Khut was high in the sky, looming menacingly above them, volcanoes visible and smoking. But to Tuvok, the huge disk was calming in its familiarity.

After graduation, he had taken an advanced degree in Tactical Strategies and Weaponry, and served a three-year tour of duty aboard the *U.S.S. Excelsior* under Captain Hikaru Sulu, and thus had once again been closely quartered with a large number of humans.

Nothing in his experiences aboard the *Excelsior* altered his basic perception of this species: although gregarious, valiant, and clever, they were ruled by emotion. Increasingly, the strain of maintaining the rigors of *cthia* while living among humans became exhausting, sapping his energy and fragmenting his mental disciplines.

He longed for retreat. He had begun to dream of the desert, of its unknowable mysteries and vast silences. It was a cleansing place, which baked confusion and disquietude from one's mind and left purity and serenity in their place.

When the *Excelsior* returned to Earth, he tendered his resignation from Starfleet and returned to Vulcan on the first ship that had passenger space. The closer the vessel came to his homeworld, the more confident Tuvok was of his decision, and when he stood before his parents some days later, he was suffused with a sense of clarity and purpose.

"I have fulfilled your wishes, and broadened my experiences. I am no longer a child, and must now determine my own path. I have decided to pursue the study of *Kolinahr.*"

Tuvok thought he detected an expression of satisfaction on his father's face, but he was more concerned with his mother's reaction. He had already determined his plan, regardless of what his parents said, but he would prefer their acquiescence because he didn't want his mind cluttered with the ragged remnants of their disapproval.

So he was gratified when his mother nodded once, firmly, signaling her compliance. "And where will you pursue this study?" she queried.

"At the Temple of Amonak," he replied. It was the most rigorous of the *Kolinahr* temples, the one where he could study with M'Fau. The temple Sophie had attended. He would remain cloistered within its walls for two years before being allowed to emerge into the world again, even for a brief visit. He had no doubt that his parents would have preferred that he choose a less stringent order for his studies. He was their only child, and had been gone from them for ten years. They had probably anticipated some interaction with him once he returned to Vulcan.

"The life of an ascetic is not an easy one," his father said. "It will test you severely."

"That is precisely why I have chosen it," replied Tuvok. "After living among humans, I must be cleansed through denial and struggle. I have become soft, and dependent on creature comforts. I require the disciplines of *Kolinahr.*"

And so it was that Tuvok, after a month in his parents' company— a month in which they found they had much to share—entered the temple of Amonak and took the oath of dedication. He was now bound to the disciplines of *Kolinahr* and he felt, even more than when he had entered his parents' house a month ago, that he had finally come home.

Tuvok spent six years in the sanctuary of Amonak, a time during which he began to achieve the mastery of his instincts that he had always thought must be possible. He realized how uncontrolled he had been during his first thirty years, when confusion, puzzlement, and uneasiness bubbled so closely to the surface. He vowed to do everything in his power to subdue those treacherous feelings.

He lived in a small cell, barely three meters square, and slept on a pallet on the floor. The walls were Vulcan sandstone, thick and white, effectively blocking both heat and sound. A small table for writing and an isochromatic lamp were the only other furnishings. No adornments graced the walls, no mementos of his prior life cluttered the table. This simplicity was not required by the brothers and sisters of Amonak, and indeed many other penitents had cells that were comfortably furnished and even decorated. The criterion dictated by the priests was "surroundings which provide the least distraction from pursuits of the mind," as they wisely realized that there were those who would be inattentive to their studies if their minds were on the austerity of their habitats.

Tuvok disdained this indulgence, which he considered luxury. He personally felt that everyone should live in the same way, with the fewest creature comforts, so that all focus would be on *cthia.* But the choice was not his to make, and he accepted that the priestesses possessed a greater wisdom than he, and undoubtedly had their reasons for this decision.

He rose each day at dawn, and ruminated that his mother would no doubt still consider him a lie-abed. He ate nothing until he had completed two hours of meditation, alone in his stone-quiet cell.

Then he would join his brothers and sisters for a simple meal of bread and fruit, which was followed by a meditative walk in the hills. On those mornings when T'Khut loomed above them, a special invocation would be chanted, an ancient prayer for T'Khut to keep her place in the sky. Of course everyone now realized the astronomical relationship between the two planets, and knew that T'Khut could not descend upon Vulcan at will, but the ancients did not understand that, and believed that fiery, violent T'Khut might at any time plunge from her perch to wield molten destruction to all the inhabitants of Vulcan. The incantations to T'Khut were considered some of the most powerful ever spoken, and even today priestesses extolled their awe and majesty.

The only other meal of the day came in late afternoon, and was as simple as the first: bread and fruit again, accompanied this time by soup. It followed classes in the temple and preceded an evening of communal meditation. Then everyone retired to their rooms to write and study, and finally to sleep.

It was an unvarying routine, broken only a few times a year for the observance of certain hallowed days: the birth of Surak; the consecration of Seleya, the holy mountain; and a few others. These observances were muted and staid, as was appropriate, and characterized primarily by the addition of music, generally the Vulcan harp, to the ceremonies.

Tuvok lived like this for six years, studying *Kolinahr,* and was more at peace than he had ever been before. The rightness of his choice soothed him, and he vowed to dedicate the rest of his life to the pursuit of mental discipline.

One day he was walking along one of the stone colonnades that ringed the temple, musing over a certain passage in Surak's writings that seemed to possess a flaw in logic, when he heard the sound of children at play. They were part of the summer program conducted by M'Fau—the same program which Sophie Timmins had once attended—and they had been at the temple every one of the six years he had spent there.

Today, however, the sound was disturbing to him, in a way he couldn't define. Something vague and uncomfortable began manifesting itself in him, and he was aware of sensations he hadn't had since his days at the Academy. He determined to identify, analyze, and then eliminate these perfidious sensibilities. To that end, he changed direction and walked to the children's yard.

There were perhaps thirty of them, ranging in age from five or six up to twelve or so. They were playing dak'lir, a structured game intended to eliminate excess physical energy—often necessary before young and undisciplined minds can be turned toward logic.

The day was a mild one, distant mountains etched against the sky (which was absent T'Khut's menacing presence), red desert sparkling in the sun. It was on days like this that Tuvok made a point of strolling the colonnades, musing on the Disciplines. Now, as he gazed at the yard of unruly young people—and no mistake about it, they were behaving in a most untoward fashion—he felt a genuine annoyance. They had interrupted his thoughts. Their noisy discordance prevented him from reentering his former reverie.

He moved closer to the yard, seeking the priest or priestess who was in charge, but he saw no adult, just the gaggle of loud children. He was further annoyed to realize that the children were unsupervised. Unthinkable! How could any reasonable person allow this intractable group to create such a clamorous distraction?

He strode toward the children, not consciously aware that his heart rate was elevated, his blood pressure rising. He merely felt justified in taking steps to right a wrong.

"Silence!" he bellowed, and was mildly surprised at the look of amazement he saw on the young faces that instantly turned toward him, eyes widened and mouths agape. He was gratified that they obeyed instantly, as good Vulcan children should, and he decided they should be commended for their swift obedience.

"You were behaving very badly, and you are fortunate that I was present in order to restore order. Your swift response to my command, however, is laudable. I trust this raucous display is now finished." He gazed at them sternly for a moment, then turned to leave.

M'Fau was standing directly behind him, looking at him curiously. Her face was heavily lined with age and wisdom, but her eyes were a deep ebony that seemed timeless, powerful. "Tuvok?" she queried.

"I have chastised these young people because they were entirely too obstreperous," he stated. He saw nothing unusual in this statement, but M'Fau's left eyebrow lifted slightly. "The adult in charge was not present to control them. You may want to determine who should have been here, and to remind them of their responsibilities."

M'Fau's voice was glacial. "I am the adult in charge, and I purposely left the children unsupervised. It is a necessary step in their learning to become masters of themselves."

"I see." Tuvok tried to keep his voice flat, but there was a strange vehemence to it. Where had it come from? "I regret my statement. I did not understand the situation."

M'Fau's expression seemed more curious than ever. She was staring at him, eyes narrowed. "Are you well, Tuvok? You seem feverish."

Feverish? Tuvok lifted the back of his hand to his forehead and was surprised to find it moist with perspiration. What could have caused it? He was perplexed. "I . . . do not know. I shall retire to my room. If necessary, I will see the physician."

He turned on his heel and marched away from the priestess, aware now of the hammering of his heart. Perhaps he was ill. He would drink an herb tea and go to bed early, after working the Disciplines with extra diligence.

But by the time of the afternoon meal, he found himself ravenous, and he rose from his pallet to join his brothers and sisters in the spacious meal gallery. He filled his tray, piling on several mugs of soup, half a loaf of nut bread, and several varieties of fruit. He sat and began devouring this feast.

The soup was excellent—both spicy and sweet, crammed with thick chunks of sorda, a vegetable he had enjoyed since childhood. The bread was freshly baked and still warm, and he tore it into thick slabs, which he used to sop up every bit of broth in the bottom of his mugs. The fruit, kuffi, was ripe and juicy, with a few more seeds than he wanted to deal with, but unusually delicious, as well. He wondered how it might taste cooked into bread, a kind of dessert dish. He determined to recommend it to the bakers.

He was in the process of deciding if he wanted to go back for more food when he became aware of a peculiar silence around him. He lifted his head to discover that the entire table of penitents was staring at him, their expressions ranging from the inquisitive to the disdainful. At the same time, he noticed that he had made a frightful mess on his tray. Soup was spilled, sodden hunks of bread had fallen to the table, and kuffi seeds were strewn everywhere. Then he realized that his face was wet with pulp from the fruit, and his hands were stained and dripping.

There was one instant of surprise as he discovered the disarray he had created, but almost immediately another response boiled up in him. He felt the white heat of anger. "What are you staring at?" he snapped at his fellows. "You are violating my privacy."

A gentle voice behind him caused him to whirl. Teknat, a priest and a friend, was holding a white cloth toward him. "May I offer you a napkin, Tuvok?" he said quietly.

Tuvok's response was to spring to his feet in a fury. "If I want a napkin, I'll find one for myself." Then he ripped the cloth from Teknat's hand and flung it on the ground. He spun around and marched from the gallery, espying as he did M'Fau's pale craggy face across the room, dark eyes following his every move.

Back in his room, he found himself pacing frenetically. For the first time, he realized how small and cramped the room was. He moved to the window and flung it open, hoping that the evening breeze might make the space less oppressive.

The heat of the desert flooded in. The room, which had been pleasantly cool, was now even more stifling than ever, making it difficult, somehow, to breathe. With a strangled oath, he slammed shut the window, and the noise it made when it collided with its casing seemed as loud as a tricobalt explosion in the tiny room. His sensitive ears rang painfully, and he swore again.

He flung himself down on his pallet, arm over his eyes, trying desperately to gain control over whatever was happening to him. He took three deep breaths and began the first of the Disciplines, but within seconds, his thoughts had fragmented like shards of broken crystal. He recalled Teknat offering him a napkin, and rage overcame him once more. He clenched his hand into a fist and pounded it against the wall. The pain that resulted was the only slightly soothing sensation he'd had all day.

In the midst of all this, a soft chime announced that someone was outside his door. "Go away!" he called in as loud and strident a voice as he could summon.

But in response, the door opened, and M'Fau was standing there.

Chagrined, he got to his feet. He noticed that his knuckles were gouged, and droplets of blood dripped green on the floor. "I . . . apologize," he said with difficulty. "I didn't realize it would be you."

She made no answer, but entered the room and perched on his chair, hands upon her knees like a scrawny raptor poised to dive for small game. "Sit, Tuvok," she said, and to his ears her voice seemed to echo as though from the depths of an ancient tomb.

He sat. Irritation and anxiety clawed at him, and he struggled desperately to maintain some measure of control. He envisioned himself putting his hands around M'Fau's thin neck, skin crepy with folds, and squeezing until her black eyes popped wide and she collapsed in a shuddering death.

". . . what has happened to you."

He realized she had been talking to him, but as he had been fantasizing about murdering her, he had no idea what she'd said. He wiped at his face and shook his head, trying to clear it and focus on M'Fau.

"I'm sorry, would you repeat that?"

"I said, I believe I know what has happened to you."

He stared at her, trying to make sense of this statement, but unable to make sense of anything. He shook his head again. "Oh?" he replied vaguely.

She leaned toward him. "I believe your time has come."

This, too, made no sense to him, though he forced his mind to try to assimilate her meaning. His time? What time?

"I do not know . . . what you mean," he said with effort.

She sighed. He discerned then that she was extremely uncomfortable, and this realization struck at him like an asp. He felt unaccountably fearful.

"Thee hast lapsed into the Pon farr," she continued, using the formal mode as a kind of shelter from her embarrassment. "What the ancients called the plak-tow. The blood fever."

"I still . . . do not know what you mean."

"That is because we do not talk about it. But it comes to every Vulcan male at some point, and every seven years thereafter. The onset can have many forms, but I believe thine hast begun."

Confusion swam in his brain, and he worked desperately to quell it. "What is 'it'? What comes every seven years? I don't understand . . ."

"The mating time. Thee must take a wife."

At these words, a powerful image burst into Tuvok's brain: he was walking down a richly appointed corridor, drawn inexorably forward by the siren song of a woman's voice humming an intoxicating melody. The sound was silken, keening, suggesting indescribable longing. His heart hammered as he drew toward a door, rich with brocades, and extended his hand to open it . . .

M'Fau peered at him, waiting for a response. Tuvok folded his hands together, forcing concentration, and felt his arms shake with the effort. "How do I find a wife?"

She seemed pleased that he could focus on the matter. "Go to thy parents. They will have chosen."

This struck him as monumentally odd. His parents—would have chosen a mate for him? When? And why had they never mentioned it? Why had they never told him of this incapacitating experience, prepared him for the disruption to his life?

But he asked none of these questions. All his rapturous energy, so diffuse and unbridled, had coalesced in an instant to a single goal, which burned within him like the white-hot tip of a tiny needle: he had to find a woman.

When he arrived at his parents' home, he was perspiring heavily. His mother took one look at him and seemed to understand what was happening, a fact which angered him but which didn't detract from his need. "We have chosen a mate for you, Tuvok," T'Meni announced confidently. "We have given this matter much thought, and have selected carefully. We think you will be satisfied."

"Why did you never tell me of this?" he queried, still finding it preposterous that such a monumental event would be concealed from him.

"We do not discuss it" was his mother's only reply. "Bathe yourself and put on suitable clothes. We will meet your bride."

And so it was that Tuvok found himself standing in the home of people he had never met, staring into the serene and knowing eyes of a young woman named T'Pel. Her skin was as soft and shining as brown velvet, and her hair hung down her back in carefully restrained curls. Her voice was low and keening, and as soon as she spoke, he could imagine her singing to him with a siren lure.

She evinced no surprise at the introduction to her mate—did everyone know about this except him?—and Tuvok imagined that he saw in her tranquil expression a satisfaction, perhaps even a pleasure, in seeing him.

A yearning more powerful than anything he could ever have imagined swept over him. He had to touch her, to caress her, run his hands over all her body, taste her skin, press against her, flesh against flesh, must *become* her, make one of their two.

The thought came to him: Was this what Lily, and Sophie, and the others had felt? Did humans live in this constant state of arousal? Now he understood the tears.

Abruptly, he turned away from her, aware that he must be making a spectacle of himself. He could not embarrass his family like this. He removed himself from the group, into a corner, and stood silently there, observing with as much decorum as he could while his parents, and T'Pel's, made arrangements for their mating ceremony.

The next day they were standing in the ritual site, Tuvok ruminating that while Vulcans inexplicably kept this powerful experience a carefully cloaked secret, once it began at least they acted with alacrity. He was grateful for this, for he wasn't sure how he could have endured one more night alone.

Now T'Pel stood before him, gracious and composed, listening as M'Fau intoned the mating ceremony. Tuvok paid little attention to what was being said; it was all he could do to hold still. The afternoon burned hot from the desert winds, and, prophetically, T'Khut loomed monstrously overhead, volcanoes belching lava. It was, Tuvok thought, an apt representation of the fire within himself, an inferno boiling within that needed eruption.

At M'Fau's instruction, he placed his fingers on T'Pel's luminous face, initiating the mating bond.

Rapturous images swirled between them. The desert in its shimmering heat became the silvery cold of the mountains became the roiling lava flow became the ecstasy of icy streams became the blistering summer storms became the chill winds of the short season. Ice upon fire, fire upon ice, as T'Pel warmed and Tuvok cooled and their minds entwined with one another, touching, blending, dancing, singing, soaring.

One. Forever.

Later, they were alone, standing apart from each other in a room that had been prepared for them with candles and incense, with wine and fruit. They gazed at one another, Tuvok hearing the beating of his heart in his ears, thundering, insisting, louder and more demanding every second until all he could hear was a roaring that propelled him forward.

His last thought before he touched her was *What if I don't know what to do?*

But he soon realized he needn't have worried.

"You have another son, Tuvok," announced his mother, and Tuvok nodded acknowledgment. His first- and second-born sons, Sek and Varith, sat with him, playing kal-toh, with which Tuvok hoped to quiet their youthful energies and teach them to focus on a mental task. It had proven daunting. Sek showed some promise, but at fourteen his attentions were drawn to more physical and exuberant games, like dak'lir. It was difficult to persuade him to sit quietly even for three or four hours.

Now he leapt to his feet, snatching the opportunity to dispense with the game. "May I go see Mother and the baby?" he asked politely enough, but Tuvok could seem him practically twitching with uncurbed energy, his wayward ringlets—his mother's hair—spilling over his bronzed forehead.

"And me!" chirped Varith, who at seven was a true challenge to Tuvok's skills as a parent. He was a stunning child, his skin the color of mulled tea, eyes large and dark, teeth white as the snows on Seleya. These teeth were frequently visible, as Varith had the unfortunate propensity to smile, no matter how hard Tuvok had labored to teach him restraint.

"We will all go," Tuvok announced. "But not until I see that you are truly focused and your emotions under control. I do not want your mother, nor your new brother, to bear witness to this unseemly vigor."

He could see the boys doing their best to obey him; both closed their eyes and drew deep breaths, and Sek seemed to gain some measure of constraint, but a telltale tug at Varith's lips bespoke his incipient mirth. "We will not see your mother, Varith," Tuvok said firmly, "until you are fully in control of yourself."

At this, Varith's hands tightened into small fists and his lips formed a rigid line. Holding himself like this, he opened his eyes and looked directly at Tuvok, as though to say, *I'm in control now, Father.*

Tuvok knew full well that true mastery did not come from a clenching of fists and a forced expression. But at least Varith was making an effort, and perhaps that was all he could expect. He turned away from them. "Come," he said, and led them into the long gallery that ran from the formal rooms of their home into the living quarters.

They lived on the periphery of the desert, as close as a habitat could be erected, for Tuvok was most at home near the vast expanse of red sand. He never tired of gazing into its Promethean depths, an occupation he found tranquilizing.

Now he paused before the great windows of the gallery and turned to his sons. "Look to the desert," he intoned. "The sight will help to quiet your minds."

The boys gazed obediently toward the great flatness, beyond which mountains loomed darkly and distantly. Seleya was beyond them. Tuvok had never seen the sacred mountain, never made the pilgrimage that was so cherished by Vulcans. Someday, he would go there and see the black shape that erupted from the desert floor, climb the ten thousand steps that had been carved in its stone, imbue himself with the power and mysticism of this most holy place.

"I want to see Mother," Varith muttered fretfully, and Tuvok drew a breath which some might deem a sigh. This child was taxing.

"For losing your concentration, we will stand here fifteen minutes more," Tuvok told them. And they did, Varith's mounting anxiety, fueled by the occasionally mewling sound of a baby's crying, notwithstanding.

When finally they entered T'Pel's chamber, Varith bounded across the room and flung himself into his mother's arms. Tuvok was disappointed that T'Pel embraced him, holding him close to her and murmuring gently to him. Such reinforcement of untoward behavior did nothing to ease his task of teaching his children the self-control they must acquire before taking their place in the adult world.

Sek, at least, was more restrained, and moved with appropriate speed to his mother's bed. "I hope you are well, Mother," he said. T'Pel extended her arm to him, as well, and both boys enjoyed an embrace from their clearly exhausted mother.

"I am well. As is your new brother. Go to him, and see what you were like in the first hours of your birth."

The boys moved toward the large cradle that stood near the bed, circling around the nurse who had come to help with the birthing. Tuvok sat next to T'Pel, holding a look in which their thoughts fled back and forth between each other, calming and reassuring.

"He is a strong, healthy boy, Tuvok. We are blessed again."

"I believe you had hoped for a daughter."

"I am grateful for my healthy boys. This one was the largest yet, and he's already suckling strongly."

Varith called out to them. "Look, Father, how tiny he is!" Tuvok turned to see Varith's teeth showing once again and realized he was smiling. "Close your mouth," Tuvok said automatically, and the teeth disappeared.

Tuvok moved to the cradle to inspect his newest son. The baby was lighter-skinned than the other two had been at birth, and his mother's curly hair lay in loose ringlets on his head. His mouth was moving in sucking motions, rather like a fish, but he wasn't crying and seemed content for the moment. His diminutive fists waved in the air, and Tuvok was reminded of the orchestra conductors he had witnessed on Terra. Perhaps this child would be musical; neither of the others had shown any propensity for music.

Varith had managed to insert his finger into the baby's small grasp and was wiggling his arm back and forth. "We're going to play dak'lir together," the child announced solemnly. "I'll show you how to dodge the runners so you can be the first one through the rings." Then

Varith looked up at Tuvok. "What's his name? What will we call him?"

Tuvok looked over at his wife and lifted an eyebrow. They had had a difference of opinion about the baby's name, Tuvok preferring a name in the Surak tradition and T'Pel preferring to bend that custom and give him a more original name. "The choice is yours," he told her. The child was healthy; a name was unimportant by comparison.

She held his look for a long moment, then finally she said, "His name will be Elieth."

Though he did not betray it, Tuvok could not have been more surprised. His aunt Elieth, who had been Eldest Mother, had recently died, leaving the mantle to his mother, T'Meni. Conferring the name of an Eldest Mother on a male child was an honor of the highest sort and could only be bestowed by the mother of the child, not the father. It was said to portend extraordinary events in the child's life.

Tuvok nodded at his wife to signify his acceptance of her gesture. It was a particularly astute way to have solved their difference of opinion, and he noted to himself that T'Pel was truly remarkable in her ability to achieve these compromises.

He returned to the cradle where Sek and Varith were both stroking the baby, talking to it, as though it were some kind of small pet, a newborn sehlat. "Children," he said, "this is your brother Elieth."

They found this pronouncement singularly unremarkable, and Tuvok made a mental note to instruct them more fully in the significance of Vulcan names. Varith might be excused for not understanding, but there was no justification for Sek's not grasping the importance of this designation.

As he regarded his three sons, grouped together now as though for a family portrait, Tuvok wondered if he was fulfilling his duties as a father satisfactorily. He had determined at Sek's birth that, unlike his own father, he would take an active role in the upbringing of his children. His father had spent his days at the temple—a worthy endeavor, to be sure—and left Tuvok's training and education in the hands of his mother. And while Tuvok had nothing but the greatest respect and esteem for T'Meni, he had often wondered if a greater presence by his father might have inculcated better disciplines in him at an earlier age.

Of course, his own efforts toward that end didn't seem to be having the desired result. His own sons were woefully lacking, in his opinion, the attributes they should have by now. What was he doing wrong? Surely an adult of his experience should be able to teach two children effectively. Determined to get to the crux of the matter, he sat himself on a chair near T'Pel's bed.

"I am concerned," he began, "with our sons' behavior. They are lacking in basic disciplines, and at times are unacceptably obstreperous. They lie abed until nearly an hour after sunrise, whereas I was always up before dawn. Their lessons go undone until I insist they be tended to—something unheard of when I was a child. They simply are not achieving appropriate control over their actions or their emotions, and certainly are not embracing the ideals of *cthia*. What can be done about this?"

Having concluded his analysis of the problem, Tuvok looked at his wife, and was startled to realize that she was sound asleep. He started to reach out and shake her gently awake, then thought better of it. She had, after all, just given birth.

He rose with a sense of purpose. "Sek, Varith, come with me." The boys looked at him with surprise, apparently hearing the determination in his voice. To their credit, they did not hesitate or complain, but followed him out of the chamber, Varith scurrying to keep up with Tuvok's long strides.

An hour later they sat before M'Fau in the temple of Amonak, the boys pale and quiet, each clutching one small container into which he had packed a few necessary items of clothing and toilette. M'Fau looked like a richly plumed nestra bird, dressed in a robe of brilliant saffron and orange, and was as intimidating.

"I commend them into your care," Tuvok informed M'Fau. "I have failed as a father and I do not want my sons to suffer because of my inadequacies. Instruct them in the proper Vulcan ways so that they may take their place in the adult world properly trained."

M'Fau made no response to this, but carefully studied the boys. Sek returned her gaze evenly, but Tuvok thought he detected something behind the boy's eyes that bespoke pain and uncertainty. And Varith's apprehension was not concealed; his lips were trembling and he clutched his container so tightly his fingers were pale and splotched.

These observations seemed to Tuvok affirmation of his decision. Properly trained children would not behave in such a way, so clearly these boys needed the firmer hands of the priests and priestesses. But M'Fau was silent, not confirming his decision. Tuvok waited patiently, sure she was being characteristically deliberate.

Finally, after a long inspection of the two boys, she turned to Tuvok. She was nearly two decades older than she had been when

Tuvok first entered the Pon farr, and her face was even craggier now; but her eyes retained their flinty intensity, and he could feel her probing him with her mind. He obediently allowed the scrutiny.

Presently she placed her fingertips together and gazed out her window. A pale light remained of the day, yellow and fading, and Tuvok was reminded of the overcast afternoons of San Francisco, when the sun struggled vainly to illuminate the city but could manage only a weak, sallow hue that seemed poisonous.

Finally M'Fau turned to him. "These boys are not ready for *Kolinahr*," she informed him. "I cannot accept them."

Tuvok was bewildered. How could she not accept them when they so clearly needed the rigorous disciplines of the order? He opened his mouth to speak, but M'Fau held up a hand, silencing him.

"When you came to Amonak, it was by your choice. You were ready because of your life experiences. The same is not true of these boys. You cannot accelerate the process, Tuvok. Your haste will create the opposite result from what you intend."

"But . . . they are not responding to their present teachers, nor to my attempts to supplement their disciplines. They require a firmer hand."

"The raising of children should be an easy task, shouldn't it? We simply teach them what they should know, and they will dutifully absorb that wisdom, growing to adulthood in precisely the way we want them to."

Her eyes flickered to Tuvok's, who remained impassive, waiting for her to make her point. "It's a pleasant fantasy," she continued, "but no more than that—a fantasy. You cannot deny them their own struggle, Tuvok. They need their own life experiences, their own obstacles to overcome. You cannot lecture them into maturity."

"But at their ages I was not so unruly—" He was cut off from the sentence as M'Fau rose abruptly and gestured to the boys. "The kitchen undoubtedly has some leftover honey cakes. Tell Cook that I want you to have some."

Sek and Varith rose with more than obedience and hurried to the door. When they had exited, M'Fau turned back to Tuvok.

"I knew you at their ages, Tuvok, so don't tell me what you were like. You were *exactly* as they are, and your mother was as concerned about you as you are about them."

Tuvok was stunned. How could this be? He had never been unruly, or undisciplined, and he had always obeyed both his parents instantly and completely.

Hadn't he?

"Had I remained on Vulcan," he began, "I would have experienced no difficulty in my upbringing. It was my interaction with humans that provided a hindrance in my growth toward self-control."

"You are possessed of an even greater proclivity to fantasy than I had realized," said M'Fau, her voice granite. "But perhaps no greater than many parents who wish to believe they were paragons of good behavior when they were the ages of their children." She moved to her table and removed one of the kal-toh sticks and replaced it, seemingly idly, but the construction shimmered and achieved its ordered state. "I will not absolve you of the responsibility of raising your children. You will have to struggle with it as does everyone else."

"I understand."

"Do you? I don't think so, not yet. But eventually, you will."

She nodded dismissal and he went to the kitchen, where he found his sons gulping hunks of fragrant honey cakes. "Would you like a piece, Father?" said Varith, his mouth still full of sticky crumbs. Tuvok almost remonstrated him for his manners, but rethought the matter and accepted a square of cake.

It was sweet on his tongue.

"What are you doing, Father?"

Tuvok turned to see the round face of his daughter Asil looking up at him. A chubby hand grabbed at his robe, clenching its plush purple folds possessively. Tuvok brushed away the thought that if it had been one of his sons who had done so, he would have chastised him. He readily acknowledged that he treated this fourth child somewhat differently from the others, but believed it was because of his experiences with the first three, rather than because of the child's gender.

She was gazing imperturbably at him now, her eyes a near duplicate of her mother's, almond-shaped, tilting slightly upward at the outer edges, ringed with lashes that were black and lacy. Her bones were delicate, almost elfin, and her neck was as long as a winter swan's. She seemed to him far older than her four years.

"I am looking at the desert," he replied.

"Is there something out there?"

"There are many things there, but not that we can see from here."

"Have you ever seen those things?"

"No."

"Would you like to?"

Tuvok drew three breaths and then sat down in the padded window seat and drew Asil into his lap. She had a disconcerting ability, for such a young child, to discern what he was contemplating. He had not felt her search his mind, but he had no other explanation for her insights.

"Yes, Asil, I would. For many years I have dreamed of making a pilgrimage into the desert, and of seeing Seleya, the sacred mountain."

"Then why haven't you?"

Tuvok hesitated. He wasn't sure how much Asil could understand about familial obligation, nor did he want to burden her unfairly with the suspicion that children might prevent their parents from fulfilling long-cherished goals.

"There is a time for everything," he replied simply.

Asil turned her small head away from him and gazed out upon the desert, which shimmered with heat in the midday glare of the sun, the red sands turned almost orange. To some it would seem an uninviting sight, cruel and unforgiving. Tuvok saw there only mystery and beauty.

"It must be very quiet there," said the child softly.

"The quiet of the ages," agreed Tuvok, marveling once more at his small daughter's insight. Most spoke of the desert's heat, or its vast expanse, the dangers contained therein. Who would think to comment on the purity of its silence?

"I'll go there someday," Asil said matter-of-factly. "Maybe we could go together."

Tuvok rubbed her back tenderly, then was aware of something plucking delicately at his mind, almost imperceptibly, as though a tiny finger strummed one string of a harp. The little minx *was* touching his mind, so daintily that he was almost unaware of it.

"What did you discover?" he asked her quietly, thinking it was best to let her know he was aware of her clandestine prowl through his mind. She looked up at him, unfazed.

"That if ever I go, I must go alone," she replied. "And so must you. But I think—and this is my thought, Father, not yours—that you must go soon."

And so it was, several days later, that Tuvok announced to T'Pel his intention to make a pilgrimage into the desert. "I wondered when you would realize it" was her only reply, although he noted that she turned away from him, as though there were an expression on her face of something she didn't want him to see.

His mother, as usual, had other thoughts. "Again, you long for isolation. Life's lessons are not learned in this way, Tuvok. Detachment and seclusion are the easy ways. It is being part of the world that is difficult."

By now Tuvok was old and experienced enough to realize that his mother challenged him as a matter of course, forcing him to examine his choices and to process them in the machinery of reason. If he had announced his intention to return to Terra and immerse himself in the bustle of humanity, she would have argued the opposite of what she was now saying.

Nonetheless, he appreciated her methodology and valued its wisdom. If a decision could hold up against the cold marble of her logic, it was unassailable.

Therefore he had not anticipated M'Fau's more rigorous examination. As he sat opposite her in the small stone chamber of the temple, her ancient eyes glittered like ebony, fathomless. "Anyone can make a pilgrimage to Seleya," she said with an oddly challenging tone. "Transports are arranged daily."

"I don't intend to transport," Tuvok answered evenly. "I will make the traditional pilgrimage—through the desert."

She made no immediate answer, and Tuvok listened to the ragged wheeze of her breathing. She was old enough that the thin air on Vulcan was taking its toll, forcing the lungs to labor in order to get enough oxygen. The sound seemed to Tuvok like the breeze through the sails of some prehistoric sailing vessel, ruffling thick canvas sheets.

"The desert is dangerous," she said finally, and Tuvok started to respond to that when she continued. "You know all about the physical dangers, of course. Heat, sun, animals . . ." She glanced sidelong at him. "I assume when you say 'traditional pilgrimage' you mean that you will take only the ritual belongings with you?"

He nodded curtly and she continued. "But there are other dangers, Tuvok. Dangers of the spirit, dangers of resolve. Those things are more perilous, and more damaging, than any lematya pride you might encounter."

"I am prepared to do what is necessary," he said simply, wishing to have this interview over with so he could begin to make preparations. But he knew he could not go without M'Fau's blessing.

"I'm sure you are. But you don't have any way of knowing what will be necessary, do you? Consequently, you can't really be prepared. That is the point I am making."

Tuvok stirred in his chair, wanting only to be done with it. "I can only prepare for what I am able to anticipate, and be ready for whatever else I may discover."

A sudden strike, like a sand viper, and she was inside his thoughts. Startled, he nonetheless gave himself over to her and sat quietly as she hunted and probed the recesses of his mind, like an explorer who crawls patiently through secluded caverns, mapping each turn, each tunnel. It was not a sensation he appreciated, this intrusion, and he found himself having to draw deep breaths in order to keep himself seated.

Then it was over, and she looked at him with an unusual expression: self-satisfaction? condescension?

"As I thought. You have a fantasy of the desert, a romantic spiritualism which informs you falsely. You possess no realization of the *reality* of the desert."

"I fail to understand how I could know something I have yet to experience," Tuvok replied, "or, in fact, how anyone could." He put his own dark gaze on M'Fau. "Have you, for instance, crossed the desert?" he asked.

There was a long moment before she answered, and he feared he had crossed a boundary in the boldness of his question. But when she answered, he could detect no coloration in her tone. "No," she said simply. "And that is because I have a respect for it that you lack. It is not my place to say that my attitude is superior to yours, but Tuvok . . ."

She paused, shimmering eyes fastened on him. "I fear for thee," she intoned. Then she turned away from him and he understood that the audience was at an end.

And so it was that Tuvok, after a month during which he made such preparations as he thought fit, walked into the great red desert with a pack which included only the ritual artifacts of a spiritual retreat: a knife, a cup, and a holy stone which M'Fau, in a final gesture of acquiescence, had given him.

T'Khut loomed fulsomely over the daytime desert in the first week of his journey. He stared at its swollen immensity, volcanoes sputtering fire and ash as they had for eons, and tried to find there some sign, some manifestation that would make clear to him the reason for his odyssey. For the truth was, for all his need to go into the desert, Tuvok had no idea why he was so compelled, and that enigma disturbed him in a way that few things had. He had become convinced that, once he entered the still purity of the vast expanse, the answer would become clear to him.

But after a week, he was no closer to understanding why he was doing what he was doing than he had been when he started.

He had examined the question from every side, bringing to bear all his formidable powers of logic. There was, for instance, the possibility of genetic predisposition. His ancestors had dwelled in the desert, had worshipped at the feet of Seleya, had endured the harsh rigors of the endless sands and the cruel sun. Encoded in his brain might be the need to experience this primal past.

But if that was so, why was every Vulcan not so inclined? Many wanted to make a spiritual journey to Seleya, but that was easily done through transport and that was the method most people chose. Tuvok hadn't heard of anyone for many generations past that had walked through the desert to the mountain.

He considered the possibility that his spiritual side, because of his father's influence, had been enhanced from the time he was a small boy, and had implanted in him this need to experience the desert's depths.

But he rejected that likelihood quickly; even M'Pau, the most spiritual being he had ever known, had never crossed the desert and, apparently, felt no need to do so.

What then, in Tuvok, compelled him? He stared upward at T'Khut, focusing his mind, turning the logical possibilities over and over, only to reject each and every one.

After a week, he realized he could no longer travel by day; he would not survive the journey. He chastised himself briefly for this most simple error in logistics; even in Starfleet Academy he had learned the wisdom of traversing intemperate landscapes by night. In his eagerness to find answers, he had stepped out boldly but foolishly; now, though he had supersaturated his body with liquids before starting out, he was already beginning to feel the effects of thirst. Had he traveled by night, he might have been able to move for another two weeks before having to address the problem of finding water.

This was a fundamental mistake, and it grated at Tuvok that it marked the beginning of his trek, for it seemed to him to taint the entire endeavor. He had lost, at the beginning, the imperative of logic, and had hastened into the journey propelled by need, not reason.

He vowed it would be the last such error.

By resting during the day and walking at night, he was able to move for almost a week more, then had to acknowledge that, without fluids of some kind, he could not continue. There was no water, and so he would have to find liquids of another sort. The most obvious of those was blood.

He had seen no obvious signs of any of the common desert inhabitants—sehlats, lematyas, asps—but he had not been looking for any. He had kept his head up, trained on T'Khut, looking for answers in the heavens rather than in the sands.

As he concentrated on finding quarry, though, he saw much evidence that he was not alone here. Faint pawprints in the drifts, droppings, spoor that carried on the dry air: all spoke of the denizens of this fierce world, and of a means to replenish his depleted fluids.

He rose before the sun had set and there was still at least an hour of daylight in which to hunt. It was an hour when smaller animals were likely to make an appearance, before night fell and the nocturnal hunters began to roam. He searched until he found what seemed to be a fresh set of prints, small tracks that led to an indentation in the sand. This would be the burrow of a merak, a small, catlike animal, and it would suit his needs admirably, being small enough to be dispatched easily, plump with blood that would slake his thirst, and muscled with meat that would refuel his strength.

He sat behind the small indentation in the sand and, using his fist, began drumming in a constant pattern on the surface, creating a vibration that would disturb and confuse the merak in the burrow. Eventually, one would come out to investigate the unusual circumstance, and meet his doom.

Tuvok pounded the burrow for what seemed the better part of an hour. He changed hands every so often, and then finally began using his feet. He began to wonder if this old folktale were true or if he were making a fool of himself, sitting on a mound of sand, pounding on it like a demented drummer.

But, eventually, he saw a slight movement, a shifting in the sand, and then a long pointed snout poked into the air, twisting this way and that, trying to find the source of the disturbance. Gradually the head emerged, protruding eyes scanning nervously, but not, fortunately for Tuvok, behind it, and then furry shoulders shook their way out of the sand, followed by the squat fleshy body.

Tuvok's knife fell swiftly; the merak went from a condition of animal curiosity to oblivion in an instant, unaware of its own doom. Tuvok turned the creature upside down and slit the underbelly, then lifted it to his lips and drank the dark warm blood that poured forth. It had a salty flavor, musky and fragrant, and he gulped it greedily, hoping to get his fill before it began to clot. When the blood was drained, he skinned the animal and then cut the muscle from its bones, eating it raw, in small bites chewed carefully, until it was gone.

Tuvok had never done anything remotely like this. Vulcans had been vegetarians ever since the time of Surak. He had read of the meat-eating practices of his ancestors, the desert-dwellers, and assumed that he would be able to do the same. But now it occurred to him how primitive an act it was to slay an animal, and how there might have been every chance that, when the time came, he would not have been able to perform it, or that he would have done it so unskillfully that it would have failed.

But those were afterthoughts. In fact, when the time came, Tuvok moved with surety and ease, instinctively doing what he must. He pondered that fact, curious as to how this behavior fit into the continuing enigma: Why was he doing what he was doing, and what would be the result?

Another two weeks into the desert, and those questions had still not been answered. Tuvok had killed and eaten twice more, and though he was not as strong as he had been when he started out, he was nonetheless able to maintain a constant pace across the sand.

In the first blush of morning light and in the waning hours of the day—the only time he saw light on the desert—he noticed that the color of the sands was beginning to change. What had once been a rust-red had paled gradually, and was now the shade of a weak tea, a light brown flecked occasionally with umber. He knew that meant he was beginning to move into the vast white sands that surrounded Seleya, and his heart quickened to realize it. He began to think of his journey as nearly over, when actually it was just beginning, and his greatest trials were yet to come.

Eventually, he lost track of how long he had been marching through the blistering wastes. There was only the vastness, the great expanse of sand, growing whiter with each day, and the broad horizon; time ceased to have meaning as he plodded in his steady pace, eyes straining to find the first sign of Seleya in the distance. He dozed fitfully during the day, then rose before the sun fell and started out once more.

T'Khut was an occasional escort, waxing and waning, staring down at him, the "watcher" of ancient yore. He continued to search its immutable face for some indication of the motivation behind his quest, but then one day he questioned why he thought he would find what he was seeking in the face of T'Khut and he realized he couldn't answer that, either.

His journey was not proving satisfying; it gave him no answers, only more questions.

Still he moved forward. Hunger and thirst were constant companions, so much so that he thought of his condition now as the natural state, and the absence of those sensations as abnormal. He found it more and more difficult to find meraks, and seemed to remember that they preferred the dark sand habitats; now he was moving into the territory of the sehlats and lematyas, and must be wary. They were a danger to him, but he also needed to hunt them, for they would be his only source of nourishment.

His first encounter with a sehlat came in the middle of one night, as he was marching steadily toward the sacred mountain, whose peak had yet to be seen on the horizon. He heard an aberrant sound, a rustling in the sand, and stopped instantly, ears tuned for the shuffling noise, his fingers already gripping the handle of his knife.

T'Khut was a slim crescent, and gave off only slight illumination, but it was enough to reflect in two red eyes some ten meters distant. A low growl told Tuvok he had encountered his first sehlat, but not what the result of that encounter would be.

They stood like that, watching each other, for a quarter of an hour. The sehlat was tensed, ready to spring, long claws digging into the desert floor, dark fur standing in an agitated ruff along his back. Tuvok acknowledged that he didn't have a clear idea of what to do. If he moved off, turning his back on the animal, it would surely attack from the rear. On the other hand, he could not stand like this indefinitely, waiting for the sehlat to retreat; he must keep moving toward the mountain.

"We must come to terms, sehlat," said Tuvok aloud, and the sound of his voice was strange in his ears, like the vaguely familiar sound of an alien musical instrument; it was the first such sound he'd heard since he left his home weeks ago.

The sehlat cocked its head at the utterance, fierce teeth bared, wicked canines glistening in T'Khut's reflected light, and didn't move.

"I must keep moving toward Seleya," Tuvok continued, "and I do not care to think of you attacking from behind."

The sehlat snorted briefly, and pawed the ground with one massive claw. Then it turned in the direction of the sacred mountain and began trotting toward it, not looking back. Tuvok watched it for a moment, and then followed. He didn't believe the animal was going to Seleya; rather, the sound of his voice had broken whatever animal tension existed between them, and the creature was merely moving off to hunt, or to find its own kind.

But by morning, the dark brown sehlat was still with him, trotting steadily toward the mountain. Again, Tuvok was uncertain. The sun was already warming the morning air, and it was time for him to rest. But if he fell asleep, there was every chance the beast would pounce, ripping out his throat and devouring him.

He stopped and sat down on the sands, creating a berm, as was his custom, to shelter him from the sun. The sehlat had proceeded on his way until he sensed Tuvok was no longer behind him, and then he stopped, turned, and stared at him. He no longer bared his teeth, and seemed to Tuvok almost quizzical.

"I must rest," said Tuvok. "You must be weary, as well. Let us sleep now, and proceed again at nightfall."

The beast eyed him briefly, then dropped on his stomach and began digging in a curious fashion in the sand. Presently his body was submerged, except for his nose, which extruded from the sand, barely noticeable. Tuvok wondered how many sleeping sehlats he might have walked near, or over, without realizing it.

Now a dilemma presented itself. He was thirsty and hungry. The sehlat would make several meals, and its blood would slake his thirst. Now was the time to creep up upon it, to plunge his knife into its skull. That was the logical course of action.

But something stayed his hand. He did not actually think the animal capable of thought, or decision, or loyalty, and yet it had not attacked him, had traveled with him for most of the night, and now seemed content to bed down in the sand while Tuvok himself slept. He didn't intend to romanticize the situation, but he couldn't avoid the sense that they had bonded, the sehlat and he, and that to kill it now was to violate some canon of the desert. And surely that would doom his venture.

And so he lay down behind his berm and closed his eyes against the sun, and trusted that he would be alive when the sun set.

For four days he and the sehlat traveled together, sleeping by day and walking by night. It was another mystery with which the desert had presented him, but Tuvok found that he no longer cared to struggle to solve these conundrums. Why the sehlat had chosen to accompany him might remain an unanswerable question, and here in the unfathomed expanse of white sand, that seemed perfectly acceptable. It simply was.

There was a growing problem, however: he had seen no signs of other animal life, and the need for food and fluid was becoming urgent. "We are both growing weaker, sehlat," Tuvok said, and the effort hurt his parched throat and lips. "This is your domain. I ask your help."

This was as he lay down behind the berm he had created and closed his eyes. Sleep came more easily every day.

When he woke it was from a dream that had promised to show him the answers to his questions: a dark presence, a black form, shapeless, hovered in his dream, the repository of knowledge. Tuvok longed to plunge within its depths, to know the unknowable, to be lost forever in its tenebrous folds. But the more he struggled toward it, the more quickly it receded, until it was gone like a shadow dissolving in the morning sun.

His eyes opened and the sehlat was standing over him, snout dripping with blood, and Tuvok startled awake, jumping to his feet.

Lying in the sand near him was the half-eaten body of a lematya, blood still unclotted and dripping onto the sand. Tuvok took it quickly and sliced other veins, drinking greedily of the thick liquid which poured out, thinking he had never tasted anything so sweet. He then devoured the flesh, ripping meat from the bones without using his knife, even as the sehlat had fed.

When he was done, his face was covered in blood, and he suddenly felt the overpowering need to cry out, to howl at the setting sun, and he did, an ancient baying that took flight on the still desert air and disappeared into its depths.

The sehlat cocked its head and regarded him; had Tuvok not known better, he would have thought the creature was mocking him.

On the fifth day of their communal adventure, Tuvok thought he saw something in the dawning sun: the tiny tip of something—a mountaintop?—on the horizon. He blinked again and again, trying to determine whether it was merely a shimmer of heat or actually was what he had been seeking all these weeks, sacred Seleya, most holy place on all of Vulcan.

Even if it were the mountaintop that he saw in the distance, he knew the end of his quest was not near; it would take weeks more to cross the sands that lay between him (and the sehlat) and the mountain.

But his heart felt lighter, nonetheless. He had survived what he was sure was the worst of the journey, and now Seleya was in sight. That thought would sustain him.

One day after that, the Winds arrived.

Every Vulcan child had heard of these fierce desert gales, the stuff of legend and myth. Winds that whipped the sands into billowing, rasping clouds, turning the desert dark for days on end, swallowing men and beasts whole like a gluttonous leviathan. It was a thrilling legend, told in the safety of warm sleeping rooms, and children shivered at the tale, then snuggled under soft covers and dreamt of desert adventures and conquering heroes.

The sehlat was the first to detect the oncoming gusts. He was restless, pawing in the sand with his claws as Tuvok prepared his berm for the day, raising his nose to sniff the wind, uttering a mewling cry, and then beginning the whole process again.

Tuvok lifted his head from his endeavors and saw, behind him, what appeared to be a puff of dust in the distance, too far away to be of any concern. He resumed his digging, only to feel the sehlat's strangely cold nose under his hands, lifting them from the task. Tuvok stood, and looked again at the puff of dust.

It was more than a puff now, rolling like a fog bank on the horizon, far across the sands over which he had traveled, but moving inexorably closer.

"The Winds?" he murmured, and then realized there would be no sleeping today. They must keep moving, try to stay ahead of this murderous storm. He glanced at the sehlat and then began moving forward with quick, purposeful strides, only occasionally looking back over his shoulder.

Each time, the dust cloud was gaining on them.

It made a noise like animals screaming, a chilling, unnatural sound, spirits wailing from the terrible underworld, tormented and suffering. That sound gradually overwhelmed Tuvok. He wanted to stay ahead of that bestial cry, which seemed more ominous even than the punishing grinding of the sand.

Neither, of course, was to be avoided. The Winds arrived by midday with a howling cry, a bray of triumph. The sands exploded on him and the sehlat, drilling them with millions of tiny needles which stung as though tipped with acid. Tuvok was thrown to his knees, and as he fell he grabbed one corner of his robe and covered his face with it, filtering the sand. The sehlat inched toward him, face wrinkled in misery, pitiful bleats emitting from his clenched jaw. Tuvok pulled the muscular beast in close to him and covered it with the other side of his robe. There, the two of them huddled, waiting out the storm.

But the winds of Vulcan are not so easily endured. Tuvok and his companion crouched in the vortex of sand for hours, tens of hours, days, and still the storm lashed at them. It had no beginning, it had no ending, it simply was, eternal, the only reality that existed: the noise, the stinging needles, the nut-colored mist of particulates comprised the totality of their universe.

Tuvok had no idea how long they had crouched like that when he began to hallucinate. First he detected a decrease in the noise level, as though a dampener had suddenly been applied, and he lifted his head to peer out. Utter silence then descended on him, and the swirling sands took on a diaphanous quality, a luminous shimmering which was utterly beguiling.

Then he was ascending through this sparkling mist, rising above the desert floor, looking down at his crouched body and that of the sehlat, far below. He hovered there, drifting in the vaporous winds— breezes, really, just gentle breezes—turning slowly and languidly above his own figure.

Curious. What was he to make of this? It was certainly pleasant up here, far more so than down in the roaring, rasping Winds, but there was something amiss about it. How could he reach Seleya like this? Was it possible to fly? The idea held a certain appeal, but he was definitely not in control of his path and was not moving in any direction—just drifting, languorous.

He tried to make himself heavy, so he would float downward, but his efforts accomplished nothing. He summoned all the concentration of his mind's powers he could, and willed himself to return to his body.

But still he wafted, effortlessly, suspended in this strange union with his body, equally unable to move from, or return to, the prostrate form.

It occurred to him that he might be dead.

Such experiences had been recounted by some who had experienced death, only to be snatched back through medical intervention or sheer happenstance: this same watching from above, seeing one's inert body below, a condition which existed until the fact of death was accepted and one's katra moved on to—wherever it went. There were, of course, no accounts of where that was, for the reporters had, by definition, returned before getting there.

Tuvok considered the possibility of his death, and was not inclined to accept it. He had come too far and endured too much to countenance failure this close to realizing his quest. "I am not yet done," his mind said to whatever forces might be at play here. "I must finish the journey to Seleya."

Below, he saw the sehlat move its nose to his face and snuffle at it for a moment, then begin to lick at his cheeks, his mouth, his eyes. He pondered the improbability of this particular sehlat's nature. The beasts were known to be vicious and cunning, driven by predatory instincts and primal urges. In their feral state they did not behave as house pets, docilely trotting alongside a master and snuggling up to him in times of strife. Nor were they known to procure food for anyone other than themselves. This sehlat was indeed puzzling.

How to explain that? Several options came to mind: perhaps it was simply his good fortune to have encountered an animal with domesticated tendencies. Or it may be that he had simply hallucinated the beast, even as he now seemed to be hallucinating this strange hovering above himself. It was even possible that the sehlat was, in some way, divine, a messenger sent to him from some unknown dimension, in order to impart—

—an unpleasant odor assaulted his nose, and his skin was being grated with an abrasive object, over and over. He frowned and struggled upright, opening his eyes slightly.

The sandstorm wailed around him, fierce and biting as ever. But he was safely returned to his own body, a fact which was a source of surprising comfort to him. The sehlat crouched over him, peering at him with what Tuvok might—had he chosen to anthropomorphize this animal even further—term anxiety. Some instinct made him reach out and scratch the sehlat gratefully on the head.

"We must leave this place," Tuvok announced, voice raised against the shriek of the Winds. "We must keep moving. We will die if we stay here." He struggled uncertainly to his feet (how much easier it had been to hover, weightless, in the air) and forced his body forward, driving it against the formidable resistance of the swirling sand. The sehlat followed and, step by difficult step, they proceeded, Tuvok hoping that whatever providence had sent him the animal would also guide him in the right direction.

In what seemed one more day the gale began to diminish, the sound abating first; then the swirling sand began to lose some of its sting, and gradually it passed by them, roaring off across the desert and leaving him and the sehlat exhausted, covered in sand, and desperately thirsty. Tuvok brushed what sand he could from his face, dusted the sehlat's with the hem of his robe, and looked around.

Seleya was a triangle on the horizon, white and tiny, but most definitely there. Tuvok's heart quickened, and he turned to look down at his companion. "Look—our destination . . ." he began, but then he realized something was very wrong with the animal.

It lay on its side, tongue lolling out, eyes blank and staring, rib cage heaving rapidly as it panted desperately. Tuvok knelt quickly and felt the nose, which was warm and dry. The rugged beast had pushed itself to its limit, but now it could go no further; it was dying.

Tuvok looked off to Seleya in the distance, the longed-for goal now manifest. He was weak and thirsty, but he knew he could go on, lured by the proximity of the sacred mountain. It was the logical course, to continue his march and accomplish what he had set out to do. Sehlats were born in the desert and died in the desert; it was the natural order of things.

But he could not bring himself to abandon the beast. He assured himself it was not an emotional decision, but an unwillingness to offend whatever spirits might be at play in this vast expanse. Inexplicable things had happened to him during this remarkable sojourn, and he felt the power of mysterious forces all about him. Things unknown were present here, and it was therefore not possible to act according to any prior set of expectations. With imperfect knowledge, one could not be in control of one's fate.

The appearance of the sehlat, his unusual behavior, his loyalty—all seemed to point to a guiding presence, and to affront that presence might be to invite disaster. To turn one's back on a benefactor was surely an insult to any being, corporeal or not.

And so he sat down beside the sehlat and stroked his head. "I can see the mountain. It gains me nothing simply to see *more* of it. I deem my journey over." The sehlat made no response.

They sat like that for a long, uncounted time, Tuvok keeping his eyes firmly fixed on the faraway triangle, wondering if in fact he had accomplished anything. The vague questions with which he started had not been answered nor even clarified, and new questions had been added along the way. And the sight of the mountain—the tip of the mountain—brought him no relief, no fulfillment. To what end, then, had he endured this travail?

He thought about that for a long time, worrying the idea like a fine point of logical debate, and had lost himself in a serpentine series of possible deductions when he realized he heard something—had been hearing something for a while, in fact, without its having registered on his conscious mind. It was a low, rumbling sound and it seemed to be coming from all around him.

He looked up and realized the sky had darkened, even though it was, by his reckoning, midday. Shadowy yellow clouds sagged above him, ominous and foreboding. In a second's astonishment, he understood that he was hearing something Vulcans heard only rarely: thunder. As the rumbling grew louder, the saffron clouds were illuminated from within by flashes of light. A rainstorm was approaching.

Rainfall was scant on Vulcan, and almost unheard of in the desert. There were stories of torrential downpours that erupted only a few times each century, but were leviathan in their immensity. Tuvok acknowledged a palpable sense of awe that he was about to witness one of these legendary events, and stood as though to greet it with proper reverence.

The air temperature had dropped quickly and a cooling breeze began to stir. It was utterly unlike the punishing winds they had recently survived, and was refreshing in its chilliness. It caressed Tuvok's body gently, as though assuaging a fever, and he shivered as he had not since his last Pon farr.

The rumbling of thunder now became louder, and assumed the form of discrete claps, which resonated through the clouds with the sound of the most powerful photon cannon, and were followed by a sharp brightening of the clouds, turning them from yellow-brown to a brilliant gold. Tuvok studied the changing palette of the sky as though evaluating a colossal painting, then he felt the strange oppressiveness of humidity in the air, and smelled the scent of moisture.

Presently, the first drops of water fell.

He turned his face toward the sky and felt the liquid plash of rainfall on his cheeks, his forehead, his eyelids, a balm of wetness that soothed and healed. He opened his mouth as the rainfall became more intense, and gulped mouthful after mouthful of the sweet liquid.

He then turned to the sehlat, who had lifted his snout as though he, too, were trying to lick at the falling rain. Tuvok cupped his hands until they filled with water, then tilted them so the liquid ran down the animal's throat. He repeated this over and over, until finally the animal rose shakily to its feet.

The rain had turned the desert sand to a caked mass; Tuvok began digging a series of bowl-like indentations, which quickly filled with water and made drinking much easier. The sehlat lapped at the puddles and Tuvok scooped handful after handful until he had drunk so much he felt ready to burst.

Another bounty was provided by the rainstorm: small, sand-burrowing animals came scrambling to the surface, lizards and voles and others Tuvok had never seen before, trying to escape the sudden flood of their burrows. Both he and the sehlat became ardent hunters, and ate rapaciously until their hunger was as slaked as their thirst.

And still the rains fell, not in a lashing, brutal attack, but in a steady torrent, a powerful cascade of water from above, cleansing, healing. When Tuvok had eaten and drunk his fill, he removed his robe and stood naked in the downpour, feeling the drenching caress of the deluge; something primal, something elemental stirred in him. His most ancient ancestors had lived in these deserts, unfettered by clothing, unabetted by technology, living a hardscrabble life of deprivation and thirst, occasionally indulging in an unexpected bounty of nature like this thunderstorm. He felt a palpable link to those ancient people, a connection that stretched over millennia, and with that joining came a sense of intensity and might, a tapping into elements of himself that he had never known existed, much less accessed.

Powerful, endowed, he turned like a dancer on the desert floor, lifting his arms to the skies in an impromptu paean to Vulcan's past and the way in which it validated him. Nearby, the sehlat sat contentedly, wet coat matting around him, regarding the strange undulations of the naked man as he paid homage to the rain.

Four nights later, the euphoria of the rainstorm had evaporated like the moisture on the desert floor. He was not hungry or thirsty; there was still an abundance of small creatures who had not yet returned to their underground existence, and he and the sehlat fed well.

But T'Khut had returned to loom above him in the night sky, and with its portentous appearance Tuvok's doubts returned. He had spent a great deal of time walking across the desert—exactly how much time he didn't know, but he was sure it was at least several months—and he had yet to feel any genuine sense of accomplishment. Seleya was there, growing larger with each night's walk, but he could only think of what he had said to the sehlat as it lay dying: what difference did it make if he got closer to it, if he got all the way to its base? He would see more of it, of course, and he could make the claim that he had endured long enough to bring his journey to completion. But what, ultimately, did that matter? Had all his effort, all this risk of his very life, been for no purpose other than to say he had completed what he started out to do?

It seemed a paltry reward.

Now that Seleya was within reach, his stomach full and thirst abated, he was more doubtful than he had been when he was near death from dehydration and starvation. This observation flew in the face of reason, and disturbed him more than he cared to acknowledge. It seemed that his expedition would end with no genuine resolution, no satisfaction, no enlightenment.

What, then, had it been for? He glanced down at the sehlat, trotting strongly at his side, and was struck again with the impossibility of explaining any of this. *The answers will come when they will come,* said a voice in his head, *not when you decide you need them.* It was a calming thought, and he decided to trust it.

No sooner had he made that decision than the ground beneath him trembled slightly. It was a mild quiver, nothing more, and though he paused for a full minute after that, uncertain whether to proceed, there was nothing more. He stepped forward once again, his eyes trained on T'Khut, which seemed to foam in the dark sky, fiery volcanoes spewing fire. He felt it was appropriate that T'Khut be visible on this, the last leg of his journey; it brought his pilgrimage full circle.

The ground shuddered again, this time more emphatically, and the sands shifted uneasily beneath his feet. Tuvok stopped, recognizing the tremor as a small earthquake. What other phenomenon of nature would this barren wasteland produce for him? Drought, wind, rainstorm, and now temblors. He glanced up at Seleya, as though its snowy summit might suddenly erupt with volcanic activity.

Another quake, and Tuvok half crouched, unable to keep his balance on the moving sand. He realized with some disquiet that there was no solidity, no permanence to sand; it was quite possibly the worst place to be during a series of earthquakes. If the tremors became violent enough, great sinkholes could develop, yawning chasms which could suck him into their depths and bury him beneath thousands of kilograms of sand. He looked for the sehlat and saw it standing, frozen and alert, dark fur standing on end.

Now the ground was shaking violently, and he fell to it, unable to keep his balance. He spread his arms and legs wide, to reduce the risk of his being swallowed by the now heaving sand. A great roar ensued, a sound that reminded him of the fierce howl of the Winds, but infinitely lower, deeper, as though a thousand tympanums were resonating. The rocking of the earth was now violent, and for perhaps the dozenth time since he began his journey, Tuvok anticipated his demise.

Then a strange darkness descended and the frenzied vibrations subsided. Tuvok dared to look up from his spread-eagled position on the now quiet sands.

T'Khut had disappeared, as had Seleya.

Confusion clawed at his mind. The earthquakes might have toppled Seleya, but how could they have affected T'Khut, who sailed majestically in orbit, unassailable by planet-based temblors?

Gingerly, he came to his hands and knees, looking upward, searching for an answer to this latest mystery. He saw only darkness above him.

And then the darkness spoke. With a searing assault, images invaded his mind, tumbling, overwhelming, drowning him in visions. He gasped from the impact of it, and then drew desperate, ragged breaths of air into suddenly oxygen-starved lungs. He saw sights he could not have imagined, strange, swirling worlds awash in color and blood, songs that he saw rather than heard, except that he heard them too, a cacophony of dissonant melodies, exotic and overpowering.

Then, with startling clarity, he understood what was happening, and he stared up at the Underlier which had risen from beneath the sands, its immensity blocking the night sky and obliterating the sight of Seleya and T'Khut. Its huge mass arched above him, gargantuan, and in its roar was contained the knowledge of the ages. Into Tuvok's head vaulted images of enormous scope: he saw the births and deaths of civilizations, he witnessed the great events of history on every settled planet; he was both an observer and a participant in the great battles of all time, from the ancient to the future; he created poetry and music and lived a million lifetimes, until he was a witness to the end of the universe, the entropy that consumed everything in the great heat death, and then he saw the form of the Other and knew he was able to grasp infinite truth, it was just beyond him, a fingertip away . . .

. . . and then with stunning intensity he possessed it: the answers to all questions ever asked, the revelation of the wisdom of the universe, the secrets of starbirth, insight into the infinite. It was a glorious, dazzling, joyous sensation, and he howled with delight, his puny voice absorbed by the Underlier, joined with it, until they became one and Tuvok's mind opened further and further and then the face of the Other was just about to be revealed to him, a great white light was bursting and it was there, there, right before him, he could reach out and touch the face of the Other—

With an enormous hiss, the Underlier began to sink beneath the sands once more. It happened remarkably quickly as the great being sank down, down, down, to the black depths where there was no light, no air, nothing but the crushing weight of the sand.

Seleya and T'Khut were in their rightful place once more, stately and serene, as though a miracle had not just taken place.

The sehlat had disappeared.

Tuvok stood alone in the darkness, trying to hold on to what he had just experienced, but everything was dancing away from him, sparkling motes in the air that he tried to grasp but which eluded him and then dissolved into nothingness.

The silence was monstrous. He put his hand on his chest and felt his heart thundering against his ribs, and he took several deep breaths in an automatic response to bring it under control. Then he sat down to contemplate what had happened.

The vast insights of his experience had vanished. He no longer understood the universe, he no longer knew infinite truth. He couldn't summon up the face of the Other. All that knowledge had been his for the briefest of instances, and then it disappeared beneath the sands with the Underlier.

But one thing that was revealed, he retained: the reason he had undertaken his journey. Though he hadn't known it at the time, it was to see the Underlier, *a'kweth,* the repository of all knowledge. For one brief and transcendent moment, he, too, had possessed that knowledge, and if he no longer did, that was as it should be; man is too flimsy to bear the weight of that much wisdom. A half-second's insight is almost too overwhelming, and one would surely perish if required to retain it any longer.

He had touched something holy, and he was fulfilled. He rose to his feet and continued marching resolutely toward Seleya, but in fact his passage was complete. He had held the infinite in his mind and no one could ask more than that.

Two days after that, when he emerged from the desert wilderness and came to the base of Seleya, he was greeted by a group of Vulcans who stared at him with barely concealed curiosity. He couldn't imagine how he must look after having lived in the desert for months, but it was a sight that obviously had an impact on his normally stoic countrymen, who spoke to him uncertainly, as though believing he must be a madman. They seemed relieved when he responded lucidly, and when he related his adventure they were almost reverent in their awe, recognizing his feat as something unique and wondrous, something they would never attempt. They arranged for him to transport back to his home as soon as he had paid whatever obeisance he had planned to the sacred mountain.

But that was now irrelevant to him. Tuvok had made decisions. He could no longer live the life of an ascetic, and he must give something back to the universe in return for the gift it had shared with him. He would never abandon his family, for they completed him, but he would petition to rejoin Starfleet, and pledge his life toward exploration and investigation. A debt must be paid.

His reinstatement as an ensign might have been difficult for some people of his age to accept, but Tuvok saw it as a just decision. He had made his choice years ago to leave Starfleet; it should be he, not Starfleet, who paid the consequences.

His only impatience came with the schedule of his return to deep-space duty. Starfleet had seen fit to assign him to Headquarters, to serve on the review board as tactical officer, and he had spent months evaluating captains' procedures with regard to weapons and tactics, a task requiring meticulous attention to detail, which suited his skills well. But it was also a limited and repetitive chore with little of particular challenge to him. His promise in the desert had to do with exploration, not with endless assessment of tactical logs.

Nonetheless, he accepted the assignment without protest, and applied his skill and intelligence to it, working diligently and thoroughly, to the delight of his Starfleet superiors. They were so enthusiastic about his performance, in fact, that he wondered if they would elect to keep him here, on Terra, at the same redundant task, until he retired.

Most of the reviews he conducted were routine. Starfleet captains didn't get to their positions by ignoring regulations, and Tuvok examined scores of logs that were models of precision and flawless performance. In general, he had only to mark "approved" on the padd and his job was done.

His immediate superior was Admiral McGeorge Finnegan, a generous, expansive man in his fifties with a thatch of red hair graying in spots, and a ready smile. As Tuvok sat in his office one gray

November afternoon, methodically studying a set of logs from the *U.S.S. Appalachia,* which had just returned from a mission to the Barnard's Star system, Admiral Finnegan rapped casually on the doorjamb and leaned in, padd in hand.

"You'll have to put the *Appalacia* aside for the moment," he announced. "We have a first-mission review that Owen Paris has personally asked to be put at the top of the list."

The Vulcan's eyebrow lifted automatically at this news. It was unusual for Admiral Paris to make such a request, and Tuvok was curious as to the reason.

"I know what you're thinking," said Finnegan with a smile. "This particular captain seems to be one of Owen's pet projects. He's been like a nervous father for the last few days."

Tuvok frowned. He felt this attitude was unsuitable, and he was reminded, as he was every day, of the willingness among humans to allow emotional involvement to determine procedure. But he had long ago stopped thinking he could change their nature. All he could do was to perform his own duties with as much intellectual rigor as possible.

When he reviewed the tactical logs of this particular captain, one Kathryn Janeway, he was appalled. For the first time, he felt his position was justified, and was gratified that the many months of studying logs had given him the experience necessary to ascertain that these particular records were abominable. Captain Janeway had taken her ship, the *Bonestell,* into the Beta Quadrant and gathered information on microsecond pulsars, and he hoped her scientific methodology was more precise than her attention to tactical matters would seem to indicate. He was somewhat amazed that a captain would dare to submit an accounting that made her look so inept.

Tuvok began taking notes on all the transgressions, and stayed in his office long into the night in order to write as thorough a report as possible. In all, he cited forty-one violations of tactical procedures, including an absence of test firings and battle drills, with only two weapons reviews during the entire six-month mission. He found it hard to imagine that a Starfleet officer would pay such lax attention to details.

When he left his office that night, he noticed lights burning in several offices of Starfleet Headquarters. Curious, he stopped to see if Admiral Finnegan were there, and found his superior in his office looking wan and haggard.

"It's a terrible tragedy," he said to Tuvok. "Owen's son, Thomas, and three other cadets were in the Vega system, practicing asteroid deflection. There was a collision. The three cadets were killed."

"That is regrettable," said Tuvok sincerely, thinking of his own children and allowing himself a flickering twinge of relief that they had chosen to remain on Vulcan and eschew the sometimes dangerous path of joining Starfleet. Although it was true that no one could predict the vagaries of life, it was unlikely that he would get a message similar to the one three sets of parents had received that day, and for that he was grateful.

Disliking these unusual thoughts, he turned his attention once more to his task. "I am sorry to inform you, sir, that my analysis of Captain Janeway, Admiral Paris's protégée, suggests an officer who is less than capable."

But Finnegan was too consumed with the recent tragedy to care about a minor tactical report. He waved Tuvok off, wearily. "We'll deal with that tomorrow," he sighed. "I'm waiting for the sensor logs in Cadet Paris's shuttle to be downloaded."

Tuvok nodded and left. He understood the admiral's priorities. But he also knew he had to keep his own in proper alignment.

The next afternoon, he checked his notes thoroughly in order to make certain they were accurate. In doing so, he noticed two more violations of procedure which, though minor, must nonetheless be included. He left a message for Admiral Finnegan that he would be with them as soon as he had corrected the entries.

As soon as he was done, he hurried to the paneled room in which reviews were always held, and found three admirals—Finnegan, Paris, and Nechayev—already there. Standing to one side was a dainty, small-boned woman who nonetheless emanated strength, whose brown hair was neatly coiffed, and whose gray-blue eyes reflected a keen intelligence. Admiral Finnegan was introducing them, gesturing to Tuvok and saying, "Captain Janeway, may I present Ensign Tuvok."

The woman extended her hand and he took it. "Captain," he intoned, and then set a stack of padds on the table. Within minutes Finnegan had turned the meeting over to him, and without hesitation Tuvok launched into his review, citing each of the forty-three violations along with his opinion as to whether the infraction was major or minor. As he spoke, he was aware that Captain Janeway was studying him intently, and he was certain she intended to argue each point with him.

When he had finished, Admiral Finnegan turned to her. "You may feel free to answer the charges, Captain."

The woman sat quietly for a moment, then rose. "Sir, I was raised in the traditions of Starfleet. I learned the precepts of this organization at an early age; I admire and honor them."

Her voice was clear and strong, and she spoke with earnest conviction. Illogically, but earnestly. When she had finished trying to rationalize her errors, Tuvok rebutted, and she rebutted that statement, and so on until they were sent into the hallway while the admirals decided the outcome of the hearing, which came quickly. As Tuvok had known they would, the admirals rebuked Captain Janeway for having violated tactical procedures.

He was caught off-guard, however, when they announced that they intended to post him to her ship, for he had not anticipated such a maneuver. But he quickly saw its definitive logic. This was a captain who could be developing bad habits, and she required firm guidance. He had no doubt that, with his help, she might yet be molded into a passable officer.

Five months later, he despaired of that task. The woman was simply the most stubborn, frustrating, impossible human he'd ever met. He had already decided to request another posting as soon as they returned from their present mission, a survey of supernova remnants in the Trige sector. In the meantime, he intended to keep insisting that she follow protocols.

"Good morning, Captain," he intoned as she came on the bridge. "Weapons systems are on-line and ready for weekly review."

"I'm sure I can leave that task in your capable hands, Tuvok."

"I have done so, as I do each day," he replied, "but regulations clearly state that at least once a week the captain is expected to review weapons status."

"Strange. That seems to imply that the captain has no faith in her tactical officer, which I assure you is far from the case. I trust you implicitly."

Was there the slightest curl to her lips? Tuvok could never be sure. Captain Janeway was always poised, cool, implacable. He had learned that human humor took many forms, and he lacked the ability to distinguish between them, especially if they were subtle. But it was entirely possible that the captain was mocking him.

"I did not think that you lacked faith in me, Captain. However, if you trust me so fully, why is it you pay so little heed to my recommendations?"

"I believe in establishing a self-reliant crew, one that doesn't need the captain looking over their shoulders all the time. Surely my time is better spent elsewhere."

Tuvok couldn't conceal a deep breath that might have been termed a sigh. They'd been at this long enough for him to know she wouldn't yield.

"Very well, Captain. I will once again review the weapons systems. My report will be in your console within the hour."

"Thank you, Tuvok. I'm so glad you understand."

He didn't deign to respond.

On that morning, however, Tuvok would not complete the weapons review, for Captain Janeway indulged another of her habits: becoming so excited about a possible scientific discovery that she put herself in mortal danger.

They were within scanning distance of a main-sequence star system consisting of seven planets, one of which intrigued the captain because it was an M-class sphere that closely resembled Earth, albeit at a much earlier stage of its evolutionary history.

"Remarkable," said the captain as she read the sensors. "It looks like Earth might have in the Mesozoic Era—one hundred and fifty million years ago. This planet might give us some insights into our own history. We've got to go down there."

"Captain, I point out that this is a highly treacherous environment. There are violent storms, volcanic activity, seismic temblors. I suggest that sensors and automated probes can perform any tasks of exploration that you might require."

But her face was shining, eyes alight with curiosity and determination. "How can I not see what it looks like? This is a chance to travel back in time, to see what our own planet might have been like millions of years ago. No, Tuvok, I'm not going to miss an opportunity like this."

"Then I will accompany you. As will a full security detail."

"And I'll want a full scientific detail, as well. We'll make a regular party of it. This is so exciting, Tuvok!"

"Yes, Captain." Tuvok's mind was already organizing the security detail, anticipating the possible problems involved in this foolish quest. What kind of captain was this to be so guided by whim and caprice? To abandon her scheduled mission on an impulse, undoubtedly endangering not only herself but the other members of the away team as well. *A party,* indeed. He renewed his resolve to request a different posting at the earliest possible moment. Perhaps he would even send a transmission to Starfleet Headquarters from the ship.

An hour later they transported to an alien surface that was as unusual as any Tuvok had ever seen. Distant volcanoes belched smoke into the hot air of a landscape dotted with odd-looking vegetation. Huge tree ferns, some fifteen meters tall, bowed and swayed with frenzied energy in the smoky winds.

Captain Janeway began running back and forth like an unruly schoolchild, tricorder scanning here, there—Tuvok was sure it was quite impossible to get accurate readings with such a scattergun approach. This mad folly wouldn't even lead to valid scientific data.

The away team stood atop a precipice overlooking the vast landscape. Behind them stretched an expanse of land upon which danced the tree ferns; below them lay a huge body of water, boiling, throwing up huge gusts of steam. A hot wind lashed them, carrying off their words as they shouted to each other. It occurred to Tuvok that this world was as frantic and disordered as humans were themselves.

Particularly Captain Janeway, who was now shouting orders to the science team, which then moved off in different directions, wielding their tricorders like wands. Tuvok himself kept a wary eye on the sky, which contained a number of reptilian birds, swooping and diving, apparently not yet having noticed the new intruders. But he was sure they soon would. He put his hand on his phaser, and nodded for his security team to accompany the wandering scientists.

He intended to stay close to the captain, whose youthful jubilation could well hamper her judgment and cause her to place herself in even greater danger than they were in simply by coming to this ferocious environment.

He was watching one particularly fierce-looking bird which was straying ever closer to them. "Captain," he began, wanting to alert her to its presence, but when he looked for her, she was nowhere to be seen.

Tuvok bolted to the edge of the precipice where he'd last seen her and looked over it, dreading what he might see—her body, broken on the harsh rocks, or sinking beneath the bubbling waves of that boiling lake . . .

What he saw surprised him even more. She was climbing, precariously, down the side of the cliff. What was the woman thinking?

Then he realized there was a large nest tucked in the crags of a rocky outcropping, and within that nest lay two eggs, mottled in brown and green.

"Captain!" he bellowed over the wind, but she gave no indication that she heard him. He looked back at the smoky sky, and saw the bird drifting closer, borne by the updrafts of the hot, humid air, giant wings spread to their full width, which he estimated to be a good two meters.

It was close enough now to see the bird's head, and he watched in curious fascination for a moment. The head looked more like the head of an animal than that of a bird. Eyes were set in front, like a predator's, rather than on the sides. And the mouth, now agape, contained a set of quite vicious teeth—teeth, he was sure, that were capable of ripping flesh from limb.

Tuvok waited no longer. He climbed over the side of the cliff and began climbing toward Janeway, cursing her, in his mind, as he did.

The noise of the wind was even louder on this side of the precipice, and powerful enough to make the going difficult, even for him. He wondered how that tiny slip of a woman could stay on her feet, but she was climbing nimbly, heading directly for the nest. Tuvok struggled toward her, casting frequent glances at the sky, but the cliff wall obscured the angle of his vision. He realized that if the bird was returning to its nest, it would be upon them almost without warning.

Captain Janeway was now near the nest, which she was scanning intently, holding on with her free hand to a jagged rock in order to keep her balance. She glanced back and saw Tuvok, and broke into an excited smile. She mouthed words which Tuvok couldn't hear, pointing toward the eggs.

In reply, Tuvok pointed to the sky—but as yet, the bird had not appeared. Perhaps this was not its nest, after all.

". . . eggs . . . may be . . . or saurian . . ." The captain's shouts were lost on the roaring winds, but there was no mistaking the genuine excitement on her face.

He was only a few feet from her now, and he hoped he could persuade her to give up this folly. "I suggest we ignore this nest, Captain," he shouted, but even as he did he realized she was not looking at him, but staring up, at something above him. Tuvok whirled and saw the predator bird diving toward them.

He drew his phaser, was vaguely aware of the captain shouting, "Don't hurt it!," but the bird rammed him before he could get off a shot. He lost his balance, teetered on the slippery rock, then grabbed for a hold with both hands, the phaser tumbling down the cliff face to the edge of the stormy lake far below.

The bird had circled away from them and was turning to make another dive. He moved to put his body in front of the captain's when he saw her pointing; he turned, and saw the opening.

Several meters from them, along a treacherous, rock-strewn path, was the opening to what might be a cave. The captain was already scrambling toward it, and Tuvok, casting a quick glance at the now-diving bird, followed quickly.

A heavy impact on his arm and then searing pain as the bird clamped down on his arm. He swung around with his other fist and hit it in the forehead, dislodging it. Then he dived into the cave.

It was small and cramped, but it would shield them from the predator bird, the opening being too small to admit it. He and Janeway crawled to the back wall of the cave and sat there catching their breath.

"You're hurt," she noticed.

Tuvok inspected his arm. His uniform was torn and there were angry green marks on the back of his upper arm, but the wound didn't look serious. "It's nothing," he told her.

"I think that bird is saurian. Or something very similar. Basically a pterodactyl—a flying dinosaur."

"And as deadly," he intoned. "I suggest we return to our ship immediately."

"Aren't you excited by what we've seen here? The data we've collected will be invaluable to paleontologists."

"I'm sure it is a discovery of great scientific significance."

She smiled and touched her combadge. "Janeway to the *Bonestell*. Two to beam up."

They waited, but they stayed where they were. "Janeway to the *Bonestell*. Do you read me?"

Silence. Janeway flipped open her tricorder, and a small frown appeared on her brow. "I'm not reading anything. There's some kind of interference in here . . ."

She waved the tricorder in all directions, apparently with the same result. She snapped it shut and settled back against the cave wall. "I guess we wait."

"For what, exactly, are we waiting? For the predator's eggs to hatch and the birds to grow large enough to fly away?"

To his amazement, Janeway burst out laughing. It was a big, hearty laugh, completely genuine, and it baffled Tuvok. What could she possibly find amusing about their situation? He watched as she rubbed her eyes, apparently having laughed herself into tears, another human trait which was mystifying.

"Tuvok, you're wonderful. I enjoy you so much."

He considered this statement, which was as puzzling as the rest of her behavior. "Captain," he said finally, "I must confess that I do not understand you. We are trapped in a small cave on a hostile planet, while a territorial predator awaits us outside, ready to attack and devour us as soon as we emerge. And yet you show no concern about the situation, and instead find it humorous. Could you explain?"

To his surprise, the captain came to him and put her hand on his shoulder, and gazed at him with eyes that seemed to emanate affection. "I'm so glad we were thrown together. I would never have chosen you, and then I'd have missed getting to know a most remarkable person."

Tuvok took three deep breaths in order to quiet the confusion in his mind. "At the risk of seeming dense, I simply don't understand. We were in conflict from the moment we met. We have remained so. You pay absolutely no attention to my recommendations, and in general ignore the Starfleet protocols I strive to effect. I have no sense that you admire, or even respect, me."

A change came over her, a twinge of concern. "I listen to everything you say. And I follow all your admonitions." There was a brief hesitation before she continued, with a bit of a lilt in her voice. "I just don't always let you know it."

What seemed to be a smile tugged at her mouth and Tuvok took a few more breaths, reminding himself of *cthia* and the power to control one's mind, which this capricious woman was in danger of undoing. "Could you explain?"

"I thought we were playing a game. It went on for so long I couldn't imagine that either of us took it seriously anymore."

Tuvok's bewilderment was now complete. "Captain, I am at a loss. I frankly don't understand anything you're saying, but it isn't necessary that I do so. I must inform you that I have decided to request a different posting as soon as we return from our mission." He glanced outside into the fierce alien environment. "Assuming we do," he added.

Janeway's face had become awash in emotions which he wouldn't begin to identify. She grasped one of his hands with both of hers, a gesture he found disquieting. "No, please," she implored. "You mustn't go. I need you too much."

"There are many fine officers who could serve you equally well—"

"No. Not as well. Tuvok, you are my rock, my ballast. You steady me in a way I've never felt before." She looked up at him, urgency giving her words a dimension he couldn't ignore. "I've been asked to take command of a new starship," she continued. "An Intrepid-class vessel called *Voyager*. It's an exciting opportunity, and I'd looked forward to sharing it with you. Please say you'll consider it."

Tuvok regarded her with as much equanimity as he could muster. "I am grateful for your confidence in me," he said carefully, "but I must have time to weigh the consequences of this decision."

"Fair enough. But I warn you—there's only one answer I'll accept." She was smiling again, and Tuvok mused that one could develop vertigo from trying to keep up with the emotional shifts in this mercurial woman.

Now she became brisk and businesslike. "Well, I'd hoped someone would have noticed our absence, but it looks as if we'll have to get out of here by ourselves." She took her tricorder from her waist and began working the controls. "I suspect an ultrasonic beam will confuse that poor flying creature long enough for us to be transported to the ship."

"I assume by 'that poor flying creature' you are referring to the rapacious predator that attacked us," said Tuvok dryly.

Janeway smiled as she reconfigured the tricorder. "She's just a mother guarding her babies," she said. "There's no need to hurt her. We're the ones invading her territory."

Tuvok started to remark that, given a choice, he himself would not have considered invading this territory, but he thought better of it. The captain looked up at him, cool and confident. She evinced no apprehension, no doubtfulness in her plan, and Tuvok had to admire her quiet courage.

"Let's give it a try," she said, and moved toward the opening of the small cave. Tuvok was right beside her.

They looked up to see the huge bird sitting in its nest, staring directly at them. It emitted a high shriek and rose to its feet, wings opening to carry it aloft. Janeway pointed the tricorder at it and activated the ultrasonic beam. The creature hesitated, folded its wings, opened them slightly. Its auditory senses were thrown off balance, and it didn't seem to know how to react.

"Janeway to *Bonestell*," the captain said after tapping her combadge. "Two to beam up."

In the brief instant before dematerialization, Tuvok realized that he had already made his decision. He could never hope to understand this complex woman, would probably always remain awash in the wake of her intricate emotional nature; but he could not deny that she was unique, powerful, and compelling. Committing himself to her would undoubtedly keep him in a greater state of turmoil than he might find comfortable, but it might also provide an experience of unparalleled adventure.

Something told him the rewards of this association would far outweigh the costs. He realized that insight wasn't particularly logical, but there was a curious satisfaction to it nonetheless.

CHAPTER

15

WHEN TUVOK WAS FINISHED, HE TURNED TO VORIK, AND THE TWO HELD A long, intense look. Clearly this remarkable tale was meant as a gift to the young Vulcan, but everyone else in the room had been awed by its telling as well. No one spoke.

Finally Tuvok looked around the room. "I think we must return to the business at hand," he declared. "Lieutenant Torres, when do you estimate the underground chamber will be completed?"

"With any luck, by tomorrow night," she replied. "We can't be sure until we actually transport someone down there, but Harry and I think by then we'll have carved out a space big enough for two people at a time."

"Then I suggest we make our attempt at that time. The longer we stay in this place, the greater the danger of our being discovered."

"And of our becoming sick and debilitated," added Chakotay. He glanced over toward Noah Mannick, who was lying on the ground, knees tucked into his chest. He had been experiencing severe cramps for most of the day, probably as a result of contaminated drinking water. Brad Harrison sat quietly by him, a comforting hand on Noah's shoulder. Illness was much to be feared in conditions like these, and Chakotay could sense Brad's concern, though the young man didn't voice it.

It was agreed that late tomorrow night, when the camp was at its quietest, they would begin the process of transporting themselves out of Hellhole and into the forest. What went unspoken was the fact that even if they were successful in doing so, they had no idea where to go from there.

Neelix was in a state of heightened expectation the next day, as the prospect of getting free of this oppressive place became more nearly a reality. He was careful, however to keep from revealing his excitement to Tassot Bnay, as they toiled in the psilminite mines, for he didn't want to arouse suspicion from any corner.

The day seemed endless. It was unusually hot, and he felt the top of his head stinging from the sun. The hours crept by in a haze of dust and noise, as the prisoners toiled to extract ore from the ground and the guards sat in the shade, chewing their mood-altering roots. It seemed to Neelix that they had become unusually noisy today, yattering and barking with laughter.

By late afternoon Neelix was all but trembling with anxiety and anticipation, willing the time to pass more quickly, compelling this day to be over. He couldn't resist another visit to the antigrav storage area to see if powder from the underground ore was still being deposited there. Once again, he feigned difficulty with one of the sleds, and then began to guide it around the periphery, out of sight of the guards and the other workers.

He returned the sled to its storage place, watching as a film of dust materialized and settled. Harry and B'Elanna were still working. Would they be finished with this interminable chore by tonight? It had been several days since they began; surely no one had envisioned its taking this long.

Neelix turned again to the dark forest, into which, if all went well, they would be entering tonight. This time, he couldn't resist investigating a bit more. He looked around carefully to make sure no one could see him, and then he crept into the thickly tangled undergrowth that flourished under the canopy of trees.

Immediately, it was many degrees cooler, and Neelix breathed the damp air gratefully. There was comfort in this tenebrous glade, respite from the relentless sun and heat. He listened for the sound of forest creatures, but heard nothing except the distant sound of the mining operation.

He continued into the forest for several meters when something made him turn around and look back out toward the storage area.

One of the Subu guards was there.

Neelix froze in the spot, reasonably sure the guard couldn't see him in the dark depths. When he had been out in the harsh sunlight, he couldn't see into the woods at all.

The guard moved along the length of the antigrav sleds, leaving footprints in the silty ground. Neelix prayed that he wouldn't walk right into a cloud of materializing ore dust, but he seemed to have moved beyond the area where it was being dumped.

The guard moved to the edge of the clearing, and then did something strange: he bent over slightly, and inserted one of his tentacle-like appendages into his mouth. Then he regurgitated a mass of partially digested matter.

Neelix's stomach quailed, but he forced himself to watch. He had no idea why the Subu was performing this indignation, and he didn't care. He only cared that he leave before there was another materialization of dust.

But the Subu continued to bend over, hacking and spitting. He was still in that position when Neelix saw the film of dust appear in the air and settle onto the ground.

Obscuring the Subu's footprints.

Neelix stared in fascination. Would the guard notice, when he returned, that the prints he had left were no longer there? Or was that a subtlety that might go unnoticed? He had no idea how basically bright these guards were—though frankly he hadn't been impressed by their alacrity so far.

The guard finally stood up and made his way back through the storage area toward the quarries. He seemed not to notice the ground, and his absent footprints, but instead continued coughing and spitting. Neelix surmised that he'd chewed too much of the narcotic root and had elected to bring it up in order to get rid of some of the substance. And if that were true, maybe he was too muddled to take close notice of what was going on around him.

The guard had almost cleared the storage area when he stopped, hesitated for a moment, then looked back. He seemed to scrutinize the ground in puzzlement. He lifted his feet and inspected the bottoms. Then he stared back at the ground, where his single set of tracks stretched behind him.

He stood like that for a full minute, shaking his head in seeming bewilderment. Finally he turned and moved back out of sight.

423

Neelix was still frozen in place as his mind reeled with indecision. Had the guard realized what had happened? Or was his brain so addled by narcotics that he was incapable of deducing why his footprints had disappeared?

He was certain the group was in more peril now than at any other time since they'd arrived here. They'd better accelerate their plans before they were uncovered. He wished he had his combadge in order to alert the others, but it had been taken to provide tuning circuits for the transporters.

He waited another few minutes, then casually emerged from the woods and took another antigrav sled, guiding it at his side, tinkering with it as though he were preoccupied with its performance. As he moved through the storage area, another deposit of dust appeared and settled to the ground, obliterating both his footprints and those that the guard had left.

The next hour passed like a week. Neelix kept sneaking looks at the guard who'd thrown up, trying to figure out if he was behaving as though he was suspicious. He didn't seem to be, sprawling lazily under the rock ledge, somnolent and dulled, staring out with hooded eyes at the activities of the miners.

Neelix had considered the possibility of feigning illness in order to be returned to the camp before the day was out. But he decided against it on several counts: it might draw attention to him and arouse even more suspicion; and the Subu guard, who didn't seem particularly leery about his experience, had settled into a torpor. There was no reason to panic.

The workday ended and the prisoners were herded together for the walk back to the camp. Neelix was eager to get back and see how close they were to putting their plan in motion. Four guards usually accompanied them, one ahead, one behind, one on either side. But today, as the group started out, the guard who had visited the storage area gestured to another one, and then, to Neelix's horror, began leading him back toward the stored sleds.

He had noticed! If he didn't understand what had happened, he had at least realized something was odd, and was bringing the other guard to inspect the area, to offer his opinion as to how it could be that footprints could disappear from one moment to the next.

And of course when they returned they'd find no footprints at all, and would probably stand there long enough to witness one of the cyclical materializations.

Neelix forced himself to be calm, walking in a measured stride with the other miners, resisting the impulse to look over his shoulder and see if the two guards had returned from the storage area. The walk back to the camp seemed interminable, and by the time they got to the wall that surrounded the stockade, Neelix was panting, not from exertion, but from apprehension.

One of the guards gave a signal, and the huge gates rolled open and the miners entered the camp. Neelix walked briskly but calmly toward their shelters, trying not to run, adopting as casual a mien as he could. Finally he was there and he ducked inside.

"Commander!" he called, and Chakotay rose and came to him. "I think the guards may have seen some of the ore dust materializing. They may not be able to figure it out, but I think they're suspicious."

Chakotay turned immediately to B'Elanna and Harry, who were tirelessly operating the transporters. "How soon?" he asked tersely.

B'Elanna shoved her hair out of her eyes. Her face was grimy and sweaty, and dark rings under her eyes testified to her fatigue. "Without going down there, I can't tell. There might be enough room now."

"I think you should check it out."

"All right. Harry—set the coordinates and get ready to energize."

Harry worked his transporter briefly, then looked up at her and nodded. "Ready."

B'Elanna took one of the three remaining combadges, retained for just this purpose, and attached it. "Send me down," she told Harry.

Torres shimmered briefly and then dematerialized. Moments later, they heard her voice. "Bring me back up," she ordered, and Harry did so.

She was back in seconds, looking pleased. "It's a little snug," she reported, "but we can get two people in there. It's going to work."

Chakotay walked to the opening of the shelter and looked out. "It'll be dark soon. We won't wait until the place has completely bedded down, but I don't want to move out until we have the cover of darkness."

"We should wait to receive our nightly rations," offered Tuvok. "Our absence at that time would be noticed."

"Agreed."

And then Chakotay gathered them all around, going over the plan one more time so that everyone knew what was expected of them. Harry Kim listened quietly, already having gone over the strategy a hundred times himself. He wasn't concerned about the logistics of their maneuver, but he was worried about something else. When Chakotay had finished, Harry approached him.

"Sir? Can I see you outside?"

Chakotay looked quizzically at him, then nodded and they both exited the shelter. The temperature had fallen quickly as the sun dropped lower, and there was a vague stirring in the camp as the heat-induced lethargy was relieved. Neelix was at the Rai' shelters, making something for dinner, keeping to his nightly routine even on this most urgent of nights.

"What is it?" asked Chakotay.

"I don't know what you have in mind, but I'd like to take Coris with us."

Chakotay was quiet for a moment and Harry, fearful that this signified his reluctance, hurried to fill the silence. "I know she isn't Starfleet-trained, but she's bright and quick and she wouldn't hold us back. I'll guarantee it."

Chakotay smiled slightly. "Of course she's coming with us," he said, to Harry's great relief. "I'd never leave her behind."

"Thank you, sir," said Harry, feeling immeasurably lighter.

Then they heard the sound of the gates rolling open. Harry looked toward the wall, expecting to see the antigrav units bearing the nightly rations, but what he saw was armed guards emerging from all sides. The prisoners instantly fell into their self-conscious activity, studiously avoiding the presence of the guards.

Harry and Chakotay exchanged a glance. What did this impromptu visit mean? Suddenly Neelix was in front of them, holding a bowl of liquid, looking a bit pale and rattled. "Commander, will you try this soup? It needs a touch of something, I think."

He poked the bowl toward Chakotay, who took it as Neelix leaned in to him, and whispered, "Something tells me we'd better get out of here now."

Chakotay peered over the edge of the bowl at the guards nearest them, about fifty meters away. Three of the Subu were upending a shelter, ripping aside walls of a meager lean-to, tentacles pawing through all the possessions of the hapless prisoners, who stood back anxiously, trying without success to look nonchalant.

Harry estimated there were perhaps a dozen shelters between the guards and *Voyager*'s people. At the rate the guards were going, they would be rummaging through the Starfleet shelters in ten or fifteen minutes, and they'd find the transporters.

It was time to move.

Harry, Chakotay, and Neelix swung into the shelter, Chakotay snapping orders as they did. "Harry, get ready to beam down to the chamber. Vorik, go to the other shelter and let them know what's happening. Tell everyone to start drifting over here one at a time, slowly, without any urgency."

"Yes, sir."

"We have to start this process now. Ready, B'Elanna?"

She nodded grimly and glanced at Harry. He picked up the second transporter and held it tightly. "Let's do it," he said, and noted that his voice sounded hollow.

"Energizing," said Torres, and at that moment a sudden movement in the back of the shelter caught Harry's eye; it was Coris, looking frightened, and Harry realized he hadn't let her know she'd be coming with them. The notion threw him slightly off balance and he took a step forward to keep from reeling. Then he felt the momentary disorientation that always accompanied dematerialization, the brief blackness when his molecules had been converted to pure energy.

When he rematerialized he began screaming. A pain so excruciating he thought he might lose consciousness was searing his right foot, and he couldn't move. Desperately, he fought against the pain, forced himself to stay conscious even as nausea welled in him.

His right foot, with which he had stepped forward at the moment of transport, had rematerialized inside the rock wall of the chamber, crushing the bones of the foot.

Harry gasped for air and switched on the small hand beacon they'd constructed from parts Neelix had cadged. Perspiring heavily, chilled, fighting nausea, Harry set the transporter to beam him out again, back a bit farther in the dank chamber. He was able to key the controls just before he blacked out from the pain.

He came to on the floor, with Chakotay's voice coming over his combadge. "Harry! Harry, answer me! Do you read me?"

Groggy, pain-riddled, Harry struggled to a sitting position. "I'm here, Commander," he said through clenched teeth.

"Did something go wrong?"

"No, it's fine. Start sending people down."

"Tuvok will be first."

Harry glanced around the chamber and realized he'd have to be standing if two people were to fit here. It was a rectangular space no more than a meter across at its widest point. Painfully, his right foot throbbing, he pulled himself upright on his other foot.

For a moment he was afraid he was going to pass out again, but he bit his lip until it bled, and his head cleared. In the next instant, Tuvok materialized in front of him.

"Okay, sir," he rasped, "I'm putting you outside the wall, about three hundred meters into the forest." He began working the transporter controls.

"Ensign, have you been injured—" Tuvok began, but he was gone before he could complete the sentence. Seconds later, his voice over the combadge announced that he was successfully in the forest, well outside the walls of the prison camp.

Harry found another part of his lip and bit down again. This was going to be a long night.

Above, in the shelter, Chakotay announced the order of descent: "Seven, Tom, Gabrielle, Neelix, Coris, Brad . . ." As he spoke, everyone was aware of the increasing hubbub outside. Coris sneaked to the opening and peered out as a clamor of shouting erupted, punctuated occasionally by screams.

"They're getting close. But they must've found something illegal in someone else's shelter. They're punishing people—burning them with the acid that comes from their tentacles."

Chakotay remembered vividly what that felt like, and felt sorry for the poor wretches who were suffering it now. But he had to stay focused on the current task. "Keep going, B'Elanna. Send them as quickly as it's safe."

Seven was dispatched, and moments later, Tom. The others were lining up in an ordered and disciplined fashion, even though worry was etched on their faces.

Gabrielle Allyn dematerialized. Then Neelix, his spots pronounced against a pale face.

"Coris, you're next," said Chakotay, looking around for the small girl.

Coris wasn't there.

Coris of Saccul moved with purpose through the crowded camp, circling around to come at them in a direction different from that of the *Voyager* shelters.

For once in her life, she would accomplish something. It had been an undistinguished life so far, noted mostly for its misery and disappointments, but a tiny flame of determination was burning in her now and she fanned it eagerly.

Finally she understood some of the things her mother's mother had told her when she was small. Her beloved Gammi, the only creature on Saccul that cared whether she lived or died, who had taken her in when her own mother had abandoned her, choosing instead to become a camp follower, lying with soldiers in return for crumbs of bread and spoons of soup.

Once, Coris had dreamed of grand and glorious accomplishments: she would sing as beautifully as the night birds of her planet; she would study the heavens and uncover their dark mysteries; she would become a priestess and guide young people in the intricacies of spirituality.

Those dreams were gone by her ninth year, when Gammi died at the hands of drunken soldiers and the greatest aspiration Coris could imagine was simply surviving for one more day.

Her own capture and imprisonment by the Subu reduced the circumstances of her life not at all, as she believed she would have died soon had she remained free. Dying in this prison camp was no different.

Until the Voyagers had come along.

She had never met such people, never even imagined them. Gammi had taught her that in the life after death there were such great beings, full of goodness and joy, but never had she thought it possible for people of this dimension to embody all those grand qualities.

She was ashamed that she'd been introduced to them because of trying to steal Harry's boots, but she was still grateful to have met them, to have sat with them and listened to their stories, to hear of their strength, their generosity, their selflessness. Night after night she had sat quietly, discovering in them a nobility that both fascinated and intimidated her.

She finally felt that she knew why one was born into low estate, into pain and squalor: it was so that one could transcend those circumstances, could toughen and hone oneself against adversity and in so doing, become noble and selfless.

She hadn't thought her opportunity would come so quickly. She'd hoped to go with the Voyagers when they made their escape, so that she could continue to learn from them, could grow stronger and more certain of herself.

But she hadn't the slightest doubt that fate had given her the very opportunity she sought right at this moment.

At the rate the Subu guards were moving, the Voyagers would never be able to move everyone out of the shelters before they were discovered. Something had to slow them down, and that was what Coris intended to do. The tiny flame nicked higher, warming her with a feeling she'd never had before, something she couldn't even identify, but which she knew she must follow.

The old transtator was heavy in her hands. This was the very first component the Voyagers had procured; she'd been with Harry when he found it and traded some food for it. It turned out not to be functional, even though it sparked and hummed and emitted a weak beam of light.

But tonight it would become invaluable.

She had now circled around so that she was ready to intercept the guards from a direction well away from the Voyagers. A few minutes was all she'd need, and she was sure she could endure the attack of the Subu tentacles for a few minutes. Pain was familiar to her, and surely in her young life she'd suffered worse.

She noticed that a few puzzled prisoners stared after her as she marched through their midst, ordinarily an undertaking fraught with danger. But with the presence of the guards, no one would think of doing anything to draw attention. She was safe from the unwanted attention of prisoners.

The guards were only a few meters away now, rampaging through a small encampment of the Yottins, who shrank in terror from the guards, their monstrous weapons, and their deadly tentacles.

Now.

She planted herself directly in front of the guards as they moved away from the Yottins and lifted the transtator, pointing it directly at them. The thin beam of light wasn't visible in the daylight, but now that night was almost on them, it shone right at the first Subu guard.

He stopped in utter bewilderment. Then took a step back, hand raised to stop the others.

His orifice opened slightly, an expression Coris had never seen on these creatures. It looked almost like a smile, but she couldn't imagine these beings smiling.

It occurred to her that it must be a strange tableau, she, a small girl, holding the heavy transtator pointed at the guards; they stopped in their tracks, uncertain, caught unawares by her strange behavior.

The guard stretched out a tentacle. "Give me that," he rasped, but Coris shook her head.

"It's mine."

"Is that the machine which turns ore to dust?"

So they did know what had happened. Coris felt her heart quicken with urgency, but her voice was clear and strong in the night air, now unnaturally hushed as the prisoners waited to see what the guards would do.

"No," said Coris, "it's a machine which will insure that you never father children."

There was an astonished gasp from the onlookers, and a heavy moment passed, charged as though in the instant before lightning strikes. Then Coris saw the guard's tentacle snake out and rip the transtator from her grasp, then pass it to one of his fellows.

Then the tentacle came whipping back for her.

Her voice, when it began screaming, seemed disembodied, a high keening that came from somewhere far away. She'd been wrong; this pain was worse, far worse, than anything she'd ever experienced. By the time blackness came, she'd forgotten her purpose, her quest for nobility, even who she was and why she was here, writhing in this crucible.

Chakotay and B'Elanna were the last to go. When the screams began, he had run to the opening of the shelter and saw Coris twisting in the deadly embrace of the Subu guard. There was nothing he could do for her now. He moved back to B'Elanna and signaled her with a nod.

He was beamed to the underground chamber thinking of Coris, whose sacrifice had undoubtedly bought them the time they needed to complete the transports.

When he materialized, it was in front of a Harry Kim who looked as though he was about to pass out.

"Where's Coris?" Harry gasped, obviously in pain.

"She decided not to come," lied Chakotay. "She was afraid."

Harry was baffled but Chakotay didn't want to get into it now. "Beam me out of here, Harry. B'Elanna still has to come down."

Harry responded as though by reflex. Chakotay knew he was in a bad way, but didn't yet know why, and for now it didn't matter; what mattered was to get all of them outside the camp and into the forest.

Seconds later, he was standing among the rest of the crew, deep within the forest which, at night, was cold and damp. Not long after, B'Elanna shimmered into view before them, and finally, Harry Kim, who collapsed as soon as he materialized.

"What is it, Harry?" said Chakotay, who hurried to his side. Harry rolled over to look up at him with eyes that were black against his pale face.

"Foot . . . crushed . . ."

Chakotay looked down to see the boot on Harry's right foot soaked in blood, the shape of the boot twisted unnaturally.

"Can't walk . . . leave me here . . ."

"Forget it." Chakotay nodded toward Tuvok and Tom, who hauled Harry up, ready to hoist him onto Tuvok's back. The Vulcan's strength would come in handy tonight.

"Which way, Commander?" asked Tuvok, and then Chakotay remembered that he was expected to guide them in the right direction.

But he felt nothing. No urge, no impulse, nothing that gave him any clue how to proceed from here. But they couldn't just stand here; their absence would be discovered soon and the chase—if there was to be one—would be on.

He turned to Seven. "It's not working. I don't feel what I did before."

She moved to him and stared solemnly at the implant on his cheek. She reached up and touched it gently. "This may cause you momentary pain," she announced, and then she drove the heel of her palm directly into the nodule on his cheek.

Chakotay felt as though his head had exploded. A jagged knife was ripping through his jaw, driving into his brain. The forest began to spin and he staggered, put his head down to get blood to it, then back up as the increase in pressure exacerbated the pain.

Gradually, it abated, and he breathed deeply. The air was cold and sweet, and helped clear the residual pain.

And as it did, he felt the unmistakable impulse to move from this place. There was something, an indefinable but potent something, pulling at him.

"This way," he said to the others, and began to plunge with unerring instinct through the forest.

* * *

Coris felt herself lifted upward, and wondered if she was going to the afterlife, and if so, if Gammi would be there. She wasn't afraid, just curious.

Then the pain returned, and she heard the wild cry of the camp's klaxons, and she realized she wasn't dead after all. She opened her eyes and looked up into the dark face of Tassot Bnay, who was carrying her in his arms as easily as if she were a rag doll.

"We will put salve on your wounds," he announced. "There may be some scarring, but it will be minimal."

Coris absorbed this information dispassionately. Only one thing mattered to her. "Did the Voyagers get away?" she asked in a voice hoarse from screaming.

"They are no longer in the camp. Whether they will succeed in their escape or not is uncertain. The Subu have apparently decided to pursue them."

Coris subsided into silence, finding comfort in the gentle jostling of Tassot Bnay's gait. She felt secure in his arms, protected. She had given of herself to help the Voyagers, and now she in turn was being aided. There was a justness to the situation that pleased her, and at that moment she knew life could be led nobly, even under the most brutal and callous of conditions, and that from this time forward, that is how she would live.

"Good luck, Harry," she whispered to herself, and then gave herself over to the comfort of Bnay's strong arms.

Chakotay and his crew had been moving through the forest for only a few minutes when they heard the sound of the klaxons. It was an ominous, alien noise, which rent the stillness of the night in a primeval way, like the trumpet of some ancient, extinct behemoth.

The sound was so startling that they all stopped for a moment, listening, but Chakotay exhorted them forward. "Move," he hissed. "We have to keep going."

A few minutes later they saw the lights of hovercraft far overhead, obscured by the thick canopy of trees, and then the powerful beams of searchlights swept by. Chakotay knew that it would be difficult for the beams to penetrate the trees and unless they emerged into a clearing they should escape detection. But it was unnerving, nonetheless.

On they plunged, Chakotay trusting the strange pull of the signal more completely now. Tuvok was still carrying Harry, who was nearly unconscious. He'd hung on until his job was done, in spite of the excruciating pain, and he couldn't fight it any longer.

"Are you doing all right?" Chakotay asked Tuvok.

"I'm fine, Commander," Tuvok replied, but Chakotay sensed the effort in his voice. Vulcans were strong, but he couldn't be expected to carry a strapping young man indefinitely.

And then they saw the lights of the vehicles.

They were antigrav units, skimming through the woods with deftness and speed, powerful searchlights plying the darkness like giant fireflies. There would be no canopy protecting them from the beams of those lights.

The vehicles were still in the distance, moving in seemingly random patterns through the woods. Did they have sensors? If so, they could surely detect fifteen people hurrying through the forest. But strangely, the vehicles weren't headed directly for them, but were circling, hunting, clearly unaware of their location.

They heard the next obstacle long before they saw it. At first it was barely perceptible, a soft rumble like the lowest notes of a bass viol. But as they moved foward the rumble became louder and more foreboding. A dampness pervaded the air and the temperature dropped still further, producing a clammy cold. What was ahead of them?

Chakotay moved unerringly in the direction of the noise, knowing instinctively that it was their destination, but without knowledge of what, exactly, it was.

Louder and louder was the sound, beyond a rumble now, a great growling as though thousands of cannons were detonating simultaneously and continuously. A mist was swirling in the air, wetting them, becoming thicker as they moved forward until finally they felt as though they were walking through a cold shower.

Behind them, Chakotay noticed that the lights of the vehicles seemed to have stopped hunting randomly and were now focused in their general direction. Had they been spotted?

In the next moment they walked out from under the protective canopy of the trees.

The sound was thunderous now, the chill mist oppressive. And before them, they were able to see the source of the noise and the moisture.

It was an unbelievably massive waterfall.

Chakotay and his group stood on the edge of a precipice; from their left, stretching farther than they could see, a torrential river several thousand meters wide swept to the head of the falls, which wasn't half a kilometer from them.

Then it plunged over a steep drop, down, down an impossibly long way until it disappeared in billowing mists of vapor which churned with the force of the gigantic fall. They couldn't see the bottom, or guess how far down it was.

None of them had ever seen such an immense display of water power. The volume of water that cascaded over the cliff and plunged downward was incalculable, the force that it generated immeasurable. It was an awesome phenomenon of nature, which the scientists of the group would ordinarily have wanted to study.

But tonight they viewed it with dismay.

"Commander—what now?" asked Tom, trying not to sound worried.

Chakotay didn't answer, just stared at the Promethean falls, mind searching for the answer. He turned, and saw the lights of the vehicles drawing nearer; they had indeed been spotted.

And suddenly hovercraft appeared overhead, lights sweeping the area in circles, within seconds of discovering them as well.

Chakotay's vision blurred and everything before him swirled into hallucinogenic images: waterfall, clouds of vapor, thick forests, arcing beams of light, the hushed, expectant faces of his crew, all blended into kaleidoscopic fragments. What was he to do? How could he get them out of this awful predicament? What had the captain intended—or was she behind this strange escape at all?

He was seized with the memory of himself as a young person, running through the woods like a deer, heart pounding, feeling like an unencumbered animal dashing headlong, at one with nature. He tried to concentrate on that memory, to strip from himself all rationality, all logic, for something was telling him strongly that only his instincts could be relied on now, only his connection with the primeval being he carried deep inside. *Father,* he thought. *Help me.*

And in his mind he heard his father's voice, saying, *Trust yourself. You know what to do.*

With that, the sensation of falling returned to him, even as it had the night the captain planted the Borg nodule in his cheek. But this time it held no terrors.

He opened his eyes, certain of their course.

The Subu vehicles were audible now, pushing through the forest, and the hovercraft were descending. There was no time to hesitate.

"We're going to jump," he said firmly. "Join hands. Here we go."

To the credit of the crew, there was no objection, no reluctance. He supposed they realized if the Subu reached them they'd be dead anyway. And maybe this mad leap was at least the more defiant way to go.

They joined hands, Harry still clinging to Tuvok's back, and as one, leapt off the precipice and began to fall.

Chakotay lived a lifetime during their fall.

He nuzzled at his mother's breast, fat and content, tugging at the nipple long past satiety, basking in comfort and succor . . . breezes blew his hair in his eyes as he stood on the hilltops near his home, carrying the desperate aroma of spring flowers . . . he felt the sweet urgency of first love searing his body, a black-haired girl ripe as a peach . . . gathering the artifacts for his medicine bundle . . . needles piercing the skin of his temple as the indigenous people of Central America etched the ritual tattoo into his forehead, his final tribute to his father . . . a woman's voice, singing in the twilight . . . he felt love, pain, longing, aspiration . . . all the myriad emotions that had driven him since infancy swirled around him, coalescing into rib-boned patterns of light, colorful serpents that twisted through, around, over him, objects now not of abhorrence but of reverence . . .

Kathryn's face, swimming in the mists . . .

They had fallen endlessly, down and down, impossibly far, forever, and still they plummeted. Chakotay felt a curious peace settle over him, a willingness to fall like this until eternity, glorying in the rapturous plunge.

And then a vision came to him.

It was *Voyager,* rising from the mists of the gorge, ascending toward them like a roc.

Chakotay realized he must be dead already, that this wondrous vision was nothing more than the last dying electrolytes of his brain, flickering with familiar images before they faded into the dark oblivion of death.

And then he felt himself dematerializing.

"I was reasonably sure Seven would recognize the homing signal," said Kathryn. "But I didn't know if you'd understand that you had to jump."

"I don't know that I did understand it. It was a sensation, an instinct. That's all."

"The only place on that planet I felt I could conceal *Voyager* was in the mists of that waterfall. It was almost three kilometers long, and produced enough energy to disrupt their sensors."

They were in her quarters, relaxing over the best meal Chakotay had had in days, and had even splurged by replicating a bottle of wine. A powerful sense of well-being suffused him, abetted by the food, the drink, and the presence of Kathryn, who looked particularly lovely this evening.

"How's Harry's foot?"

"The doctor said it was badly mangled, and it might take a number of osteogenic treatments, but it should eventually be almost as good as new."

Chakotay nodded, and the image of Harry standing upright in the underground chamber, in agony but steadfasting carrying out his duty, came to him. He was silent, remembering the sacrifices every member of that group had made, their courage, their resourcefulness, their unflagging willingness to make that final plunge with him, the ultimate leap of faith.

He felt a soft hand on his and realized Kathryn had taken hold of him and was looking into his eyes with concern. "What is it?" she asked softly.

He hesitated. How could he tell her? How could he communicate what had happened to them in the course of that extraordinary adventure, describe the immensity of feeling that had come of their imprisonment and escape?

Maybe he couldn't. He felt incapable of re-creating the closeness, the intimacy they had all shared. Maybe it was an experience that would have to remain private, to be remembered and abreacted only among those who had lived it.

"I was thinking," he said carefully, "about that blue robe you had on when you visited the camp. Where'd it come from?"

"From people called the Murr. They're wealthy traders who do business with the Subu."

"I'd give a month of replicator rations to see you in it again."

Her mouth turned in a slight smile. "I think that could be arranged," she said.

They sat like that for a while, easily silent, hands joined, looking out at the sweep of the warp stars.

In a few moments he realized that of course he must tell her everything, must communicate every moment, every nuance of the experience, must make her feel as though she had been there, too. Because if she weren't a part of it, he would be somehow incomplete.

The touch of her hand was warm. He could feel the beat of her pulse in her wrist, and it seemed to him that his heart must be beating in rhythm with hers. The stars streaked by, breathtaking ribbons of white, defiant, transcendent, an ecstasy of light, and he gazed at them, mind quieted by their hypnotic power.

Presently, he began to speak.